Who Woul e Thought It?

María Amparo Ruiz de Burton

Edited and introduced by
Rosaura Sánchez and Beatrice Pita

Recovering the U.S. Hispanic Literary Heritage Project Publication

Arte Público Press
Houston, Texas
1995

This volume is made possible through grants from the National Endowment for the Arts (a federal agency), the Andrew W. Mellon Foundation, and the Rockefeller Foundation.

Recovering the past, creating the future

Arte Público Press
University of Houston
Houston, Texas 77204-2090

Cover design by Mark Piñón

Ruiz de Burton, María Amparo, 1832–1895.
Who would have thought it? / María Amparo Ruiz de Burton ; edited and introduced by Rosaura Sánchez and Beatrice Pita.
p. cm.
ISBN 1-55885-081-3 (paper)
1. New England—Social life and customs—19th century—Fiction. 2. Mexican-American women—New England—Fiction. 3. Young women—New England—Fiction. 4. Family—New England—Fiction. I. Sánchez, Rosaura. II. Pita, Beatrice. III. Title.
PS2736.R53W48 1995
813'.4—dc20 95-11585
CIP

The paper used in this publication meets the requirements of the American National Standard for Permanence of Paper for Printed Library Materials Z39.48-1984. ∞

Our past is, has been, and will

be in your future.

SECTIONS

INTRODUCTION[1]

> It was the anniversary of some great day in New England [...] some great day in which the Pilgrim fathers had done one of their wonderful deeds. They had embarked, or landed, or burnt a witch, or whipped a woman at the pillory, on just such a day. [*Who Would Have Thought It?* 62]

On board the steamer *California* in late summer 1872, a San Francisco newspaper correspondent met María Ampario Ruiz de Burton, who was returning to San Diego after her train trip from the East. The newspaperman, who had learned that she was the "authoress" of the recently anonymously published novel *Who Would Have Thought It?*,[2] made known to her his wish to publicize her name as the author, but she asked that her name not be revealed "because everyone would then criticize the work," and would think to have discovered defects which otherwise no one would notice.[3] Ruiz de Burton was concerned that readers knowing that English was not her native language would be more inclined perhaps to find fault with the text. However, the correspondent did not accede to her request and in fact published a review of her novel giving the author's name and speaking of the "descriptive and narrative power" of the work as well as of the author's "critical though perhaps too cynical habit of observation" [ibid.]. The article recommends the satirical work, but notes its controversial nature as follows: "The book will be read with pleasure on this Coast at least, even though the sentiments contained therein may be considered contrary to received opinion."[4]

The critical perspective noted in the Ruiz de Burton novel, *Who Would Have Thought It?*, needs to be seen in the context of Congressional Reconstruction (1867-1877), a period of dramatic economic, political and social changes in the United States. A native of Baja California who came to Alta California in 1847, Ruiz de Burton would have a front-row seat at the turbulent events of the decade of the 1860s when her husband, Colonel Henry S. Burton, was ordered East to serve in the Union Army. Her novel, published in Philadelphia in 1872, provides a historical perspective from the vantage point of an outsider who was a citizen,[5] and had spent almost two-thirds of her life in the United States as a member of what soon after the U.S. occupation of California became a dispossessed and disempowered Californio community. In *Who Would Have Thought It?* Ruiz de Burton carries out an aggressive demystification of a series of national foundational ideologies. By variously deploying allegory, satire and parody, the author effects a critique driven by a perceived crisis in the body politic of the United States itself.

As in the case of her second novel, *The Squatter and the Don* (1885),[6] published under the pseudonym C. Loyal,[7] Ruiz de Burton considered her status both as a member of a conquered population and as a woman to be disadvantages for an author interested in inveighing against the government and its policies and particularly bent on challenging dominant opinion. Further weighing against full disclosure was the fact that by the time of the novel's publication, Ruiz de Burton was a widow. Her husband, a breveted Brigadier General in the Union Army, had died in 1869, after contracting malarial fever while serving in Florida during the Civil War. Burton, a West Point graduate, was a native of Connecticut, but his wife, a Latina, a Catholic, and Spanish-dominant, was an outsider in Yankee territory, even after several years of residence in various Eastern cities. For nearly a decade she had lived back East while her husband was stationed first at Fortress Monroe (Maryland) and later in command of Fort Delaware, before being deployed to Pittsburgh and participating in the Richmond campaign, the battles of Cold Harbor and Spottsylvania Courthouse, and the bombardment of Petersburg. Ruiz de Burton's experiences on the East coast, particularly in New York, Rhode Island and Washington D.C., in a predominantly Protestant region where Irish Catholics were a discriminated low-wage working-class sector, are undoubtedly a source of many of the insights recorded in *Who Would Have Thought It?* Crucial also is her personal history as a member of a displaced ruling class in California that was conscious of Mexico's loss not only of half of its territories to the U.S. but of its immense mineral resources.

Ruiz de Burton's background thus afforded her a certain critical distance and alternative points of reference; her extended stay on the East coast provided an opportunity for first-hand observations and assessment of the U.S. Republic as it was torn apart during the period of the Civil War and was reconfiguring itself immediately thereafter. Reconstruction after the Civil War, which displaced the old plantation ruling class in the South, would no doubt also trigger memories of what had taken place in Alta California, where after occupation the ruling Californios were reduced to a subaltern minority. Her outsider status also allowed her to view major political and economic changes taking place in the United States within a global context, one affecting Latin America, especially Mexico, a country, by 1872, already devastated in quick succession by the U.S. invasion of 1846, internal strife and civil war, and a French invasion.

By the time Ruiz de Burton left California, the state was already undergoing significant changes, but not nearly to the extent that was taking place in the East, where rapid urbanization and industrialization were much more in evidence, even before the war, given its "widespread factory system, an integrated railroad and telegraph network, and a permanent laboring class."[8] The Civil War would have profound consequences on the nation's economy, allow for further industrial expansion, usher in a new and accelerated phase of capitalist development, and give added impetus to gender and racial civil rights movements that would in some cases take over one-hundred years to come to fruition. The social and political landscape of the U.S. during the ante-bellum period as well as the Civil War and its aftermath are configured in the Ruiz de Burton novel. An analysis of the figuration of these various elements in the novel necessarily implies an examination of genre discourses and narrative framing strategies.

Novels of Domesticity

> "I do not object to her dark skin, only I wish to know what position she is to occupy in my family. Which wish *I* consider quite reasonable, since I am the one to regulate my household," said Mrs. Norval... [*Who Would Have Thought It?* 19]

Who Would Have Thought It? does not adhere to the precepts of the typical romance of domesticity, for it takes women from the domestic sphere into public domains and readers into the space of politics, a sphere from which nineteenth-century women were to a large extent excluded given their lack of suffrage and inability to hold public office. The novel, with a national and international focus, situates the U.S. as a modernizing and expansionist nation, within which the family domain is also transformed. Shifting between these parallel spheres, the political and the domestic, enables a transcoding of two social contracts, metonymically related: marriage (the family formation) and the Constitution (the republic), each governed by its own conventions and boundaries. The allegorical transcoding of power-relations, violations of conventions and deception is matched by an ironic transcontexualization of several nineteenth-century narrative genres.

Who Would Have Thought It? is a parody of both the early sentimental novel and the mid-nineteenth-century novel of domesticity, if by parody we understand, with Hutcheon, "the acknowledgment of recognizable, stable forms and conventions" as well as the transgression of generic limits.[9] As Hutcheon often notes, parody is "repetition with difference" [32] or "imitation with critical ironic distance" [37] and its target is always another text or a generic code. Parody is, however, but one vehicle used in Ruiz de Burton's novel to satirize nineteenth-century socio-political structures and practices in the United States. To ridicule politicians and other cultural icons of the period, the novel uses not only burlesque and elements of the picaresque to produce comic and caricatural representations—laying out for the reader an entire rogues' gallery—but elements of the adventure romance and *testimonio* alongside realist and historical reconstructions of the antebellum and Civil War periods. The overlapping of satire and parody enables a virulent attack and consequent demystification of a number of nationalist common places, a ridiculing of particular social types, and the mocking of a series of social and literary conventions.

The construct of domesticity in many nineteenth-century novels is one of the conventions that served to reinforce the notion that women were limited to the home and hearth; yet whether in fiction or history, it should not surprise us to find, as Ryan has indicated, "Victorian women, even Southern ladies, in the public arena."[10] The gendered distinction between the public and the private is highly—and rightfully—contested today within feminist theory. One can, according to Ryan, choose to challenge the gendering of the spheres while retaining the concept [4], but one can also question the very notion of this type of binary and exclusionist spatial construction given the compenetration of the domestic and the public. One should not lose sight of the fact that nineteenth-century women also necessarily had a role to play in public places, but this was not, however, the primary concern of novelists constructing a domestic sphere governed by women, one that fit in nicely with capitalist development and modernity and posited the teaching of principles of discipline, self-reliance and individualism within the home, that is, in preparation for socialization and integration within a capitalist system and within a particular political sphere. As Davidson indicates, nineteenth-century discourses of domesticity and republican motherhood "extolled women as specially gifted for the crucial task of rearing children,"[11] providing in this way a new focus on the mother rather than on the father for the upbringing of children. As the Reverend William Lyman argued:

> Mothers do, in a sense, hold the reign of government and sway the ensigns of national prosperity and glory. Yea, they give direction to the moral sentiment of our rising hopes and contribute to form their moral state. To them therefore our eyes are turned in this demoralizing age, and of them we ask, that they would appreciate their worth and dignity, and exert all their influence to drive discord, infidelity, and licentiousness from our land. [quoted in Davidson, 134]

The emerging "bourgeois" home as an ideological site and apparatus, as a sphere within which women "could most effectively exercise their power" as the "moral guardians of their husbands and children," and as the "standard-bearers of piety, decorum and virtue in Northern society,"[12] is constructed in numerous mid-nineteenth-century novels of domesticity. Whether at a given historical moment the home is a site for the reproduction of dominant culture, a site itself of oppression within which women negotiate power, or a site of resistance and change within which women develop critical perspectives—or potentially all of these—is a suggestive question, particularly in a period of economic and political transition, like that reconstructed in Ruiz de Burton's novel.

The "cult of domesticity" itself implies changes from the late eighteenth-century sentimental novel, which had focussed on young women before marriage, to nineteenth-century novels with new notions of republican motherhood [Davidson, 134]. After 1818 the seduction plot of the virginal girl seduced by fortune hunters, abusive men or scoundrels in good measure disappears from sentimental fiction [Davidson, 135], except perhaps for the case of *The Scarlet Letter*;[13] the didactic dimension, however, is retained, but now with "matronly" middle-class young wives, like Eva van Arsdel, in Harriet Beecher Stowe's domestic novel, *We and Our Neighbors*,[14] who assumes the role of moral and practical adviser of young girls preparing for "middle-class" marriage or in need of redemption from a life of prostitution. In novels from 1820 to 1879 Baym finds that the "overplot" is generally that of a self-reliant woman who, left destitute, struggles for economic independence.[15] Harris, on the other hand, suggests going beyond the formulaic overplot or coverplot to examine how these very formulaic plots are subverted and literary conventions challenged in nineteenth-century women's fiction.[16] It is these challenges—generic and ideological—that we propose to examine in our study.

Douglas' analysis of nineteenth-century novels also distinguishes between the representation of women in sentimental novels during the late eighteenth and early nineteenth centuries and the later mid-to-late century romances, all in relation to economic and political structures in a state of flux. In the earlier period, the republican mother, restricted to the domestic sphere—where she cultivated in her family the principles of the republic—was depicted as an active participant in domestic production through her cottage industries. Then, as now, in effect, the private was also public. In time, as manufacturing developed further and clothing became easily accessible, cottage industries faded away and women's "mother power" was seemingly disestablished.[17] The shifting status of the matron from producer to consumer led to new roles for women and to a new cult of motherhood [Douglas, 75]. Women came to be seen as a "moral and religious influence" [Douglas, 60] within now fully constituted notions of "the private." As consumers, middle-class women in the Northeast assumed a new role within the home and within the economy: "Fashion was the back door through which middle-class northern women re-entered the American economy" [Douglas, 61]. In novels like *We and Our Neighbors* by Stowe, female characters are happily involved in "the making of bright happy homes" (Stowe, 1875, 463) and concerned as much with their furnishings and house plants as with their apparel, all of which must be brightened up with ribbons and lace. In these narratives, the warmth of women and hearth creates an appropriate place for social interaction and for enlightening feminine conversation. The home is thus the appropriate "nesting" place for the workings of "middle-class" marriage—a dominant social contract within capitalist society—and the ideal locus for the consumption of women's literature, hence the proliferation of novels and popular magazines published with a female readership in mind [Douglas, 62].

The other key domestic sphere, here as in other novels of domesticity, is the Church—a feminized social space [Douglas, 98] and a complement to the home—which is itself structured by religious faith and matronly wisdom. Women's changing roles and powerful position within the family accompanied the feminization of religion and the abandonment of the authoritarian, male-dominated Calvinist notion of the Atonement; in place of a stern patriarchal God stood a maternal, affectionate, nurturing God [Douglas, 124]. Religious faith would now be defined "in terms of family morals, civic responsibility, and above all, in terms of the social functioning of churchgoing" [Douglas, 7]. As women became the primary parishioners (with the disestablishment of churches, and the ministers' financial need to attract members), there developed a close relationship between ministers and their female congregation. The popular press of the 1860s and 1970s, in fact, included accounts of a number of "ministerial sex scandals" [Douglas, 100]. Interestingly, preachers began to appeal to their flocks in much the same language used by sentimental literature. Instead of the fiery preachers of yesterday, clergymen often were the writers of novels or newspaper columns themselves [Douglas, 40, 101]. Preachers also lost their eminent position of earlier times and now were often impoverished: "the commercial classes treated the clergy disdainfully as powerless, ill-informed 'people half-way between men and women' " [Douglas, 43]. It is then not surprising that ministers should figure so prominently in women's novels of the nineteenth century [Douglas, 104], which, as noted, also stressed the moral and religious influence of women, often portraying them as the equal of preachers in their capacity to minister to lost souls, as missionaries, in "edifying bedroom scenes" or merely as housewives engaging in their own "daily self-sacrifice" [Douglas, 111, 128-129], like Eva van Arsdal in Stowe's *We and Our Neighbors*. This simultaneous secularization and feminization of religion and culture, in the midst of a growing consumer society rocked by political and financial scandals and the rise of powerful monopolies, are, in fact, some of the social conventions satirized by Ruiz de Burton.

The overlapping of satire and parody is evident from the start in the Ruiz de Burton novel. Here it is the dominant "cult" of women's "moral authority" that will be parodied through a plot of "fallen republican motherhood." Jemima Norval, as we shall see, can be taken as a descendant of Hester Prynne, but now refashioned into a bourgeois subject with pragmatic as well as passionate interests. Feminine subjectivity while posited is, however, deconstructed in the narrative as it proves to be grounded in deception and thus only temporary. Republican motherhood (embodied in Jemima Norval) is, in part at least, a metaphor for the republican nation, also fallen during the Civil War, but more importantly the construct introduces an operation in which a whole constellation of ideological myths is collapsed. The novel implicitly argues that this national practice of misrepresentation and concealment and self-deception is so engrained that only on occasion is it unmasked; as one of the characters comments rhetorically: "Surely we Americans have got to be great liars, or else some fearful lies are being told to us.'"[18] And what better way to take to task and disarticulate myths and misrepresentations than by focussing on the Bill of Rights and on a historical moment, the Civil War period, when freedom of expression was repressed? Romantic idealization of the political is in this way disrupted and satirized in *Who Would Have Thought It?* as is the notion of a tolerant, just nation that ostensibly values dissent.

In the Tracks of Scoundrels

> What would the good and proper people of this world do if there were no rogues in it—no social delinquents? The good and proper, I fear, would perish of sheer inanity—of hypochondriac lassitude—or, to say the least, would grow very dull for want of convenient whetstones to sharpen their wits. Rogues are useful. [*Who Would Have Thought It?* 9]

Satire, as Hutcheon explains, is a "critical representation, always comic and often caricatural" of reality [49]. Its strategies for ridiculing social types, practices or ideologies may involve the picaresque, the burlesque, irony or even parody, all techniques to be found in Ruiz de Burton's novel. Satire is, however, generally of a reformist bent, harking back to better bygone times, and as a rule oriented towards correctives within established norms. The picaresque mode, in evidence too in *Who Would Have Thought It?*, is a useful framework of analysis in this respect, for, as Davidson indicates, the tracking of characters cast as rogues allows for a confrontation of political controversies from a variety of perspectives; likewise the techniques of irony and hyperbole in effect enable a blurring of oppositions into ambiguities and provide a certain narrative irresolution [Davidson, 152, 164, 165]. Scrutinizing the utilization of this mode is especially fruitful in the work of Ruiz de Burton, who given her outsider's perspective "within the belly of the monster," as Martí would later put it, doubtlessly enjoyed confronting diverging and contradictory rhetorics across the ideological spectrum within the U.S. Nevertheless, her more acerbic and/or burlesque discourses inevitably are targeted against one particular side; despite the fuzzy field of ideological ambiguities created within the text, there is a definite interest in mocking certain widely held "truths" and unmasking dominant myths.

As a rule, however, picaresque novels (except for a few that Davidson terms "female picaresque," where the female character often crossdresses and travels about like a *pícaro*, disguised as a man) do not focus on women. As Davidson has indicated, "the picaresque virtually excludes women precisely because women *were* excluded from the politics of the new Republic and also from the more perfect, imagined *polis* formulated by most of early American political visionaries" [152]. And yet, despite the inclusion of an outsider, marginal like the *pícaro* but angelic in true romantic fashion, who travels from the Southwest to the East coast and comes face to face with social contradictions in ante-bellum and bellum society, *Who Would Have Thought It?* is not a true picaresque novel, although a certain picaresque mode, as evident in certain satirical or comic strands, structures this romance. The novel presents the reader with an entire gallery of rogues, all "useful whetstones" [5] for the author's representation of the vices and venal character of nineteenth century middle-class society. All receive ridiculous, pompous or comic names, beginning with the preachers (Hackwell and Hammerhard), the neighbors (the Cackles), and their sons, all with high-sounding classical names (Julius Caesar, Mark Antony, Marcus Tullius Cicero, Mirabeau Demosthenes), Hackwell's aides and associates (Mssrs. Hooker and Skinner, Aeschylus Wagg, Sophocles Head—a.k.a., Scaly-wagg and Sophy-head, respectively), and others such as Mr. Albino Skroo, Mr. Blower, and of course the Honorable Le Grand Gunn. The wealthy belles of New York's upper crust suffer the same ridicule in being given names such as the Misses Squeezephat, McCods, Van Krout and Pinchingham. The novel's sardonic allusion to classical Greek and Roman dramatic and historical characters (Miltiades, Themistocles, Clytemnestra, Antigone, Electra, Darius, etc.) serves as well to ridicule the petty nature of the narrative's chief scoundrels and their minions.[19] Ruiz de Burton's novel also gives us the typical picaresque mobility from one geographical site to another, a displacement which allows for a charting of a variety of both domestic and public spaces within nineteenth-century East-coast society.

Who Would Have Thought It? satirizes American politics, an emerging consumerism, and dominant representations of the nation itself, often through a mocking of divisive political discourses and practices of the period set against the backdrop of idealized constructs of domesticity and nationhood. The novel is thus an amalgam of romance, hyperbolic picaresque and realism that invites multiple readings. Unlike other nineteenth-century novels written by women, Ruiz de Burton's narrative is not a typical example of woman's fiction, inasmuch as the work is only satirically concerned with the "self-realization" and "self-improvement" of women [Baym, 233, 236]. However, it does dialogue extensively with the romance of domesticity, which it parodies, and in the process retains some conventions and subverts others.

Who Would Have Thought It? is divided into sixty chapters followed by a Conclusion. The first ten chapters deal with events between 1857 and 1861 (the attack on Fort Sumter), through flashbacks taking us back to 1836 (the marriage of the Norvals) and 1846 (the kidnapping of Doña María Teresa Almenara de Medina, Lola's mother). The next fifty chapters deal with events during the Civil War (1861-1864). The novel's Conclusion, a case of "writing beyond the romantic ending,"[20] takes up the narrative after a seven-year hiatus, wraps up the romance and situates the reader in "real time" as it were, in the midst of political events of 1872. The geographical mobility of the main characters takes us to the U.S. Southwest, Massachusetts, New York City, Washington D.C., several Civil War battlefields and Confederate prison camps, and Mexico, as the novel shifts from domestic social spaces to public, primarily political and military, spaces. Viewing the novel as a mapping of social geography will further allow us to reconstruct the boundaries between gender spheres as well as to see how the novel presents the limitations of liberal democracy and the emergence of consumer society in the Gilded Age.

Whiter Than White

> "I think Lola might teach us the secret of that Indian paint that kept her white skin under cover, making it white by bleaching it. I would bargain to wear spots for a while," said Emma. [*Who Would Have Thought It?* 232]

Recent historical studies on the Civil War have given rise to a diversity of interpretations of the war itself, slavery and abolitionists. The "new political historians," for example, have tended to de-emphasize national and economic issues to concentrate on ethnic and cultural conflicts.[21] Foner, however, points to the danger in ahistorical accounts that focus on specific variables (religion, ethnicity, nativism, class, etc.) in isolation, as if they existed independently of historical context [1980, 18]. Clearly, in order to grasp more fully the historical processes, what is needed, in addition to a political history that focuses on micro-structures and the individual, is a social history that provides a more global picture of the interplay between all these forces [1980, 30]. Novels of the ante-bellum and Civil War period published in the nineteenth century are particularly rich in elucidating historical variables such as ethnicity, gender or religion and should in fact be tapped for this micro-structural type of political history. But novels, as historians are increasingly recognizing, can also be fruitfully mined to evoke a more general and broader view of society, both of the political and social context, despite the evident gaps and absences inherent in any text, fictional or not.

In this regard, *Who Would Have Thought It?* allows for a recasting of our understanding of the ante-bellum period by focusing not on the issue of slavery—glaringly absent in the novel—but on ethnocultural and ideological conflicts and their impact on an emerging empire. The key ingredient, or rather enabling agent, that exposes these conflicts and contradictions will be the wealth of the young Lola Medina, first introduced when Dr. James Norval, after a four-year absence doing geological research in the newly appropriated Southwest, returns to Massachusetts in 1857 with an added surprise: the dark-skinned ten-year-old María Dolores (Lola) Medina, along with several enormous boxes of what look like rock specimens collected in the Southwest. The reaction of the abolitionist Mrs. Norval to the dark child in the red shawl, whom she sees as black and would prefer sending to eat in the kitchen with the servants, will expose the deep-seated racism among abolitionist Yankees. The novel in fact reveals significant racial and class contradictions during the ante-bellum period in the North, where, as Foner indicates, "racial prejudice was all but universal" [Foner, 1980, 77]. It bears remembering that in the decade of the 1850s, Massachusetts and the rest of New England were considered the centers of Abolitionism where an anti-slavery ideology had been present since the colonial period. This did not, however, lead to an open critique of slavery until the 1830s, when a new concept of a society of competing individuals emerged and displaced older notions about an organic and harmonious social order [Foner, 1980, 22-23]. It would thus be notions of individual rights that would lead to a condemnation of slavery. Abolitionism did not, however, mean the end of racism.[22] Moreover, we should remember that in the North, anti-slavery sentiments were more often a rejection of an unfree labor system at the threshold of modernization than support for racial integration and equality.[23]

Unlike many novels of the postbellum period often intent on mending a rent nation, the question of slavery stays in the background in the Ruiz de Burton novel; foregrounded are issues of religion, nativism, class relations, democracy, liberalism, women's suffrage, imperialism and modernization. What is, however, central to the novel is the issue of racism, linked closely to nativism and set forth from Chapter I, figuring prominently in a plot that combines the rescue of a captive girl with the despoliation of Mexican wealth. In this regard, Lola's deliverance from bondage and her mother's dictated narrative evoke the period's slave narratives and bring to mind Frederick Douglass' critique of the racism to be found in the North.[24] Racism will also serve as an obstacle to the novel's romantic plot. The abolitionist movement is only dealt with tangentially, with respect to its ideological impact—or lack thereof—on supporters of the anti-slavery movement, like Mrs. Norval (said to be a strict Garrisonian and follower of Wendell Phillips' teachings), the Cackles, Hackwell and Hammerhard, all middle-class Yankee advocates of abolitionism, temperance and internalized self-discipline. This social type, often presented as possessing "the character traits demanded by a 'modernizing' society" [Foner, 1980, 25], is held up to close scrutiny and ultimately unmasked in the novel; here abolitionists reveal themselves to be racists, temperance-promoting preachers to be drinkers, and the apparent self-restraint of the "pillars of the community" to be a sham. When personal gain and individual desire intervene, individualism, considered the very core of the Protestant work and moral ethic, overturns and lays waste all notions of order, self-discipline and righteousness, previously so vehemently supported. In effect, the representation of the Norval family's weaknesses and desires and its later fragmentation are a transcoding not only of the Republic but of the North itself, divided along political and economic lines even in the midst of the Civil War.

The Abolitionist Republican Mrs. Norval, who reacts to Lola's darkness "with a slight shiver of disgust" [17], further reveals herself to be a nativist and to hate all things foreign, unlike her Democrat husband, who sends his son Julian to study in Europe and introduces his brother-in-law Isaac to European cuisine and wine. In his absence, however, Mrs. Norval brings her son back home to study in a "proper" Boston college. The New Englander's racism is also seen to be based on unmitigated ignorance, as in the comic scene in which the Norval family, contemplating Lola, the doctor's latest "specimen," discusses the differences between Indians and Blacks and posits the existence of a tribe of "Pinto" Indians whose skin is splotchy, like that of pinto beans. Both the family and the preachers reify the child, making all kinds of ignorant suppositions and observations in her presence, only to find that the child speaks English and has understood every word. In much the same vein, and ignoring Hackwell's lesson on geography, Mrs. Cackle, undaunted, goes on to insist that, in her mind, all non-Anglos are foreigners and cannibals: "To me they are all alike—Indians, Mexicans, or Californians—they are all horrid" [11]. Selective application of the right to religious freedom is also exposed in the same section which presents Mrs. Norval as a staunch advocate of freedom of religion, but not when it comes to Catholicism, which she dismisses as that religion of "abominable idolatry" [24]. Her less dogmatic husband, on the other hand, advocates "the right to choose our religion" whatever it might be since, according to him, they all serve the same function [66]. From the opening chapters of the novel to its conclusion, in numerous instances such as these, the discrepancy between "anti-slavery" discourses and racist practices is clearly laid out.

As Dr. Norval later recounts to his wife, between puffs on his pipe (while the child, sent to the maids' room but unable to bear the stench and the snoring of the Irish maids, sleeps out on the floor in the hall), the child he has brought home is an orphan, the daughter of a pregnant Mexican woman, Doña Teresa Almenara de Medina, kidnapped by the Apache Indians in Sonora in 1846 and brought north to the Colorado River area where she was sold to the Mohave Indians and made the woman of the Indian chief. Here the narrative makes it a point to indicate that the girl's mother is of Spanish blood and her father, Spanish as well, although Austrian by birth. To keep them from escaping and from attracting attention, the Indians made the two captives dye their skin and thereby pass for Indians. Doña Teresa had not attempted, however, to escape, for she no longer felt herself "fit" to return to civilization or to see her family again and only wished to help her daughter escape, to be baptized and brought up as a Roman Catholic. She conceives the violation of her body as a violation of her marriage vows, a debasement too shameful for the family, i.e. the men in the Medina and Almenara families, to bear. In true martyr form, she places their honor above her suffering.

Class, gender and race, here interconnected, reveal cultural constraints on women and their consent to norms that subordinate them significantly, the novel shows, as much in Mexico as in the United States; the novel also counters stereotypical notions of Mexicans with a construction of upper-class Latino/as as white, a perhaps defensive—though not defensible—move on Ruiz de Burton's part, in view of the fact that Congressional records of the period refer to Mexicans in the Southwest as "a mongrel race." Unlike a novel like Lydia Maria Child's, *A Romance of the Republic*,[25] which in its critique of slavery focuses on miscegenation as an intrinsic part of U.S. society and on the greed, self-indulgence and sexual activities on the part of Southern slave owners, Ruiz de Burton uses the child's artificial darkness, explained but initially disbelieved, as a mechanism for laying bare Yankee hypocrisy and racial attitudes and racism, in the process revealing "opposing versions of America" [Davidson, 158]. Ultimately the thorny issues of racism and miscegenation are conveniently sidestepped in *Who Would Have Thought It?* by making Lola's blackness only "blackface," and later allowing for an "acceptable" marriage, within the parameters of the romance. Lola's blackness is only one of the masks that will fall in the novel, but it does highlight the New Englanders' preference for concealment and masking. Thus masks and deception are more often than not found to be more credible than logical explanations and the stereotype of Mexicans as dark will prove to be enduring as we find Rev. Hackwell commenting years later, on the arrival of Lola's father: "the accursed blue-eyed Mexican. [...] Who ever heard of a blue-eyed Mexican" [253]. Yet even after Lola's skin returns to its natural color, she will continue to be the dark Catholic outsider to xenophobic Mrs. Norval, portrayed in these episodes as the witch whom the child must avoid and yet obey. For "the dreaded Mrs. Norval" anything foreign is diseased and to be kept contained, or at least at arm's length. Thus, as the dye on Lola's skin begins to fade, Mrs. Norval assumes the spots to represent "some sort of cutaneous disease" [79]. As a result of her "condition," Lola is constantly humiliated in the Norval home.[26] Lola, never totally idealized like little Eva in *Uncle Tom's Cabin*,[27] is nonetheless portrayed as beautiful, virtuous, intelligent and reserved; she is the object of both scorn and desire but, positioned on the margins, functions as a counterpoint to Jemima, without doubt the central character in the novel. Although defenseless and powerless within Jemima's household, Lola is beyond moral reproach, incorruptible, much to Hackwell's chagrin. She is also presented as having her own class/cultural identity, even as a child, seen ostensibly in her notions of cleanliness, her repugnance at the thought of sleeping with the Irish maids, and her unshakable religious faith.

Significantly, especially once she falls in love with Julian, Lola too becomes exceedingly concerned with the whitening of her skin, lest he think her an Indian or black. The child's whitening thus functions as a socially symbolic act, working out social contradictions while at the same time containing them. The performance of blackface will serve to make transparent the deceptions and hypocrisy of the New England community, but in the end, when her whiteness is revealed, it serves to maintain the norm of whiteness within the romance and within dominant upper-class New York society, where she will now be admissible. The narrative thus uses the issue of Lola's changing skin color and even the possibility of miscegenation as a way of censuring abolitionist racism.

The Plunder of Mexican Gold

> "To me they are all alike—Indians, Mexicans, or Californians—they are all horrid. But my son Beau says that our just laws and smart lawyers will soon '*freeze them out.*' That as soon as we take their lands from them they will never be heard of any more, and then the Americans, with God's help, will have all the land that was so righteously acquired through a just war and a most liberal payment in money. Ain't that patriotism and Christian faith for you?" added Mr. Hackwell. [*Who Would Have Thought It?* 11]

Whatever repugnance Mrs. Norval might harbor towards the dark Lola, "the horrible little negro girl" [25], it does not however extend to the wealth that accompanies her person. In fact, Jemima comes to see Lola's fortune as rightfully her own, as part of her manifest destiny, she being of a superior race. Here again cultural stereotypes are foregrounded in the text as we have Julian asking that his mother invite Lola, who is about to finish her schooling at a Catholic boarding school, to come to New York, to their new home, bought with Lola's money. Knowing Lola is not welcome there, Julian threatens to marry Lola right away unless she is allowed to come live with them. Hearing this and not wanting to be separated from Lola's wealth, Mrs. Norval calls Lola "a good Mexican," who "knows how to put the dagger to the throat," but Julian counters the insult: "Pshaw! In this instance the simile is bad, for we have appropriated the purse, not she" [180]. The only thieves are of course the Norvals, who have appropriated for themselves Lola's wealth.

The arrival of Lola Medina thus not only unmasks the racism and nativism of abolitionists but also introduces into the narrative agenda a new issue, the appropriation of Mexican space as a result of the U.S.-Mexican War. While Ruiz de Burton's 1885 novel, *The Squatter and the Don,* will deal more specifically with the dispossession of the Californios, *Who Would Have Thought It?* provides an allegorical reading of the modernization and expansion of the United States through corruption, war, and usurpation. While backgrounded and in good measure subordinated to the narratives of romantic love and intrigue, Ruiz de Burton's novel deals with several forms of accumulation of capital, especially with the war effort, which accelerates investment and industrialization. But, as noted above, there is also a discussion of a more primitive type of accumulation that is more akin to the conquest, plunder and piracy practiced by European colonizers in the Americas. Just as colonization and the ensuing plunder of gold and silver would have an enormous impact on European development, on the industrial revolution and on the Enlightenment, so too the conquest of the Southwest and its bonanza of gold and silver mines in California, Arizona and Nevada would stimulate the modernization of the United States.

The plunder of the Southwest is allegorized in *Who Would Have Thought It?* in the Yankees' appropriation of the Mexican girl's gold and jewels and warrants closer examination. The narration of Lola's displacement from the Southwest begins, as we know, with Norval's geological expedition to the Gila region near the Colorado River, where he and his party come across a large group of Indians returning with several wounded after attacking a wagon train and fighting the U.S. cavalry. To avoid being killed, Norval and his party assist the Indians at their camp and meet the chief's wife, *ña-Hala*, who shortly thereafter reveals her identity as Teresa Almenara de Medina to Norval and requests his assistance in saving her daughter Lola. It is in exchange for his services that Doña Teresa offers him half of the cache of gold, diamonds and gems that for ten years she has accumulated in a ravine, intending with it to save her daughter and see that she is educated. The subsequent departure of Norval with the child and close to a million dollars worth of gold and gems hidden in specimen boxes (once Doña Teresa has dictated her *testimonio* in Spanish to one of Norval's assistants) is too much for the mother to bear and she, as befits her role in the romance, dies as her child leaves in Dr. Norval's care.[28]

The allegorical "plunder" of the Southwest will create new millionaires back on the East coast and rapidly produce a number of social changes, putting to the test and melting in the process a number of supposedly "essential" social constraints. The transformation is evident from the start as we have the description of Mrs. Norval kneeling before the enormous specimen boxes, overwhelmed and absorbed by the gems and gold, the "glittering fortune," that unfortunately belong to the "despised black child" [30]; we see her scooping out the treasure by the handful: "The sedate, sober, serious lady of forty was a playful, laughing child again" [25]. The arrival of the gold in Massachusetts will strip the veneer of the righteous Puritan and transform Mrs. Norval into a desiring and plotting woman. The chests of gold function, then, as a Pandora's box, unleashing repressed desires of all sorts. The orphan Lola, a mere child of ten, will be defenseless against the greed and voracious appetite of Mrs. Norval for what is not hers—just as the U.S. had long lusted after the Mexican territory and the wealth contained therein. Thanks to the not insignificant infusion of capital, the family's fortunes improve, with a new home, carriages and horses, although Lola is treated like an odious stepchild by the matron, who grudgingly provides for her. In true romance fashion, the *testimonio* manuscript awaited by Dr. Norval for details on Lola's origins so that he can search for her father, will however fail to arrive, as it ends up in the "dead-letter" file at the Washington post office. It will be the fortuitous finding of the manuscript by Norval's brother-in-law Isaac and his tracking of the Medina-Almenara family in Mexico several years later that will allow for a happy resolution of the romantic emplotment involving Lola and Julian.

The Prison Camps

> "What a debasing thing is war, when it suggests to man such horrible, ghastly ideas, and his fellowman applauds him for them, and instead of calling him an inhuman monster, calls him a great man." So reasoned Lavvy, like a true woman, losing sight entirely of the main point of Mr. Blower's argument. [*Who Would Have Thought It?* 115]

U.S. expansionism and empire-building would be put on hold by the Civil War, another crucial social space in the Ruiz de Burton novel.

Who Would Have Thought It? does not describe the actual military campaigns of the Civil War, but does allow for a glimpse of what occurs behind the scenes: the flight of soldiers and officers, the wounding of Julian, the viewing of the spectacle by Congressmen from a safe distance, and the putative heroic actions of cowards, like Julius Cackle. The Union Army's 1861 defeat at the battle of Bull Run, which historically led to the capture and imprisonment of about fifty officers and approximately a thousand enlisted men in Confederate prison camps,[29] initiated both formal and informal policies of prisoner exchange between North and South. In the novel, Isaac Sprig is one of the prisoners taken by the Confederates. As a prisoner of war, Isaac continues to languish in a southern prison camp long after that battle without being exchanged; the reason: he has been practically erased from official memory due to the mean-spirited intervention of a member of Congress, Le Grand Gunn, the Cackles' ally, who, as "second assistant to the Secretary of War" was in charge for a time of prisoner exchange. A personal fight between the two over the affections of the quadroon belle, Lucinda, had triggered Le Grand Gunn's spiteful deletion of Isaac's name from the list of prisoners to be exchanged.

Historically, we know that commanders of both armies would sometimes exchange prisoners on the field, but the U.S. government at first preferred not to negotiate any exchange to avoid recognizing the Confederacy. In 1862 a cartel for the formal exchange of prisoners was signed, but this agreement would be short-lived, given a series of irresolvable conflicts. The North, for example, asked that Black soldiers be treated as prisoners of war, but the Confederates insisted on returning recaptured slaves to their masters [Hesseltine, 103-104]. The North also feared that exchanged Confederate prisoners would return to the firing line again. Each side accused the other of poor treatment of prisoners of war, but clearly, as the novel stresses, the South was so ravaged that it could not adequately feed, clothe or shelter its own soldiers, much less provide for Union prisoners.

The novel goes to great pains to expose the "barbarous policy" [117] of the North that called precisely for *not* exchanging Union soldiers held in the South in order to deplete further Confederate soldiers of supplies ("because they help to consume the resources of the South" [114]) and to add additional distress to the rebels. Never formally approved by Congress, such a measure, undoubtedly, would not have been popular with the soldiers' families in the North ("And do THE PEOPLE of the United States—I mean *the loyal people*—do they approve of their brothers being left to starve in the South?" [115-16]). Lavinia, who searches for information on her imprisoned and forgotten brother, is encouraged by a lobbyist to be "a patriotic girl" and resign herself "to the misfortune that made [her] brother one of the noble victims selected by Providence to be the means of subjugating the wicked traitors, and thus putting down a rebellion *never equaled for its magnitude and want of cause*" [italics in original, 114]. Lavvy, in a reprise of the Antigone role, finds the measure monstrous:

> What a debasing thing is war, when it suggests to man such horrible, ghastly ideas, and his fellow man applauds him for them, and instead of calling him an inhuman monster, calls him a "great man"! So reasoned Lavvy, like a true woman, losing sight entirely of the main point of Mr. Blower's argument. [115]

This seemingly quick and condescending dismissal of Lavinia's reaction is meant to underscore the obvious, the lack of humanity in the government policy, so clearly evident to a woman, and simultaneously to mock a man's defense of what is deemed a magnanimous policy of starvation as a concept and course of action "beyond [women's] sphere of thought" [115]. The "people" here are feminized by those in power and deemed incapable of understanding these policies. As the lobbyist condescendingly indicates to Lavvy:

> Ours is a popular—ahem!—government, my dear lady, but our leading men do not lay before the people all new great measures, some of which the unthinking multitude could not grasp at once; not until time and trial have shown their wisdom. [116]

Lavvy, however, is not one to be taken in by Mr. Blower's rhetoric. Let those that form part of "the best government on earth" go down to the prisons themselves, she says: "They would not be so heroic if they were starving in a horrid prison on the other side" [116]. Her ally Congressman White, on the other hand, finds the very idea of an unwritten policy of no prisoner exchange unconscionable and seeks to deny the lobbyist's pragmatic and undemocratic assertions, adding that to believe that Congress would approve of this barbarous policy, this "soul-sickening holocaust," is to slander Congress [117]. The fact that over 22,576 Union soldiers (of a total 270,000 prisoners) would die in Confederate prisons of starvation, diarrhea, dysentery, small pox, maggots, exposure to the elements from lack of clothing, blankets, tents, and from other diseases might of course give the ultimate response to this debate. Confederate soldiers would not, however, fare better; in fact, their death rate in Northern prisons would be higher. Of a total 220,000 Confederate soldiers in northern prisons, 26,436 died.[30]

Lavinia first enters the public sphere when she becomes the charge nurse of a hospital ward. She makes use of her contact with wounded soldiers and exchanged prisoners of war in Washington D.C. to inquire after her missing brother Isaac in hope that someone has seen him at one of the prison camps. Her conversations with these ex-prisoners will allow for one of the more realistic, even naturalistic, representations in the novel: the reconstruction of the hunger, sickness and desperation in the Confederate prisons. It bears recalling that by 1872 when *Who Would Have Thought It?* was published, several accounts had been published of life in Southern prisons [Sprague, 142]. Among them, the eye-witness account of Homer B. Sprague would tell of the deaths of hundreds of prisoners abandoned to starvation. Hesseltine in his 1930 study of Civil War prisons reviews an account by prisoners of one particular episode at Belle Isle which involved the capture of the prison commandant's pet poodle by prisoners, who in desperation ate it [Hesseltine, 124]. In the novel, an episode closely resembling the account in Hesseltine is related to Lavinia by the exchanged prisoners.

However, while going into detail about the misery of war prisoners,[31] the novel fails to recount or even make mention of the Draft Riots of 1863, although the Norval family is by then in New York City. Historically, the draft, instituted after Gettysburg, generated a great deal of anger among the populace because it allowed the wealthy to buy themselves out of conscription; it was the poor white laborer who had to go fight.[32] By focussing strictly on the middle and upper classes in the North, and on the earlier volunteer soldiers and officers, the novel ignores much of the social strife of the North as well as the plight of the poor, primarily Irish immigrants, and their cramped living conditions, although there is some attempt to describe the rat-infested quarters of two rank and file soldiers working under Hackwell.[33]

The novel does not, however, ignore that, for some, wars have always proved economically profitable—"A long war was good for the Cackle family" [164]. The Civil War, we know, would speed up production of materials and supplies needed in the battlefield and lead to an economic boom. The need for uniforms, for example, meant contracts for local clothiers, although the quality of the material used was not always satisfactory, as occurred historically in the well-known case of uniforms produced by Brooks Brothers with shoddy cloth [McKay, 73].[34] In *Who Would Have Thought It?* the Cackles are likewise involved in selling shoddy goods to the government [290]. Without going into detail, the novel makes clear that rogues like the Cackles were ready to use the war for profit-making through government "contracts" of rotten blankets and of shoes made of burnt leather" [290]. It is known, of course, that the production of military materiel and ordinance proved profitable to Northern businessmen [McKay, 78]. Machine shops profited from war contracts for iron forgings, castings and marine engines, metal, timber, etc. In not a few cases profit came before loyalty, and materials, be it wagons, medical supplies or rifles for the Confederacy, were shipped from the port of New York to Matamoros or Nassau, despite Congressional orders to block all illicit trade with the South [McKay, 223-224]. Consequently, a new segment of millionaires, making their wealth "through political contacts and outright corruption" [McKay, 220], would dominate the business world and join the ranks of the "old money." As the war came to a close, new scandals were revealed as rivals took turns accusing each other of taking advantage of the war and selling shoddy blankets, uniforms, and guns to the government. These exposés, and in some cases court trials of profiteers and corrupt officials, would achieve the status of spectacle in the post-war period.

If the uniforms and weapons were shoddy, the ad-hoc recruited troops were also in good measure untrained and not ready to engage in a war of maneuver; often they panicked and retreated in the midst of battle. Civil War history is replete with such cases, as is the novel in its account of the cowardly desertion of Julius Caesar Cackle, whose encounter with Le Grand Gunn, a fallen and fleeing battle spectator, ended with Cackle's half-hearted efforts to aid him, all of which, ironically, resulted in Cackle's promotion. In a second incident, the novel again mocks now "General" Cackle, whose runaway horse is mistaken for a sudden charge upon the enemy, again unjustifiably earning him even further laurels as a hero and fearless leader. The guilefulness and cowardice of Hackwell, who shot himself in the leg while trying to get away from the battle scene, and the Cackle brothers and other untrained men who were granted the rank of colonel, major or general without meriting it, are derisively portrayed in the novel and contrasted with the patriotism and courage of Julian Norval and others, both officers and enlisted men. Thus, in its representation of the social field of the Civil War era, the novel specifies that with the war came certain opportunities—not only economic, but in terms of professional advancement—all part of larger scale socio-economic changes that would transform the nation. Just as these changes facilitated upward mobility for some, for others, women especially, they made for the removal of restrictions that allowed for greater social mobility and interaction, for example, in Jemima's Norval's life—and most notably in her sister Lavinia's, as we have seen.

The Fall of Republican Motherhood

Was it Hackwell alone who had caused this change in the rigid pink of blue propriety, or had external influences—MONEY—helped him? [*Who Would Have Thought It?* 173]

Nineteenth-century domestic novels, like the Stowe text mentioned before, are often centered around the home and the church; religious faith and preachers who serve as friendly advisers [Baym, 44] are constructed as having an important impact on the moral fiber of republican families. Countering from the start this idealized framing of church and preacher, Ruiz de Burton's novel opens in a picaresque mode as it follows two parsons, Rev. John Hackwell and Rev. Hammerhard, riding in a rickety wagon led by an old nag on their way to the train station to pick up the returning Dr. James Norval. In a community where the consensus is abolitionist, anti-Catholic and self-righteous, Dr. Norval, the non-conformist scientist, is portrayed as a pseudo-rogue, the whetstone of the townspeople that keeps tongues wagging as they censure him and his "deviant" ideas. The real rogues are of course the parsons themselves, who are soon revealed to be opportunists, seducers, and hypocrites and yet have enormous influence over the town's womenfolk. While preaching temperance, these two imbibe their whisky behind closed doors and are not beyond blackmail, deception, false representation and violation of others' rights. The novel thus begins by satirizing all that is idealized in nineteenth-century romantic literature and counters notions about Latin America and "popery" by showing these New England women to be "parson-ridden" (as opposed to "priest-ridden") and overly influenced by their preachers.

The prodigal Norval returns home from the Southwest to find in his wife Jemima a powerful matron whose word has been law during his four-year absence. After nineteen years of marriage, Jemima Norval is "a model of matronly virtues and a stickler for propriety" [251]. The family lives in a small Massachusetts town, away from the farm where the couple first met and where we are told Jemima Sprig, like other women, was involved in domestic production of eggs, pickles, butter and applesauce for sale in the Boston market. While close to the manufacturing centers of Boston, this small town is still dependent on the production of its yeomanry who, like the Sprigs or Cackles, work nearby family farms. Marriage to the college-trained geologist meant leaving the farm to become a housewife and mother, in effect the ruler of the hearth, although the family continued to depend on income from Norval's farm [121]. By 1857 cottage industries, however, are no longer in the picture and the now middle-class Norval family, though considering thrift a Puritan virtue, has two maids, and Mr. Norval has his own personal servant. Presented as a strong-willed and resourceful woman in control of her family (her three children and her younger brother and sister), her domestic help (the two Irish immigrant maids) and the purse strings, which she holds tight, Jemima Norval is quite unlike her generous husband, who is presented as always ready to help the Sprig family as much as his neighbors and other townsfolk in need. Within the home, Jemima rules as a tyrant, as her sister Lavinia recognizes [138].

The novel's entry into the homespace of the Norval household allows us to see how market capitalism has led to the separation of the home from the workplace, converted the family into a private institution, and reconstructed the home as a domestic sphere under the control of women. This privatization of the domestic is captured in the narrative by the description of fenced houses. Neighbors dying for a bit of gossip, like Mrs. Cackle (whose sons owe their political placement in Washington D.C. to Dr. Norval), must now wait at the fence till some member of the family makes an appropriate gesture to invite them on the premises. The boundaries of the private sphere are not however totally closed as each household is ever in relation with the rest of the community, contact mediated for the most part through the various churches. Members of the Norval family, for example, belong to two churches, Reverend Hackwell's and Reverend Hammerhard's, and there is frequent socializing of Church members and parsons. As Douglas indicates, church-going had become the dominant form of religious practice by mid-century [7]. But though the more orthodox version of Calvinism might be on the wane, Jemima Norval continues to have traditional values and strict notions about proper behavior, notions applauded by the minister of her church. The church in effect serves as a second domestic sphere dominated by clergymen and women. Social differences are marked by power of acquisition and consumption, already evident here as they serve to exclude particular young ladies from socializing, especially if their mothers, like Jemima Norval, prefer thrift to consumption of articles in fashion.

In *Who Would Have Thought It?*, republican motherhood will find itself disestablished by market forces, consumerism and urbanization, all attributable to the emerging new industrial order in nineteenth-century U.S. society. The novel reconstructs aspects of modernization that gave rise to the production of new social spaces and new social constructs, providing in the process new roles for middle-class women. No longer co-producers of staples, women were now reconstructed in domestic novels and popular magazines as the pillars of family values (morals) and civic responsibility; their power now lay in their exertion of moral influence and their economic power as consumers [Douglas, 17, 68, 117].

As played out by Ruiz de Burton in *Who Would Have Thought It?*, the "modernization" of the Norvals can be traced to the family's sudden acquisition of wealth. Their usufructuary appropriation of Lola's fortune becomes the turning point in the fortunes of the family, signaling a changing class position that corresponds to a new phase of production in the North. The infusion of capital will radically alter the Norval household and will transform the matron from a prim and proper Pilgrim into a nineteenth-century consumer and lady of leisure. Again working against the grain of the dominant fiction of the day, Ruiz de Burton's novel focuses not on woman's "moral and religious influence" [Douglas, 60] but on her hypocrisy and even moral corruption; ironically, this counter-moral behavior is the result of a type of self-reliance, leading to the emotional and sexual realization of the republican mother, although in the end at the price of her consenting to her own deception and debasement. Dr. Norval's self-exile and announced death, along with the family's new wealth, are the catalysts that will loosen social constraints on the matron and facilitate Hackwell's conniving, not so much against her, but rather, significantly, with her. Thus it is that Jemima, head of household and in control of Lola's wealth, this "strict hater of popery, a pious, proper churchwoman" [173], whose only passion has been "her religious bigotry" and whose only ambition has been to save "more pennies and five- and ten-pieces than any of her neighbors" [231], finds herself seduced and thrilled beyond measure by none other than "her spiritual adviser," the now ex-Reverend Hackwell, a non-combatant officer in the Union Army, who makes "her heart throb [...] in such unmatronly, unpresbyterian tumult" [173]. Her clandestine marriage to Hackwell follows soon after his suggested move to a bustling New York City.[35] The insularity of New England is now replaced by intense social interaction. By dipping liberally into Lola's fortune, the Norval family moves into the circle of the leisured class, receives company at home and attends gala events. The secret marriage between Mrs. Norval and Hackwell becomes one more urban enterprise "manageable" in a mansion on New York's Fifth Avenue with secretly connecting adjoining bedrooms. With their new upper-class status comes the voicing of a repugnance for the lower classes; the novel pointedly condemns those like the Cackles and Ruth Norval who, once in the money, claim to hate poverty and poor people in order to distance themselves from their yeomanry background [288]. In this, *Who Would Have Thought It?* adopts a stance of patrician disdain for the social parvenu, presented as ignorant, uncouth, unscrupulous and mean-spirited, the nouveau riche that through questionable dealings and corruption moves into a higher socio-economic bracket and becomes a contending force in society.

Ruiz de Burton's mapping of public and private spaces in her novel is thus a mapping of the social, economic and cultural transformations taking place as the country moves from country to city, from incipient manufacturing to industrial revolution, from competitive capitalism to corporate/monopoly capitalism. As the novel charts the nation's social and ideological spaces, it also provides a critical commentary of U.S. republicanism, monopoly capitalism, political and economic corruption, and individual opportunism. In this way microstructural spaces are transcoded to the level of macro-structures. The narrative functions thus as an allegory of the "modernization" of the United States through plunder, corruption and war. Constructing this transformation at both an individual and structural level is carried out through various strategies of containment. Social and political problems are contained through two leading strategies in the novel: violation and deception. Implicit in both operations is the idea of a social contract (at both a micro- and macro-structural level) that has been breached. The breach or violation will, however, be at first successfully concealed, yet constantly in danger of being revealed. The novel traces the dialectic of concealment and deconcealment within two major overlapping spatial dimensions: family and public spaces. The constant threat of revelation or disclosure of particular secrets or "truths" at either the family or national level serves to advance novelistic action and to unmask discrepancies and contradictions within the political framework. These opposing narrative strategies of concealment and unmasking reveal the novel's rich interplay of multiple and contradictory perspectives contained within a façade of acceptability and hypocrisy, ever more accessible in a volatile urban setting which banks on appearances and façades.

The novel's coverplot of seduction takes us from Jemima's moral conceit to her fall and eventual quasi-redemption, if retreat into madness and later the steadfast support of a "good husband" can be read as "redemption." The fall of "republican motherhood," read allegorically, marks the violation of the marriage contract, just as Norval's persecution, as we shall see, will signal a violation of the Constitution. Also significant is the fact that Mrs. Norval's transgression will be concealed from all but the reader and the villains involved. Jemima Norval, thinking, and later hoping, her husband dead, will assume that her clandestine "marriage" to the recently widowed Hackwell (performed by co-conspirator Hammerhead) is legal, although she will consent to hiding the relationship from the rest of the family and live in constant fear of "some dreadful calamity," that is, the announcement that her husband is alive [251].

The matron's fall is initiated in the small town in Massachusetts and consummated in New York City. Here in the city, portrayed as the site of consumerism and accelerated living, concealment is easy. Social interaction is both public and private, with the latter now open to a larger social circle and given to more formal receptions, generally in the late evening.[36] The city also promotes greater consumption. As part of a commodity culture, daughter Ruth, for example, who previously sublimated her desires for consumption through the reading of women's magazines, can in New York give full rein to her consuming passion; she is constantly absorbed by the latest fashions and entirely involved with her latest purchases. There is as well a new pace in urban society, as evident in the description of the trip taken by Hackwell's subalterns, who eat on the run. Like the rest of the country, the U.S. population is said, for example, to prefer eating fast food and gulping it down, suffering frequent dyspepsia [157]. In this, *Who Would Have Thought It?* thus traces how by mid-century social practices have undergone change in conjunction with the production of new social spaces.

Mrs. Norval's repressed consumerist proclivities are also revealed. Jemima (now referred to by the less severe sounding "Jenny" by Hackwell), who previously had prudishly hated theatre, now, dressed in the latest fashions and looking several years younger, accompanies the dashing and younger Hackwell and her family to the opera. She now dresses very well, has her hair done every day, and adopts "womanly" gestures: "She had grown younger and improved in appearance rapidly since her arrival in New York" [171]. Jemima Norval is never more feminine than when she falls in love with the dashing Hackwell and never more willing to effect a radical transformation of her life than when she foregoes her Puritan upbringing and submits to her passion. But it is not only Hackwell's "love" that has changed her, the narrator mockingly reminds us, but wealth, money taken from another, that allows her to spend to her heart's content.

> ...she loved this new state of being. She had so far degenerated that she regarded her youth as misspent, her life a blank, until she loved Hackwell, until she was past forty. Poor woman! to have been a chrysalis all her days! Who would not excuse this avalanche of the snows of forty years? [173]

The ironic portrayal of Jemima's transformation into the younger-looking Jenny serves to mock not only the sexually-realized Puritan matron but the social and economic transformation of society taking place as well; with the increased circulation of commodities comes, in effect, the increased "circulation," mobility, of women within public spheres. But, at the same time, the narrator considers this circulation a degeneration of values, comparable to a historical and political degeneration at the level of nation. And so it is that, at her age, Jenny discovers passion and ardor, the degree and intensity of which surprises even the "preaching scoundrel" Hackwell [39], whose report on "the madam" leads the Reverend Hammerhead to call her a veritable "Yankee Popocatepetl" [177]. Hackwell, ever insightful, "moralizes" as follows:

> There is more latent passion in one of those women who live with frozen-up souls half of their lives, than in those impetuous, susceptible children of feeling who have burnt their hearts to a cinder before they are thirty-five. [174]

Here again the novel overturns the stereotypical description of passionate Latin women by mockingly describing the repressed passion of a good Puritan woman, "a model of matronly virtues, and a stickler for propriety" [251]. The stern Mrs. Norval is given to us as unable to respond to "the devotion, the generosity and the kindness" [174] of a good man, but ready to yield to the conniving pretense of a villain, an unscrupulous man consumed by his own demons and passion for another, about which Jenny did not know: "no wife ever does," notes the narrator in an understanding aside [251]. The narrator voices a tongue-in-cheek understanding of Jenny's situation and deals half-compassionately and half-moralistically with the poor woman's weakness. The characterization of Jemima and her fall, in fact, undermine and mock the reader's expectations of a domestic novel, although perhaps not entirely, as in the end, knowledge of her husband's survival (information concealed from the start by Hackwell and Hammerhard) and his return drive the poor woman insane, for she is unable to deal with the "horror" of her "debasement" and its revelation [267]. In Mrs. Norval's case, unlike Teresa's, the matron's debasement is presented as self-inflicted. Here again we have the representation of the repression of women (where sexual transgression is punishable by madness or death) and of women's consent to their own subordination as central themes in *Who Would Have Thought It?*

The tracking of the trajectory of the morally virtuous, up-right and previously thrifty Jemima through to her fall is central to *Who Would Have Thought It?* It is the fall of the cult of motherhood itself, but it is also a concealed fall, for the icon will remain unsullied before the eyes of all the world, save those of the villains involved. Her madness will be explained away as resulting from the shock of learning that her husband is still alive. The tension and "glaring gap between the public morality officially espoused and the private behavior of the characters in the sentimental novel" [Davidson, 135] sums up the picaresque contradictions constructed in Ruiz de Burton's narrative. The rogue Hackwell is throughout presented as a typical unrepentant *pícaro*, a scoundrel capable of self-reflection and analysis but willing to deceive and con his way to his objective. As a rogue operating in an unprincipled and therefore unfixed ideological field, Hackwell also serves as a weathervane turning from side to side as best serves his immediate circumstances, in the process voicing opposing ideological discourses. It is Hackwell, then, who can speculatively look to a day when the patriarchal system will be overthrown and women will gain a chance to right the world. But it is also Hackwell who is willing to put patriarchy to his service by entrapping Lola into what he will construe as a common-law marriage, by threatening to reveal to the whole world the fate of Teresa Medina at the hands of the Indians, and by threatening to expose Jemima's adultery, all this in order to win Lola. The former preacher is thus presented as a symbol of all that is decadent and, ironically, attractive to women; for his part Hackwell is vain enough to trust in his final success. Ironically, it takes a scoundrel, such as Hackwell, to know, expose and willingly exploit the flaws of the patriarchal system and to show women's complicity with it.

If in the telling of the fall of Mrs. Norval *Who Would Have Thought It?* parodies the seduction plot typical of women's fiction in two sub-plots, the novel reproduces it as well. These sub-plots involve the seduction of young ladies. Lavinia Sprig, for example, was seduced and then abandoned by Hackwell, to whom she was engaged, and was later courted but cast aside as well by the other parson, Rev. Hammerhead. Both "divines" marry the better-dressed, upwardly mobile Dix sisters. In the case of Lola, the Rev. Hackwell will attempt to seduce her, but she rejects his amorous offers, as she is in love with Julian. In the end, Lola will be able to escape his entrapment unscathed, thanks to Julian's intervention, as well as the fortuitous reappearance of her father and the intercession of a series of "helpers" including Isaac, Lavvy, and Mina.

Satire and parody thus come together in this picaresque portrayal of the preacher. We should bear in mind that we are speaking of a period in which clergymen were viewed as cultural "stars" in many communities, as the moral pulse of the nation; within this context the depiction of a preacher as scoundrel and the mocking of dominant moral discourses as dissembling serve to satirize the nation's moral standards as well as to mock women's fiction. It is no longer the question of a preacher seduced by a Hester Prynne, but rather the preacher as seducer of a matron. Hackwell is the antithesis of the sentimental, sensitive, delicate minister of nineteenth century fiction [Douglas, 104]. The representation in the text of Hackwell's un-parson-like behavior and highly compromised morality is undoubtedly meant to recall other scandals of the period, particularly that of the renowned anti-slavery preacher of the period, Henry Ward Beecher.[37] The Reverend Henry Ward Beecher was then the eminent pastor of the fashionable Plymouth Church in Brooklyn ("the most successful church in America" [Shaplen, 57].[38] It was Beecher's dramatic style and his capacity to assume various roles and make people either laugh or cry that packed the church every Sunday [Shaplen, 18, 20].. In 1870, two years before the publication of *Who Would Have Thought It?*, Elizabeth Richards Tilton, a woman of thirty-five and mother of four children, confessed to her husband Theodore Tilton that she had committed adultery with Reverend Beecher, himself a married man, and that the affair had been ongoing since 1868. The revelation of this affair would be reported nationwide and lead to a sensational public trial and two church councils that would rock the nation, a scandal reminiscent of present-day cases of adultery of well-known preachers. Because prominent pastors were then the equivalent of Hollywood or sport stars today, extensive newspaper coverage made the case a veritable nineteenth-century soap opera, with supporters defending the pastor's innocence and detractors accusing him of being an adulterer, perjurer and fraud [Shaplen, 5].[39]

Beecher's greatest sin, according to Frank Moulton, a mutual friend of the involved parties who became the mediator, was not adultery but hypocrisy [Shaplen, 94]. While Moulton tried to reconcile the parties and they in fact seemed willing to forgive and to conceal the affair's sordid details, it would be the advocate for "free love," Victoria Woodhull, in a May 22, 1871 letter to the *World* editor, who would first expose the scandal.[40] Woodhull would print a full exposé of the

Beecher-Tilton scandal story in her own *Weekly* [Shaplen, 157, 159] in 1872—the year *Who Would Have Thought It?* was published—the very year that Woodhull would be the first woman nominated for the presidency of the United States (as a candidate of the Equal Rights Party, with Frederick Douglass as her running-mate).

The Hackwell-Norval case is similar though not identical to that of Beecher-Tilton, as the Ruiz de Burton characters do not become involved in an affair until both are presumably widowed; yet Hackwell's behavior with Lavvy before the death of his wife does indicate that he felt no compunction at being a faithless husband. The preacher's lack of scruples, his fortune-hunting, his ability to seduce the matron under false pretenses—knowing full well her husband is alive, as he has kept Norval's letters from her—and his premeditated enactment of a fraudulent marriage all point to his villainy. A similar deception, although not involving a minister, is also to be found in Child's *A Romance of the Republic*, where the Southern plantation owner deceives the mulatta beauty, Rosabella, into thinking they have been married. The primary strategy in both narratives is thus deception, for nothing is as it appears and women's position allows them to fall into the scoundrels' hands. In the case of Jemima, outwardly the epitome of "republican motherhood" and "the pink of propriety," her fall is predicated on her deception and on her collusion with Hackwell, for behind closed doors both are shown to be willing to deceive themselves. As noted in the previous sections, the discrepancy between what is avowed and what occurs in practice is at the same time a commentary on the national social contract. In that sphere, the novel points out, there is also an implicit consent to being deceived.

Public Domestic Spaces

> She became from that day more firmly convinced than ever that ladies with hearts and brains were absolutely necessary to her country's cause [. . .] thoughtful women, who could judiciously order as well as obey in an emergency like this, which ended so tragically. [*Who Would Have Thought It?* 129]

The outbreak of the Civil War takes Julian Norval to the battlefront and Lavinia, Jenny's sister, to serve as a nurse in Union hospitals.

The Civil War—like subsequent wars—would afford women, previously circumscribed within the domestic sphere, entry into public spaces as a rule off-limits to them. Women would gain a public space during this period by again converting the domestic sphere into one of production for the Union cause, in the preparation of rations, clothing, blankets, bandages and other goods and articles, and by serving as nurses in Army hospitals and prison camps. Hospitals serve as an extension of domestic spaces into public space, thereby marking the continuity between private and public spheres and in effect blurring the distinction between these sites. The novel's argument for the competence and power of women within these spaces is especially clear in the case of Lavinia, who proves to be an excellent nurse and "runs a tight ship" on her hospital floor, much like her sister Jemima does at home. Her efficiency is essential, we find, as the one day Lavvy is absent and does not keep close watch on her ward, several soldiers die needlessly.[41]

Lavinia is not however constructed as a feminist, although historically women involved in the war effort would also figure prominently in the struggle for gender-specific interests, especially suffrage.[42] These women were also known for their social-reform work, be it abolitionist, temperance or labor related; yet in their various struggles for gender interests they often continued to adhere to all the patriarchal constraints placed upon moral, virtuous women.[43] A few women did, however, seek to break out of the mold of "republican motherhood." Susan B. Anthony and Elizabeth Cady Stanton were known, and reviled, for example, for their demands for more liberal divorce laws and for the right of women to propose to men [Shaplen, 14]. This was also the period of radicals like Woodhull, who advocated "free love" [Shaplen, 37].

Allusion to nineteenth-century feminist struggles forms a sort of backdrop in *Who Would Have Thought It?* It is the Norvals' French maid Mina, for example, who advocates free love and is far more astute and sophisticated—and ultimately loyal—to Lola than either of the two Norval daughters. Through her wiles and contacts, Mina will obtain information on Hackwell's intentions and plans, all of which will serve to save Lola from Hackwell's grasp. But, ironically, the one female character who gains a certain measure of liberation, emotionally and sexually, even if only for a short period, is, as we have seen, the severe Jemima, the cold and proper matron prohibiting all expression of affection at home, who later becomes effusive and passionate with Hackwell. The novel, however, "understandingly" mocks this "liberation" of passions which accompanies unrestrained greed, a total subordination to the scoundrel, a neglect of motherly duties, and an unenlightened view of race and foreigners. What should not go unremarked, however, is that in her allegorical function, Mrs. Norval's willingness to compromise all her presumed family values and to yield with slavish submission is constructed as akin to the nation's consent to its own subordination before blackguards like the Cackles and Hackwells. In fact, Jemima's willingness, as she says, to have Hackwell as her God [174], transcodes as a blind acquiescence to political domination in exchange for a limited freedom or liberation. Thus gender and other counter-ideological struggles interconnect in the novel at a number of suggestive levels.

Historically, the alliance between feminists and abolitionists disintegrated after the war, once it became clear that "national reconstruction" had no place for women's suffrage. Writer Child voiced bitterness in the face of women's exclusion from representation in a letter to Charles Sumner:

> If I were to give free vent to all my pent-up wrath concerning the subordination of women, I might frighten you.... Suffice it, therefore, to say, either the theory of our government is false, or women have a right to vote. [quoted in Foner[44]].

Similar frustrations with women's lack of power in public, i.e. within political spaces, are presented in *Who Would Have Thought It?*, especially in the case of Lavinia's futile attempts to try to get information from the War Department on her imprisoned brother Isaac. The government's failure to negotiate his exchange, despite his early capture and the exchange of many subsequent prisoners is beyond her comprehension. For Lavvy, a trip to the War Department is futile, for even the young officer acting as receptionist in the Secretary's office treats her with a lack of courtesy and dismisses her inquiries. Lavinia braves the snubs and condescension she faces as a woman in the very bosom of male power and reflects on the demeaning experience, realizing that it is not she, but her gender that is at the root of her mistreatment:

> Lavinia was becoming very tired, and was reflecting that no matter how much a woman, in her unostentatious sphere, may do, and help to do, and no matter how her heart may feel for her beloved, *worshiped* country, after all is but an insignificant creature, whom a very young man may snub simply because he wears very shiny brass buttons and his uncle is in Congress. "What a miserable, powerless thing woman is, even in this our country of glorious equality! Here I have been sitting up at night, toiling, and tending disgusting sick-

> ness, and dressing loathsome wounds, all for the love of our dear country, and now, the first time I come to ask a favor—a *favor*, do I say? No. I come to demand a right,—see how I am received!" [106]

Lavinia, shown here to be conversant with notions of "rights," is presented as expecting more than is forthcoming from "great men": "She had believed all she had read in printed political speeches delivered just before election times" [106]. Dismissed by the Secretary, she then leaves crying ("a common occurrence with the sex," according to her driver [106], and seeking recourse heads for the Capitol, which she finds populated by corrupt lobbyists and indifferent and sell-out Cackles. The fact that the Cackles are "at home" in the capital rotunda speaks volumes about the direction taken by the country.

Lavvy's naive notions of "rights" and her frustration with dominant discourses of "equality" suggest an emerging consciousness and the acquisition of strategic discourses. Although she is said to be "no advocate of 'woman's rights,'" Lavvy does begin to attain a certain critical perspective to see her situation in terms of gender and its relation to power: "[she] did not understand the subject even, but she smiled sadly, thinking how little woman was appreciated, how unjustly underrated. *She* could obtain *nothing* from the government,—the Cackles, *all*!" [129].

The character Lavvy, ridiculed earlier in the novel for pining away for her seducer Hackwell and for pathetically putting all her canaries to death to save them from a worse fate, is "rescued" and ultimately vindicated as a character when she moves from domestic to public spaces, developing in the narrative into the one admirable Sprig woman, wiser, unselfish, loyal and more kind than her sister or nieces, with a strong sense of right and responsibility. Her hospital experiences are crucial in this regard, allowing Lavinia to textually constitute herself as a middle-class woman in her own right, "with heart and brains." When, for example, in her absence from the hospital, several soldiers die due to the incompetence of the paid nurses, she resolves never to let her own concern for Isaac and Dr. Norval stand in the way of duty:

> She became from that day more firmly convinced than ever that ladies with hearts and brains were absolutely necessary to her country's cause. Not merely paid menials should attend the sick and wounded, but thoughtful women, who could judiciously order as well as obey in an emergency like this, which ended so tragically. [129]

Thus while the hospital serves, undoubtedly, as an extension of the domestic space, it will allow Lavinia to construct herself as female within a collective class identity and to challenge dominant notions of women while at the same time reinforcing classist biases.

Women like Mrs. Cackle, on the other hand, are presented as ignorant, gullible and mercenary. While Mr. Cackle enjoys reading the classics, and had in fact named all of his children after Roman or Greek heroes, his wife has little use for literature—classical or religious. She is, on the other hand, accepting of everything the government or newspapers say:

> ...as she was a good American woman, she believed firmly in "Manifest Destiny," and that the Lord was bound to protect the Union, even if to do so the affairs of the rest of the universe were to be laid aside for the time being. [159]

She therefore does not question the North's position on prisoner exchange nor doubt that it will win the war, for the war was good, "the best thing that could have happened," as it not only would free the slaves but also make her sons distinguished Congressmen and Generals [159]. Mrs. Cackle, like other citizens, both male and female, is portrayed as incapable of independent thought or of questioning political policies, especially when they buttress her family's economic interests and upward mobility.

Gullible and ignorant women characters are not the only ones satirized in *Who Would Have Thought It?* The novel is especially acute in its censure of vacuous and mercenary women, like Ruth, Norval's daughter. Ruth's love for wealth and consumption is paralleled by her lack of appreciation for anything not reducible to material profit. Upon the now rich Major General Julius Caesar Cackle's proposal of marriage to her, she sees "her life-dream realized":

> She saw herself the leader of *American bon-ton*, quoted and imitated by all the fashionable belles of New York and Washington, of Long Branch and Newport—all the well-dressed women who have a perfect right to be silly and trifling because their husbands conduct the mighty affairs of the nation; who have a perfect right to be spendthrifts because their husbands have, by extortion and driving hard bargains, accumulated princely fortunes—all these beautifully-dressed ladies who slander as they drive by in *their own* carriages, richly cushioned in damask; who backbite from their bay windows hung with costly satin; who snub and ignore old acquaintances if

> seen driving in the Park in a hired hack—all of this fortunate class Ruth wished to lead, and she felt equal to the task. [287–88]

Here again the collusion of women with their oppression—and that of others—is made clear in the novel in its representation of Ruth, whose "metallic heart" beats rapidly at the thought of her marriage to Julius Caesar Cackle and his "lard and salt-pork contracts" [290]. She is likewise only too happy to stimulate the market through the accelerated consumption of luxury goods. *Who Would Have Thought It?* does not therefore assume a blind defense of women, for it at all moments sees the articulation between gender, class and culture, and sees women as capable of assuming various positionalities, not all of which are positively portrayed.

Ironically, it is Hackwell, who, following the privileges of the rogue to refute himself, serves to point to a series of contradictory conditions within Gilded Age society and to construct the perspective of marginal elements, in this particular case, that of women. Thus the novel presents us with a scoundrel within mainstream society (and what can be more mainstream than a Presbyterian preacher) who becomes the ex-preacher voicing a dissonant perspective. In what is a parody of the hero's reflective soliloquy, *Who Would Have Thought It?* makes the reader privy to the scoundrel Hackwell's not-so-far-fetched notions on the nation and its governance. It will be Hackwell who notes society's penchant for "success" at whatever cost, taking particular aim at a society of men that rewards the arrogant and guilty and holds to male superiority:

> I think the sooner we give over to women the management of public business, the better it will be. If we did not have such brute arrogance and unblushing conceit, we would long ago have seen the justice and propriety of hiding our diminished heads. But no. Because we have the physical force to beat women at the polls with our fists, we maintain that they have no right there as thinking beings. And because we make the polls indecent with our profane language and drunkenness, we remain masters of the field. Glorious! Behold the result! How well the world is governed! [271]

Gender and nation are again brought together in Hackwell's discussion of the subordination of women and empowering of men on the basis of their gender and physical force, paralleling the subordination of "the people" to what is construed as a repressive government:

> And what and who is the government? At present, of course, *our* government is the Secretary of War: that we all know. But I mean, speaking in general, What is a government? Ah! it certainly is a terrible impersonality of a republic—an irresponsible tyrant that can neither blush nor be guillotined. And for this reason we call ourselves *a free people*! And with perfect sang-froid we can see a cabinet officer make a cat's-paw of a President! And we say we are the "*model government*" because, as long as the mob is cajoled, no matter how much *individuals are tyrannized over*, a cabinet officer can crush any one opposing him and make it all right with the President by telling him and the mob that it is done for the glory and interest of *the people*. [271–72]

It is not coincidental of course that in Ruiz de Burton's novel this cynical critique of the republic and its farce of democracy follows the tirade on gender oppression, for, as we have seen, gender assumes a double role in the novel: it serves both to feminize "the people" as a citizenry dominated by tyrants in the government and without the power to adjudicate responsibility or determine outcomes, and to critique gender subordination by showing, on the one hand, how women are in good measure precluded from the public sphere and, on the other, how when in power, like Jemima (Jenny) Norval, are as capable as men of being tyrannical. Hackwell's previous argument that women in control would do better is in part thus disarticulated, as the novel points to a diversity of women: tyrants like Jenny, devoted and level-headed women like Lavinia, empty-headed consumer "belles" like Ruth, sexually liberated women like Mina, and angelic ingénues like Lola. It is this combination of women's complicity, power and impotence that *Who Would Have Thought It?* configures in its parody of romance.

Violations of the Social and Political Contract

> "For you know that by fair or foul means the Cackles must hold to their power," added Beau.
> "You are always logical, my boy," said the elder. [*Who Would Have Thought It?* 295]

The transformational impact of the Civil War, which in addition to accelerating the development of a new phase of capitalism promoted the construction of a national identity, is one of the central emplotments in *Who Would Have Thought It?* In particular, Ruiz de Burton's novel deconstructs notions of a unified "imagined community" on which the nation predicated itself (a national identity only fully constituted as a mass phenomenon after the Civil War [Foner, 1980, 53]. This is achieved by the narrative's focussing not only on political divisions within the North but on divisions between the political system and the mass population, "the public." The problems facing the nation are thus reconstructed as going beyond the issues of slavery and sectional conflict. In effect, the novel posits another type of slavery, not the "wage-slavery" that workers in the North denounced "to describe the plight and grievances of the labor movement" [Foner, 1980, 59], but a comparable "white slavery,"[45] that of whole sectors of the population denied political power and the rights of liberty and democracy.

These issues are represented most directly in the scenes having to do with the unresponsiveness and irresponsibility of government to the claims of its citizens. Thus when falsely accused and subject to dismissal without a trial, Colonel Julian Norval, in an outburst before President Lincoln, exclaims in exasperation: "I am a Pariah. No, I must resign. I wish to have my freedom. If the negroes have it, why shouldn't I. I did not bargain to surrender my freedom to give it to Sambo" [241]. At a moment when slaves have been emancipated by Proclamation in the states which have seceded and where consequently the Presidential edict has no effect, it is ludicrous, even racist, for Julian to speak of surrendering freedoms granted to slaves. But clearly "slavery" has become a metaphor for disempowerment and disenfranchisement. It is the meaninglessness of "citizenship," the fragmentation of the union and with it any illusions of national identity, as well as the glaring discrepancies in the social contract, ably concealed by ideological discourses, that most concern the novel.

The apparatus of national representation had produced several myths, among them conceits and idealizations of the Pilgrims [62] we see satirized in the novel. Through sarcasm and tongue-in-cheek comments, the novel pokes fun at these and other sacrosanct constructs in American historical accounts, satirical thrusts which go hand in hand with Ruiz de Burton's parody of the romance framework. In effect, both satire of social and political conventions and parody of generic conventions are posited as products of the same system of representation which creates an illusion of transparency,[46] unmasked in the text. This shared illusion is evident in the romanticization of ideological constructs, like, for example, that of democracy. Thus the celebration of dissent, said to be central both to romanticism and democracy,[47] figures prominently in the novel as a sham to reveal the fallacy of a romantic conception of politics. Unmasking discrepancies within the social contract[48] thus implicity entails a countering of romantic representations. Thus the violation of the social contract in the novel is not merely the violation of marriage vows, but the abrogation of the guarantees provided for in the Constitution, especially the denial of freedom of expression. Dissent, as guaranteed by the first amendment, is shown to be neither desired nor tolerated, as evident in the persecution of Dr. Norval, who, critical of Lincoln's policies, has to leave the country to avoid what some say are imminent orders for his arrest. Norval, who in the novel represents the Peace Democrats,[49] underwrites a regiment of Union soldiers before leaving but is nevertheless considered a Copperhead for having supported Senator Crittenden and others "in their efforts to avoid a war with the South" [64].

In its partial reconstruction of the complex ideological battlefield of the period, the novel criticizes the suspension of individual rights under the cover of a state of emergency with the outbreak of the Civil War, much as occurred during and after World War II although in a perhaps more blatant fashion. Historically we know that the North was far from unified with respect to the secessionists or to the war effort. Many in the North unabashedly supported the South, like New York Mayor Fernando Wood and Congressman Daniel Sickles, who proposed seceding with the south [McKay, 33]. Others, like inventor Samuel F. B. Morse, for example, saw slavery as a 'divine institution,' considered abolition a sin [McKay, 15], and felt despair before what they saw as the destruction of the union and the creation of "an overwhelming hatred":

> "I see no hope of union," he wrote. "If there was a corner of the world where I could hide myself, and I could consult the welfare of my family, I would sacrifice all my interests here and go at once. I have no heart to write or do anything. Without a country: Without a country!" [Morse quoted in McKay, 132]

The elder Norval is described as feeling this kind of hopelessness upon the walkout of the Southern Congressmen in Washington and the outbreak of the war [64]. Norval's critique of government policies would again become an issue after the 1862 Battle of Antietam, when Lincoln announced his Emancipation Proclamation; by some it was hailed as striking a blow for the abolitionist struggle, but some like Morse and others considered it a usurpation of executive powers that defied the Constitution [McKay, 159]. Democrats, like Norval in the novel, would also strongly oppose the President's suspension of the writ of habeas corpus and a number of resulting arbitrary arrests in New York City [McKay, 161].[50] It is these persecuted dissenting positions that Norval, despite his unwavering support for the Union cause, represents in the novel's mapping of the complicated political landscape of the Civil War period.

The novel does not condemn dissenting Peace Democrats like Norval who, once war breaks out, patriotically joins the Union effort. He and his son Julian, a Union officer, are presented as examples of the "best men" in society, enlightened, free of hypocrisy, generous and non-chauvinist. In a country ostensibly founded on principles of free speech, the persecution of dissent and of men like the Norvals is seen as one more instance of the disjuncture between theory and practice. Dr. Norval, although not an abolitionist, is represented as more free of racism and in fact more generous to blacks seeking to buy their family's freedom, for example, than his abolitionist yet miserly wife. Portrayed as an ethical and morally righteous intellectual, willing to share his good fortune with his neighbors, long before he became rich, he is also cast as a wise and prudent investor who with the help of advisers is able to double Lola's riches, keeping for himself and his family, he insists, only that stipulated in his agreement with Lola's mother. It is his political dilemma, arising from taking seriously Constitutional guarantees of freedom of expression, that the novel marks as proof of the degeneration of democratic values and the faltering of the republican ideal.

The novel's exposé of the sham of individual liberty and protection of rights is restated as well in the episodes involving both Lavinia Sprig and Julian Norval. What Lavinia finds in her visit to Congress is that discourses of rights and equality are false and, moreover, manipulated to deceive the people. Those in power conceive of a naive—feminized—public not capable of knowing what's best and therefore not consulted. Democracy in *Who Would Have Thought It?* is in fact represented as a myth for public consumption and not a reality; what is determined by those in positions of power is often *a posteriori* attributed to "the will of the people" [120]; there is, in effect, no informed consent of the governed as the novel points out, but rather corruption and influence peddling everywhere, even in the highest circles of government, where democracy degenerates into demagoguery. This is further confirmed when the twice-wounded war hero Julian Norval, mistaken for his father, comes close to being dismissed and humiliated on the basis of rumors brought to President Lincoln by self-serving cronies of the elder Norval's political enemies.

Julian here stands for the typical patriotic citizen who "with the grand simplicity of a true American [...] has accepted—au pied de la lettre—in all sincerity the lofty theories of republicanism, and honors his country and his government with a manly reverence truly noble" [210]. He thus cannot understand the preferential treatment accorded to the few, that is, to the smiling men who go in and out of Lincoln's office while he cools his heels outside for days, waiting, along with many others, without any possibility of seeing the President. Among those waiting are the mothers of war prisoners, women whom the President is too busy to see, to Julian's disgust, for he believes that "in a country of equals, every man's concerns are as important as any other's" [209]. He is "disenchanted": "[he] felt that it would take a long time before he should again believe that in America there is not as much despotism as in Europe" [244]. Convinced that he will be disgraced and dismissed unless he meets with the President and clears his name, thus proving himself worthy of Lola, Julian decides to search for the President in the White House, all the time muttering to himself about his rights as a free man. The President, in what is a highly critical representation of an iconic figure, cannot, however, even recall dismissing the young Norval, nor even his name; Julian smiles bitterly as he says:

> American citizens as individuals, then, had lost the importance, the sacredness of old. Now they only counted as masses on which leaders might tread to stand high,—as masses to be hurled at the cannon's mouth.... He thought too, that it was of ominous augury for the liberties of the Americans if a man who was on the field defending that Union loved by all so dearly, exposing his breast to the bullets of its enemies, should be dismissed, and the case be considered so unimportant, or of so common occurrence, that it was immediately forgotten! [215]

Any accusation or dismissal of the type Julian was subject to required at least trial by jury, but he was being denied his individual rights on the caprice of his accusers, "high officials" who, the novel insists, had the ear of the Executive. The suspension of the writ of habeas corpus, like the *de facto* abrogation of the First Amendment, are taken to mean that the social contract, the Constitution, is a sham. In Julian Norval's case this travesty of justice is however mitigated, if not fully rectified, when allies of his, notably men of political and financial influence, intercede on his behalf. An individual without connections, on the other hand, is thus shown to be powerless and even the President is represented as weak and manipulated by his close advisers.

Underlying the novel's satire and caustic critique of the political degeneration of the republic is of course the notion of a more just society predicated on a generally conservative or reformist longing for bygone days, for as Jameson comments, "the great satirists have thus been predominantly conservative, and their golden ages ideological fictions."[51] Thus Julian's idealized notion of relations between the government and the governed presupposes a former historical moment in which the notion of rights itself was sacred, as he laments: "Has *might* usurped the place of *right* in this free, beloved land of ours? Am I a free man, or an abject slave?" [213]. Political satire here, perhaps ironically, implies a romantic notion of the republic, a utopian moment in which "an American citizen and a patriot defending [his] country" could have access to "the guardian of the people" and the ear of what is sardonically termed, "his absolute excellency the President" [237]. The character is cynical enough to mock this idealized notion of a simple, more democratic community as a "delusion of old times," yet he is clearly also full of unmet political desires; thus upon seeing the same "anxious faces of people who had come there day after day in the vain hope of seeing the President," Julian asks:

> "And why don't they see him?" asked Julian, naïvely, laboring under the delusion of old times, when the President held it to be his highest honor to be called *the servant of the American people*. [209]

Implicit in Julian's remarks is a nostalgia for a past utopia; this utopian past will also be subsequently demystified, but it does serve here as a critique of the national degeneration.

Julian Norval's is not the only case of false accusations. Hackwell too finds himself falsely accused of having appropriated government funds, a theft in fact perpetrated by his head clerk Skroo. Unlike Julian, who cannot bear the ignominy of a tarnished reputation, Hackwell—ever the blackguard—can only repent of not having allied and cut a deal with Skroo:

> I wish I had made a confederate of that scoundrel Skroo, and stolen two or three million. I never yet acted honestly—that is to say, like an ass—that I did not have occasion to repent. And I hate repentance. [271]

The scoundrel Hackwell laments his failure to take advantage of the situation and his "loyalty" to the government, all of which again ironically engage him in a long diatribe critical of the republican framework, portrayed as an inanimate structure that cannot be beheaded but that empowers tyrants who cater to the mob, deny individual rights and sell out to the highest bidder and monopolies. Here too the rogue—behind closed doors, of course—mocks the notion of a "free people" [271] and attacks the abuse of power by cabinet members as well as the abuse of dominant rhetoric, especially the overuse and misuse of phrases like "the people." The gullible people are deceived, he says—doubtlessly in unison with the narrator's voice—by discourses of a "model government" and of the U.S. as the "best government on earth," constructs that operate as received truths. It is these dominant ideological discourses that the novel dismantles and attacks; the fact that the words are voiced by a scoundrel provides an added twist that makes them all the more worth remarking and points to Ruiz de Burton's strategic and ambivalent handling of a narrative displacement of the narrator's voice.

The severity of the critique uttered by Hackwell is countered and partially undone by the rogue's own numerous deceptions, for which, however, in true scoundrel form, he feels no remorse: "Only the bigoted Roman Catholics believe in the efficacy of remorse, which they call *Contrition*" [272]. His conniving to blackmail Lola and Julian, his threats to retain Lola on the basis of false and contrived allegations, his mock marriage with Mrs. Norval, his tampering with the U.S. mail and hiding Dr. Norval's letters from his wife, his unauthorized opening of the Norval will and his manipulation of Mrs. Norval's money, will all go unpunished. As a savvy former lawyer as well as *pícaro* preacher, Hackwell is too well versed in how to manipulate the system not to get away with his crimes. The picaresque is—like satire more generally—in the last instance, generally a fundamentally conservative literary form, despite its critique of society, for, traditionally, in the end the socially mobile *pícaro* ultimately conforms and confirms the status quo. Here, in the typical Ruiz de Burton narrative twist, the *pícaro* confirms the corruption of the status quo, to which he happily conforms.

The Best Men

> It was a sight that would have done your patriotic heart good, reader—for I suppose you *have* a patriotic heart—we all have in this country... [*Who Would Have Thought It?* 288]

By 1872, when Ruiz de Burton's novel was published, a new set of ideological discourses was framing political thought and policies in the United States, bent on undoing what changes radical Republicans had instituted during and immediately after the Civil War. A national identity, rather than regional or state identity, was being forged, accompanied by new structuring concepts of liberal democracy that were taking the nation from eighteenth-century notions of classical republicanism with its elitist civic humanism to nineteenth-century economic liberalism, that is, liberal republicanism, positing government's function as ensuring "the conditions for liberating man's self-actualizing capacities."[52] This changing vision and conception of civil society, harking back to debates between Federalists and Jeffersonians, is the basis of the critique in the Ruiz de Burton novel of the U.S. republic, with the text ambiguously playing off both positions, siding as much with those like Jefferson, who advocated the protection of individual rights, particularly freedom of expression, as with those like Hamilton and Adams, who saw more to fear from people than from rulers [Appleby, 324]. Yet despite assertions of a compact guaranteeing individual liberty and equality, representative democracy in the U.S. in the 1860s was still very much restricted to white men with property, as the novel suggests. Women of the middle class, though denied voting rights, were for the most part complicit in maintaining the status-quo.

As we have seen, the novel notes with scorn how the interests of "the people" are set aside to serve those of opportunistic capitalists and rising professional politicians; the rulers are portrayed at best as overwhelmed and ill-advised, and at worst incompetent in the face of self-interested and corrupt cabinet members and congressmen. Other historical issues serve to further complicate the political debate reconstructed in the novel. Closely linked to mid-nineteenth-century liberal policies that advocated "free land and free trade" [Appleby, 313] were policies of expansionism promoting westward migration and the occupation of Mexican land. In the novel, these imperialist practices of the republic, justified as part of a "manifest destiny," are closely linked to nativism, racism, regionalism and economic interests.

In spite of its acerbic critique, Ruiz de Burton's novel is not at all populist. On the contrary, it favors an elitist standard, that of an intellectual "aristocracy," that is, of an enlightened professional class, a perspective akin to that of the Liberals of 1872 who supported rule by the "best men" [Foner, 1990, 214]. The notion itself is elitist and presupposes an ignorant and subservient "public," like that represented in *Who Would Have Thought It?*, a "public" consenting to rule by an irresponsible government increasingly allied to capital. By ideological training (the very task assigned to women during the mid-nineteenth century), this "public" is predisposed to an unquestioning acceptance of all governmental rhetoric and to value profit and economic success above everything else, argues the novel's narrator. Like the British, who worship success above all else, according to the quoted Thackeray, the "free-born American resembles his proud progenitors in this so well, that he is ready to do homage on his bended knees." The narrator, assuming towards the novel's end a much more prominent voice, goes on to say:

> The Eastern worshipper saying to his idol, "Crush me if thou wilt, to worship thee is my delight, my pride," is not more subservient than the "equal of kings," the free-born American, before the successful man, before the millionaire, before the railroad kind,—monopolists. [119]

The myth of "America's uniqueness" is thus unmasked, with the population at large constructed as being as subservient as Europeans, if not to an aristocracy of nobility, to capitalists. The novel's commentary on politics under monopoly capitalism will note not only the industrial growth, expansion of railroads, and increased accumulation of capital, but also the widespread corruption, reaching the highest echelons of the political structure, conditions which give rise to a call for reform.

The end of the Civil War revealed corruption in industry and government to a degree hitherto unknown and brought what Foner calls the degradation of Gilded Age politics [1984, 490]. The Tweed Ring of New York, for example, "epitomized the symbiotic relationship between corruption, organizational politics, the political power of both railroad men and the urban working class, and the misuses of the state" [1988, 491]. This was also the period of Reconstruction, which saw federal intervention in southern states to ensure the civil rights of the newly emancipated blacks, and the dramatic growth of organized labor, a phenomenon often reductively linked to "Butlerism," named after Benjamin F. Butler, a Republican congressman from Massachusetts, a populist associated with "a new kind of mass politics" that was said to have "infused American public life with 'the spirit of the European mob'" [1988, 491].[53] In this climate there arose a group of liberal reformers, often designated as "the best men," who voiced the "outcry of a middle-class intelligentsia alarmed by class conflict, the ascendancy of machine politics and its own exclusion from power" [1988, 492]. These "best men" were economic liberals but political conservatives, in favor of free trade, the law of supply and demand and the gold standard, but concerned with monopoly capitalism and the "eclipse of smaller" industries. Yet these intellectuals were "alarmed by a growing political danger from below," [1988, 488] from emergent sectors and practices, that took the form of labor strikes and demands for eight-hour workday legislation and state regulation of business, child labor and factory safety. Concerned with "the dangers of unbridled democracy and the political incapacity of the lower orders" [1988, 497], these reformers were ready to put an end to governmental intervention in the south to protect the freedmen and in effect "retreated from democratic principles altogether" [1988, 492], much like present-day efforts by the political right seeking to overthrow Affirmative Action and other hard-fought Civil Rights protections. In a period of political machines, elaborate campaigns with millions of pamphlets and other literature distributed across the land, and the growing influence of lobbies, those reformers, who felt excluded by political machines and increasingly threatened by a growing urban working class, would meet as Liberals, both Republicans and Democrats, in Cincinnati in 1872 to oppose Grant's re-election as President. Although unable to agree on a number of issues, the Liberals resented taxes to pay for Reconstruction, arguing that "it was now up to the freedman to make their own way in the world" [1990, 212]. They nominated the former abolitionist Horace Greeley, now against relief efforts to help the freedmen, whom he denounced as "an easy, worthless race, taking no thought for the morrow" and sentenced to fend for themselves with his injunction: "Root, Hog, or Die!" [quoted in Foner, 1988, 502]. By the summer of 1872, Greeley had been endorsed as well by the Democratic Party [1988, 506], but Grant would still win the election with the largest majority between 1836 and 1892 [1988, 510].

In its critique, the novel shares much with the perspectives of this "American intelligentsia" who saw abroad the mass uprising of the Paris Commune [1871] as a harbinger of things to come in the U.S. and was particularly upset with the likes of the Democratic machine of "Boss" William M. Tweed.[54] Equally reprehensible to the "best men" was "Butlerism," which is figured satirically as "Cacklism" in *Who Would Have Thought It?* and is especially condemned by the liberal Ruiz de Burton. The entire Cackle family, satirized as opportunistic and populist parvenus, serves to portray the perceived weaknesses of democracy. The absurdities and self-aggrandizing stupidities pronounced by Congressman Beau Cackle, the novel says, are "celebrated by the American people" [296]. In its populism, its pro-freedman stance and anti-Southern oligarchy and anti-discriminatory advocacy, "Cacklism" is indeed a figuration of "Butlerism," positions that are mocked and ridiculed in the novel by an obviously elitist narrator who sees the travesty of justice inflicted on Julian and James Norval as enormous in comparison to the denial of a seat to Frederick Douglass on a steamer [298]. Contradictorily, however, "Cacklism" in the novel is also linked to anti-Grant politics, when in fact it would not be Butler, who supported Grant [Foner, 1988, 509], but the Liberals who would oppose the moderate Republican Grant along with radical Republicanism in the contested and conflictive political arena of the 1870s.

Foner recalls that the "best men" rejected egalitarian ideas on the basis of what they considered the political incapacity of the working class and on the basis of racism against Irish, Black and Asian workers [Foner, 1990, 211–212]. Reaction against Reconstruction policies and against federal protection for the rights of Blacks would bring sympathy for the Southern whites, who were "increasingly portrayed as the victims of injustice" [Foner, 1990, 212]. This sympathy for the South's devastation and intolerance for incompetent rulers pervades the entire Ruiz de Burton novel, aligning her with the elitist "best men." Yet the novel is contradictorily supportive of Grant, praised for his "gentlemanly consideration [...] of the vanquished enemy" and his "moderation and good sense" [294], and supported as preferable to any Cackle-led ticket. Linking these anti-Grant Liberals and the heterogeneous coalition that formed around them at the political convention held in Cincinnati in 1872 to "Cacklism" is thus problematic. But like the Cincinnati Liberals, whose nominee would be endorsed by the Democratic Party, Beau Cackle in his "momentous" speech in Cincinnati urges that those for Cacklism be "logical" and join the Democrats against Grant. Historically, this division of the Republican Party signalled the death of Radicalism and the Liberals' growing influence [Foner, 1990, 216].[55]

The perspective in the novel is thus fuzzy in this regard, not unlike the contradictory ideological field prevalent at the time, with Cacklism serving for a critique both of opportunistic politicians who all too easily switched from the Democratic to the Republican Party and back again (as did the Cackles, in step with the prevailing political winds of the moment) and for a repudiation of mass politics, mocked and censured for allowing the self-serving, incompetent and corrupt Cackles of the North, the former farmers, now rich from their "unsavory" salt-pork and lard contracts, their "contracts of rotten blankets and of shoes made of burnt leather which they had sold to the best of governments" [290], to determine the fate of the nation in Congress. And although the novel assumes a perspective akin to that of "the best men," it also takes aim at these very same Liberal Republicans who in 1872 broke with Grant. Historically, these Liberals were very much opposed to

Radical Republicanism, yet, in the novel, with regard to Grant's "slighting" of Frederick Douglass, the Cackles, as made clear by Beau Cackle, seemingly continue to espouse selected Radical Republican notions in what is described as a hot-button political campaign designed to gain votes by resorting to any means, despite contradictorily determining to ally with the Democrats opposed to these very ideas [298]. The Cackles, as *Who Would Have Thought It?* demonstrates, were eminently flexible, ready to espouse whatever position seemed to be gaining momentum. Since Cacklism is parodied and presented as a caricature of what democracy has come to mean in the United States, rule by unprincipled opportunists, the novel, in picaresque and parodic style, can rail against both radical and moderate Republicans. At bottom is the unmasking of American politics in the 1850s, 60s and 70s, an exposé of corrupt governmental practices and a demystification of dominant ideological constructs, shown to be façades for the only thing that counts in the Gilded Age: profit and power. In opposition to "Cacklism" and the politics of convenience are of course the "best men," enlightened, honest and true democrats, figured in the novel in the persons of James and Julian Norval.

Two Republics

> "We are living on the credit of our fathers and squandering the inheritance of liberty left to us, but we want to humbug posterity by loudly insisting that we have greater riches, more freedom." He laughed. [*Who Would Have Thought It?* 244]

The "best men" of the 1870s, as indicated, were for the most part middle-class reformers with aristocratic notions of politics and bourgeois interests seeking to protect a capitalist project. The situation in Mexico at the time is different economically and politically, but ideologically, given the opposition between pro-capitalist, anti-clerical Liberals and pro-monarchy, pro-oligarchy conservatives (church and landowners), debates similar to those of the late eighteenth century in the U.S. were taking place in regard to the desirability of a republican form of government. *Who Would Have Thought It?* will prove very insightful in its reconstruction of these debates and its constructed distinction between economic and political liberalism[56] and democracy.[57] We have a situation, then, in which the novel, on the one hand, advocates support for individual political freedom and equality for women, but, on the other, is ambivalent in its judgment of democracy as mass politics. In effect the novel sees no democracy in practice; the "unthinking multitudes," as described by lobbyist Blower are never consulted by "our leading men" and are only informed after the fact, practices, moreover, said to have been "adopted from the time of Washington" [116], thus refuting the possibility of upholding any nostalgic notion of a utopian past [209]. The "people" in fact are seen as easily duped and falling prey to deception through the use of rhetoric that calls for their making "sacrifices to vindicate the principle upon which is founded *the best government on earth*" [116]. Other contradictions are evident: at the same time that the novel points to the need for the regulation of monopoly capitalism, it also supports entrepreneurial competitive capitalism and the type of capital investments made by the banker Sinclair and Norval in the novel.

These various ideological issues, discussed throughout *Who Would Have Thought It?*, come to the fore in the section dealing with Mexico. Here domestic political questions are closely linked to the impact of imperialism. Both French and U.S. displacement of the narrative to Mexican social spaces in effect provides a necessary distance to denounce U.S. imperialism and to offer a critique of a republican form of government, seen as ineffective and given to corruption. Foreign/domestic spatial constructs are foregrounded in a central episode which begins with Isaac, who upon his unofficial release from the Confederate prison camp, goes back to the North for an unexpected confrontation with "the Honorable" Le Grand Gunn, whom he thrashes for engineering the erasure of his name from the list of prisoners to be exchanged. Fearing grave consequences, and "sick of his country and countrymen for what he thought their heartless ingratitude in leaving him forgotten in a prison" [192], Isaac, like Dr. Norval, decides to leave the country. He travels to Mexico in self-imposed exile with the secondary intention of searching for the Mexican father mentioned in that forgotten manuscript found years before in the dead-letter file at the post office, where he had worked after being unjustly dismissed from another position as a result of his nemesis Gunn's machinations. The recovered manuscript is, we later come to know, of course, none other than the *testimonio* narrated by Doña Teresa Almenara de Medina, Lola's mother, before her death.

In Mexico, Isaac finds Don Luis Medina and Don Felipe de Almenara, the respective father and grandfather of Lola, although Isaac is at this juncture unaware of the connection to the girl brought home by his brother-in-law Norval. The romantic plot does, however, pause to allow narrative comment on the political situation in Mexico. The two wealthy, cultivated gentlemen Isaac meets are both Liberals, supportive of Juárez's republican government against the French invasion. Don Luis, of Spanish descent but born in Austria, is a citizen of Mexico and an officer in the republican army [197]. Don Felipe, Lola's grandfather, is a *criollo*, also of Spanish descent but born in Mexico. Around the time of Isaac's visit, December of 1863, the two tell of receiving letters indicating that the monarchists have offered the Archduke Maximilian the throne of Mexico and that there is a likelihood that he will accept. Don Luis, who has been fighting to repel the French, is, however, less than eager to fight against an Austrian prince. The elder Don Felipe is likewise not ill disposed to the idea of restoring Mexico to a Hapsburg monarch, that is, in his mind, to a lawful heir of Queen Isabella and Charles V [197], especially in view of the civil and political turmoil besetting Mexico. The two in fact see the establishment of a republic in Mexico as a mistake and are of the opinion that a monarchy[58] would conform to the popular will:

> I am convinced that a republican form of government is not suited to the Mexicans, and it is well that the change be made with their [the people's] free approval. [198]

Almenara further goes on to argue that the only reason Mexico has become a republic is on account of the undue influence of the United States:

> Of course the ideas of this continent are different from those of Europe, but we all know that such would not be the case if the influence of the United States did not prevail with such despotic sway over the minds of the leading men of the Hispano-American republics. If it were not for this terrible, this fatal influence—which will eventually destroy it—the Mexicans, instead of seeing anything objectionable in the proposed change, would be proud to hail a prince who, after all, has some sort of a claim to this land, and who will cut loose from the leading strings of the United States. [198]

Through these characters, the novel acknowledges the French imperial threat to Mexico and sees an even more imminent and powerful threat from its northern neighbor, a U.S. in which—before and even after the Civil War—there were sectors favoring continued expansionism south. The U.S. by then had its eye on the Dominican Republic, Cuba, Puerto Rico, Baja California and other parts of Mexico. Already it sought to dominate the Latin American nations economically and politically and did not welcome any other foreign power's intervention in what by then it construed as its "natural" sphere of influence. As Martí would so eloquently warn a few years later, "Whoever says economic union says political union."[59]

The upper-class Mexicans represented in *Who Would Have Thought It?* support a liberal economic policy (as would Maximilian, who surprised his conservative supporters by proposing liberal policies similar to those of Juárez),[60] but reject a republican form of government, one that the novel sees as lending itself in the U.S. to tyrannical power by cabinet ministers and to corruption and rule by profit-mongers, all to the disservice of the populace. The political and the personal are linked up once again in the discussion. In Medina and Almenara's mind, "a stable government [...] would bring [...] peace and prosperity" [196] to Mexico, for they blame existing and previous Mexican lawmakers for their particular personal grief: "If Mexico were well governed, if her frontiers were well protected, the fate of Doña Teresa would have been next to an impossibility" [201], referring here to the abduction by Indians of the pregnant Doña Teresa on Mexico's northern frontier. Both men are disposed to fight against any invader, in this case the French, but argue that if the type of government is left to choice, then they favor a popularly supported monarchy, an option that by 1867 would be militarily rejected in Mexico.[61] Yet in Ruiz de Burton's text the debate is resuscitated to make a point against the pitfalls of inoperative republican governments.

Whether Ruiz de Burton herself favored a liberal monarchy in Mexico is not clear nor really at issue. What is clear is that by 1872, having lived in the United States for about 25 years—about two-thirds of her life—she had a highly developed sense of self as a Latina in opposition to Anglo-dominant society. What particularly concerned her was, on the one hand, the perceived misrepresentations of the U.S. as regards its democratic and egalitarian principles, and on the other, the subordinate status of Mexicans, especially Californios in the United States, and U.S. imperialist policies towards Mexico. As she had indicated to fellow Californio Mariano Guadalupe Vallejo's son, Platón,

> ...[the Americans'] boasted liberty and equality of rights seem to stop when [they] meet a Californian. Witness the Land Commission! We are a child's handful in their mighty grasp; they can crush us with impunity. They know it and broke their faith as solemnly pledged at Guadalupe Hidalgo; broke it by stooping to a miserable stratagem. How shameful this, in this, in the conquering, the prosperous and mighty nation.[62]

In his reply to her letter, the elder Vallejo's response indicates that he found her position to be ethnocentric:

> A thousand times you have said to me, "our race" and the "Anglo-Saxon race" and I confess to you candidly that even now my attention has been aroused to such a degree that I take the liberty of asking you, "What do you mean in those two distinct phrases?" [Mariano Guadalupe Vallejo in Emparán, 317]

Ruiz de Burton, like Martí not too much later, saw the conflict between the United States and Latin America as economic, political and cultural, with the U.S. advocating the superiority of "the Anglo-Saxon race over the Latin" [Martí, 372]. In part, at least, a defense of a Latin—i.e. French—model for Mexico was predicated on an indictment of U.S. policies, a strategic rejection of U.S. imperialism externally and an indictment of political practices internally. It is through this counterpoised discourse of "*latinidad*" articulated in *Who Would Have Thought It?* that the novel denounces Anglo-Saxon "barbarism" and corruption during the Civil War era, turning the tables and refuting the standard stereotypes applied to Latinos.

The critique of the U.S. republic carried out in *Who Would Have Thought It?* is thus written from the perspective of one critical of failed promises under a republican form of government. The novel is, however, ambiguous here, even circular in its argument, for its critique of the U.S. government, as has been noted, revolves precisely around the transgression of guarantees protected by the Constitution and Congress. In many cases it is the government's failure to follow its own precepts that is criticized. Thus it will be its failure to be as democratic or as representative as it purports to be and its failure to expunge corruption and opportunism from the government that give rise to this satirical representation of the republic. As in picaresque novels generally [Davidson, 165], there is a great deal of narrative and ideological irresolution because the perspective is reformist and ultimately in good measure elitist.

Conclusion

> But by all thy nature's weakness,
> Hidden faults and follies known,
> Be thou, in rebuking evil,
> Conscious of thine own.
>
> Whittier

[title-page epigraph to *Who Would Have Thought It?* 3]

We have argued that *Who Would Have Thought It?* constructs an allegory of the modernization of the U.S. attained through plunder, corruption and war. The novel transcodes this historical narrative through a romantic emplotment that involves deception, intrigue, adventure, fraud, disguise and plotting by rogues who seek to gain access to the domestic centers of power. These family spaces in *Who Would Have Thought It?* have their correlates in a number of public spaces, particularly national political spaces, wherein similar machinations, mergers of convenience and acts of corruption are enacted. At the domestic level the "best men" eventually intercede to disarm and displace the scoundrels, redirect energies, control "deleterious" passions, and see to it that social interaction is restored and resolution attained.

Achieving narrative resolution in the political sphere and at the level of the nation will prove to be more problematic, for in the novel's conclusion, or its "writing beyond the romantic ending" [293], the political structure as constructed in *Who Would Have Thought It?* is clearly still at risk and witnessing the entrenchment and institutionalization of "Cacklism." Once again in its "repetition with difference," [Hutcheon, 32] the romance-parody acknowledges its parodied conventions and its romantic iconizing, but the narrator's iconoclasm intercedes forcefully at the end, as narrative time collapses in what is an eloquent parody of vacuous political rhetoric of which today's political scene is all too reminiscent.

Who Would Have Thought It? is ultimately subversive in its ironic manipulation of parody, for the novel goes beyond an attempt to parody the literary conventions of romance. In fact, an alternate reading of *Who Would Have Thought It?* could argue for a reading of the novel as a sardonic, yet realist, narrative wherein parodic strategies are simulated as a dissembling strategy to cover for what is, in fact, conceived as a critical historical and realist construction of the Northeast U.S. during the period of the Civil War and as a virulent critique of the empire from within. In doing so, *Who Would Have Thought It?* carries out an incisive demystification of an entire set of dominant national myths, many of which are, unfortunately, still very much with us today, a hundred years after Ruiz de Burton's death in 1895. Who would have thought it?

—Rosaura Sánchez
—Beatrice Pita
San Diego, 1995

Notes

[1]Our thanks to Lauro Flores, who first made this nineteenth century text available to us.

[2]*Who Would Have Thought It?* was first published by J. P. Lippincott & Co. in Philadelphia in 1872. Although published anonymously, it was copyrighted in the Library of Congress as the work of Mrs. Henry S. Burton.

[3]"'Who Would Have Thought It?' A Native Californian Authoress. A Literary Incognito Lost in an Interview. A New Sensation for the Public," in San Francisco *Daily Alta California*, September 15, 1872, p. 1.

[4]Clearly the ever-enterprising Ruiz de Burton hoped that she, like so many other women writers, would "make it" with her writing, lifting her out of her precarious financial situation. With this work she engages in the nineteenth-century push of women as professional writers.

[5]María Amparo Ruiz de Burton automatically became a citizen of the United States, like other Mexicans residing in the Southwest, under the provisions of the Guadalupe-Hidalgo Treaty of 1848, which marked the end of the U.S.-Mexican War and Mexico's loss of half its national territory.

[6]María Amparo Ruiz de Burton. *The Squatter and the Don.* Edited and introduced by Rosaura Sánchez and Beatrice Pita (Houston, Texas: Arte Público Press, 1993). Originally published in 1885.

[7]See Rosaura Sánchez and Beatrice Pita, "Introduction," to María Amparo Ruiz de Burton. *The Squatter and the Don*, 1993.

[8]Eric Foner, *Reconstruction. America's Unfinished Revolution* (New York: Harper & Row, 1988), 19.

[9]Linda Hutcheon, *A Theory of Parody: The Teachings of Twentieth-Century Art Forms* (New York: Methuen, Inc., 1985), 75.

[10]Mary P. Ryan, *Women in Public* (Baltimore: The John Hopkins University Press, 1992), 3.

[11]Cathy Davidson, *Revolution and the Word: The Rise of the Novel in America* (Oxford: Oxford University Press, 1986), 134.

[12]Christine Stansell, *City of Women. Sex and Class in New York 1789–1860* (Chicago: University of Illinois Press, 1987), xii.

[13]*The Scarlet Letter* by Nathaniel Hawthorne (1804–1864) was published in 1850.

[14]Harriet Beecher Stowe. *We and Our Neighbors* (New York: J. B. Ford & Co., 1875).

[15]Nina Baym, *Woman's Fiction: A Guide to Novels by and about Women in America 1820–70*, Second edition (Chicago: University of Illinois Press, 1993), 35.

[16]Susan K. Harris, *Nineteenth Century American Women's Novels: Interpretive Strategies* (New York: Cambridge University Press, 1990), 20.

[17]Ann Douglas, *The Feminization of American Culture* (New York: Oxford University Press, 1977), 48.

[18]María Amparo Ruiz de Burton, *Who Would Have Thought It?*, 239.

[19]Curiously, one of the principal targets of the novel's critique, Lincoln's Secretary of War, Edwin M. Stanton, is alluded to only obliquely until well into the narrative, when he is revealed as one of the "high officials" wielding power tyrannically, and is called by name.

[20]Rachel Blau du Plessis' term quoted in Harris, 200.

[21]Eric Foner, *Politics and Ideology in the Age of the Civil War* (New York: Oxford University Press, 1980), 17.

[22]As Foner points out, abolitionists in the North did not necessarily represent anti-racist sentiments; in fact, most northern states denied blacks the right to vote and to attend public school, segregated them in transportation and excluded them from many labor markets [Foner, 1980, 77]. Streetcar segregation would not be outlawed in New York until 1864 [Ryan, 93]. Property requirements, that is, ownership of property worth $250, effectively denied suffrage in New York to 80% of blacks [Ernest A. McKay, *The Civil War and New York City* (Syracuse, N.Y.: Syracuse University Press, 1990, 21]. Democrats supporting the Wilmot Proviso excluding slavery from the territory acquired from Mexico did so on the assumption that this meant the exclusion of blacks from these lands, rather than on the basis of a repugnance for slavery. Senator John A. Dix, for example, like the author of the Proviso, would support this exclusion and reject white association with blacks on the basis of "Negro inferiority" and his contention that the destiny of the U.S. was to be populated exclusively by the white race [Foner, 1980, 83–84].

[23]While many, especially Republicans, saw slavery as "a threat to northern free labor and democratic values" [Foner, 1980, 49, 74] and therefore supported the anti-slavery movement, others, especially white laborers, rejected slavery, all slavery including "wage slavery" but feared that "emancipation would unleash a flood of freedmen to compete for northern jobs and further degrade the dignity of labor" [Foner, 1980, 60], but in effect, as McKay indicates, it was black labor that was replaced by Irish in the North, especially in the low-wage jobs.

[24]See Frederick Douglass, *Narrative of the Life of Frederick Douglass, An American Slave. Written by Himself*, published in 1845. The 1988 edition is published by Harvard University Press in Cambridge, Massachusetts.

[25]Lydia Maria Child. *A Romance of the Republic*, [Boston, Mass.: Ticknor and Fields, 1867.]

[26]The motif of contagion is not limited to Lola's "singular spots," [79] but is picked up as well in the Cackle *pater familias'* fear of contagion of Lavinia Sprig's "lack of luck" when she is figured as a leper to be avoided: "Mr. Cackle now was so overpowered by fear that, entirely forgetting his lately-acquired gallantry, he dropped his arm, and then shook off that of Lavvy resting on it and retreated a few steps, as if in involuntary dread of contagion. He thought of his son Beau's maxim of flying from unlucky people as if they were lepers, and the Norvals were not exactly in luck then" [110].

[27]Harriet Beecher Stowe, *Uncle Tom's Cabin or Life Among the Lowly* (New York: Penguin Books, 1981). First published as a book in 1852. It first appeared serially in an anti-slavery newspaper, *The National Era*.

[28]It should be noted that the wealth Doña Teresa hoards as her daughter's "dowry" is entirely naturalized and masks the plunder of Indian lands and resources.

[29]William B. Hesseltine, *Civil War Prisons: A Study in War Psychology* (New York: Frederick Ungar Publishing Co., 1978), 7. The book first appeared in 1930.

[30]Homer B. Sprague, *Lights and Shadows in Confederate Prisons. A Personal Experience 1864–65* (New York: G. P. Putnam's Sons, 1915), 146.

[31]The novel does not report on prisons in the North for both Confederate soldiers and Union deserters, but these too like the Southern prisons were horrendous, with many prisoners packed into a space that would accommodate a handful of men. Some prisons in the South would be even worse, like that of Andersonville in Georgia, where men slept on the ground in the cold winter and died by the thousands, but in the North, often the prisoners and deserters had to take turns sleeping on bare floors, with lice, vermin and refuse on the floor [McKay, 186].

[32]Former New York mayor Fernando Wood warned that the draft "would compel the white laborer to leave his family destitute and unprotected while he goes forth to free the negro, who, being free, will compete with him in labor" [quoted in McKay, 196].

[33]Historically, the shortage of housing and high rents meant thousands of people lived in cellars; cholera and typhus ran rampant in working-class areas because of the lack of adequate sewage systems. With the war came military contracts that allowed the garment industry to flourish; women working in these shops were paid as little as 17 cents for a 12-hour day; the more experienced made 68 cents for 14 hours of work to make a boy's suit. Discontented workers began organizing and business did its best to destroy the unions, especially the molders' and machinists' unions, by blacklisting them. Employment increased and in some cases wages improved. These working-class conditions are absent in the novel.

[34]In many cases N. Y. soldiers were sent to battle with ill-fitting uniforms and shoes: "In contrast to the well-equipped New England troops that marched through the city, many of the New Yorkers appeared to be half-clothed with basted uniforms, wooden-soled shoes, inferior muskets or none at all and no wagons for sick or wounded" [McKay, 75].

[35]New York is by 1861 a bustling city, port and manufacturing, commercial and financial center of eight hundred thousand [McKay, 4], a city undergoing profound economic changes.

[36]By the 1860s it is common to see women in public, that is, on the streets, shopping, watching parades, attending ceremonial festivities and by 1877 even participating in parades themselves [Ryan, 47]. As the novel demonstrates, women traveled on streetcars, and in the cultural domain, attended theatres, etc.

[37]In his work *Free Love and Heavenly Sinners*, Robert Shaplen narrates the story of the Henry Ward Beecher scandal of 1870. [Robert Shaplen, *Free*

Love and Heavenly Sinners. The Story of the Great Henry Ward Beecher Scandal (New York: Alfred A. Knopf, 1954), 5]

[38]The wealthy Congregationalist church had two thousand members and is said to have been the largest in the country [Shaplen, 18].

[39]The affair with Tilton's wife was reportedly not the pastor's first, for he was said to have been involved with others, including the wife of Henry Bowen, the publisher of *The Independent*, the newspaper edited by Beecher and Tilton. It was Bowen who had brought Beecher and his wife, Eunice Bullard, daughter of a New England Puritan family, to Plymouth Rock [Shaplen, 7–8] from Indiana. As assistant editor of *The Independent*, Tilton was also known for his abolitionist stance, his support of women's causes, including a more liberal divorce, and his belief in evolution, as well as for contributions in his newspaper from the most noted men and women of the day. The young Tilton and Beecher were the best of friends and Tilton was in part responsible for Beecher's liberal ideas and anti-slavery position [Shaplen, 29–31]. Tilton and his wife Elizabeth were famous for their evening gatherings of intellectuals to discuss issues of the day, much like Eva and Harry in Harriet Beecher Stowe's novel, *We and Our Neighbors*. Among Beecher's causes was the issue of women's suffrage, which his wife did not support, for Mrs. Beecher, called "The Griffin," was rigid in her precepts and advocated traditional roles for women.

[40]An advocate for "free love" and a well-known radical spiritualist, Woodhull would rant in the letter against those who attacked her but practiced "free love" in secret [Shaplen, 124]. Woodhull, who was a proponent of woman suffrage and of a single standard of morality for both sexes, as well as the first woman, with the help of Benjamin Butler, to address the Judiciary Committee of the House of Representatives on the subject, would be suddenly "made the darling of the suffragist movement" and it would be from Elizabeth Cady Stanton and from Elizabeth Tilton's mother that Woodhull would learn the details of Beecher's affair [Shaplen, 129–130].

[41]Historically, women organizing for the war effort included a number from prominent families. Women like Elizabeth Blackwell, the first woman in the country to receive a medical degree, Dorothea Dix, who would become superintendent of nurses in Washington, and Louisa Lee Schuyler, who led a women's movement to help the sick and wounded soldiers [McKay, 66, 82], are clearly models for the representation of Lavinia Sprig and the Cackle women, who volunteer to serve as nurses in Washington, D.C. hospitals.

[42]Elizabeth Cady Stanton (1815–1902), Susan B. Anthony (1820–1906), Lucretia Mott (1793–1880), Matilde Joslyn Gage (1826–1898) and Andrea Jenks Bloomer (1818–1894) struggled for many years for women's right to vote and in effect paved the way for the Nineteenth Amendment granting women the right to vote in 1920.

[43]Dorothea Dix (1802–1887), who served as the superintendent of nurses in Washington during the Civil War, for example, was known for her work with the mentally ill and her school for girls in Boston. During the war she

would accept only women who were thirty years of age or older as "the morals and modesty of young women had to be protected" [McKay, 66].

[44]Eric Foner, *A Short History of Reconstruction* (New York: Harper & Row, 1990), 205.

[45]For a discussion of how Ruiz de Burton takes up the issue of "white slavery" in another context, the Californians *vs.* Railroad monopoly antagonism of the 1880s, see the Introduction to Ruiz de Burton's *The Squatter and the Don* by Sánchez and Pita.

[46]Henri Lefebvre, *The Production of Space* (Cambridge, Massachusetts: Basil Backwell, 1991), 27–28,

[47]Steven H. Shiffrin. *The First Amendment, Democracy and Romance* (Princeton, N.J.: Princeton University Press, 1993), 142.

[48]Louis Althusser. *Politics and History: Montesquieu, Rousseau, Hegel and Marx*. London: NLB, 1972.

[49]The Copperheads or Peace Democrats were, for the most part, advocates for mediation to end the war.

[50]In 1863 these Peace Democrats formed the Society for the Diffusion of Political Knowledge, with Morse as president. The society was organized to discuss the constitutional transgression of Lincoln and to attack efforts to silence their critiques with charges of disloyalty [McKay, 174]. Members, who considered that the governed had the right to rebel [McKay, 188] would be quickly attacked in the press as disloyal Copperheads [175]. While many within New York City supported these Copperheads, others outside the city considered them to be corrupt and traitorous scamps like ex-mayor Wood and his brother, both of whom would be elected to Congress in 1862 [McKay, 167]. These historical figures also no doubt enter into the composite caricature of the ridiculed Cackle phalanx.

[51]Fredric Jameson, *Fables of Aggression* (Berkeley: University of California Press, 1981), 137.

[52]Joyce Appleby, *Liberalism and Republicanism in the Historical Imagination* (Cambridge, Mass.: Harvard University Press, 1992) 299.

[53]"[Butler] flamboyantly supported causes that appalled reformers: the eight-hour day, inflation, and payment of the national debt in greenbacks. He further horrified respectable opinion by embracing women's suffrage, Irish nationalism, and the Paris Commune. 'Butlerism' became a shorthand for a new kind of mass politics that had infused American public life with 'the spirit of the European mob'" [Foner, 1990, 210]. Benjamin Butler (1818–1893) was a prominent attorney at Lowell, Massachusetts, and a Breckinridge Democrat in 1860 who supported the Union after the Civil War broke out and was appointed an officer in the Union army. He served for a time as major general in command of Fort Monroe, Virginia, and participated as an officer in several expeditions, not always with success. He was infamous for his occupation of New Orleans, where his measures were considered by Copperheads to have been unscrupulous, dishonest and profitable; for this reason he was known as the "Beast" of New Orleans [McKay, 279–280]. General Butler was an agent for the exchange of prisoners of war for a period of time, much like the charac-

ter Le Grand Gunn in Ruiz de Burton's novel. After the war he became a Radical Republican and supported Reconstruction measures in the South. He advocated impeachment of Johnson and was a strong supporter of President Grant until 1878 when he broke with the Republicans to back the Greenback Movement. In 1882 as a Democrat he was elected governor of Massachusetts and was a candidate for President of the Greenback Labor Party and of the Anti-Monopoly Party. Although accused of corruption, he was never found guilty.

[54]Tweed, who not only "plundered the city of tens of millions of dollars" but also "controlled city patronage, forged an alliance with railroad magnates Jim Fisk and Jay Gould, established close ties with labor unions and fashioned an unofficial welfare system that used municipal funds to aid Catholic schools and provide food and fuel for the poor." For his patronage and protection Tweed was supported by lower-class voters, even after his corruption was exposed [Foner, 1990, 210].

[55]By 1875 most of the gains for freedmen instituted by Reconstruction were being reversed by state governments with the support or unwillingness to intervene of a federal government that increasingly upheld political repression of blacks on the basis of states' rights [Foner, 1990, 223–227]. By 1877, with the election of Hayes, Reconstruction was dead and the protection of the civil rights of blacks and, as became clear, of workers was no longer to be considered important in national politics. Among Democrats, Southerners and Northerners, the notion of enfranchising blacks and the very notion of a collective national community that included blacks were strongly repudiated [Foner, 1990, 122–123]. This racism coupled with both violence and fraud would in effect cause the struggle for civil rights to take a hundred years more to attain basic voting rights and the end of legal segregation. Racism, of course, has survived buttressed by the class division of society.

[56]Chantal Mouffe, "Democratic Citizenship and the Political Community," in *Dimensions of Radical Democracy*. Edit. by C. Mouffe (London: Verso, 1992), 11.

[57]C. B. Macpherson, *The Real World of Democracy* (New York: Oxford University Press, 1981), 6–7.

[58]Historically, those favoring French intervention in Mexico would accuse Juárez of selling out to the United States. The choice then was formulated in cultural-nationalist terms: Latin vs. Anglo-Saxon culture. France represented "Latin Civilization" with the capacity to form a Latin empire which would extend from Texas to Panama [Noel Salomón, *Juárez en la conciencia francesa, 1861–1867* (Mexico: Secretaría de Relaciones Exteriores, 1975), 133]. Cultural links were in fact a representation of economic, political and territorial interests. The monarchists accused Juárez of making land concessions to U.S.-British colonization companies and through the proposed MacLane-Ocampo Treaty (never approved by the U.S. Senate) of guaranteeing the U.S. access to the Rio Grande, to the Isthmus of Tehuantepec and to the Gulf of California for entry into Arizona [Salomón, 133]. For entering into these commercial transactions with the United States, to which the Liberals appealed for arms and diplomatic support to defend the constitutional government against

the French, Juárez was labeled a traitor by French supporters in Mexico and by the French diplomats and press. In effect, France, or at least Napoleon III, had similar interests, specifically the acquisition of Sonora and Tehuantepec, according to the Mexican ambassador in Washington, Matías Romero, as payment for the Mexican debt to France [Salomón, 136]. More importantly, France was interested in having the whole of Mexico as a French colony and market. The fact that Romero apparently preferred granting these lands to the United States, rather than to France, if it became necessary to save the rest of the national territory, was cause for alarm for many Mexicans, who saw in this proposal by the Juárez minister a continuation of U.S. usurpation of Mexican territory, only a few years after the Mexican loss in 1848 of half its territory to the United States.

[59]José Martí, "The Monetary Congress of the American Republics," in *Inside the Monster: Writings on the United States and American Imperialism* (New York: Monthly Review, 1975), 372.

[60]Daniel Cosío Villegas et al., *Historia mínima de México* (Mexico: El Colegio de México, 1977), 113.

[61]In its place was established rule by "the best men" of Mexico, the liberal cabinet around Benito Juárez, which included Sebastián Lerdo de Tejada, José María Iglesias and Matías Romero [Cosío Villegas, et al., 118]. Yet this combination would not be able to avoid the continuing civil strife that would lead to Porfirio Díaz's presidential challenge of Juárez in 1867 and 1871 and to armed revolt. By 1877 Díaz would be in power.

[62]Ruiz de Burton quoted in Madie Brown Emparán, *The Vallejos of California* (San Francisco: University of San Francisco, The Greeson Library Associates, 1968), 317.

Who Would Have Thought It?

María Amparo Ruiz de Burton

WHO WOULD

HAVE THOUGHT IT?

A NOVEL.

" But by all thy nature's weakness,
Hidden faults and follies known,
Be thou, in rebuking evil,
Conscious of thine own."

WHITTIER[1]

PHILADELPHIA:
J. B. LIPPINCOTT & CO.
1872.

Original title-page of the 1872 edition of the novel.

[1]Ruiz de Burton begins the novel with these verses from the poem "What the Voice Said" by Massachusetts poet John Greenleaf Whittier (1897–1892).

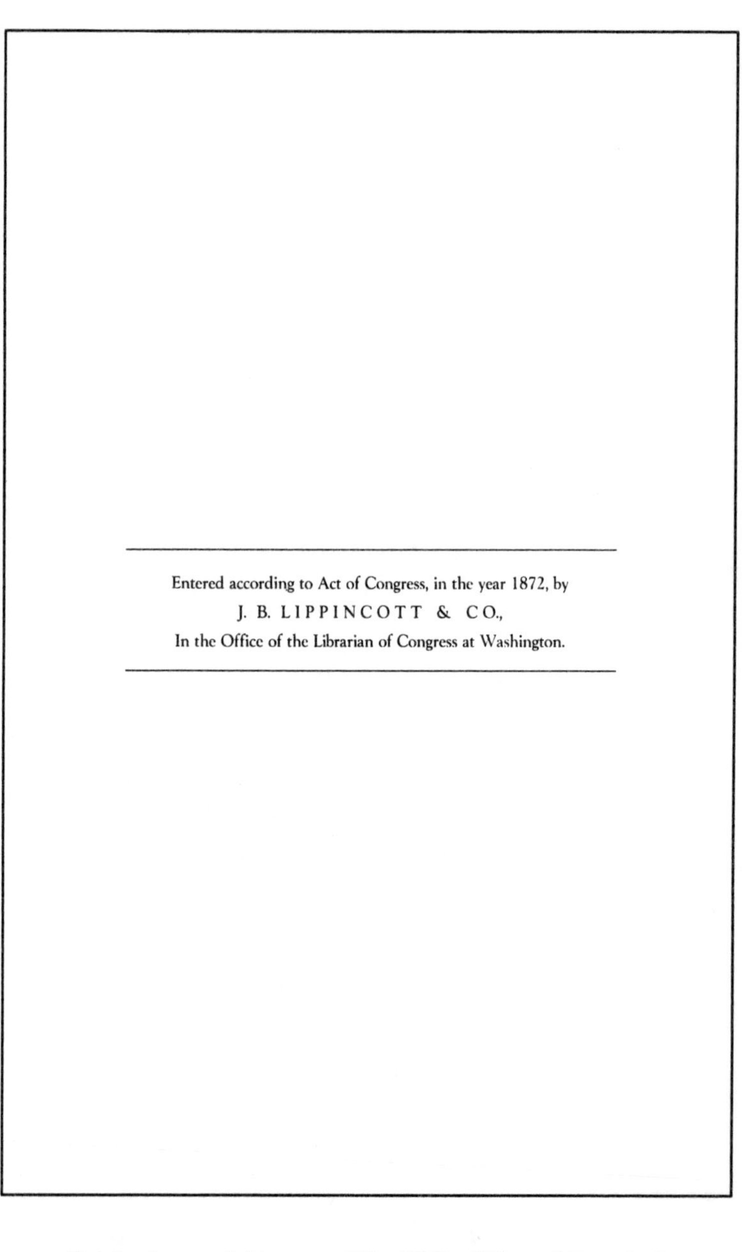

Entered according to Act of Congress, in the year 1872, by
J. B. LIPPINCOTT & CO.,
In the Office of the Librarian of Congress at Washington.

Original copyright page of the 1872 edition of the novel.

CONTENTS

CHAPTER I

The Arrival

"What would the good and proper people of this world do if there were no rogues in it—no social delinquents? The good and proper, I fear, would perish of sheer inanity—of hypochondriac lassitude—or, to say the least, would grow very dull for want of convenient whetstones to sharpen their wits. Rogues are useful."

So saying, the Rev. Mr. Hackwell scrambled up the steep side of a crazy buggy, which was tilting ominously under the pressure of the Rev. Mr. Hammerhard's weight, and sat by him. Then the Rev. Hackwell spread over the long legs of his friend Hammerhard a well-worn buffalo-robe, and tucked the other end carefully under his own graceful limbs, as if his wise aphorism upon rogues had suggested to him the great necessity of taking good care of himself and friend, all for the sake of the good and dull of this world.

"May I inquire whether present company suggested the philosophical query and highly moral aphorism, and, if so, whether I am to be classed with the dull, good or the useful whetstones?" asked Mr. Hammerhard, the reverend.

Mr. Hackwell smiled a smile which seemed to say, "Ah, my boy! you know full well where we ought to be classed," but he answered, "I was thinking of Dr. Norval."

"Of Dr. Norval! And in what category?"

"In that of a whetstone, of course."

Mr. Hammerhard looked at his friend, and waited for him to explain his abstruse theory more clearly.

"I was thinking," Mr. Hackwell continued, "how, in default of real rogues (there being none such in our community, eh, Ham? ahem!), our good and proper people have made a temporary whetstone of Dr. Norval's back. Which fact goes to prove that a social delinquent—real or supposed—is a necessity to good people. As for the charity of the thing, why should people who have all the other virtues care to have charity?"

"An excellent text for next Sunday," said Mr. Hammerhard, laughing.

Mr. Hackwell joined in the laugh, and with a series of pulls and jerks to the reins, he began to turn slowly the big head of a yellow horse of a Gothic build and slow motion, in the direction of the railroad depot, for the two divines were going to meet Dr. Norval, who was expected to arrive from California on the six p.m. train from New York that evening.

The yellow beast hung down his big head, put out his tongue, shut tight his left eye, and started, looking intently at the road with the right eye opened wide, as if he had been in the habit of wearing an eyeglass, which he had just dropped as he started.

Hi! hi! hi! went the crazy buggy, as if following the big-headed beast just to laugh at him, but in reality only squeaking for want of oiling and from great old age.

"Confound the brute! He squints and lolls his tongue out worse than ever!" exclaimed Mr. Hackwell. "And the rickety vehicle fairly laughs at us! Hear it!"

Hi! hi! creaked the buggy very opportunely.

"Look here, Ham, it is your turn to grease the wheels now. I greased them last time," added Hackwell.

"Greasing the wheels won't prevent the crazy, dilapidated concern from squeaking and going to pieces, any more than your sermons prevent some members of your congregation from gossiping and going to the devil," answered Mr. Hammerhard sententiously.

"I wish I could send them there in this wagon—all, all, the palsied beast, and the rotten wagon, and the penurious Yankees, that won't give us a decent conveyance," said Mr. Hackwell.

"All the rich people of our town belong to your congregation—all the rich and the good. Make them shell out, Hack. You are the fashion," Hammerhard observed.

"Yes, that is the reason I drive this fashionable turnout. No, they won't give except it is squeezed out of them. They are *so good*, you know. My only hope is in Dr. Norval."

"Because he is a whetstone?" asked Ham.

"Exactly. Because he is the only man who don't pretend to be a saint. Because he is the only one in this village who has a soul, but makes no parade of the trouble it gives him to save it."

"His virtuous wife and Mrs. Cackle will save his soul for him. You would think so if you had heard Mrs. Cackle's conversation today with my wife."

"The old lady gave us a hash of it well spiced. We went over the vast field of Mrs. Norval's virtues, and the vaster one of the doctor's errors, all of which have their root in the doctor's most unnatural liking of foreigners. That liking was the cause of the doctor's sending his only son Julian to be educated in Europe—as if the best schools on earth were not in New England—and Heaven knows what might have become of Julian if his heroic mother had not sent for him. He might have been a Roman Catholic, for all we know. That liking was also the cause of the doctor's sending Isaac to be a good-for-nothing clerk in sinful Washington, among foreigners, when he could have remained in virtuous New England to be a useful farmer. And finally, impelled by that liking, the doctor betook himself to California, which is yet full of '*natives*.' And as a just retribution for such perverse liking, the doctor was well-nigh 'roasted by the natives,' said the old lady. Whereupon, in behalf of truth, I said, 'Not by the natives, madam. The people called '*the natives*' are mostly of Spanish descent, and are not cannibals. The wild Indians of the Colorado River were doubtless the ones who captured the doctor and tried to make a meal of him.' 'Perhaps so,' said the old lady, visibly disappointed. 'To me they are all alike—Indians, Mexicans, or Californians—they are all horrid. But my son Beau says that our just laws and smart lawyers will soon "*freeze them out*." That as soon as we take their lands from them they will never be heard of anymore, and then the Americans, with God's help, will have all the land that was so righteously acquired through a just war and a most liberal payment in money.' Ain't that patriotism and Christian faith for you?" added Mr. Hackwell.

"For yourself, since it comes from one of the pillars of your congregation," answered Mr. Hammerhard, laughing, Mr. Hackwell too joining in the laugh, and touching up the horse, which tripped as he always did when pretending to trot, and the quickened motion caused the crazy vehicle to join in also with a series of squeaks, which made Mr. Hackwell's blood curdle, and set his teeth on edge, although a philosopher.

Whilst the two divines thus beguiled their way to the depot, the subject of their conversation—Mrs. Cackle—made hers laboriously towards home, thinking what pretext she could invent to be at Dr. Norval's when he arrived.

"I would give worlds to know his version of his conduct. Maybe —like Mr. Hackwell—he won't admit that the native Californians are savages; of course not, being foreigners. Mrs. Norval, though, will soon show him we ain't to be fooled."

Hi! hi! hi! she heard, and the squint and the lolling tongue of the parson's horse passed by her as if in derisive triumph.

"The aggravating beast!" exclaimed Mrs. Cackle—meaning the horse—just as Mr. Hackwell bowed to her most politely. "Going for the doctor?" said she to the divines, as if she thought the turnout needed physic. But the answer was lost in the squeaking of the wagon. "I know they are. I'll go and let Mrs. Norval know it," said the old lady, and walked briskly on.

Jack Sprig—Miss Lavinia Sprig's poodle—sat bolt upright upon Mrs. Norval's front doorsteps, watching the shadows of coming events whilst supper was cooking, as Mrs. Cackle came sneaking by the picket fence. Jack was happy, sporting a new blue ribbon around his white neck, and the fragrance of broiled chicken and roasted turkey came gratefully to his nostrils, whilst to his memory came the triumphant recollection that *he* had helped to catch that turkey who was now roasting, and who had been his bitter enemy, pecking at him unmercifully whenever he dared venture into the chicken yard. Jack wagged his tail, thinking the turkey could peck nevermore, when lo! the round face of Mrs. Cackle, like a red full moon in heated atmosphere, peered over the picket fence. Jack's tail dropped. Then a growl arose to his swelling throat. Would that he could put Mrs. Cackle beside the turkey! And who has not felt like Jack? He was a good hater, and ever since he could remember there had existed between himself and Mrs. Cackle a "magnetism of repulsion," of such peculiar strength that, after going to the very extreme, it curled back on itself, and from a repulsion came out an attraction, which made Mrs. Cackle's feet almost dance with longing to kick Jack, and made Jack's mouth water to bite the well-fed calves of Mrs. Cackle.

"There is that miserable poodle, with his wool all washed up white, adorned with a new ribbon!" exclaimed Mrs. Cackle, holding to the pickets to catch breath, for she had walked fast. "That old maid Lavvy Sprig, I suppose, has decked her thousand cats and her million canarybirds all with ribbons, like her odious poodle." And Mrs. Cackle looked towards the house, but she saw no decked cats there, though the hall door and all the windows were open. In a few moments, however, she espied Ruth Norval—eldest daughter of Dr. Norval—sitting by one of the parlor windows, rocking herself in a chair, reading a fashion magazine.

"There is Ruth, as usual, studying the fashions. If her father's funeral was coming, she would do the same," said Mrs. Cackle, and peered at the other window. "Who is there?" said she, putting her fat chin over the pickets to take a better view. She then distinguished a face so flattened against the windowpane that it had lost all human shape. But she rightly conjectured that the face belonged to Mattie Norval—youngest daughter of Dr. Norval—inasmuch as Mrs. Norval was too dignified to go and mash her face against the window glass, and Lavinia's high nose would have presented the same obstruction as her sister's dignity. Mrs. Cackle saluted the flattened mass, but it "gave no token," only it looked more flattened than ever, as now Mattie riveted her gaze more intently in the direction of the railroad depot, saying to her sister Ruth, "Don't look up, Rooty; study the fashions. There is old Cackler's moon-face on the pickets saluting, but I don't see it. 'Deed I don't. I am looking down the road."

"Tell your mother I heard the whistle!" bawled out the old lady, holding to the pickets.

"I wish she had heard the last trumpet," said Ruth. "Don't answer her, Mattie. She wants to be invited in. Why don't she go home? I see all the young Cacklers in their '*setting room*'—as she very properly calls it—all watching for papa's coming to begin their cackling."

"Ruth, I have told you not to make puns on Mrs. Cackle's name. It is very unkind to do so, and in very bad taste," said Mrs. Norval from the corner.

"In bad taste!" replied Ruth. "La, ma! the exquisite Mr. Hackwell makes puns all the time. I asked him why he kept 'The Comic Blackstone' among his theological books, and he answered, 'In abjuring all that pertains to the worldly profession of the law, I permitted myself the privilege of keeping this innocent punster.' And the 'innocent punster,' Mr. Hackwell the divine keeps between Kant and Calvin—above Martin Luther, ma!"

"Here he is!" screamed Mattie, interrupting her sister, and all flocked to the window. A light wagon, followed by another so heavily loaded that four strong horses could hardly pull it up, approached the gate.

"What upon earth is he bringing now?" exclaimed Mrs. Norval, looking at the light wagon in alarm.

"More rocks and pebbles, of course. But I don't know where he is to put them: the garret is full now," said Ruth, looking at the large wagon.

"He will store them away in the barn loft, where he keeps his bones and petrified woods. He brings quite a load. It is a government wagon," added Lavinia, also looking at the large wagon.

"I don't mean the boxes in the large wagon. I mean the—the—that—the red shawl," stammered Mrs. Norval. And now the three other ladies noticed for the first time a figure wrapped in a bright plaid shawl, leaning on the doctor's breast, and around which he tenderly encircled his arm.

CHAPTER II

The Little Black Girl

So astonished were the ladies at the sight of that red shawl, that not one of them—not even Mattie, who was more impulsive than the others, and had looked for her father's coming with more affectionate impatience—thought of answering the doctor's nods and salutations which he began to send them, full of smiles, as he approached the gate.

The light wagon stopped in front of the gate; the large one behind it. The Rev. Mr. Hackwell alighted, then the Rev. Mr. Hammerhard: the divines, in consideration for the doctor's feelings, had left their own carriage at the depot and ridden with him. The doctor alighted next, and then the mysterious figure in the bright-red shawl, which was handed carefully to the doctor by the driver from the wagon. Then all proceeded towards the gate, the doctor again tenderly throwing his arm around the female in the shawl—for it was a female: this fact Mrs. Norval had discovered plainly enough.

The meeting with his family, after an absence of four years, would have been cold and restrained enough for the doctor, who had felt nothing but misgivings since he passed Springfield, fearing, like a runaway boy, that even the fact of his return might not get him a pardon. Not a single smile of welcome did he see in the scared faces of his daughters or the stern features of his stately wife. But a happy and unexpected agency broke the spell of that ominous gloom and scattered the gathering storm. And this potent agency, this mighty wizard, waving no wand, only wagging his woolly tail, was no other than Jack Sprig, who, unable to contain himself any longer in the midst of so much excitement, ran out as Mrs. Norval's champion to bark at the red shawl. The female screamed, frightened, and clung to the doctor for protection. In her fright she dropped the obnoxious shawl, and then all the ladies saw that what Mrs. Norval's eyes had magnified into a very tall woman was a little girl very black indeed.

"Goodness! what a specimen! A nigger girl!" exclaimed Mattie, whereupon all the ladies laughed and went out to the hall to meet the doctor.

When the first salutations were over, and the first cross—very cross—questioning done by Mrs. Norval, the doctor ran out to see about bringing in his big boxes from the large wagon. They proved to be so heavy that besides the drivers of the two wagons, and Dandy Jim—the doctor's body-servant—it was found necessary to call in Bingham, the gardener, and the doctor himself lent the aid of his muscular arms to roll the boxes into the hall. Mrs. Norval came out to remonstrate against such heavy boxes full of stones being brought into the hall to scratch the oilcloth, which was nearly new, but the doctor would have them in the hall, so that Mrs. Norval was obliged to desist, and the work of rolling in the boxes continued.

Mrs. Norval asked the two reverend gentlemen to stay to tea. Mr. Hackwell accepted readily, but Mr. Hammerhard declined, as Mrs. Hammerhard's baby was only three weeks old, and she felt lonely without him.

Whilst Dr. Norval was busy rolling in his heavy boxes, the ladies and the Rev. Mr. Hackwell turned their attention to the little black girl, upon whom the doctor evidently had bestowed great care, making now and then occasional remarks upon the well-known idiosyncrasy of the doctor for collecting all sorts of rocks.

"The doctor is not content with bringing four boxes more, full of stones, but now he, I fear, having exhausted the mineral kingdom, is about to begin with the animal, and this is our first specimen," said Mrs. Norval, pointing at the boxes in the hall and at the little girl, who was looking at her with a steady, thoughtful gaze.

"The next specimen will be a baboon," added Ruth, "for papa's samples don't improve."

"I have been looking at this one, and I think it is rather pretty, only very black," the Rev. Hackwell observed.

"Of course she is pretty," put in Mattie. "Look what magnificent eyes she has, and what red and prettily-cut lips!"

"How could she have such lips?—negroes' lips are not like those. What is your name?" cried out Miss Lavinia, as if the child were deaf.

The girl did not answer: she only turned her lustrous eyes on her, then again riveted her gaze upon Mrs. Norval, who seemed to fascinate her.

"How black she is!" uttered Mrs. Norval with a slight shiver of disgust.

"I don't think she is so black," said Mattie, taking one of the child's hands and turning it to see the palm of it. "See, the palm of her hand is as white as mine—and a prettier white; for it has such a pretty pink shade to it."

"Drop her hand, Mattie! You don't know what disease she might have," said Mrs. Norval imperiously.

"Nonsense! As if papa would bring anyone with a contagious disease to his house!" said Mattie, still holding the child's hand. "How pretty her little hand is, and all her features are certainly lovely! See how well cut her nose and lips are. And as for her eyes, I wish I had them: they are perfectly superb!"

"Isn't she pretty?" exclaimed the doctor, bringing in the last box. "And her disposition is so lovely and affectionate, and she is so grateful and thoughtful for one so young!"

"How old is she? Her face is so black that truly, it baffles all my efforts to guess her age," said Mrs. Norval dryly, interrupting the doctor.

"She is only ten years old, but her history is already more romantic than that of half of the heroines of your trashy novels," answered the doctor.

"She is a prodigy, then—a true emanation of the black art!" said Mrs. Norval, smiling derisively, "if so much is to be told of a child so young."

"Not of her personally, but of her birth and the history of her parents—that is to say, so far as I know it."

"Who were her parents, papa?" asked Mattie.

"Indians or negroes, or both," Ruth said. "Any one can see that much of her history."

"And those who saw that much would be mistaken or fools," retorted the doctor warmly.

"Well, well, even if she be Princess Sheba, let us not have a discussion about it the minute you return home. Suppose we change the subject to a more agreeable one," said Mrs. Norval.

"I am perfectly willing," the doctor replied, drawing to his side the little girl, who had stood silently listening to the conversation, looking wistfully from one face to the other.

"I suppose you got my letter telling you I had sent for Julian? And now he is in Boston, where every New Englander should be educated," Mrs. Norval said boldly.

"But where not every New Englander is willing to be educated. Julian writes to me that he doesn't like his college," the doctor replied.

"Julian is perfectly ruined by his unfortunate trip to Europe," said Mrs. Norval, addressing Mr. Hackwell, "and, like Isaac, he will never get over his fondness for foreigners."

Happily, Hannah, the waiter-girl, came to interrupt the conversation by announcing that tea was ready.

"Take this child to the kitchen," said Mrs. Norval to Hannah, pointing to the little girl.

"What for? She is very well here," the doctor said, putting his arms around the child's waist.

"Doctor, you certainly do not mean that we are to keep this creature always near us—you can't mean it!" exclaimed Mrs. Norval, half interrogatively and half-deprecatingly.

"And why not?" was the doctor's rejoinder.

Mrs. Norval was too astounded to say why not. She silently led the way to the tea table.

"I beg you to remember, Mr. Hackwell," said the doctor, following his wife and holding the poor little girl by the hand, "and to draw from that fact a moral for a sermon, that my wife is a lady of the strictest Garrisonian school,[2] a devout follower of Wendell Phillip's teachings,[3] and a most enthusiastic admirer of Mr. Sumner.[4] Compare these facts with the reception she gives this poor little orphan because her skin is dark, whilst I—a good-for-nothing Democrat, who doesn't believe in Sambo[5] but believe in Christian charity and human mercy—I feel pity for the little thing."

[2]William Lloyd Garrison (1805-1879), U.S. journalist and radical abolitionist, whose newspaper *The Liberator* (1835-1865) campaigned against slavery in the U.S.

[3]Wendell Phillips (1811-1884) was a superb speaker, abolitionist crusader and close associate of W.L. Garrison. He condemned the federal Constitution for its compromises over slavery, and after the Civil War supported full liberties for freedmen, as well as women's rights and universal suffrage.

[4]Charles Sumner (1811-1874), U.S. Senator from Massachusetts (1652-1874), abolitionist and powerful Chairman of the Senate Foreign Relations Committee (1861-1871).

[5]Derived from the Latin American term *zambo*, a caste category for persons of mixed Indian-Black ancestry, "Sambo" in the U.S. was used as a disparaging term for African-Americans.

CHAPTER III

The Mysterious Big Boxes

"Where is the child to eat her supper?" asked Mrs. Norval of her husband, without making any answer to his last remarks.

"Here by my side, of course," the doctor replied.

"I am glad you have abjured your old prejudices against the African race," said Mr. Hackwell, without making allusion to Mrs. Norval's sentiments upon the subject.

"Yes, but the evil spirit has not left our house, for it has only jumped out of me to take possession of my better half," said the doctor, laughing. "Since when have you changed, wife, that a dark skin has become so objectionable to you?"

"As for that, you are mistaken. I do not object to her dark skin, only I wish to know what position she is to occupy in my family. Which wish *I* consider quite reasonable, since I am the one to regulate my household," said Mrs. Norval, taking hold of the teapot to serve tea, but with a look that suggested a wish on her part to welcome her husband by throwing it at his devoted head.

"Her position in our family will be that of an adopted child," said the doctor.

Mrs. Norval's hand shook so violently on hearing this that she poured the tea all over the tray, but little of it fell in the cup where she meant to pour it. With assumed calmness, however, she said, "In that case your daughters and myself will have to wait upon your adopted child, for I am sure we will not find in all New England a white girl willing to do it."

"And that, of course, speaks very highly for New England—abolitionist New England, mind you. But I'll warrant, madam, that you shall have plenty of servants."

Mrs. Norval was too angry to speak. There was an awkward pause, which happily Mattie interrupted, saying, "Has she got any name, papa?"

"I suppose her name is Rabbit, or Hare, or Squirrel. That is, if she is an Indian," said Ruth, laughing.

"You ask her," the doctor said.

"What is your name?" asked Ruth.

The child looked at her, then at the doctor, and went on eating her supper silently.

"She doesn't understand," said Ruth.

"Yes, she does. But, not liking your manner, she disdains to answer your question," replied the doctor.

Mrs. Norval suppressed a groan. She could not swallow a single mouthful.

"Indians are as proud and surly as they are treacherous," observed Lavinia. "I suppose she is a mixture of Indian and negro."

"Your supposition, being very sagacious and kind, does honor to your head and heart, but it happens that this child has no more Indian or negro blood than you or I have," said the doctor testily, evidently losing patience.

"I thought she might be Aztec," said Lavinia apologetically. But the doctor did not answer her, and there was another awkward silence.

Mr. Hackwell was sorry he had stayed to tea. He had anticipated a very pleasant conversation and amusing accounts from the doctor, who was very witty and told a story charmingly. But instead of this there had been nothing but sparring about the little black child. Mrs. Norval had utterly lost patience, and the doctor seemed in a fair way to the same point. Mr. Hackwell stirred his second cup of tea slowly, thinking what he should do to change the conversation. He would first propitiate the doctor by showing some kindness to the child. How should he begin? He took a slice of bread and buttered it nicely. Then he took some jelly, spread it on the butter, and presented it to the child with a smile.

"Thank you, sir," said the little girl, in very good English.

"Why, the little 'possum! She speaks English, and very likely has understood what has been said," Mattie exclaimed.

"She has understood every word," the doctor answered, "and doubtless is impressed with your kindness."

"That is a pity," said Mr. Hackwell and, addressing the child in his blandest manner, he asked, "What is your name, my little girl? Won't you tell me?"

"My name is María Dolores Medina, but I have been always called Lola or Lolita," she answered in the plainest English.

"And have you understood all we said since you arrived?" asked Mattie.

Lola nodded her head in the affirmative and stole a furtive look toward Mrs. Norval, which was very piquant. The doctor and Mr. Hackwell laughed, and so did Mattie. But, as Mrs. Norval colored with vexation, Lavinia did not dare to join in the laugh, whilst Ruth was too deeply absorbed in thinking how she could fix her old grenadine dress to give it a new look for the christening of Mrs. Hammerhard's baby.

As soon as tea was over, the doctor called Bingham, the gardener, and asked him if he had found the men to help with the boxes, to which Bingham answered in the affirmative. The doctor then told him to go and fetch them.

"What is the matter now?" exclaimed Mrs. Norval, seeing seven men enter the hall, preceded by Bingham and followed by the doctor's body-servant, Dandy Jim.

"The matter is, that these men have come to take my boxes upstairs," said the doctor. "Put them in Master Julian's room, Jim."

"Why not take them at once to the garret? In Julian's room they will tear the carpet to pieces," Mrs. Norval remonstrated.

"We'll risk that. I don't want to take my specimens to the garret until I assort them. Besides, the boxes are too broad to go up the narrow staircase of the garret-rooms."

"Then why not leave them where they are? Afterwards you can assort your specimens down here."

"Because I propose to do that upstairs."

Mrs. Norval bit her lip. She could almost have cried with vexation. The doctor was more persistent than ever in foolish whims. What a miserable wife she was! But now Mr. Hackwell said some kind words to her, praising her great forbearance and amiability under so many exasperating trials, then, pressing her hand to bid her good night, took leave of the doctor in the hall, where he was superintending the moving of his boxes, bowed good night to the young ladies, and left.

Lavinia sighed, watching his retreating form, and Ruth smiled contemptuously, whilst Miss Mattie stood up and made a motion with her foot as if giving a kick to some imaginary object before her.

"For shame! you are no longer a child, miss, to indulge in such unlady-like antics!" said Mrs. Norval sternly. But the doctor laughed and patted Mattie on the back. And Mattie hung on her father's neck and whispered something which made him laugh more.

After all the boxes were safely deposited in Julian's room—which adjoined Mrs. Norval's bedchamber—there was one more discussion to get through, and that was the most difficult to dispose of. The question as to where Lola was to sleep had to be decided.

The doctor said she should have a room to herself, and, as there was none ready for her, she should occupy either Julian's room or share that of the girls with them: Lavinia's being too small to admit another bed.

But Mrs. Norval was so shocked at this that the doctor, tired as he was in body by his journey, and in mind by all the harassing little incidents and disputes which had occurred since his arrival, left the matter for that night to his wife's discretion. The child, then, was sent with Hannah to share her room for the night.

The doctor kissed Lola several times and embraced her to bid her good night, and she, sobbing as if her heart would break, and looking back several times as she left the room, went away to sleep the sleep of the orphan under that inhospitable roof.

CHAPTER IV

What the Mysterious Boxes Contained

"Don't you know, doctor, that you kissed that Indian child more affectionately than you kissed your own daughters?" Mrs. Norval said fiercely to her husband when they had closed their bedroom door to the outer world.

"Maybe I did, for I pity the poor orphan. My daughters, thank God, have yet their parents to take care of them, but this poor little waif has no one in the world, perhaps, to protect her and care for her but myself."

"As for that, she'll get along well enough. She is not so timid as to need anybody's particular protection. Her eyes are bold enough. She will learn to work—I'll see to that—and a good worker is sure of a home in New England. Mrs. Hammerhard will want just such a girl as this, I hope, to mind the baby, and she will give her some of her cast-off clothes and her victuals."

"Cast-off clothes and victuals!" the doctor repeated, as if he could not believe that his ears had heard rightly.

"Why, yes. We certainly couldn't expect Mrs. Hammerhard would give more to a girl ten years old to mind a little baby in the cradle."

"And how is she to go to school, if she is to mind Mrs. Hammerhard's baby for old clothes and cold victuals?"

"Doctor," said Mrs. Norval, tying her nightcap with deliberation, "I said nothing about cold victuals. She can eat her victuals cold or warm, just as she likes: this is a free country. But I do say this, that this is the first day I have laid eyes on you for four years (you left in '53, and now we are in '57), and I think it is very hard that this first day we should have so many disagreeables about a stranger, and that an Indian child. I'll do the best I can for her: I shall do *my duty as a Christian woman*. But she can't expect to grow up in idleness and be a burden to us. She must learn to work and earn her living. In the winters, perhaps, she might go to school at nights; I'll see what I can do about that. She will go to our Sunday school, of course, but—"

"She will go to Sunday school if anyone will teach her the Catholic Catechism, but certainly not the Presbyterian," said the doctor, pulling his coat off, as if making ready to fight on that point. "And as for her learning to work, she will learn to do what ladies learn, and she will suit herself in that, when she has finished her education."

"Finish her education! A Catholic Catechism!" faintly echoed Mrs. Norval, letting her cap strings go and sinking into her armchair.

The doctor, in his shirt sleeves, crossed his arms over his breast and, standing before his wife, also repeated, "Finish her education, Mrs. Norval, yes, and a Catholic Catechism. I said those words, Mrs. Norval; and I mean them, too, madam."

A contemptuous smile played around the pale lips of the agitated Mrs. Norval, as she said, "And pray who is to teach her that abominable idolatry here? And who is to pay for her magnificent education? For I suppose she must have several *masters* to teach her foreign languages, and music, and painting."

The doctor nodded his head in the affirmative, entirely disregarding his wife's sarcasm, and, taking a bunch of keys from his pocket, said, "If you will follow me, madam, I'll show you with what Lola's education is to be paid." And the doctor, taking a candle, led the way to Julian's room. Mrs. Norval followed her husband, not knowing but that he had gone crazy and meant to set the house on fire with the lighted candle he carried.

The doctor set the candle on the bureau, and Mrs. Norval seated herself on the chair, silently waiting to see what he would do next.

The doctor selected a key from the bunch he held in his hand and opened a trunk from which he took a screwdriver. Then he went to one of the heavy boxes, brought with so much labor, and began to unscrew from the lid several large screws, saying, "Arthur Sinclair is to blame for these boxes taking this trip up to New England. I told him distinctly that I wished them to be left at his brother's in New York, and he must, of course, go to work and ship them by express all the way here. When I went to William Sinclair's office to see if the boxes were there, he told me they had been shipped that morning. I went to the depot to stop their coming up, but only two boxes had not been put into the baggage car, and those I sent back to Sinclair's. The other four came up, and now I shall have to take them back."

"So you were bringing six boxes full of rocks?"

"But only to New York."

Now the doctor took out the last screw, opened the box with the key, and began by taking out some articles of clothing. Mrs. Norval smiled. Then he came to some specimens of ores, very rough-looking stones. He lifted a piece of canvas, on which these rough stones were laid, and said to his wife, "This is what will pay for Lola's education."

Mrs. Norval stood up, uttering a cry of delighted surprise, then, clasping her hands, remained silent, with open mouth and staring eyes, transfixed by her amazement and joy.

"But is it *real* gold?" she whispered hoarsely, after some moments of bewildered silence.

"All is not gold that glitters," the doctor replied smiling, "but *this* is."

"And whose is it? Ours? Yours? Whose?"

"Don't you guess? If I say it will pay for Lolita's education, it is because it belongs to her."

"What?" ejaculated Mrs. Norval, falling back in her chair. "You are jesting; you can't mean that. No, no! I can't believe that this horrible little negro girl—"

"Once and for all, let me tell you that the blood of that child is as good as, or better than, yours or mine; that she is neither an Indian nor a negro child, and that, unless you wish to doubt my word, my veracity, you will not permit yourself or anybody else to think her such."

Mrs. Norval was incapable of controversy now; her soul was floating over those yellow, shining lumps of cold, unfeeling metal. She made no reply to her husband, but, as if obeying a natural impulse, she knelt by the chest, and with childlike simplicity began to take pieces of gold and examine them attentively and toss them up playfully. Then she took a handful, then two handfuls, trying to see how many pieces she could lift up. The sedate, severe, sober, serious lady of forty was a playful, laughing child again.

The doctor watched her and smiled, but his smile was sad. He had not seen that expression on her face since they were gathering apples and he asked her to marry him, twenty-one years ago!

"I think that Lola, instead of being a *burden* to us, will be a great acquisition. Don't you think so?" said the doctor, after his wife had toyed with the gold for some time.

"How much is it?" asked Mrs. Norval in a scarcely audible voice tremulous with emotion.

"I really can't tell how much is in this one box, but, according to our calculation in San Francisco, there must be about a million dollars in the six boxes."

"A million!" screamed Mrs. Norval.

"Hush, wife! If you indulge in such loud exclamations, someone will hear you, and I don't want it to be known that there is so much gold in my house. I shall certainly send it back to New York as soon as possible."

"But what will you do with so much gold? Won't they steal it from you?"

"I'll look out for that. William Sinclair is an honest man, and he will take charge of it. I arranged all that with him. He is to have the gold coined immediately, and will take it for three years at six percent interest, giving me good securities on real estate."

"But the child doesn't want sixty-thousand dollars a year," said Mrs. Norval deprecatingly, as if speaking to the gold, and in a timid, plaintive voice—she was so subdued, so humbled, before the yellow god!

CHAPTER V

The Rough Pebbles

"No, Lola doesn't want sixty-thousand dollars a year, nor the fifth of that," said the doctor. "But what we don't spend on her we will invest in real estate, or stocks, or anything else that Sinclair thinks advisable, so that by the time the little girl is twenty, she will be very rich, and people wouldn't call her Indian or nigger even if she were, which she is *not*."

"I am glad she is not, because—because—if she be of decent people, then—why—then, of course, a decent man would marry her."

"Just so, and she will be beautiful, as that black skin will certainly wear off," said the doctor, busily putting back in the box the things he had got out of it and beginning to screw the lid down as it was before.

"Have you thought that Julian or brother Isaac might take a fancy to Lola? and—"

"No. I am the last man to plot matrimony. And, take my advice, you let it alone, too. No good comes of that kind of managing."

"You have not told me how you came across this child and her gold," said Mrs. Norval as they walked back to their bedroom again.

"Her mother deposited both under my care, as the poor lady died on the banks of the Gila River."

"But what was such a rich woman doing there? Why did she leave her child and gold with you? Had she no husband or relations? How came she to die in that wild country among savages?"

"Well, the poor lady's story is a long one, and unless you let me smoke my pipe while telling it to you, we'll have to put it off until tomorrow. And now let us go to sleep."

Mrs. Norval allowed the pipe. Though very obnoxious, it was better than to go to bed and not be able to sleep thinking about the probable history of such a rich woman.

Whilst filling his pipe, the doctor prefaced his recital by saying, "I am very sorry I could not bring with me the narrative in writing in the very words of Lolita's mother herself, as Lebrun wrote it in shorthand. The poor lady knew well that she would soon die, and begged that I should make a memorandum of what she was going to tell me, so that I could let her husband know it if I ever found him. I called Lebrun to the bedside of the poor lady, and, as Lebrun is a stenographer, he took in shorthand all she said, and will soon send me the manuscript when he puts it all in plain English. So, about the previous history of the lady I don't know much, except how she got the gold and the diamonds little by little, and—"

"What diamonds?" interrupted Mrs. Norval eagerly. "What do you mean? You have not mentioned diamonds to me."

"No, nor the emeralds and rubies I have not," said the doctor with provoking nonchalance, lighting his pipe leisurely and puffing the smoke at long intervals. "I had not mentioned the"—puff, puff—"diamonds and emeralds and opals;"—puff, puff—"I hadn't got to that"—puff, puff—"point in my story. The poor lady did not give them to me until the day she died—after we had sent off the gold, and after she told us how she was carried off by the Apache Indians and then sold to the Mohave Indians, and how Lolita was born five months after her capture. So you see how Lolita's blood is pure Spanish blood, her mother being of pure Spanish descent and her father the same, though an Austrian by birth, he having been born in Vienna. These particulars I remember well, as Lebrun and I thought them so very strange, and the fate of so highly-born a lady so sadly unfortunate."

"But how did she keep the diamonds and save so much gold all this time?" asked Mrs. Norval, intent upon her own thoughts and caring very little for the sad fate of any woman just then. "Where are the diamonds? Let me see them, before you go on with your narrative."

The doctor, again taking the bunch of keys from his pocket, went to his traveling-trunk, and, opening it, took out a buckskin bag, and from it a piece of cloth in which were tied a number of pebbles of nearly uniform size. He spread the pebbles on the table, and said to his wife, "Here they are, and I can pick you out each of the different stones by the color showing through those little places where the rough coating is rubbed off."

Great disappointment was depicted in Mrs. Norval's face as she saw those rough pebbles spread before her eager eyes. She was unable to withhold the expression of her contempt. She exclaimed, "Pshaw, doctor! These can't be *real* diamonds. They must be what they call

'California diamonds,' which are a sort of bright pebble, but no diamond."

"I flatter myself, wife, that I am a pretty good judge of precious stones, though I am no jeweler, and I tell you these are splendid gems, in size and in quality. The poor lady was no fool, and she made her selection quite as judiciously as could be done by the best judge of gems. She had some diamond rings on her fingers when she was captured, and with those rings, she told me, she managed to scratch the surface of these rough pebbles and ascertain that they were diamonds. Accidentally, whilst bathing in a small stream which is a tributary to the Colorado River, she saw a very bright, shining pebble. She picked it up, and, as she had some knowledge of precious stones, she saw it was a large diamond, though only partly divested of its rough coating. Then she looked about for similar pebbles, and found many more. Afterwards she followed the little rivulet from which they seemed to come down, and, following it, was led up to the side of a hill and down a ravine, where, as if they had been washed thither by the rains, she found opals and larger diamonds. Afterwards the Indians brought her emeralds and rubies, seeing that she liked pretty pebbles. Thus she made a fine collection, for she took only the largest and those which seemed to her most perfect."

Mrs. Norval now condescended to examine the pebbles. Yes, they all showed shining spots—more or less bright, more or less large—and the places where the poor captive had scratched them with her ring. On further examination, Mrs. Norval discovered larger spots of light, which showed that most of the pebbles had been rubbed hard against each other, as the bright spots corresponded in size and shape. The same was the case with the emeralds. No, there was no doubt in Mrs. Norval's mind; they must be real gems. And yet she frowned. Then she said, "And these diamonds also belong to the little nig—I mean the little girl?"

"Of course they do. To whom should they belong but to Lola?"

"Didn't her mother give you anything for taking charge of her daughter for life?"

CHAPTER VI

Lola Commences Her Education

"The mother did not leave the child with me for life. She wished me to take care of Lola whilst I make inquiries about her family. When Lebrun sends me the manuscript of her narrative, I shall know the names of her relatives and where to look for them. In the meantime, my duty is to take care of Lolita, send her to school, or have her taught at home, and invest her money judiciously."

The face of Mrs. Norval fell. All this glittering fortune which she—vaguely as to the way, but clearly as to the intent—had resolved to share—all this brilliant fortune might leave her house too soon for her to mature any plan to participate in it. The despised black child she now would give worlds to keep. She would go on her knees to serve her, as her servant, her slave, rather than let her go. Oh, if Lebrun only would keep that manuscript forever! Yes, so that the doctor would not be able to find her relations and Lola remain with them! Thus ran the thoughts of the high-principled matron. But never once did it occur to her that she had sent the child to sleep with the cook and the chambermaid, and she did not know that the little girl was now crying as if her heart were breaking, calling her mother between sobs, sitting up in a dark room, and with the snoring of the two Irishwomen for sole response to her impassioned apostrophes. Lola had refused to share the bed with either of the two servants, and both had resented the refusal as a most grievous insult.

"I am shure I don't want to slape with any of the likes of ye, naither. Niggers ain't my most particliest admirashun, I can tell ye, no more nor toads nor cateypillars. Haith! I think, on the whole, I prefer the cateypillars, as a more dacent sort of a baste," said cook, giving Lola a withering look. Then, with the dexterity of a conjurer, she gave a pull to certain strings about her stomach, whereupon the whole structure of her apparel came tumbling down magically, to Lola's great astonishment, who had no idea but what that hoop skirt was part of the cook's mortal coil.

With dilated orbs, Lola gazed upon the fallen hoops and skirts, then upon that figure clad in an inner garment (which hardly reached to the corrugated knee), standing in the center of the circle like a stubby column in the middle of a blackened ruin. Cook, being a good Catholic and a lady of spirit, crossed herself earnestly but hurriedly, shook her fist threateningly at Lola, and bolted into bed, leaving behind, in the middle of her hoop skirt, a pair of shapeless shoes, like two dead crows, and carrying with her to bed a pair of stockings which had been blue, but were now black, and had the privilege of ascending to her ankles, where they modestly coiled themselves in two black rings, and went no farther.

Hannah, the chambermaid, was not so repulsive to look upon. Still, the thought of sharing her bed was to Lola very terrible. Trembling with fear of giving yet more offense to the sensitive Irish ladies, the poor child timidly asked them if they could spare for that night a blanket and a pillow, to go to sleep by herself on the floor.

"I knew that. I knew she would like the floor much better. She ain't used to a nice, dacent bed—that is the nature of her!" said the indignant cook.

Hannah gave Lola a blackened pillow, but told her she could not spare a blanket. Lola said her shawl would do, and Hannah put out the candle. Then the two offended ladies began their nasal duo, and Lola her heart-breaking laments. The louder the Irishwomen snored, the more terrified Lola felt at the darkness and silence beyond that discordant noise, until, almost frantic with terror and desolation, and almost stifling with the foulness of the air, the child, trembling with fear, staggered out of the room and went to lie in the hall—anywhere, only as far from the Irishwomen as possible. She groped her way along the hall until she felt a door, and at her feet a carpet: it was the mat before Mrs. Norval's door. Suppressing her sobs, Lola lay down on the mat, quietly wrapping her shawl around her shivering body. Jack was lying at Miss Lavinia's door, and kindly came to nestle at her side, wagging his tail apologetically, as if not sure that Lola would appreciate his feelings.

Seeing that his wife made no observation after his last remarks, the doctor continued, saying, "Yes, my first care must be to invest the gold. Then I'll see to the cutting of the stones. It seems to me they will make more jewelry than Lola wants: I might sell part of them."

"Of course you ought to sell the greater part of them. It will only make the child vain to have so much jewelry. She doesn't want them," said Mrs. Norval warmly, for she had already begun to form a little plan to buy cheap some of these rough pebbles, with the gold she meant to take out of the boxes for her husband's services. For, Mrs. Norval argued to herself, if the doctor was foolish enough to take so much trouble and care for a strange child, for no pay, she did not mean he should. She meant that his services should be well paid. He had a family which he had left for four years, and whilst he was looking after the interests of this strange child, of course he ought to be paid, and must be paid.

"No," the doctor said, and Mrs. Norval started, as if he had read and was answering her thoughts—"no, I can't sell the gems, for I remember now that the poor lady repeated that *all*, *all* should be made into jewelry for Lola, as the gold would be enough to support her until her father was found, and who being rich, will not want Lola's gold—so she said several times."

"She did not know the gold was a million dollars?"

"No, she had collected it gradually, but she had no idea how much it was. She was only anxious that there should be enough for Lola's expenses and education, until her father was found," said the doctor. But he did not say that Lola's mother had told him to take half of the gold for his services.

"And didn't she give you anything for your trouble and your kindness to herself and her child?" inquired Mrs. Norval again.

"Indeed she did pay me royally, like a noble woman that she was. I have yet about ten-thousand-dollars' worth of the prettiest gold nuggets ever found, besides five thousand I left in Sinclair's bank, and all I spent in California, after paying all my debts."

"And you consider that a sufficient remuneration for all that we are to do, besides what you have already done for them?" asked Mrs. Norval, a slight sneer curling her lip.

"Of course I do. She must have given me something over thirty-thousand dollars. Besides, in using Lola's money, of course we can derive a great many advantages, for I don't mean to stint the income, only I shall take mighty good care of the principal."

Mrs. Norval's eyes brightened. The doctor added, "And, as a matter of course, all the surplus income shall be well invested. The expenses of the child can't be very great, no matter how extravagant we choose to be. Her income will be mostly turned into capital."

His wife gave him a withering look of wrath and contempt. How stupidly, how provokingly honest that man was! His wife almost hated him for it.

"But now it is getting late, Jemima. I must hurry with my narrative, for I am tired with traveling all day," said the doctor, unconscious of his wife's unuttered, unutterable wrath. "Where was I? I forget how much I have told you about that poor lady's story. Let me see. I think I shall have to fill up my pipe again to finish my tale, which, as I said, is not very long, for I trusted to Lebrun's manuscript to refresh my memory."

Mrs. Norval scarcely listened. She made no answer. Her whole soul was oscillating between the bundle of rough pebbles and the box containing the yellow nuggets. What should she do? Who could help her to execute a plan to stop her husband from taking the gold away, or in some way to get a hold of it? Ah! a bright thought! The image of the Rev. Hackwell presented itself. Yes, he was "*smart*," and—and—honest. The thought of Mrs. Norval *stammered* at the word *honest.*

"Well, here is my pipe filled again. But I must hurry, for it is past twelve," said the doctor, sitting by his wife to resume his narrative.

CHAPTER VII

Lola's Mother

"Let me see," said the doctor, looking at the clouds of smoke which, for the first time in the twenty-one years of Mrs. Norval's married life, floated in her bedchamber, such is gold's power. "We were on our way down the Colorado River, intending to follow its course to its junction with the Gila, or perhaps to the Gulf of California, and we had encamped to take a two days' rest, when we were surrounded by a large party of Indians. We took our arms, and got together to make fight, if necessary, but it was not. The rascally Indians had had enough of shooting just then. They were returning from a fight with an emigrant train and some government troops. The chief and two of his sons were badly wounded, and perhaps would have died if my medicine chest and my surgical instruments hadn't been so good. The village of the Indians—called ranchería—was only about a mile from our camp, and the chief told me he wished to send for his wife and daughter, and remain in my camp with his two sons, that I might attend to their wounds. I gave the three wounded Indians my tent and went to share Sinclair's with him. That same evening, after I had dressed the wounds of the chief and his two sons, and was yet busy attending to other warriors who had been winged, Lola and her mother came, accompanied by an Indian woman. The chief told me in broken Spanish, which he and I spoke about alike, that 'Euitelhap'—pointing to Lola's mother—was his wife and had come to take care of him, and said to her, '*Ña Hala*, this is the good man doctor who is going to cure me and my sons, and has already relieved us.' The *ña Hala* looked at me with a pair of large, mournful eyes, but made no answer. She evidently did not feel very enthusiastic on the subject of the chief's recovery. The chief, however, seemed to feel the greatest respect for the *ña Hala* (which, in the language of these Indians, means *my lady*), and all the Indians the same, obeying her slightest wish. A day or two after, when the wounded Indians were taking their midday siesta, the *ña Hala*, feeling better acquainted, asked me if she could trust me with a secret, and begged me to do her a favor, for the love of God, and for humanity's sake. I answered I would do what I could. Then she told me that her name was Doña Theresa Medina, that she had been carried away from Sonora, in Mexico, ten years ago, and she had never had an opportunity to escape until now; that she had made an oath to the chief not to try to escape because in that way he would relax his vigilance, and she be enabled to send her little girl away. I told her that she ought to try to regain her liberty, that her oath to the chief could not be binding. She insisted that it was, for she had voluntarily made it; that she did not wish to see her family now, after ten years of such life as had been forced upon her; that she only wished to save her daughter from a similar fate, and then to lie down and die. She said also that she would pay me well if I would take her child away and care for her until I found her family (she told me the name of the place where her family lived in Mexico, but I have forgotten it), and that I must promise to try to find Lola's father. This, of course, I promised her. Then she told me that she had 'enough gold to fill up those boxes' (pointing to our mess and provision chests), which she would put under my care for Lola, and for me to pay myself for my trouble; that she had the gold in a little ravine not far from the spot where our camped was pitched. At first I could hardly believe what she said, but she did not let me doubt long. That same night she brought me a buckskin bag, which she could hardly carry, full of gold nuggets, and gave them to me, saying she would give me as many more as I wanted if I only would take her child away from among savages and bring her up as a Christian, and educate her myself in case I should not be able to find her father.

"Sinclair and Lebrun had gone down the river on a sort of reconnaissance and would not be back for a week. So I told the lady that when my companions returned, we would make the necessary arrangements to carry Lola away, and the gold she wished to give her, and that she must keep quiet in the meantime. But she was too anxious to wait. Every night, accompanied by her Indian woman, she made four or five trips to the little ravine where she kept her treasure. By the time Sinclair and Lebrun returned, she had transferred nearly half of it, and she and I had packed two of our chests full of gold nuggets, leaving room only to put some specimens of ores and pieces of quartz on the top. As soon as Sinclair and Lebrun came, I took them aside and asked them if they were willing to discontinue our expedition for the present, and make ten-thousand dollars each clear of expenses. They said yes, particularly as we were obliged to stop for a while on account of the freshets. Then I pledged them to secrecy and told them what Lola's mother had said to me, and of my promise to carry the child away.

"The Indian chief, as well as his two sons, was fast convalescing, and it was advisable to hasten our departure before they were strong enough to give us trouble, whilst Doña Theresa herself was visibly declining in health, and daily becoming more weak and emaciated. The prospect of being forever separated from her child was rapidly killing her, and she knew it full well. But such was the self-sacrificing devotion of that lady, that sick and weak as she felt, with a sinking heart and no hope for herself, she never swerved from her purpose to set her child free, and then, literally, lay down and die.

"The day fixed for our departure came. We had thrown away, unknown to our escort, at night, when everybody was asleep, the greater part of our specimens—breaking from each, to keep, a small piece—to make room for the gold. We packed it all in two of our wagons, putting some ores and other traps which we had used in our expedition on the top of the gold, and then we were ready to start.

"I told the chief that, as he was on a fair way to get well, and both of his sons the same, I would now go on my journey down the river; that I would leave him my tent, where he could stay three or four days longer, if he wished. He begged me to remain a few days longer, as he was afraid that *ña Hala* was very sick. I told him I would see the *ña Hala* and ascertain whether she required my services.

"That night, about midnight, Sinclair started with the gold and Lola and all our escort, leaving only Lebrun and Jim with me to follow next morning on horseback.

"When it was scarcely daylight, the Indian woman so devoted to Doña Theresa came to tell me that her mistress had 'lain down to die,' and wished to see me; that they had both gone with Lola part of the way, and when the *ña Hala* felt that she had no strength to go farther, they returned, and had just arrived.

"In a miserable Indian hut lay the dying lady. The surroundings were cheerless enough to kill any civilized woman, but the bedclothes, I noticed, were as white as snow, and everything about her was clean and tidy. She smiled when she saw me, and said, 'Thank God, Lolita is away from those horrid savages! Please do not forget that she must be baptized and brought up a Roman Catholic.' Her voice failed her, and she made a sign that she wished to sit up. We raised her, and, after drinking a little wine I gave her, she said she would like me to make a memorandum of some things she wished to tell me, so that if I ever found her husband, or her father, I would be able to give them news of her and some idea of her terrible history since she was carried off by the Indians. I told her that Lebrun understood Spanish better than I, and, moreover, being a stenographer, he could take her words down as she spoke them. She was very much pleased at this suggestion, and I called Lebrun to take down her narrative as she told it. Lebrun will send the manuscript as soon as he transcribes it.

"Poor woman! That was a clear case of 'broken heart.' She died of sheer grief, and nothing else."

"But she gave you the diamonds before that?" asked Mrs. Norval.

The doctor looked at her, then arose and began to undress without answering.

CHAPTER VIII

"The Trophies of Miltiades Do Not Let Me Sleep"[6]

Miss Lavinia Sprig might never have read about the battle of Marathon, but certainly there was a similarity of thought and feeling between Themistocles[7] after Marathon, and herself as she sat with the poker in her hand contemplating the dying fire. Like the Greek general, she mourned for the laurels that *might have been* her own, and the good fortune of rivals kept her awake. She was thinking of Mrs. Hammerhard and Mrs. Hackwell, and how their husbands—both—had made love to her, and then run off and married them. And they had two babies each now—her two victorious rivals were happy mothers—whilst poor Lavinia was not even a wife! And that thought kept her awake.

Miss Lavinia was sadly looking on the receding past, though her gaze was fixed upon the darkening grate, full of ashes. Was she drawing mental comparisons between that grate and her own virginal bosom?

¿Quién sabe? But true it is that she suddenly gave the fire a tremendous thrust with the poker, exclaiming, "Villain!" A few bright

[6]Miltiades (570?-489 B.C.), general of the Athenians, defeated the Persians at Marathon (490 B.C.) and ended King Darius' Greek ambitions. Thucydides, an Athenian historian, tells of Miltiades' exploits in his history of the Peloponnesian War. Husbandless and childless, Lavinia Sprig here views the two babies had by other women as the war "trophies" denied to her as a result of Hackwell's fecklessness.

[7]Themistocles (c. 528 B.C.-462 B.C) Athenian statesman and general, responsible for the victory against the Persians at Bay of Sálámis (480 B.C.), a great victory for the Greeks. Ten years earlier, after Marathon, Themistocles could only have envied Miltiades' victory, yet it was he who nevertheless recognized the need for the creation of an Athenian sea power. Thanks to his foresight, when the Persian king Xerxes attacked in 480, Athens was ready.

sparks flew up from the expiring embers, and Miss Lavinia commenced a mental soliloquy, partly uttered: "Yes, their babies! They are happy mothers, eh? I wonder if God will punish those two men for their lies and treachery to me? It is all I can do every Sunday to keep from screaming out from my pew to Hammerhard in his pulpit, 'You liar! you liar!' It would do me good if I did. And if I were to go to Hackwell's church, I don't think I could be able to contain myself, for he was the greater scoundrel of the two. Hammerhard proposed to me, and went off and married Lizzie Dix, but I wasn't positively engaged to him. But Hackwell was solemnly pledged to me—the scoundrel, preaching scoundrel!" Here Miss Lavinia gave a hard blow to the grate, muttering, "How very wrong girls are in permitting any liberties to men to whom they are engaged! How foolish! how silly! Who can tell what miserable liars they may not turn out to be? For I believe that men would rather lie to a woman than speak the truth. Who would not have trusted those two men? They are trusted now. My own sister believes all Hackwell says even now, and doesn't believe that he engaged himself to me. Oh, the rascals, the hypocrites, preaching morality every Sunday! Faugh! what nasty beasts men are!" And here Miss Lavinia, as if the word *men* filled her mouth with some of the ashes in the grate, spat in disgust, and poked the fire vigorously in continued thrusts.

"What is the matter, Aunt Lavvy? Are you sick?" asked Ruth, who, standing unperceived by Lavvy, had been a silent spectator of that lady's last performance with the poker.

Lavinia started, and dropped the poker, which rolled down from the grate to her feet with a loud noise and clatter.

"No. I was thinking, that's all. But what makes you sit up so late? I thought you were in bed."

"So I was, but I couldn't sleep. I went to your room, for I wanted to ask you something, and, not finding you there, I came down to look for you in your favorite place: watching the fire, with the poker in your hand. I remember you told me this afternoon that I was angry with you, and I thought you would tell me the reason now."

"Oh, that is of no consequence. I only thought you were angry because I did not tell you to wear my things to Mrs. Hammerhard's christening. But you may. I am not going, and you can have them. I was thinking of something else when you said that if I went you couldn't go, because you needed some of my evening things. You can have what you like that I own—which is little enough."

"It is more than I have, and I thank you, aunt. I only want your lace collar and sleeves, and your fan and pearl set. It is too bad that I don't own one bit of jewelry in the world but my cameo, which I wear every day of my life. I think mother is entirely too stingy, and I mean to tell papa that I ought to have a few things which girls must have. To think that I am twenty years old (and the daughter of a gentleman), and never in my life had one silk dress besides my black silk! And those two papa bought for me, and mamma scolded when he did it. She never would buy me a bit of jewelry. I always look like the Old Nick[8] himself, and I feel mortified and disgusted with life. I know I shall look as if just out of Noah's ark, with my old grenadine (I've been fixing it up), by the side of Julia Dix, who always dresses elegantly."

"Yes, those Dix girls always gave all their souls to their ribbons."

"That may be so, but I know that out of eight sisters seven are married, and Julia is engaged to a New York banker. Lizzie Hammerhard and Mary Hackwell are the only two of all the eight sisters who did not marry rich men. They married for *love*," added Ruth, maliciously. Lavinia arose hastily. But Ruth continued, saying, "Even old Lucretia Cackle looks better dressed than Mattie and I. And Emma Hackwell, who certainly is poorer than we are, she, too, is a great deal better dressed, and they look at our shabby clothes and sneer. But I always say to everybody that if mamma wasn't so economical we wouldn't be so shabby, and all know it is so."

"But you ought not to tell it."

"But I shall, and I'll speak to papa, too, the very first chance I get. Now I'll go to sleep. Thank you for lending me your things. I hope I may some day return the kindness, though there exists at present but a poor prospect, for who on earth is to marry such a shabby-looking girl as me? I don't think even any of the Cackle boys would think of proposing to me." So saying, Ruth ran upstairs and got into her bed again. After she was cozily wrapped in the bed covers, close to Mattie, she heard her Aunt Lavvy come slowly upstairs and go to her room. "Poor Lavvy!" said Ruth, laughing. "I wonder which of the two divines she likes best?"

"Old Hacky, of course. I can see that plain enough," said Mattie without opening her eyes.

"What! Are you awake, too?"

"You awoke me with your racket downstairs, and I think you awoke mamma and papa, too, for I heard them go into Julian's room."

"I made no racket. It was Aunt Lavvy apostrophizing her faithless parsons with the poker in her hand, hammering the grate for Hammerhard, and hacking it for Hackwell."

[8]"Old Nick" refers here to the devil.

"Bah! that isn't original. That is one of Julian's puns," said Mattie, hugging her sister.

Slowly Lavinia hung a nightgown on the two peaks which formed her shoulders and got into bed. But not to sleep. Those babies—those "trophies of Miltiades"—kept her awake. Her nose was red with crying, and her eyelids were heavy, but not sleepy.

"Do you hear Aunt Lavvy's sighs?" asked Ruth, in a whisper, and both sisters laughed.

"Poor aunty! it is too bad of those parsons to have fooled her so cruelly," said Mattie. "I don't like them for it, particularly that smooth, conceited, deceitful Hackwell. I don't see why mamma likes him. He is handsome, but what is that to mamma? She don't care for his looks."

"Of course she don't, or she thinks she don't. But looks are *a heap*, Mat, and no mistake, and that is why I think it is so mean in mamma to dress us so shabbily, and I was telling aunt I will speak to papa about it. And so you ought, for he loves you the best."

"No, he don't. Julian is his favorite."

"He loves us all well enough to feel ashamed of seeing us dress in old rags," said Ruth.

After which aphorism both sisters fell asleep, just as Lola crawled out of the servants' room in search of less foul air, and to avoid the snoring duo, which almost set her crazy, and went to lie at Mrs. Norval's door, with Jack's sympathy for consolation and his woolly body to keep her warm.

CHAPTER IX

Potations, Plotting and Propriety

Some months had elapsed since Dr. Norval's return from California. It was now Christmas night, and the reverend gentlemen—Hackwell and Hammerhard—having preached two long sermons each, now wanted a good dinner. Married to sisters, and being in many ways congenial, the two divines were very intimate, and passed almost every evening together. Particularly after a hard day's preaching, they were sure to meet in Mr. Hackwell's sanctum to criticize their own oratory, and if anyone could have heard the peals of laughter that issued through the keyhole of the sanctum, he would have guessed that their mutual criticisms were not severe. Whilst thus engaged, their two wives sat in the parlor, and compared their husband's flocks, also for relaxation.

This evening, after a very jolly dinner at Mr. Hackwell's, the two sisters, as usual, sat in the parlor to discuss the absorbing topic of the village—the sudden prosperity of the Norval family—and their husbands retired, as usual also, "to have a quiet smoke."

"All the Norvals wore new dresses to church, new cloaks, new furs, and new bonnets, again. There seems to be no end to their money," said Mrs. Hammerhard.

"Mrs. Cackle told me that Mrs. Norval said that the doctor is going to buy an open carriage to ride next summer, and keep the closed one only for winter. Isn't that grand?" observed Mrs. Hackwell. "I invited Mrs. Cackle for this evening."

"I wonder how much the doctor brought from California. Do the Cackles have any idea?"

"Mrs. Cackle thinks that those boxes which the doctor took back to New York so soon after he came were full of gold quartz, and that he got gold out of the quartz," said Mrs. Hackwell.

"Nonsense! that is one of Mrs. Cackle's wonderful stories."

Thus went on the two sisters, and thus was going on the whole village, wondering how much gold the doctor brought. And Mrs. Cackle was invited to tea by all the principal ladies of the village, because Mrs. Cackle was next-door neighbor to Mrs. Norval and was her *friend*, besides being a very observant and communicative lady.

"Here we are," observed the Rev. Hackwell, closing the door and locking it. Mr. Hammerhard knew that they were there, and *what for*, too. He knew it by experience. Without further preliminaries, his reverence Hackwell went to a closet (which he always kept locked), and, unlocking it, took out of it a gallon demijohn, a deep tray holding two tumblers, two spoons, two lemons, a sugar bowl, and a china mug which could hold about three pints. Then he took out a brass kettle, and, filling it with water, put it on the fire.

The sympathetic little kettle soon began singing the tune he knew the two divines wished to hear. Mr. Hackwell cut a few pieces of lemon peel, and, measuring his whisky (for whisky it was that his reverence kept in the hidden demijohn), put the required sugar and liquor and lemon peel in the tumblers and poured the hot water in, taking care to put in the spoons, that the hot water might not break the glasses. Whilst the Rev. Hackwell brewed the punch, the Rev. Hammerhard filled the pipes. Now, punch and pipes being ready, their reverences sank into their easy chairs to enjoy them, with their feet upon the high fender.

After some moments of silence, in which only by winks and nods they signified how very nice the punch was, Mr. Hammerhard opened the conversation.

"I have often thought I would ask you a question, but always put it off."

"Out with it! What is it?" said Hackwell.

"Well, I have wanted to ask you how it was that when you gave up practice for preaching—"

"Very good," interrupted Mr. Hackwell, taking a good, long sip at his tumbler. "I see that you have not preached away all your brains. Go on. Practice for preaching, you said."

"Yes. When you gave up hard practice for easy preaching, why didn't you become a Methodist or an Episcopalian—anything more human than a blue Presbyterian?"

Mr. Hackwell laughed, and answered, "Don't you remember that when we were in college the boys used to call me Johnny '*whole-hog*'?"

"Yes, I remember that."

"Well, it was on account of a tendency of mine, which has not left me, never to do anything by halves, but to go the whole length in anything I undertake. If I had left the practice of law to become an Episcopalian preacher, I would not have stopped there—I would have ended by being a Catholic priest. Then I could not have married. And imagine what a loss that would have been to the ladies! Think of that!"

"I think the ladies would have been the gainers thereby," said Hammerhard with a knowing wink. "I think you would have made a lovely father-confessor." At which witticism both divines laughed heartily.

"Moreover," continued Hackwell, when their laugh subsided, "as I intended to settle in New England, I knew there was no risk of my going too far as a Presbyterian. One can't be too blue in these regions, you know."

"That is a fact. But, *apropos* of the ladies, I say, Hack, didn't we miss it in jilting poor, susceptible Lavvy? The Norvals now are certainly rich, and to be in the family would not be a bad thing for a poor preacher."

"I have often thought of that myself, particularly since the new carriage and horses arrived. But now it is too late to enter by the side-door—Miss Lavvy—or the front ones—the Misses Norval—since we are married. We must manage to enter by some crack. What a pity that neither of us can be father-confessor to Mrs. Norval!"

"You can be as bad as—I mean as good—as if you were her confessor. Being *her pastor*, you can be her spiritual adviser."

"I wish I could, Ham, but she doesn't want any advice. She isn't that sort of a female."

"I tell you, Hack, you are mistaken. She does want a friend and a confidant. And, as she thinks you are next to perfection, I say, old boy, there is your chance—jump at it."

"What do you mean? Speak plain."

"I mean that from the hints she has thrown out in my presence (and no doubt she has given many more to *you*) about the Mexican child, and how she ought to be educated, and all that sort of thing, it is quite clear that there is a contest going on between the madam and the doctor about the child and about money matters. And if her mind is perplexed, she is no woman if she isn't longing for '*moral support*' and all that sort of thing, which *you* can give her."

Mr. Hackwell blushed. Mrs. Norval had said a good deal to him in the shape of hints and regrets that she had not "spoken frankly to Mr. Hackwell." If Dr. Norval had not taken his gold boxes away so very soon, Mrs. Norval would have asked for Mr. Hackwell's "*moral support*" in extracting a few lumps. Now that couldn't be done, but Mrs. Norval felt confident that if Mr. Hackwell was practicing law, she then could have managed to put Lola's money in his hands. She had *hinted* that much, only she did not say that the money was Lola's: oh, no; she wanted people to think it was theirs.

Mr. Hackwell blushed, as I said, because, on hearing Mrs. Norval's hints, the very thoughts expressed by Hammerhard had also crossed and recrossed his active brain. Hammerhard continued, "You see, you being her *pastor*, there will be no impropriety in offering advice, and you can suggest, mildly, that, having been a lawyer, you understand money transactions, etc."

Mr. Hackwell studied for awhile, then exclaimed, tapping his forehead with his pipe stem, "I have it!"

But just at this moment Mrs. Hackwell tapped at the door too, saying that all the Cackles were in the parlor, having come to pay their respects to their dear pastor Mr. Hackwell, and thank and congratulate him for his edifying sermons of that day.

The reverend gentlemen, with exclamations not at all edifying, washed their mouths to banish all odor of whisky, and went into the parlor where about a dozen Cackles awaited them.

CHAPTER X

How a Virtuous Matron Was Kept Awake

Mrs. Cackle certainly brought startling news from Mrs. Norval's, whose home she had just left. The Norvals were to have not only another carriage, another pair of horses, another man-servant, but *another house*. The doctor was going to buy Esquire Nugent's house, with its splendid gardens and greenhouses, where grapes were raised in profusion.

The company was speechless with astonishment. Mr. Hammerhard was the first to break the silence by saying to Mrs. Cackle, "But, with all your sagacity to find out things which no one else can find out, you haven't got hold of the source or the amount of their gold."

"That is not so easily ascertained, as neither Lavvy nor the girls seem to know anything about it, and Mrs. Norval evidently don't want to speak a word on that point. But with all that, one thing we can guess easy enough."

"And what is that?" several voices asked.

"That the little black child is in some way connected with the money. My son Beau, who is certainly very smart at guessing, thinks that the child's mother must have been some Indian woman who told the doctor where he could find rich gold diggings, and that the doctor, out of gratitude—for he has such funny notions—wants to educate the child and bring her up like a white girl."

"The doctor is a truthful man, and he says that the child has neither African nor Indian blood in her veins," observed Mr. Hackwell.

"If she had, Mrs. Norval would not take the girl in her carriage. Mrs. N. ain't that sort of person," said old Mr. Cackle.

"Mrs. Norval is a great abolitionist, and doesn't mind negroes. Besides, doesn't Lavvy take her poodle too?" Mrs. Hammerhard remarked.

"Mrs. Norval is a good abolitionist in talk," replied Miss Lucretia Cackle with a sneer, "but she ain't so in practice. Polly, the cook, told our cook that the night the doctor arrived with Lola, Mrs. Norval insisted that the child should sleep with Hannah, or with the cook, but as she, the cook, despises niggers, she plainly told Mrs. Norval that she 'wouldn't have sich a catteypillar' in her bed. And as Hannah wouldn't have the black thing neither, Lola had to sleep on the floor in the hall. But when the doctor found it out next morning, he 'kicked up such a rumpus' and carried on so that Mrs. Norval was afraid he would 'bust a blood vessel'. And when he was very angry, he told Mrs. Norval that if she didn't treat Lola just the same as her own daughters, he would take her and the gold to New York and put her under the care of Mr. William Sinclair, the banker, and Mrs. Norval should not have half an ounce of gold. Then a room was fixed up for Lola by Mrs. Norval herself."

The party at Mr. Hackwell's were not the only *friends* busily engaged in guessing the origin, amount, and present destination of Dr. Norval's gold. All the village was similarly occupied. If the boxes had not been so heavy and so large, the guessers could have approached nearer the truth. But how could well-balanced Yankee minds ever lose their poise to the degree of imagining such fairy-tale balderdash as that enormous amount of gold? The truth of the thing was what baffled their wise calculations, for certain minds are impervious to certain truths.

The fact of Mrs. Norval tolerating Lola in her carriage, at her table, in her parlor, was also very astonishing. They all knew that "Mrs. Norval had never been known to give a poor nigger a penny," and plenty of the poor wretches had been about the village, trying to raise subscriptions to buy the freedom of their children or their parents. The doctor was the one to give to the poor darkies; he always gave more than any other, though he never would put his name down, because, he said, he was "a good-for-nothing Democrat."

Whilst the village was guessing, the doctor invested all the money well. The rough pebbles had been sent to Europe to be made into jewelry and had been pronounced first-class gems.

After a while the sets ordered came. The remaining stones not used came already cut for setting. The doctor remembered that Lola's mother had told him to take half of the stones, if he wished, so he thought he could conscientiously take a few of the smallest and have some pins and earrings made for his girls. He would also have a handsome breastpin and earrings for his wife, though he knew she would not wear diamonds.

Ruth's set was made of emeralds and diamonds, Mattie's of opals and diamonds, and that of Mrs. Norval of diamonds alone.

None of the ladies at Dr. Norval's slept the night the jewelry arrived. Ruth and Mattie kept awake with pleasure, Mrs. Norval with rage, and Lavinia with mortification. Poor Lavvy's eyes and nose were red next morning and the doctor felt sorry to have forgotten his sister-in-law. In a few days, however, Lavvy's birthday came and then she received a beautiful topaz set and a lovely diamond ring. When the doctor had thus, as he believed, propitiated all the ladies, he bought a coral pin and earrings for Lola, and thought they ought to be satisfied. But Mrs. Norval, as usual, thought differently. That night, when they retired to their bedroom, after she had read the Bible a long, long time, so that the doctor had nearly gone to sleep, she said, tying her nightcap, "And are these the things which you brought to us all that came out of your magnificent diamonds, and emeralds, and opals, and rubies?"

"Bless you, no! They are made out of the smallest stones, and the diamonds in those of the girls are the cuttings of the larger diamonds in Lola's sets," answered the doctor ingenuously.

Mrs. Norval felt as if she would smother or choke with rage. Her husband continued: "If it wasn't for the risk, I would bring up for you all to see, the beautiful sets made for Lola. Certainly, those French people do make splendid jewelry! There are six full sets of different stones: all have diamonds, and all are very handsome. There are several pins and crosses and aigrettes,[9] besides the full sets—enough to turn half a dozen women crazy."

"Describe the sets," said Mrs. Norval.

"Well, as to that, I don't know that I am equal to it," said the doctor, lying on his back. "Let me see: one is all diamonds, worth two-hundred thousand dollars" (Mrs. Norval held her breath and closed her lips tightly); "then there is one of emeralds and diamonds, which, I believe, is worth eighty-thousand dollars; then one of pearls and diamonds, also worth eighty-thousand dollars, or perhaps more—I don't exactly remember; then one of opals and diamonds, worth forty-thousand dollars; then one of rubies and diamonds, worth twenty-thousand dollars. But the prettiest of all, to my thinking, is one of all those stones and pearls mixed. The breastpin is like a bouquet, and the necklace and ornament for the head and bracelets are like wreaths of flowers all sprinkled with diamond dewdrops: it is the prettiest thing in jewelry I ever saw! I am glad I took those stones to that house in New York, for they have acted very honorably with me. If they had not suggested to

[9]jewelry with the figure of an egret, fashionable at the time.

me the idea of exchanging some of the cut stones for pearls, I would never have thought of it. But they did, and they have made jewelry for the little girl handsome enough for a duchess. The value of the jewelry—all of it—is over half a million. Isn't the little thing rich? Sinclair tells me that in three years he will double her money."

"Where is all that jewelry?" asked Mrs. N.

"It is all locked up in an iron safe," the doctor answered, turning over to sleep.

Mrs. N. could not do that. She did not want the jewelry for herself, and she could not exactly approve of her daughters wearing such expensive things. But it made her heart ache to think that the black child would have these things. The doctor might speak about the child getting lighter by-and-by: she did not believe that. And would that little nigger be so rich, and her girls so poor? Their new carriages and splendid horses and handsome house, after all, did not make Mrs. N. happy.

Mrs. Norval could not sleep, thinking of Lola's magnificent jewelry. She was "too shocked to sleep."

CHAPTER XI

Mrs. Norval Did Not Enjoy Her Buckwheat Cakes, and Julian Wouldn't Write Any More Poetry

The Norval family had floated on a delightful stream of prosperity for nearly three years when the eventful 1861[10] dawned upon the land in all its gloom of political clouds.

Few men as yet believed that there would be a war, and one of these few was Dr. Norval.

"Sinclair writes me he is going to send his wife and daughter to Europe for a year or so, until things get clearer in this country," said the doctor one morning at the breakfast table. "Don't you think this is a good opportunity for the girls to go, too? Mrs. Sinclair says she will be very glad to take charge of them, if *you* don't go."

"*I*!" exclaimed Mrs. Norval, letting her buckwheat cakes drop from the fork.

Mattie made a rush at her father and kissed him fervently, saying, between her kisses, "You are the darlingest old papa anybody ever had! You are, you are!"

"Sit still, Mattie. What a rough, unladylike girl you are!" said Mrs. Norval sternly. "I am very much obliged to Mrs. Sinclair, but I have no wish to send my girls to foreign countries when we have a better one of our own—a *great deal* better one."

"Oh, mamma!" ejaculated the apathetic Ruth with a flush on her usually calm face, "it ain't possible you'll let us lose such a splendid chance to go to Europe?"

"Doctor, I am very sorry you mentioned this thing here. Why didn't you tell it to me alone? Now I shall have no peace, I know."

[10]The text here, in making reference to the year 1861, when the U.S. Civil War began, notes that three years have elapsed since Lola came to the Norval household.

"I didn't tell it to you alone because I knew you would be horrified at the idea of it. So I thought I would let the girls know that they can go if they wish, and you can settle the matter among yourselves," said the doctor, rising and taking his newspaper to peruse it by the fire.

"Oh, what a man! what a man! He makes it his study to do, and say, and suggest always what *he knows* will make me wretched."

"Bah!" said Mattie. "Everybody knows that papa is the best husband and the best father in these United States."

"Hold your tongue, miss! You are intolerably saucy, and your father encourages you."

Ruth gave Mattie a very expressive look, which Mattie evidently understood. Ruth was a diplomat by instinct. She liked to *manage* her mother because she was *the power* of the family. Besides, she had made up her mind to have a trip to Europe. Not that she cared to see Europe for its historical or classic associations or treasures of art: she wanted to go to Europe because in her two trips to New York she had discovered that it was genteel to talk of having been to Europe, and that you were not considered "tip-top" exactly until you spoke of Paris and the Coliseum, and going up the Thames and down the Rhine, and up and down the Danube, and being presented to crowned heads.

Nothing more was said then, but as she got into bed, Ruth told Mattie that night, "Consider yourself bowing to Queen Victoria," and then turned over to sleep.

Lola was decidedly too black and too young for Julian Norval to take a fancy to her, whilst she, the poor, lonely little soul, idolized Julian, and in her heart she couldn't compare the handsome boy to anything but an archangel.

Lola's black skin and youth were not the principal reasons of Julian's indifference. The principal reason was Emma Hackwell, the Rev. Hackwell's sister, a young lady of five-and-twenty who had lately come to make her home with her brother. With this young lady—she being five years older than himself—of course, Julian fell desperately in love. He would have run away with Emma and married her the first week of their acquaintance if that young lady had felt inclined to marry a boy seventeen years old—very handsome, it is true, but whose impetuosity was to Emma alarming, being to her way of thinking unnatural in a good New Englander, and not to be trusted by a sensible Yankee girl. She would not even engage herself to him; not until he was twenty-one years old, when he would be better able to know his own mind. Julian wrote wild love ditties and desperate Byronic sonnets, and for two sessions and one vacation, he threatened to kill himself. But on the second vacation—Julian being near twenty—his ardor began to calm down somewhat. Emma was too calculating and matter-of-fact to keep his poetical glow alive. He began to foresee the day when he would write to her altogether in prose, and, maybe, begin his letters with "Dear Friend," or "Dear Miss Hackwell," and not have to sign himself, "Your ever-loving Julian."

But in proportion, as Julian's love began to diminish, Emma's began to increase, or rather to become alarmed at his coldness. She wrote to him asking what was the cause of that change. He denied his having changed, *only* he was very busy with his studies, as he would graduate that spring. Moreover, he said, people spoke about the probability of a war, and as, if there was to be a war, he would be a soldier, he thought it was well that they were not engaged, though, "of course, he felt for her as he always would, etc., etc., etc."

Emma was frightened. She consulted her brother. He asked her to show him Julian's letter. After reading it he threw it on Emma's lap, saying, with ill-suppressed anger, "Serves you right! I told you to make sure of the boy in some way. But no, you must go and, like a fool, let him off. He is not engaged, and he'll go off and take a fancy to someone else. You'll never have such another chance, I can tell you." And his reverence walked off in great indignation.

Poor Emma! It was bad enough to be forgotten by her lover, without being scolded for it. But, though Mr. Hackwell scolded, he did not lose hope. Indeed he was not the man to let such a brilliant match for his sister slip without clutching at it with eager fingers. What would be the use of his great favor with the stately matron Mrs. Norval, who now always consulted Mr. Hackwell in every important occurrence in her family wherein she wished for anyone's advice? Thus they had many *tête-à-têtes*, which Mr. Hackwell meant to turn to account.

Just about the time when Emma received Julian's letter, the question of the proposed trip of Ruthie and Mattie to Europe came up.

Nothing could have suited Mr. Hackwell's plans better. He advocated it, and, a few days later, Mrs. Norval gave her consent.

"The girls will be out of the way," said Mr. Hackwell to himself as he walked home from Mrs. Norval's. "And that is something. I wish Emma had not been so stupid! As if a boy is to love a red-headed, uninteresting woman after he gets to be a man! Absurd! Of course he'll bolt. But the girls will be off in two weeks, and then we'll see what can be done to mend Emma's affair."

Ruth felt no more now the pangs of other days, when she had lain awake at night thinking how she could fix up her old dresses to make them look like new, when she used to go to church to watch with enraptured gaze the lovely bonnets of Julia Dix, while Mr. Hammerhard delivered his demolishing sermons. *Now* the Misses Norval—and even poor Lavvy—had been for three years the leaders of fashion.

In their handsome carriage, dressed in costly silks, the Misses Norval drove around to all their friends' houses to bid them good-by. In old times Ruth and Mattie used to walk all over the village almost daily in the summer, and in the winter would walk to a hill two miles off to slide downhill on sledges with the Cackle boys and girls, and they did not mind the violence of that exercise. Now they seldom walked. Since their new elegance, Ruth had found out that the reason why Spanish ladies have small feet and delicate ankles is because they walk so very little. Ruth's foot was large, and her ankle solid, with well-developed sinews, like Mrs. Norval's. Still, she hoped at least to make her feet softer, less rebellious to going into small shoes.

On the morrow the Misses Norval would make their farewell appearance in church, and the day after would start for New York.

CHAPTER XII

Something about the Sprig Pedigree

Before seeing the elegant Misses Norval off to be presented to the crowned heads, we must give some attention to a member of Mrs. Norval's family who is of great importance in these pages, although he has been mentioned only casually. I mean no other than Mr. Isaac Sprig, Mrs. Norval's youngest brother.

This gentleman wrote to his sister that he, though entirely blameless, had got into "the most sticky scrape that ever a fellow could trip up into," and that unless Dr. Norval went to pull him out of that hole, he—Isaac—did not see a way to crawl out of it.

Mrs. Norval was very indignant with Isaac. But when she came to that part of his doleful letter in which he said that he and Julius Caesar Cackle were in the same scrape, but that as Cackle had two brothers just elected to Congress, he had only changed places, and from the Treasury Department had been merely transferred to the Post-Office Department, whilst he—Isaac—was turned out of office, the heart of Mrs. Norval swelled, and throbbed, and ached. Her indignation against Isaac was lost in the greater one she felt against the government of the United States of America.

Oh! the idea that a Cackle should be transferred from one department to another, whilst a Sprig—her brother—was turned out! And who were those Cackles? And how came they to have more influence than Isaac? This very Julius Caesar Cackle got his clerkship through Dr. Norval's influence, and the doctor even lent him money to pay his expenses to Washington, after getting him the place. And as for these two brothers—Mirabeau and Cicero Cackle—who were now just elected members of Congress, why were they so? Because Dr. Norval had lent them the necessary money. If it had not been for the doctor, instead of giving themselves airs at Washington, they would now be at home, plowing, or minding their cattle in the barn, instead of representing their constituents at the capital. All this was too much for a rich woman to bear. She would send her husband to demand that her brother be reinstated, and that without any assistance from the ungrateful Cackles, those Cackles who might be M.C.s,[11] but were nevertheless *Cackles*.

Isaac, it is true, was a scapegrace, not at all a sober-minded, economical, thrifty, New Englander. He was free with his money, he liked foreigners, and had a most lamentable penchant for gallantry. Mrs. Norval thought of all this, and yet she—the paragon of all matrons—preferred this black sheep Isaac to all her family, excepting her children.

I heard a crusty bachelor once say that women of a severe cast of mind were sure to have folds and creases in the heart, where preferences for scamps were always certain to hide themselves. This theory perhaps accounts for Mrs. Norval's preference for Isaac—this Isaac, who had done nothing but shock her feelings and her rigorous sense of propriety. Isaac would prefer Havana cigars to a pipe or a chaw of tobacco, and those miserable sour wines to a good drink of whisky, old Mr. Sprig said. And the information only increased Mrs. Norval's fear that Isaac would come to no good end. Lately, too, Mrs. Norval had learned that Isaac went often to the theatre, and also to hear the singing of the Catholic Church, all of which was the same thing to the strict New England matron, and in her heart she blamed her husband. Yes, Dr. Norval had either developed or created those tastes in Isaac for every abomination which the well-regulated mind of a New Englander repudiates. The doctor had taught him to drink Rhine wine once when they were looking for mineral specimens in the mountains of New Hampshire. The doctor had taught him to smoke cigars. The doctor had taken him to the opera, and to the Catholic Church.

On hearing of this last performance, old Mr. Sprig had said to the doctor, "Though we owe everything to you, sir, still, I hope you will not be offended if I say that my old woman says she's very uneasy in her mind about our Isaac going to places of sin. And though we owe everything to you, sir—"

"Goodness, father! You repeat that every time you see James. What is it, after all, you owe him, that you should be so humbly grateful to him?" interrupted Mrs. Norval, provoked with her simple-hearted father.

"Nothing, my dear, of course," said the doctor.

[11]M.C., abbreviation for "member of Congress."

But a glance at Mrs. Norval's history previous to her appearance in these truthful pages will show that old Mr. Sprig was about right.

Old Mr. Abraham Sprig lived on a small farm with his family, which consisted of two girls and two boys. Jemima and Lavinia were the girls, Abraham and Isaac the boys. They lived very happily. They raised poultry and vegetables, which the boys took to market in Boston every Saturday morning. The old lady and Jemima put up pickles, and made butter and apple-sauce; all of which articles, being of good quality, commanded high prices in the Boston market. The Sprigs had lived in this Yankee Arcadia for many years, and Jemima had attained her twentieth year, when one morning—a Saturday morning—as she was counting the eggs to send to market, a young man, dressed as a college boy, stood by the henhouse door, and, without previous salutation to announce his arrival, said to her, "Will you have the kindness to tell me if I may walk through this field over to Mrs. Norval's house?"

So astonished was Jemima to see that handsome young gentleman standing there with hat in hand, speaking to her in a soft, gentlemanly sort of deep-toned voice, that she let three eggs drop—all of which got broken—and on that account she was not able to send twelve dozen, but only eleven, to market, which caused her great chagrin and disappointment.

But though Jemima colored up with vexation, still, she told the young man quite politely he could walk across the field if he wished.

"The buggy I was coming in got broken, and that was the only conveyance I could get at the station. I have had to walk four miles, and I'll have to walk two more if I don't cut across those fields," said the young man apologetically. "I am anxious to get there because they telegraphed to me that my uncle is very ill. Do you know how he is? Mr. Norval, I mean: he being your neighbor, you might know how he is," said the young man timidly.

"It is all up with him," said hopeful Isaac, snapping his fingers.

"Hush, Isaac!" said Jemima to her brother. Then to the young man: "I have not heard this morning how Mr. Norval is, but last night he was very low, sir, I am very sorry to say. My mother and father are now with Mr. Norval, and if I can be of any service to you, I hope you will not hesitate to command me."

"Thank you, thank you very much," said the young man, hurrying off.

The dying man had barely time to bid his beloved nephew adieu, when, giving him his blessing, he closed his eyes forever.

This uncle had been young James Norval's guardian and his only near relative. James felt his loss most keenly, for he had been very tenderly attached to him, and for a time he seemed inconsolable. But young Norval was a college boy, at the susceptible age of nineteen, so the warm sympathy of fine-looking Jemima Sprig gradually consoled the affectionate heart of the orphan boy, who wanted nothing better than to be consoled; for his cheerful, healthy mind instinctively rejected sadness.

From gratitude nothing was easier than to glide into love, on a quiet farm, with a fine girl constantly showing him all sorts of attentions, and his young heart longing to love someone. So the ardent college boy fell head over heels in love with Jemima, and would not return to college until he had declared his love. Jemima saw what was coming, and she took care to give him a chance.

One day Jemima said she was going to gather apples for the cider-press, and young Norval, of course, most naturally went to offer his assistance. They had a basket almost full of apples, when the college boy fell on his knees by the basket and told his love. Just at that time the boys, Abraham and Isaac, came into the orchard with the cows. The two lovers pretended to have upset the basket and to be very busy collecting the scattered apples.

But the nineteen-year-old lover was not to be balked in this manner, and he had to return to college next day.

CHAPTER XIII

What Mr. Isaac Sprig Found at the "Dead-Letter Office"

That night whilst Jemima was paring apples to make her celebrated applesauce (which brought such a good price in the Boston market), the doctor—that is, young Norval—proposed and was accepted. He did not fall on his knees again, because Jemima was so surrounded with apple peelings that there was no place near her where her lover could have rested his knees.

The match was a very brilliant one for Jemima Sprig. The marriage took place as soon as young Norval received his diploma. The young husband took upon himself the duty of ameliorating the fortunes of all his new family. Old Mr. Sprig had many more acres and more cattle added to his farm, and his son Abe plenty of hands to help him with the farming. Lavinia went to live with her sister, and attended school, being then only eight years of age. Isaac was two years younger than Lavinia, but very soon he also was sent to school, and when he was old enough to learn *a "trade,"* as he disliked New England, he was sent to New York to study law: that he didn't like, either. He was placed as a clerk in the banking house of Sinclair & Co., but there he had a difficulty with another clerk and became dissatisfied. Then Dr. Norval got for him an appointment in the Treasury Department in Washington, where he remained until the occurrence which Isaac called an "awful scrape," and which has led me to say so much of the Sprig family.

Isaac's penchant for gallantry was the cause now, as it often had been before, of his being in trouble. Isaac had the audacity to admire a lady of the demimonde whom a distinguished member of Congress also admired. One night when he, the Hon. Le Grand Gunn, was visiting the fair Lucinda, Isaac and his friend Julius Caesar Cackle, who were boarders of the house, went into the parlor and made themselves at home. To make matters more aggravating to the Hon. M. C., Isaac absorbed the attention, smiles, and sweet glances of the charming Lucinda until the infuriated Gunn rushed out of the house in a rage. Lucinda laughed aloud while the Hon. was yet within hearing, whereupon that gentleman, forgetful of his distinguished public position, came back to ask, in a very insulting manner, if Sprig had laughed at him. Sprig colored with anger, but said he had not, whereupon Mr. Gunn, shaking his finger at him, said, "You had better not."

"I did not laugh, but you are certainly laughable," said Isaac, "and I think you will make me laugh if you don't go soon."

The Hon. ordered Sprig out of the house, and Sprig told him to go himself. And from words they came to blows, and had a most ignominious fistfight in the presence of the quadroon belle.

Sprig came out victorious. Cackle had to go for a hack to convey Mr. Le Grand Gunn to his lodgings, as the Hon. gentleman was not able to walk because he could not see out of his swollen eyes. His bloody nose, lacerated to a large size, gave Lucinda great desire to laugh, but that inclination this time she held in check until the distinguished politician was well out of hearing.

The Hon. Gunn, of course, swore vengeance on the audacious clerk, and as soon as the state of his swollen visage permitted, he went to a friend of his who had great influence with the cabinet just formed, to request that the two clerks should be dismissed.

"What have they done? I know those two young men, and I think them efficient and well-deserving," said the influential friend.

"Well-deserving of h—!" roared Mr. Gunn. "This is what they have done—at least one did, whilst the other laughed and never came to my rescue," said the Hon., showing his friend a black eye, which he still kept bandaged under pretext of neuralgia in the left side of his face.

The influential gentleman laughed, but promised that the clerks should be dismissed forthwith.

"You needn't say anything about my black eye. They are both Breckinridge Democrats;[12] that is enough, I should think," said Mr. Gunn.

"Plenty," replied his friend, making a memorandum of the case.

That afternoon Sprig and Cackle received their dismissals.

[12]Breckinridge Democrats were southern Democrats who, instead of backing the Illinois candidate, Senator Stephen Douglas, for the presidency in 1860, nominated their own man, Kentuckian John C. Breckinridge, president James Buchanan's vice-president. The Hon. Le Grand Gunn maneuvers to exact vengeance on Sprig and Cackle and brings up the fact that both were "Breckinridge Democrats" to justify their dismissal from their posts.

Dr. Norval found great difficulty in having his brother-in-law reinstated. In fact, it could not be done. Sprig was a Democrat, and so was the doctor. All that the doctor succeeded in doing was to get Isaac a place in the Post-Office Department. Six months earlier, the doctor could have obtained anything in Washington; six months later, he could have obtained nothing. Now, however, the public opinion was in that transition state when no one could truly say to which side it would incline—like the waters of the sea just before the tide changes, said to be stationary for a moment, to flow soon in the opposite direction. The American people had been educated to believe that every man had a right to his opinion, and, at the breaking out of the rebellion, individuals were courteously asked their sentiments. Even officers of the army were consulted before giving them orders which might conflict with their sentiments; should these be in favor of the South, they were asked if they objected to do so and so. An officer of the army got a letter from one of General Scott's staff officers in which this passage occurs: "The general would like you to take command of ——, but he wishes first to ascertain your sentiments. If you are for the South, let me know it frankly. But I sincerely hope you are not, as the general thinks highly of you, and believes you are in every respect fitted to take the position of," etc.

Politicians, therefore, were out of humor with each other, but, as yet, they had not begun to teach the masses intolerance. As for persecution, it was a thing of abhorrence to the American mind. The political leaders, of course, saw that a change was on the eve of arriving, but *the people* still spoke of liberty in all sincerity. The door was not shut and bolted for Isaac; it was yet left ajar, and he slipped into his clerkship at the post office.

His friend Cackle was already there, and his pleasure at seeing Isaac seemed so genuine that the easy-tempered, forgiving Isaac soon forgot that the Cackles had not offered to help him in his distress.

But Sprig and Cackle had to content themselves with very humble positions compared to those they had occupied before. They were placed in the dead-letter department and the salary wasn't large. But Isaac had plenty of cash. The doctor's purse was at his disposal, and Isaac often dipped his fingers into it.

One morning, as Sprig and Cackle were busy opening "dead letters," Julius said, "Here Isaac, you who have a turn for romance, and a hankering for foreigners and their yarns, you'll like to read this, I know." And, so saying, Cackle threw a roll of paper to him.

Sprig caught the roll of paper as it fell, and, opening it, saw that it was a manuscript written in bold, clear hand, with the following heading:

"Account given by Doña María Teresa Almenara de Medina, on her deathbed, of the matter in which she was captured by the Apache Indians in Sonora, in December, 1846, and then traded off to the Indians of the Colorado River."

Then at the bottom of the last page, it said:

"I certify on honor that the above is a correct, faithful copy, faithfully transcribed from the stenographic original. I wrote as Doña Teresa spoke.

"ADRIAN LEBRUN.
"SAN FRANCISCO, CAL., December, 1857."

Sprig read a page, then said to Cackle, "Where is the envelope of this manuscript? It is very interesting."

"I knew you would think so. I don't know where the envelope is; it was stamped 'dead' and I pitched it off with the others."

"Let us look for it; I want to know to whom it was addressed," said Isaac. And both friends searched for the envelope, but in vain. Isaac was very much disappointed at this, but Cackle consoled him, saying, "What is it to you to whom it is addressed? Take it and read it, if you like."

And as he was told that many clerks took home "dead papers," Isaac did not see any objection to his taking the interesting manuscript.

CHAPTER XIV

The Doctor Was Rewarded for Listening to Mr. Hackwell's Sermon

It was the anniversary of some great day in New England when the Misses Norval were to make their farewell appearance in church before leaving for Europe—some great day in which the Pilgrim fathers had done one of their wonderful deeds. They had either embarked, or landed, or burnt a witch, or whipped a woman at the pillory, on just such a day. The reverend gentlemen of our acquaintance were to hold forth to their respective congregations, who idolized them, and would have mobbed and lynched anyone daring to hint that the two divines solaced themselves with a jug of whisky after those edifying sermons; that it was "John Barleycorn, and not John the Baptist," Mr. Hackwell said he liked to consult after church. They did not know how many puns the witty Hackwell had made on Demi-John[13], and Saint John, and Jolly-John, which last was himself.

The open carriage, with its handsome pair of black horses, stood at the gate, waiting to convey the Misses Norval to church. The doctor and Mrs. Norval would walk. Mrs. Norval did not wish to harass the ladies of the village to the verge of distraction by having her *two* carriages at once at her gate. Unless the weather was too inclement, she always walked to church; in fact, she walked everywhere most of the time, for she knew that many of her neighbors were nearly thrown into convulsions to see her daughters drive out through the village, and Mrs. Norval did not wish to be hated, although she did not particularly desire to be loved either. Her mind loved dignified repose, that was all.

[13]A "Demi-John" is a small barrel used to contain wine or another liquor. Ruiz de Burton here has the scoundrel reverends make ironic post-sermon plays on their being "saints" and "jolly" with their glasses of whiskey and cigars at hand.

At the gate the doctor's family always separated; he and his wife went to Mr. Hackwell's church, whilst the girls went to Mr. Hammerhard's. At first Mrs. Norval had insisted on Lola's going with her, but the child cried so much, or behaved so irreverently at church, that Mrs. Norval with great reluctance permitted her to go with Lavinia and her daughters to the other church. This was better than to allow her to learn anything about popery. Now, however, Lola had been for a year at school in the neighboring town, where she could get a better music-teacher, and also lessons in French and Spanish, but where there was no Catholic church. Of this Mrs. Norval had been very careful. She did not object, however, to her sister and daughters going to a different church from her own—an inconsistency which had made the doctor smile. To him it seemed a laughable freak of his serious, dignified wife, to be so careful about the religion of the child she disliked so intensely, whilst she seemed almost indifferent about that adopted by her own daughters. He was thinking of this whilst helping his daughters into their carriage; and Mrs. Norval, noticing his smile, asked him what caused it. The doctor answered, as they walked towards church alone, "I was thinking of the parallel that the Frenchman made between his country and ours."

"And what was that?" asked Mrs. Norval.

"He said that the greatest difference between France and the United States is, that 'in France there is great variety of sauces, and only one religion; whereas in the United States there is great variety of religions, but only one sauce, and that is *buttersauce*'".

"How I do hate foreigners!" exclaimed Mrs. Norval vehemently. At which exclamation the doctor laughed, saying, "I am glad that hating foreigners agrees with your constitution so well. It is well to have something to stimulate the liver. Hatred is your stimulant."

Mrs. Norval only gave for answer one of her lofty stares, and they walked to church without further conversation.

The doctor behaved very well at church. He did not smile, as he sometimes did, when Mr. Hackwell meant to be most edifying. Mrs. Norval had on one or two occasions heard her husband mutter to himself, "What a smart rogue he is!" and this when she felt her eyes fill with tears drawn forth by "the beautiful eloquence," as Mrs. Cackle expressed it, of Mr. Hackwell. On this day, however, the doctor listened attentively, and Hackwell surpassed himself. His theme, to be sure, was the hackneyed one of the sublime love of religious freedom, which made the Pilgrim fathers abandon home, civilization, and friends to come to a comfortless wilderness to encounter horrible savages and privations of all kinds, all for the sake of that one thing dearer to them than all else, viz., "FREEDOM OF OPINION," which is the "individual liberty of the soul," said Mr. Hackwell, and launched forth with renewed vigor upon the threatened rebellion and called the Southerners and their *Northern friends* all the names to be found in the Bible most derogatory to mankind, commencing with Beelzebub and ending with Judas Iscariot. Many of the remarks were evidently aimed at the doctor; at least so Mrs. Norval thought; and she nodded her head slightly in approbation, which caused Hack's eloquence only to glow the more and emit brighter sparks. The congregation also noticed this decorous by-play and began to look at the doctor, but he did not seem to notice anything. He sat still and listened attentively.

When the service was over and the congregation had gone home, various were the comments upon the sermon. The majority, however, were of the opinion that if Mr. Hackwell had "really meant to lash the doctor, it would only be serving him right."

There was no doubt that the mind of New England was greatly exasperated by the doctor. All New England knew that the doctor had gone down to Washington expressly to help Senator Crittenden[14] and other influential men in their effort to avoid a war with the South. The doctor might say what he pleased about loving his country too well to have too much partiality for *one section.* They, the New Englanders, knew better, and if the doctor had not felt too strong a partiality for the wicked South he would have stayed quietly at home, and then have gone and thrashed them back if they rebelled.

Moreover, it was known that the doctor was in the Senate when the Southern senators delivered their farewell addresses and retired as aliens from the halls in which they had legislated as distinguished citizens. The doctor wept as each stately senator, with sad but resolute mien, arose, and, bidding farewell to his colleagues and fellow citizens, bowed a head grown gray in the service of a common country, and then departed, as he thought, forever.

The doctor staggered as he arose from his seat in the Senate gallery, as if he had received a blow upon the breast. He leaned his throbbing head upon the cold marble balustrade, then, feeling calmer, went down slowly with downcast eyes. Mr. Mirabeau Cackle, the newly elected member from the doctor's district, wrote home that the

[14]Senator John Crittenden of Kentucky proposed a compromise, known as the Crittenden Compromise (1860), on the slavery question that in part allowed the new territories to decide on the question of slavery and indemnified owners of runaway slaves. It was never approved. It is implied here that Dr. Norval was sympathetic to the Crittenden position of finding some solution—other than war—on the matter of slave states and the impending secession of the South.

doctor was crying like a child as he went downstairs. Mrs. Cackle, of course, took care to repeat what her distinguished son Beau had written.

The doctor had not been the same man (his *friends* said) since he came back from Washington after the South had seceded. He was no longer the cheerful, genial man. He was silent and serious. He read or wrote all the time, never made any visits, saw but few visitors, and never spent an evening with his family. Immediately after tea he would retire to his own room to read or write.

The evening after Mr. Hackwell's sermon the doctor spent with his family, and conversed quite cheerfully with the many friends who came to wish the young ladies a pleasant journey. On the morrow the Misses Norval, accompanied by their mother as far as New York, would leave for Europe. The friends bade their adieus; the family retired for the night.

The doctor put out the light and lay down by his wife.

Wonderful to relate, and to the utter astonishment of the doctor, his wife put her arm around him (a thing she had not done since the wicked Southerners had fired on Fort Sumter),[15] and said, "I am glad you liked Mr. Hackwell's sermon."

"Yes. I approve of letting everybody enjoy freedom of conscience," said the doctor, patting her hand.

"So do I," said she, slightly pressing his.

"I am glad to hear you say so. I was afraid you would oppose me. The more I think of it, the more plainly I see that it is my duty, and that I am in honor bound to obey the wishes of Lolita's mother and send the child to be educated in the faith of her ancestors. That was the last prayer of the unfortunate lady, and I must obey it. Don't you think so?"

[15]Fort Sumter was the site of the first battle of the U.S. Civil War, April 12, 1861. Located in South Carolina, it was attacked by the South and forced to surrender. In response to the attack, President Abraham Lincoln, inaugurated a month earlier, called out 75,000 volunteers for three month's military service.

CHAPTER XV

Mrs. Norval's High Principles Begin Their Work

Gradually Mrs. Norval withdrew her arm, and slowly turned on her back to prepare for controversy. The doctor waited patiently to hear the answer.

"Unless you yourself think that the idolatry of the popish rites is religion, I don't see how you can conscientiously send the girl to be brought up to believe in such mummeries," said the lady.

"That is not the point. The mother did not leave it to my conscience to choose the child's religion. I shall be abusing her confidence if I force upon her child other than the faith she designated. If you had died, leaving your children young among Catholics, would it not have been your last and most earnest injunction before dying that your children should be brought up Protestant?"

"Of course it would. But my religion is a rational one, not an absurd belief in images, and saints, and relics, and holy water."

"I am not defending the Catholic religion itself (though I must say I think it answers the purpose of all religions as well as any other). What I am holding is, *the right to choose our religion*—the freedom which Mr. Hackwell lauded the Pilgrims for defending. Parents choose it for their children, although children in this country are generally an exception. Witness *our own*, whom you have never been able to bring to your church, and now—"

"My children and their religion have nothing to do with our discussion," interrupted Mrs. Norval. "The point is this: you say that parents ought to choose religious faith for their children. You occupy the place of Lola's parents; you ought to choose her religion."

"That would be a better argument if the child's own mother had not most positively chosen it herself. She also wished the child to be sent to a convent, and really I feel I have done wrong not to comply with her wishes. But from day-to-day I thought I would get the manuscript from Lebrun, and if I found her father he could then do what he pleased. As the manuscript never came, and Lola is now nearly fourteen, I do not think I ought to delay sending her to a convent, and I wish you to write to her tomorrow to get ready to go to any convent she may prefer in this country, or she can go to Europe if she likes."

"I declare, you are enough to set any woman crazy!" said the doctor's better half, sitting up in bed, for she felt when lying down as if her ire would suffocate her. "You are not satisfied with shocking the whole community with your absurd sympathy and treasonable defense of those wicked rebels, who have just now carried their audacious villainy to the extremity of firing upon Fort Sumter—of firing upon our holy flag, which represents *the best government on earth*—but you must now come out, too, as an advocate of popery. Oh, it is too much! Everybody pities me, for everybody knows my principles, and how horrible it is for me to have my husband writing letters against our glorious government, and making speeches against our best prominent men, and trying to help the rebels, or excuse their treason. And now, to finish all, he must defend popery!"

"I do not defend popery, any more than I excuse the South for seceding. And as for my writing against our government, whoever has told you that has told you a wicked lie, and I am ready to prove it. But that is not the point in question. The point is, to send Lola to a convent. That must be done, and I hope you will not fail to write to her about it tomorrow."

"I shall do nothing of the kind. I shall be no party to sending a child to be taught wicked idolatry, which I cannot think of except with horror and detestation. You forget yourself when you ask such a thing. Your next request perhaps will be that I give my consent to send Julian to help the rebels fight our government."

"Wife, you are too excited. Why do you insist upon bringing on a political discussion between us? You know that instead of asking you to send Julian to help the rebels, I have given him the funds to raise a company to fight the rebels. Today I wrote to Sinclair to let Isaac also have funds to raise a company. To the Cackles I have lent the money to raise another company also. This does not look as if I am helping the rebels, does it?"

"It may not, but all you have said can't be called back."

"Nor do I wish to take back anything I have ever said on the subject. I shall speak and act as I see fit. I am as good an American as any of those who accuse me."

"And you see fit to act very absurdly. Who on earth but you would lend money to the Cackles?"

"As the money is for raising troops, you at least ought to approve of my lending it. I told Julian he might raise a regiment if he liked, and I'll back him with the necessary funds."

"Is it possible that you have arrived at that point of lunacy?" she exclaimed.

"Bah!" said the doctor, turning on his side.

"All your throwing money away to raise troops won't help you. You are put down as a rebel sympathizer on account of your treasonable letters and your treasonable words, and no matter what you do it won't help you any, that I can tell you," said the lady, also turning her back on her lord, with something of exultation in her voice.

"All right," said the doctor; "let us go to sleep now, and let them put me down what they please."

Mrs. Norval was a sagacious lady, and she understood her community even better than did her easy-going, generous-hearted husband.

"You will not be so indifferent if you are not more guarded. My prayer is that your wicked sympathies may not injure Julian and Isaac."

"Bother my sympathies! No, Mrs. N., don't be afraid of that. I have received a letter from Arthur Sinclair inviting me to join him in a trip up the Nile, and to Abyssinia. I shall accept his proposal, and will join him somewhere in the Mediterranean next October. Does that make your mind easier? If I were ready, I would go with the girls now, but I must first see Julian fitted out, and Lola placed in a convent, then in August I'll start."

"Of course, Lola!—always that black girl," said Mrs. Norval to seize upon some rope of an argument to pull herself out, for she felt herself getting beyond her depth in the discussion. The doctor made no answer, and after some more futile efforts on her part she relinquished the contest.

A few days after, the Misses Norval sailed for Europe, and Lola went to a convent to be educated as her mother wished.

"The proclamation of the President! Seventy-five thousand volunteers called to defend the nation against treason!" shouted the newsboys in all the cities and towns large enough to have a newspaper. And the voices of the little urchins thrilled a great nation, for they were saying things of fearful import, though intent only on making pennies.

Men and women were electrified! What! to dare to plot against "the best government on earth!"

Martial music resounded in the air the length and breadth of the land. Volunteers flocked to Washington daily, and Julian, Isaac, and two of the Cackle brothers were among the first to offer their services to the government.

The Cackles were Republicans, and felt great desire to crush the rebels. Isaac was a Democrat, but was very angry with the rebels for their folly in "spoiling the Democratic party," and wanted to whip them. Julian did not care for politics, but he felt that every American was in duty bound to defend the Union.

With the influence of Mirabeau and his brother Marcus Tullius Cicero Cackle (both just elected to Congress), the other two brothers, Mark Antony and Julius Caesar, and also Julian and Isaac, backed by Dr. Norval's money, promptly received their commissions. Julian and Isaac got captaincies.

Julius Caesar Cackle also was made a captain. Mark Antony was Isaac's first lieutenant.

The three companies were ready by the 1st of June, 1861; the young officers had displayed great energy and capacity in enlisting and organizing their troops. Their mothers and sisters were full of enthusiasm and admiration for the young warriors. The battle of Bull Run[16] was soon to be fought.

Like two Roman matrons, Mrs. Norval and Mrs. Cackle waited to hear the announcement of the coming battle. They waited and made lint for the wounded. Lavinia did more. We will give a whole chapter to her patriotism in due time.

[16]The battle at Bull Run (July 21, 1861) was a catastrophe for the Union Army. The ill-trained troops led by General Irvin McDowell into Virginia panicked and scattered under attack.

CHAPTER XVI

"Veni, Vidi, Vici"[17]

The Northern army at last marched upon the South, and was met at Bull Run by the Southern one. With flying colors and full bands playing stirring melodies, battalion after battalion went down Pennsylvania Avenue, down Seventh Street, to the Long Bridge out of Washington. The zouaves,[18] with their gay uniforms, marched out saluted by enthusiastic shouts of the boys, and the ladies waved with their handkerchiefs their farewell. Among the zouaves there marched two young men whom we will again meet in these pages. They labored, under the classic names of Æschylus Wagg and Sophocles Head, up their rugged path in life, and now shone in the red breeches and blue jackets of the zouave uniform. The First Rhode Island Regiment also marched out gallantly, cheered and saluted by the white handkerchiefs of the ladies. Many of the fair enthusiasts followed the brave warriors beyond the Long Bridge, and carried bouquets and garlands to decorate them. Even the horses which the warriors rode were decorated with flowers. Garlands made by fair hands hung around the horses' necks. The army seemed to be on its way to a festival rather than to deal death and desolation.

[17]According to Suetonious, these words were uttered by Julius Caesar. It is also the inscription on Caesar's Pontic Triumph monument in Rome. Here these words are turned ironically against Caesar's namesake, Julius Caesar Cackle, whose deportment in battle was less than legendary yet won him honor and fame.

[18]The zouaves were the precision-trained Chicago soldiers, patterned after Algerian mountain warriors imitated by the French. The Chicago Volunteer Company imitated the French Zouaves in their methods and colorful uniforms of billowing trousers, loose tunic and fez.

Isaac Sprig, too, wore a wreath around his hat, which the trembling hands of the pretty Lucinda had placed there, leaving a tear shining like a diamond on a red rosebud.

History has recorded the result of the Bull Run battle. This narrative has to do only with our friends Julian, Isaac, and the Cackles.

The companies commanded by Julian and Isaac were among the first to go into action. Julian was severely wounded and carried off the field within an hour after the firing had begun. Isaac, also, was wounded and made a prisoner with his first lieutenant Mark Antony—called for short *Tony*—Cackle. They had the grief of seeing their company and their whole regiment run as fast as heels propelled by panic could carry them, whilst they were picked up by the rebels.

The company of Julius Cackle was more fortunate. No one in it was wounded or made prisoner, though many were terribly scratched in their frantic running through the bushes.

As for Julius himself, the stampede made his fortune. He was one of the foremost leaders of the flight, and soon he distanced the fleetest. As he ran madly in the van, his luck—having determined to be propitious—brought him slap against a horse and buggy also going towards Washington. The horse took matters more philosophically than the scared Cackle, and he grazed along the road wherever he found a tempting tuft of grass.

When the horse heard Cackle's footsteps, he started at a jog-trot, but when the voice of Cackle sent a quivering shout to him, the animal, to the great joy of the frightened warrior, stopped still and waited. With trembling eager hands the panic-stricken captain seized the reins which rested on the dasher, and the whip, and commenced to lash the horse to put him at his full speed.

The captain had not traveled long at this furious rate, when he came to a brook which seemed rather deep. The horse stopped, and Cackle gave a disconsolate imploring look at the surrounding shrubbery. A little farther up, the brook seemed more shallow: he directed the horse to that spot, and began to cross the little stream. A moan and a sob attracted his attention. There on the opposite bank, in front of him, he saw a man lying on his back who lifted his trembling hands imploringly to him.

Cackle was too frightened to be merciful; he was going on his way, leaving the prostrate man where he was, but the latter gave such a doleful bawl, expressive of so much terror and pain, that the horse of his own accord stopped, as if determined to teach the captain that "to do unto others," etc., should not be forgotten.

"For the love of God, do not leave me,'' said the prostrate man, and, as the horse was standing still, Cackle thought the shortest way would be to see if he could take the man with him. But, not wishing to lose precious moments by getting out, he said to the man, "Come on, then. Make haste.''

"I can't walk. Do help me, my dear Cackle. Don't leave me here."

"Who are you?" said the captain, getting out. "You seem to know me. Ah! what the devil are you doing here?" and Cackle involuntarily carried his hand to his revolver, for his first impulse was to shoot the prostrate man—being no other than the Hon. Le Grand Gunn, who had caused his dismissal together with that of Isaac.

"My horse threw me; he got frightened seeing so many soldiers running past us. He began to run so fast that I couldn't keep in the saddle, and I fell off. Then I ran on foot until I could run no more. I am entirely exhausted. If you don't take me in your buggy, I must die here," said Mr. Gunn in a very faint voice.

"But what business have you here, anyhow? What brought you to Bull Run on the day we were to have the battle?" asked Cackle.

"We came to see the battle from the distance. We thought it would be such a splendid sight. So three or four of us representatives, and two or three senators, got together to have some fun coming over to see the fight."

"And you have seen it, and I hope you are satisfied, you and your friends, with the d—d fun you politicians have made for us all," said Cackle, too terrified to be diplomatic, and forgetting his own uproarious loyalty besides.

But he got out of his buggy, though with many glances askance towards the south, and helped the exhausted M.C. on his legs.

"I am utterly used up. I can't drag my legs to the buggy even," said Mr. Gunn.

"Then I must drag you, for I have no notion of being nabbed by the rebs," said the captain, taking the faint M.C. in his arms, which plowing and mowing had made as strong as if of iron, and, placing him on the buggy, started off at full gallop.

The Hon. Gunn was not forgetful of the great service rendered by Cackle. He took care that he should be promoted. He made a most magnificent panegyric of the heroic behavior of the captain, so that he got him appointed colonel and breveted brigadier general. Soon after, the lucky Cackle was made brigadier general. His friend Gunn had argued well that a man who could run so judiciously as Cackle did would certainly make a good leader.

As for Mark Antony Cackle, captured with Isaac, he was immediately exchanged and made colonel, *vice* Cackle, promoted.

And Isaac: what of him?

CHAPTER XVII

Julius Caesar Cackle, a Modern Darius[19]

In justice it must be said that Julius and Tony Cackle both thought of their generous friend Sprig, who had been so free with his money, and was now perhaps in want, languishing in captivity. They endeavored to interest their influential brothers, Mirabeau and Cicero, in his behalf. Those two noble legislators took the matter rather coldly at first; then they flatly told their brothers that as Dr. Norval was a "suspected sympathizer," the least they had to do with any of the Norval family the better it would be for all the Cackles, though they owed him money.

Julius then tried to propitiate the Hon. Le Grand Gunn, believing that, in consideration of Isaac's being now suffering for his country's cause, the patriotic M.C. would forgive the unfortunate encounter in Lucinda's presence.

But in thus judging the Hon. Gunn, General Cackle only displayed great ignorance of human nature, without serving his friend. No sooner had Julius said the first words in behalf of Isaac, than the Hon. Gunn became very red in the face, and replied, "Look here, Cackle, I'll do anything for you *in reason*, for you did me a great service. But to expect that I'll do anything for that dandy, that cursed puppy, after the—the—that—he—that he gave me, is—is to expect too much of human nature! No, sir! he shall rot in prison as long as I can contrive to keep him there. He shall—and serves him right. I have made up my mind on that point. He has got what he deserves. Lucinda's eyes will be red with crying, for she

[19]Ruiz de Burton continues the parodic portrayal of the "warrior" Julius Caesar Cackle, comparing him here to Darius I, known also as Darius the Great, king of Persia from 521 B.C. to 486 B.C. Legend holds that seven Persian princes agreed that he whose horse neighed first should be king. Darius' horse neighed first when he tethered a mare near it. So too would Cackle's horse play a central role in his military "exploits."

has a silly fancy for the infernal puppy. But I reckon she will be consoled when she finds that he ain't a-coming."

Julius was thus silenced. And in the evening, as the four distinguished brothers and their father were having a family talk by themselves, Beau—being the leading spirit of the Cackle family—said to the brothers who had been pleading in behalf of Isaac, "Listen to me, Tony, and you, too, Ciss. Do you want to succeed, or to spoil your good luck?"

"Of course we want to succeed," they replied.

"Well, then, leave Isaac to his fate. Never undertake to lift a fallen man; never associate your fortunes with an unlucky dog like Isaac, by trying to help him when luck is so set against him. Bad luck is contagious, I tell you. Don't you touch any one that has it—any more than if he had the leprosy: '*Room for the leper! Room!*—make way for the unlucky man!'"

The brothers and the old man were so impressed with the wisdom and eloquence of Beau's injunctions, that they were afraid to mention their old comrade's name, and never again spoke of getting him out of prison.

"He will be exchanged anyhow, when the time comes," Julius once ventured to say to his brother, Colonel Mark Antony Cackle.

"Of course he will; indeed he might already be on his way up," said Tony. And with this consolatory remark they justified their ingratitude in their own minds, and were very glad to forget Isaac.

The philosophy of Beau was corroborated by daily increasing prosperity. No sooner was the unlucky Isaac dismissed from their thoughts, than fortune, which had certainly smiled on them, seemed to be in a constant broad grin with the Cackles.

The two members of Congress—Beau and Tool—were making money as fast as if by magic. Dr. Norval had put in the capital, and the brothers had got several Government contracts, in other persons' names, by which they made enormous profits. The Cackles would certainly be rich and renown, and influential at the same time. Beau and Tool were foremost among the political leaders of the day, whilst Julius and Tony made themselves famous, and their names were in the newspapers all the time for deeds of daring surpassed by no one in modern or ancient warfare. If I were to recount in detail their wonderful achievements as minutely as an impartial press did at the time, I would fill these insignificant pages with them. But I am not so ambitious. I will only record briefly—though not chronologically for the event happened at a later date—how Julius Caesar Cackle, like the great Darius the First, ascended higher in the path of glory, and became greater, through the humble agency of a horse: the neighing of a horse.

It happened—I think but a few months after the battle of Bull Run—that, at one of the greatest battles ever fought by men determined to destroy each other, General Julius Cackle commanded a division temporarily. On that memorable day the general was riding a horse which had been captured from the rebels. This horse happened to be the mate and companion of another horse which a rebel officer was riding on the same day right in front of General Cackle's division.

There was a lull in the firing of the wing where General Cackle's troops were fighting. Columns were changing position, and, by a movement of the rebel troops, before General Cackle knew it he and his staff were in close proximity to the rebel line.

Suddenly the neighing of a horse was heard very distinctly. At the sound of that neigh, the ears of the general's horse became erect. The general spurred the charger toward his own division, but the horse turned suddenly around and, taking the bit in his teeth, ran, as if frenzied, toward the point whence the neighing had come.

The gallant Cackle pulled the bridle with all his might in vain. Then he shouted to the running horse to stop: also in vain, so far as the horse was concerned. But the staff seeing their general charging the enemy so gallantly and heroically thought that he, with his characteristic perspicacity, had discovered some splendid opportunity to make a brilliant charge, and was now shouting to them to come on. So they all shouted also, and charged after him. The two or three regiments which stood nearest followed the staff, and then the whole division followed the regiments, though they had received orders to make a different movement, and were now waiting the command to advance. The rebels were so surprised at this mad charge that they broke ranks and, becoming disorganized, fled to the center of their line, leaving the heroic Cackle in possession of the artillery and munitions, and master of the field.

General Cackle was the hero of the day.

His gallant charge had turned the tide of victory in favor of the right cause.

The valiant general was thanked by the commander-in-chief on the battleground—the newspapers said—and the President wrote him an autograph letter. His friends said that the general ought to receive the thanks of Congress, and that some poet ought to compose an ode on his exploit like Tennyson's "Charge of the Six Hundred."[20]

[20]Ruiz de Burton makes reference to Alfred, Lord Tennyson's (1809-1892) poem, *The Charge of the Light Brigade*, in which he exalts the bravery of British soldiers in their Balaklava cavalry charge against the Russians in the 1853-1856 Crimean War, to further mock the "warrior" Cackle.

CHAPTER XVIII

Lavinia to the Rescue

Lavinia's heart pranced like a war-horse at the sound of martial music, making the chest of the maiden resound with its galloping. Her patriotic fire spread to the Misses Cackle, until nothing but making sacrifices for their country's cause would satisfy them, and Lucretia and Artemisia—the two eldest of the Misses Cackle—aided and abetted by Lavinia, prevailed upon old Mrs. Cackle to accompany them to Washington, where they would devote themselves to the care of the sick and wounded. When this heroic resolution became known all over the land, many were the matrons and maidens who, impelled by the same sentiments, wrote and came in person to enlist under Mrs. Cackle's patriotic banner.

For weeks and weeks, the Misses Cackle and Lavinia canned beef tea and made jellies and jams in the daytime, and lint and bandages and havelocks at night. They knitted a great number of stockings also. They made underclothes, and large, very large, night shirts, for these patriotic ladies seemed to take measure by their enthusiasm, and very possibly imagined that the heroes for whom the shirts were made must all be as large in size as in deeds.

"As Julian is to be brought home, you will not go with us now," said Mrs. Cackle to Lavinia, as they were packing jellies and havelocks, and jams and stockings, and lint and canned beef tea in boxes to be sent to Washington.

"Yes, I will go, too. Julian has his mother and father to take care of him, whilst—just think of the poor, poor soldiers who will be sick and wounded far away from home and friends!"

"But, as the girls are in Europe now, Mrs. Norval might want you to stay to help her in case she has to sit up at night with Julian."

"The doctor writes that Julian's wounds are not dangerous now; that he is only very weak from loss of blood. Besides, if Jemima wants help, Lola will be here: the doctor wrote for her to come."

"I thought Mrs. Norval objected to let Lola come, on account of those spots she has on her skin," said Miss Lucretia Cackle.

"That was before the girls went to Europe. The doctor says that those spots are not contagious and will all pass off in time. Lola began to have them soon after she went to school, nearly three years ago, and as yet no one has been infected by them. So they can't be very contagious."

"Emma Hackwell told me that her brother thinks Lola must belong to a tribe of Mexican Indians called 'Pintos,' who are spotted," said Artemisia.

"No, that ain't so! Mr. Hackwell said that if Lola was an Indian, the spots *might* indicate that she belonged to the Pintos," Miss Lucretia observed.

"But as the doctor says that she is not an Indian, then those ugly spots can't be accounted for, except on the theory that they are some disease," said Mrs. Norval, coming in and joining the conversation.

"With all due respect to the doctor, it seems to me clear, as you say, that the girl is either of the Pinto tribe, or her spots are a disease," Mrs. Cackle averred, as she always did, in support of any opinion of Mrs. Norval.

"Of course. So, as Lavvy is going with you, I accepted Emma's kind offer to come to help me with Julian, should I require it, and I told Mr. Hackwell I would send word to Emma when to come. In this manner, there will be no excuse for Lola to go near Julian's room. I am glad Lavvy is going, so that no one but the doctor need go near the girl, and neither Julian nor Emma nor myself will have much to say to her."

"Poor child, I pity her!" said Lavinia. But, as Mrs. Norval frowned, none of the Cackles dared to venture upon any show of commiseration for the orphan, and all remained silent. Mrs. Norval remarked that she had not heard lately whether the spots had disappeared, but she hoped they had, and Lola might be now all black or all white, no matter which, only not with those ugly white spots. Then she changed the conversation.

The doctor and Julian arrived that night. The invalid was past danger from his wounds; he was only very pale and weak from loss of blood. There would be no necessity to sit up to watch him at night. The doctor and Jim had done that for him in Washington the first two weeks after he was wounded. Still, Mrs. Norval sent for Emma. Mr. Hackwell had been so earnest in his request that Emma should be sent for to assist Mrs. Norval, that this lady, always glad to please Mr. Hackwell, had promised to do so.

Miss Emma, therefore, came to be Julian's nurse. His bed, for convenience, was placed in the back parlor.

Two days after the arrival of Julian, the doctor received a telegram from the convent where Lola was, saying that she would leave for home that morning. The doctor went to meet her at the depot in the evening. He loved the poor little orphan girl, whom he regarded now more than ever as his ward, since he had never received from Lebrun the statement of her dying mother, by means of which he had hoped to find her relatives and establish her identity.

When the doctor met Lola, his kind heart beat with pleasure. The unfortunate spots had almost entirely disappeared; Lola's skin was white and smooth, and she was very pretty. Still, there were some spots yet on her neck and arms, though almost imperceptible, and he feared that Mrs. N. would insist on regarding them as some sort of cutaneous disease.

In this the doctor was not mistaken. His wife clung to the opinion that if Mr. Hackwell's theory of the Pinto tribe was not the correct hypothesis, then the spots must be contagious. So when Lola came up to her to salute her with a kiss, Mrs. Norval drew back with a gesture of disgust, saying, "Don't, child! You know how afraid I am of your singular spots." Then she added, addressing Julian, by whose side Emma sat, "Take care, Julian. Don't touch Lola's hand; we don't know whether those spots might not be contagious."

"Oh, mother! how can you say that?" Julian pleaded.

"Lola has no right to feel hurt if we are afraid of being infected," Mrs. Norval replied.

"Being damned!" exclaimed the doctor, banging the door as he left the room.

"No sooner does this girl come into my house than your father is changed from a courteous gentleman and a Christian into a rough and a Hottentot," said Mrs. Norval, not paying any attention to Lola, who, wounded and humiliated at the reception she met, had sunk on a chair and leaned her head upon the table. Julian looked at the bent form of the child, so expressive of mental suffering, and, lifting himself painfully on one elbow, said, "Come, Lola, I am not afraid of those spots. In fact, I believe they are fabulous—they don't exist. Come, shake hands with me. I haven't seen you for four years. If I wasn't looking so forlorn, I would ask you to give me a kiss. Come."

Lola did not move or answer.

"Is she crying?" Julian asked Emma, in a low voice. But Lola heard him, and, raising her head, replied, "No, sir; I am not crying. I have cried enough in this house. I was making a resolve to cry in it as little as possible."

Julian smiled, as if amused or pleased. Mrs. Norval frowned, and the doctor, who entered the room as Lola was speaking, said, "That is right. That is the resolve I would advise you to make. Cry as little as possible, and keep up your courage. You will be perfectly independent, and will want nobody's favors. But whilst you are a child you will of course be more dependent, and that is my principal regret in going away—that I have to leave you, my poor little girl. However, Julian will stand by you *like a man*. Come to my room. I wish to speak to you alone, and, since we are not wanted here and we have an hour before supper, let us have our talk now, at once."

"I must speak to you *first*," said Mrs. Norval, rising in evident agitation and detaining her husband.

"Well, what is it ?" the doctor inquired, stopping.

"Not here. In your room." Then turning to Lola, who was about to follow, she said to her, "Stay!"

Lola stopped. But the doctor, who was walking behind his wife, made a sign to her to follow them.

CHAPTER XIX

Mrs. Norval's High Principles on the Rampage

Lola stood perplexed. She wished to obey the one through love, the other through fear. She looked back at Julian, as if asking him to advise her what to do.

"Obey my father, of course," said Julian, in answer to her appealing look. "He wishes you to follow him." Lola went.

There was no light in the doctor's room. He began to feel about for the matchbox, but Mrs. Norval stopped him by impatiently exclaiming, "Never mind a light. What I have to say can be told in a few seconds and in the dark. First, I wish to know if it is your intention to disclose to Lola what you know of her mother's history. Judging by what you just now indicated, I infer that you are going to tell her that she is the owner of the money we have been spending, and impress her with the idea that we have been robbing her."

"No, for that is not so. I will tell the child nothing that is not true, and only what will be of service to her in case I die or be killed, and do not return before she is of age."

"I suppose you'll tell her about the diamonds?"

"No, I will not. But I hope that, if the girls delay their return, all those sets of jewelry will be sent back. It was very wrong of you to take advantage of my confidence to carry those jewels surreptitiously away, and still more blamable to allow your daughters to take them away to Europe when you know they belong to Lola."

"What of that? Lola can't wear them yet, and my daughters will not hurt the jewels."

"But they might lose them, and we certainly cannot replace them. What pained me the most was to be obliged to assent to a falsehood to cover yours, for you told Sinclair I had given you the order *to keep* the jewels, when it was only that he would send them for you and the girls to *look* at them, after which they would be returned. I never thought you capable of doing such a thing."

"I did not come here to be scolded. If you had seen how crazy your daughters went when they saw the stones shining before their eyes, and how they cried, and begged, and implored, you would not be so hard on me for yielding to their tears. I knew full well that you would not spare me, but my two poor children almost went on their knees, and I consented. Mrs. Sinclair said she would take good care of the jewels, and always keep them in some bank. The set made all of diamonds, which is the most costly, they did not take. I trust you will say nothing to Lola about this, for you will only be doing your children great injustice, and, possibly, harm. In fact, I don't see any necessity of your telling her anything. If there be any need of disclosing any facts before your return, I can do that."

A ring at the doorbell, and the voices of Mr. and Mrs. Hackwell in the hall, interrupted Mrs. Norval, who was obliged to go to receive her friends and leave the doctor to his interview with Lola. As the stately matron passed out, the little girl stepped behind the door and was hidden from view.

The doctor struck a light, and immediately saw by Lola's position that she must have heard what had been said. He observed, quietly, "You heard what we said?"

"Yes, sir, unintentionally. But you need not regret it, for I knew almost all. I remember very well that my mother told me she had given you all the gold we collected in the cave by the brook, and the diamonds she had kept for me. She told me they were for me, but also for you. I know you are taking care of those things for me."

"Yes, Lola, I am. And your jewelry shall be all returned to you, for I will tell Julian how everything is. Besides, I have put all down in my will, so that if Julian and I were to die, your gold and jewelry, as well as other property we have bought for you, all will be secure, and you will be rich and independent. Still, for all that, I wish you to obey my wife in my absence, for she will have charge of you, unless your relatives appear (well-identified) to claim you, as it would be their right to do. But if none such come before I return, then my wife is to be your mother—your guardian, I mean," added he, correcting himself—"and you are to be guided by her until you are of age. When you are twenty-one years old, your property will be at your control. I have made every arrangement for that, and you will have no difficulty, even if my dear boy Julian loses his life during the war. Mr. Sinclair, your banker, and Mr. North, our lawyer, are both honorable men, and will take care of your interests. In the meantime, all I ask of you is to try to get along with my family as well as you can, for my sake. Will you do that?"

"Yes, sir. I will do anything you wish."

"If I have not returned the day you are twenty-one, my will is to be opened. But if you are to be married, or if your relatives claim you before then, Mr. Sinclair and my wife are to open my will. Mr. Sinclair will render an account also of the increase of your wealth up to that time, and how your money is invested. In the meantime, I have arranged with Mr. Sinclair that he is to have four per cent of the interest your capital is now paying, and keep six per cent subject to my order or my wife's order. This will only be taking ten per cent of the profit of your money. And I felt justified in so doing, because your mother authorized me to take one-half of the whole. This I would not do, but I think six per cent is not too much, and your expenses are defrayed from it. Do you understand me, Lola?"

"Oh, yes, sir! And I think you ought to take the half, as mamma asked you to do."

"No, that would be too much. I told Sinclair to invest whatever was not used out of the six per cent. I don't think we will spend it all, as we don't live in such grand style. Even if we were in New York, we could not spend all, for you must know that your money has more than doubled, and Sinclair says he has some safe speculations in view by which he can treble it. He has bought you ever so many handsome houses in New York, too. But you must not speak about this to Mrs. Norval. I don't want anyone but Sinclair to know how much property you have. I told my wife you are to have a liberal allowance at school and all the money you wish when you come out. I am glad you are progressing so well in your studies. You must write to me as often as I let you know there is a chance of your letters reaching me. You must promise me that."

"But where are you going, sir? And for how long?" asked Lola, her eyes filling with tears.

"I am going to Africa, to Abyssinia, with Mr. Arthur Sinclair and other gentlemen from England. Heaven knows how long I shall be away. Very probably as long as the war lasts, unless some unforeseen reason obliges me to return sooner. Pray for me that I may see you again in happier days."

Lola, prompted by an irresistible impulse, went up to her beloved guardian, and, throwing her arms around his neck, burst out crying, pouring on him a shower of most emphatic kisses. The doctor was much moved; he had not been caressed thus, with all this innocent fervor, since his children were little ones—before their mother had scolded them, with cold dignity and great propriety, into learning to curb all emotion and check all show of feeling. Julian, boy though he was, had been the hardest to teach the self-restraint which Mrs. Norval thought the great desideratum in a well-organized family. But Julian was now a man, twenty-one years old, and he had long since ceased to caress his warm-hearted father, who had almost forgotten what it was to be caressed.

The doctor was taken by surprise with this loving avalanche. His heart, however, quickly responded to it, throbbing and warming up at the passionate pressure of the little arms thrown around his neck, and the kisses which fell pell-mell on his forehead, his eyes, his cheeks, his neck, and his ears. He pressed the little girl to his heart, and the man felt as much an orphan as did the child.

He made her sit on his knees, and he laid on his breast the little head, so graceful and perfect in shape, with its wealth of silky, wavy black hair. The doctor had not felt as he now did for many years. Why could not his daughters be affectionate like this poor little orphan? he thought. Because their mother hated anything like a show of affection, and imperiously prohibited it. He sighed, and thought that if his home had not been made so cold and comfortless perhaps he would not have felt so deeply the injustice of the threatened persecution for his political opinions, which was the cause of his voluntarily exiling himself from his country. Lola was the only creature who showed any affection for him, and now he was going to leave her exposed to the harshness of Mrs. Norval. Poor little dear! He wished so much he could leave her elsewhere.

They had been thus clasped in each other's arms for some time, when they were startled by a voice at the door, saying, "Pretty business, doctor, you are discussing with your little Indian!" And the tall form of Mrs. Norval appeared in the doorway.

CHAPTER XX

Lavinia Outdoes the Spartan Women

From those gloomy days in which the Rev. Hackwell and the Rev. Hammerhard proved so faithless, Miss Lavinia Sprig had devoted herself to raising canary birds. The little innocents were the recipients of Miss Lavinia's pent-up caresses, and thus were useful as well as ornamental, for no doubt they had saved Miss Lavvy from many a fit of hysterics. In the sunshine of Miss Lavvy's love, the canaries, thrived, as though in a genial atmosphere, and by the time the wicked Southerners fired upon Fort Sumter she had no less than twenty-one birds: viz., ten couples, and the ancestor of all—an old widower called "Jule," short for Julian, and who was a very dignified singer.

The little birds were Lavvy's delight and amusement. They knew many tricks which she had taught them. They evidently loved her, judging from the way in which they shook their little wings and flew to meet her as soon as they heard her voice. They knew their own names, too, and would stand still if Lavvy, addressing them one by one, told them to be quiet, or would fly to her in the order in which she called them.

When Lavinia's patriotic enthusiasm reached its highest pitch, and when making lint, or havelocks, or beef tea, or stockings, was not sufficient for the maiden's sacred fervor, then the little darlings were neglected. With a sad heart Lavinia saw that she had neglected her pets, and that they didn't sing as before. She was a conscientious maiden. She saw she had to decide between her country and her birds, and her heart seemed to collapse with pain.

But Lavvy's soul was Spartan. It soon leaped higher, and a sublime resolve invaded her spirit.

"Oh, my little darlings! Must it indeed be so? And yet, if I leave you, you will die of hunger, or some miserable cat might devour you, one by one! Yes, my little angels, it is best that you pass away without pain. Sleep, sleep, sleep forever!"

And Lavinia, though Spartan, or, what is the same, a New England lady trained to do her duty no matter how painful, clapped her hands to her face and wept. Poor Lavvy! She was, after all, but a woman.

When this natural ebullition of tenderness had abated, Lavinia stood erect with clasped hands and fixed gaze, her mighty effort racking her bosom. She felt that what she was about to do, only an Electra, or an Antigone, or some such classic heroine, could have done outside of New England. Then she stalked with majestic stride towards the room in the garret where the doctor kept his fossils and chemicals. There, from several flasks standing on a shelf, she selected one labeled "*Chloroform.*"

Then she walked back to her room and sat by the side of the cages containing her pets.

"You shall not be devoured by nasty cats. You shall not starve to death," said she, tenderly.

Then, with more courage than Virginius[21]—for he slew only one, and at one blow—she took her little pets, one by one, calling each to her by its name, and, plunging their little heads inside the flask, put them to sleep—the sleep that knows no waking—one by one.

She laid them in couples, in a row. Yes, there they were. They had innocently flown to her to be killed, as she uttered the celebrated names which Isaac had given them. Lavinia's thoughts, as she contemplated her dead darlings, reverted to that day when Isaac, after naming all the males, was naming the females. He was saying, "Now we have plenty of classic names; let us have some modern ones. This one is Jenny Lind[22]; this stately lady is Sontag; this is Gazzaniga; this one, with the

[21]In mocking Lavinia's act of killing her beloved canaries rather than see them suffer a worse fate, Ruiz de Burton again makes use of a classical reference, here the Roman Virginius who slew his daughter Virginia at the Forum as she was about to be delivered as a slave to Appius Claudius Crassus, one of the *decem virs*, saying: "There is no way but this to keep thee free." Virginius would thereafter organize a revolt against the *decem virs* and restore the old order of government (449 B.C.). The issue of Roman slavery, relevant to the novel, goes, however, uncommented.

[22]Jenny Lind, née Johanna Maria Lind Goldschmidt (1820-1887), was a Swedish soprano known as "the Swedish Nightingale." Engaged by P.T. Barnum, she opened a two-year tour of the U.S. with a premiere at New York's Castle Garden. Sontag, both Pattis, Gazzaniga and Grisi were other noted singers of the period. Isaac Sprig's familiarity with their names is meant to underscore his liking for "things foreign."

white wings, is Carlotta Patti; and this one, with the golden necklace, is Adelina Patti, for she is my favorite, and this one here is Grisi."

"You might as well call them Clytemnestra, or Jezabel, or Messalina[23] as to give them the names of actresses," Mr. Hackwell had said. Mrs. Norval had added, "I think so, too. And Lavinia, being a Christian girl, will not call her little birds by the names of horrid actresses. I positively object to it."

"Stuff!" the doctor had said, and he and his wife had had a very warm discussion, for it had branched off to the subject of Isaac's "corrupted love for drama and foreigners," which the doctor had fomented, and from that they had passed on to the equally obnoxious subject of Julian's sojourn in Europe.

On that day, on account of that discussion, her poor brother Isaac had resolved to go away from home because Mrs. Norval was so severe. And now the innocent occasions of Isaac's voluntary exile were all dead! And Isaac, poor, unfortunate Isaac, where was he? Was he dead? Perhaps he was!

So lost was Lavinia in this sad labyrinth of reminiscences, that she forgot to kill Jule, the widower, or to shut the door of the cage. Now Jule was left all alone. He had watched Lavinia with profound attention all the while, and, as in all the days of his life he had never seen her act thus, he began to be suspicious. Whilst Lavinia was lost in thought, Jule kept very quiet and very near the cage door, but as soon as his mistress raised her head and looked towards him, he gave one little squeak and off he flew, Lavinia after him. For one moment he rested on the banister, then, as he saw his mistress come out from her room calling him, away he went downstairs and out of the front door. Downstairs Lavinia rushed after the fugitive, with her eyes fixed on him and with outstretched arms, screaming, "Jule, Jule!" She felt she ran into someone. She looked. She was in the arms of the Rev. Mr. Hackwell. She fainted.

"Bless my soul!" exclaimed the Rev. Hack. "What can possibly be the matter? Here, please, some water! Mrs. Norval! Doctor! Emma!" called he. But no one came. Hack put his hand to feel Lavvy's heart's pulsations, but he felt none. The reverend gentleman smiled, as if not at all alarmed, and yet not the slightest throb could he feel. He smiled, because he remembered having heard Mrs. Hackwell and Mrs. Ham-

[23]Clytemnestra, Jezabel and Messalina are invoked by Hackwell, and seconded by Mrs. Norval, as disreputable and evil women, implying that actresses, singers and foreigners in general are wicked and always suspect and consequently not "proper" names to be uttered in a Christian household.

merhard observe that Lavinia had a very handsome bust now, when, previous to the sudden prosperity of the Norvals, she was as flat as a pancake. And these ladies had said—all *en famille*, for they were the wives of divines and had to set a good example—that to the New York dressmakers Lavvy was indebted for her fine figure, etc. When the Rev. Hack remembered this, his thoughts, which had never been what should be in the head of a parson, got altogether very far from the church. He looked all around, and, seeing no one near, he thought he would experiment on Lavvy. He would try the effect of a kiss.

"If she is unconscious," thought he, "she will never know it. And if she is pretending, she expects it."

So saying, his reverence applied his lips to those of the fainting Lavvy. She did not move; she did not open her eyes, but his reverence thought he saw a faint pink color rise to her face. He tried another kiss, and then another. Lavinia sighed, but did not open her eyes.

"This is becoming interesting," thought the Presbyterian divine. "It seems that kisses are better than cold water for fainting maidens," and he changed his position slightly, kneeling on one knee to approach Lavinia closer. But, in doing so, he turned his head a little, and perceived Lola standing by him with Jule the fugitive in her hand.

The reverend gentleman started, colored very red, and, dropping the form of Lavinia, rose to his feet. Lavvy, without the tender support of his arm around her waist, rolled down upon the carpet very ungracefully.

"How long have you been here?" asked his reverence, frowning and looking uneasily about him.

"Since you called," Lola answered roguishly.

"Why didn't you speak, then?"

"I didn't think you would like to be interrupted."

"What is the matter? Who speaks of kissing me? It is false! Oh, the wicked bird! Take him away! No, he must die, too! He must not be left to be eaten by cats or starve to death!" Here a flood of tears and sobs came to relieve Lavinia's heart. Hackwell smiled. Lola, amused, looked from one to the other.

"They are all dead! All! All! My two lovely Pattis went first!" sobbed Lavvy.

"But who killed them?" asked Lola.

"I did. I did it to save them from pain, from the cat's claws, from starvation! Jule, too, must die!"

"Oh, no. Please give him to me!" pleaded Lola. "He is Julian's namesake. I am perfectly sure that if you kill him, Julian will be killed too. I know it!" said Lola, crying. And so earnest was she in her entreaties that Lavvy yielded, and Jule was spared, becoming the property of Lola.

CHAPTER XXI

Julian and Hackwell Inspect the Horrid Spots

Julian was out of danger. A few days more and he would be strong enough to join his regiment. He leaned on his stick when he walked about, but still he did walk all over the house, the flower garden, and the lawn. He had been very anxious to get well during the first days after his arrival, which anxiety was not at all complimentary to his devoted nurse Emma. But now, when he was better, he hated the idea of going; hated to think that soon after he left, his father would go, too, and that he might never return. At first Julian had tried to dissuade him from the idea of such an expedition. But when the doctor explained to him his reasons for going, Julian ceased to object. Father and son had several good long talks together all alone, and they understood each other perfectly.

Julian would, therefore, have gone in comparative peace of mind, but his leaving in that manner did not suit Mrs. Norval. There was a thing that must be settled before he went.

"Julian, you and I have got to settle that point," said Mrs. Norval two or three days before the one on which Julian was to leave.

"Yes, mother, you have told me that several times. Now, however, Lola and I are to play a game of chess. Come, Lola, your men are all arranged."

"There is Mr. Hackwell coming," suggested Mrs. Norval. "Play with him."

"Why should I? I prefer to play with Lola."

Mrs. Norval colored with annoyance and looked towards Emma, who sat by the window reading, then, with a cold glitter in her eyes, at Lola, who stood waiting for Julian to arrange his chessmen.

"Do you think Lola will ever have those spots, any darker? Will they remain so?" said Mrs. Norval.

"Bother the spots! Come, Lola, to the light; let me see those frightful spots" ejaculated Julian.

Lola's face was crimson with shame and resentment, but she did not even look at Mrs. Norval. She went with Julian and stood in the full light of the sun pouring through the window. Mr. Hackwell came in and approached her also.

Oh, Mrs. Norval, if you had known what was to be the consequence of this examination, I am sure you would never have brought it about.

Julian looked at Lola's eyes and lips, and he forgot all about the spots. His gaze became fixed on hers, and a thrill went through his whole frame from the little soft hand he held in his.

And the reverend Hackwell—why did he become so pale? Lola fixed her eyes on him for a few seconds only, and then withdrew her gaze. She was a child, only fifteen years of age. She had no design in her look. But her soul was up in revolt, and was grandly shining in her glorious eyes, making eloquent speeches, which Julian and Hackwell alone seemed to hear or understand. But neither found an answer. Their feelings were too deep for words.

"Well, what makes you both so silent?" exclaimed Mrs. Norval, knitting vigorously. "I guess you see I am right, and that it is a cutaneous disease peculiar to the Indians of her tribe."

Julian swept off the board the chessmen arrayed for battle, tumbling bishops and queens irreverently into their box, saying, "It is stifling here! Come, Lola, let us go and have our game of chess under your favorite maple tree. I wish to run the risk of infection all alone." And he marched off, followed by Lola, to the end of the garden.

Their game had not progressed far when Mrs. Norval, carrying her everlasting knitting, and followed by Emma and her brother, came to sit by, under the same tree. Mr. Hackwell observed, as he sat down, "Julian is right in selecting this spot for *his* game. The breeze is lovely here, Mrs. Norval. Your boy is extremely judicious."

Julian made a wrong move. Lola took his queen.

"Don't lose your head next," sneered Mrs. Norval.

"If it goes with my queen, I am willing," Julian retorted. Lola said, "Checkmate." Mr. Hackwell applauded.

"You must give me my revenge," said Julian, rearranging the men. "I played like a schoolboy, not at all like a soldier."

"Emma, take Lola's place. I have an errand for you, Lola, come with me," said Mrs. Norval, motioning to Lola to go before her.

The doctor had not intended to leave for three weeks yet, but on that day he received letters from Washington which made him change his mind and resolve to go within the next four days. He met his wife as that lady was coming with Lola, thinking what on earth she should do to keep her away from Julian. Even Mrs. Norval could not deny—to herself—that Lola was growing prettier every day. As this fact became more and more palpable, the hatred of the Christian matron increased in proportion. She had always hated and despised the black creature ever since she had appeared before her eyes encircled so tenderly by her husband's arm. But Lola was rich, and for her money's sake the matron had concealed the throbbings of aversion of her mercenary heart. For money Mrs. Norval would do almost anything; but the idea of Julian taking a fancy to Lola, when she wanted him to marry Emma, was now unbearable to her.

"Wait for me in the library," said she to Lola.

"Doctor, come here in the parlor. I must speak to you about this affair of Julian and Emma."

Lola sank into a chair in the hall. She did not do so on purpose to listen, but because her strength failed her when she heard these words of Mrs. Norval.

"There is no use," continued Mrs. Norval, "in denying that Julian is growing more and more fond of Lola and less and less so of Emma, and that won't do, doctor."

"Why? It seems to me you were the first to think that Lola would be a good match, and that, too, when she was dark and young, and when nobody could be sure that she would grow up to be so beautiful."

"You are very provoking, doctor. You know why I said that. We were poor then. But now I suppose you have money invested somewhere, for you are too conscientious"—here she smiled derisively—"too scrupulous, to be spending so freely if the money wasn't yours. That being the case, there is no reason why Julian should not marry one of his own race and religion. I hate foreigners and papists."

"We all know that."

"Yes, you know it, and yet you bring this girl to my house. Sometimes I think the gold wasn't hers, and that you told me that story to make me put up with her." Mr. Hackwell had suggested the idea—Mrs. Norval was not original. Seeing that the doctor did not look in the least disconcerted, she continued: "Julian is to leave tomorrow, and he has not said one word yet to Mr. Hackwell about his engagement with Emma. I think you ought to arrange it, if Julian feels bashful about it."

"*I*!" exclaimed the doctor.

"Yes, you. Why not?"

"Because I don't like the match. The girl is well enough, I suppose, but I don't like Hackwell, and will not help my boy to become his brother-in-law."

Mrs. Norval, for some moments, was too angry to speak, but when she was able to articulate, she said, "But I think it is your duty to insist on your boy's keeping his pledged word. I expect almost anything from you, but I must say I did not think you would countenance your son in violating his word of honor." So saying, the indignant matron went back to the party under the maples.

The doctor came out of the parlor, and, seeing Lola sadly leaning her head on a table, said, kindly, "Lola, I am going tomorrow with Julian as far as New York, and will take the first steamer for Europe. Come to my room. Let us have one last talk alone while I pack up."

Mrs. Norval resumed her seat, her knitting, and her conversation with her revered pastor, and thought Lola safe in the library waiting her orders.

Lola, in the meantime, was busy helping the doctor to pack his trunks and valises. After an hour and a half thus employed, the doctor said, lighting a cigar, "I thank you, my dear. You are certainly very good at packing up. Now I have only to put away a few papers and I am ready. I shall go and tell Julian that I am going with him."

When the doctor joined the party under the trees, it had increased. Mr. and Mrs. Hammerhard and Mrs. Hackwell were there, and all were excitedly discussing what seemed to be a topic of great interest.

Julian and Emma had finished their game. Julian had been sulky and indifferent at first, and allowed her to take his queen, two knights, and a bishop, all with two pawns. Then he savagely turned his men around and checkmated her in three moves.

A letter just received from Mrs. Cackle, from Washington, was the cause of the excitement. Mrs. Cackle had written the day after her arrival at the capital of the great republic. She could not have slept, she said, if she had not written at once.

CHAPTER XXII

"The Awful Little Bell" Described by Mrs. Cackle

Mrs. Cackle's letter was addressed to the wife of her beloved pastor, Mrs. Hackwell, but with the request that the contents should be made known to her beloved friend, Mrs. Norval. "For, though my son would be furious if he knew I divulged State secrets," the old lady said, "still, I cannot keep such an awful thing from Mrs. Norval. My heart tells me that Mrs. Norval ought to know in what danger her husband is, for though the doctor is imprudent, and has so much pity for the rebels, still, I remember he also had pity for the colored people, and always gave them money when they asked him. But all this will not do him any good (my son Beau says), nor his having helped to raise troops for the Union neither. He has written treasonable letters, my son Beau says, and he will be imprisoned if he doesn't leave the country. And my son Tool says that they are after these letters, and will have them. And Beau says that the doctor is a friend of the Habeas Corpuses[24] (I don't know who they are), and I am sorry, for they can't be good, as both my boys hate them. But the worst of all is, that there is a powerful man here in this city—I heard my two sons talking about him—a very powerful man, who, under the Constitution, has the right to ring a bell and send any man to prison. If I understood right, I think he is going to ring his awful little bell and send the Habeas Corpuses all in irons to Fort Lafayette. All the telegraph wires are attached to that little bell, so by

[24]Ruiz de Burton here pokes rich fun at the ignorance of Mrs. Cackle who, understanding nothing, goes on at length on "Habeus Corpuses" who are to be imprisoned and "the awful bell" connected to telegraph wires that is to toll for Dr. Norval and his "friends," the Habeas Corpuses. More seriously, however, the presidential suspension of the Writ of Habeas Corpus at the outbreak of the Civil War (*casus belli*) would lead to a number of arbitrary arrests protested especially by the Peace Democrats.

just touching it with the tip of his finger, and mentioning the name of the person the great man wants to send to prison, all the wires repeat the name, and no matter where the man may have gone to hide himself, he is found, at any hour of the night, and put in irons and carried off to a dark dungeon. I couldn't sleep, thinking they might do so with Dr. Norval, who got my boys into Congress, and lent them money and made us all rich. But he will certainly be taken as soon as the great man of the bell takes a notion to do it. I haven't told poor Lavvy about this awful little bell, for I know she loves the doctor so much. It will go rather hard with Julian, too, I know, and poor Lavvy is so worried about Isaac, who is yet somewhere in prison in the South. But she is as determined as ever to serve her country, and we are going to begin with our hospital work tomorrow." Here the old lady added two pages more about the hospitals and the wounded and concluded by begging Mrs. Hackwell to burn the letter, and never let any of her children know that she wrote it.

"I am really very thankful to Mrs. Cackle," said the doctor, when Mrs. Hackwell had finished reading.

"I don't understand what she means by the *awful little bell* which the great man rings under the Constitution," said Mrs. Norval, "and putting Habeas Corpuses in irons."

"Poor Mrs. Cackle! How innocent she is in her sarcasm!" the doctor said, smiling. "No, it is not easy to understand such things in this country, but we'll get used to it by-and-by. I am all ready to go, so, if the powerful man is to ring his little bell for me, he will have to make haste."

Just then the dinner bell rang, and, laughing at the coincidence, the party broke up. Mr. and Mrs. Hackwell remained to dinner; the Hammerhards declined and went home.

In the twilight, Mrs. Norval sat in her favorite seat at the deep bay window. Julian was walking in the front garden with Lola. Mrs. Norval called him, gave him a seat beside her, and said, "Your father is going away, and you also. I think before you both leave, this matter between you and Emma ought to be settled."

"I don't know what you mean," said Julian.

"You ought to know, Julian, for you have been encouraging Emma for five years, and I think it is time that you were formally engaged and that the engagement was announced."

"Goodness, mother! Since I made love to Emma in verse, and offered her my heart because it rhymed beautifully with '*dart*' and '*my hand*' because it rhymed with '*fairy land*,' and which offer Emma had the good sense to decline in very matter-of-fact prose, I have never spoken a word to her about marriage."

"Emma did not refuse you; she only allowed you to postpone your becoming engaged until you should be twenty-one. You are of that age now, and as a man of honor you should of course renew your offer. They expect it—"

"Who are '*they*'?"

"Emma and her brother, of course."

"I thought so. It can't be that Emma wants to catch a man and hold him for life with the flimsy meshes woven out of a boy's folly. I hope she is too kindhearted and too much of a lady to do that. No, mother, I do not love Emma. My boyish fancy for her has long since passed away. I can't marry her."

"Your fancy has only passed from her to another, I fear. But honor is as binding to an honorable man as the marriage vows. To my way of thinking, you are pledged to Emma, and cannot break off from that pledge honorably."

"Julian, come out here a moment. I want to speak to you," said the doctor's voice from outside. Julian arose to go, but his mother caught him by the arm, saying, "You must not go without settling this matter in one way or another. I have promised that you would, and *I* at least know how to keep my word."

"Very well, mother, keep your word, and settle the matter by saying that I have considered it settled since I was sixteen-years old, and that I do not wish to revive it."

"This is outrageous! Emma can sue you for breach of promise; I shall be her principal witness."

"Very well; let her try it. But I don't think she will. The parson is too good a lawyer to try that."

Mrs. Norval saw that threats were of no avail. She changed her tactics. She began, "Oh, Julian! you would not break that girl's heart with disappointment and shame. At least let matters be as they are, and let her refuse you if she will."

"But it appears she won't," said he, laughing.

"She has too much self-respect, of course, to wish to force herself on you when she sees that you have changed. Let this year pass, and if your engagement is not renewed now, when you are twenty-one, she will then, of course, see that—that—you don't wish it to be renewed, and she will consider herself free to marry anyone else."

"Well, as for that, I have no objection. Let she and I part good friends, and that is all I ask."

"I'll tell her so. But don't hurt her feelings."

"I hope not. I don't want to offend the girl. She has always been most kind to me."

"Well, well, you may go now."

And Julian, glad to get away so cheaply, was off with a bound.

CHAPTER XXIII

"It May Be for Years, and It May Be Forever"

"I called you to me," said the doctor, when Julian joined him, "because I overheard one or two words which make me think that your mother is after you, as she was after me this morning, about your marrying Emma Hackwell. Now, I want you to understand that you can marry that girl if you wish, but I cannot give a willing consent."

"Shake hands on that," said Julian, laughing.

The doctor gave his hand, and continued, "I am very glad you don't want to marry her, but I am afraid that they'll make you."

"*Make* me!" exclaimed Julian, arching his brows in disdainful surprise.

"Yes, for Hackwell has set his heart on that match, and he is as cunning and unprincipled as—as the devil! You look out for him. He has more influence over your mother than any one else—least of all myself—and they'll circumvent you somehow, if you are not on the lookout."

"But how? What can they do?"

"I don't know, but, to prevent mischief as much as I can, I wish you to promise me, solemnly—to swear it—that you will not marry Emma until I return. If they drive you to the wall, you can say that you will not marry before my return, and without my consent, because you took an oath that you would not do it. Then, if Emma chooses to wait until I come, she may. You will, of course, leave her at liberty to marry anyone else if she pleases."

"Certainly. And I take the oath," said Julian, raising his hand and slowly saying, "I solemnly swear not to marry Emma Hackwell before my father returns, and never without his consent! I shall keep my *oath*, father."

Mrs. Norval could not hear the words, but she saw Julian's gestures. She feared the doctor was making him promise to marry Lola. A great fear seized her. She opened the window and called out, "James, Julian—tea is ready."

Lola did not make her appearance at the tea table. The doctor inquired for her, and sent a servant to call her. She was not in her room. She was not in the house. She did not come.

Mrs. Norval and Emma did all the talking during tea. The doctor and Julian scarcely spoke. And no sooner were they from the table than Julian went out to look for Lola.

"Don't stay long, if you are going out," said Mrs. Norval. "Several people will be here this evening to bid you good-by."

"I am not going far. I shall be back in a short time." And, so saying, he directed his steps towards the maple trees, the favorite spot where Lola was sure to be found. Julian walked upon the turf, avoiding the graveled walks, so that Lola should not hear his approach.

She, sitting on the turf, her head leaning on the bench, was sobbing convulsively, all alone.

"Why are you weeping so bitterly?" said Julian, sitting by her and leaning his elbow on the bench where she reclined her head. She looked up, frightened, but seeing Julian alone, and not the dreaded Mrs. Norval, she answered, "Because you and your father are going away, and I shall be left all alone. And—and—because—because—"

"Because why?"

"Because—Oh, I can't tell you!"

"Yes, you must, else I shall think you don't care for me and have no confidence in me."

"Don't say that, please. I'll tell you. I heard Mrs. Norval talking with Emma and Mr. Hackwell, and they said you are to marry Emma."

"And do you wish me to marry her?"

"Oh, *no*!" said Lola, emphatically. Then, thinking she had betrayed herself, added, "Unless you would be unhappy without her."

"I wouldn't be unhappy without *her*, but I shall certainly be very wretched without *you*."

"Oh, Julian, don't make fun of me! I am a child yet in years, I know, but I have felt so much in my lonely life that I have learned to think more seriously than you suppose."

"I am not making fun of you, Lola. Don't think so meanly of me. Listen to me. I don't want you to promise to marry me, because you are young, and you will, in all probability, meet someone whom you will like better. But if in two years you don't like anyone better, will you then promise to be my wife?"

"Your mother says you are engaged to Emma," said Lola, in a scarcely audible voice, so agitated was she.

"I know she says so, but it is not the truth. She has a fancy for Emma, that's all."

"But you did love her."

"Yes, when I was but a child. She was the only girl I knew, and I fancied I loved her, and wrote verses to her. But let me tell you, I never felt for her as I do for you. And, child though you are, you have more power over me than any woman I have ever met. I know I shall love you with all my soul, all my life, and—and, Lola, I thought you might care for me a little. Can't you? Tell me you'll try. I may never come back, you know. You might give me the pleasure of thinking you love me, and, if I am killed, I will have that comfort before I die."

Lola could not resist this last argument. She told him, in her impetuous, passionate language, how she had loved him all the time, even when she saw he was in love with Emma, and how she had cried in the misery of her heart because she thought he despised her. She said, "I saw that your mother detested me, and Ruth had a sort of repugnance for me, and Miss Lavvy and Mattie, though they didn't dislike me, never took any interest in me. No one but your father was kind to me. I could bear all this, but I could not bear to think that to you, too, I was an object of aversion because my skin was black. And yet I was too proud to tell you that the blackness of my skin would wear off, that it was only stained by the Indians to prevent our being rescued. My mother also was made to stain her lovely white skin all black. Once, when the dye had worn off our faces, we were followed by some soldiers who were encamping near our village. From that time, the Indians never permitted the dye to wear off our faces. As soon as it became a little lighter, they immediately made us paint ourselves over again. I wanted to tell you this many times, for, though I didn't care whether I was thought black or white by others, I hated to think that you *might* suppose I was Indian or black. But I did not say anything to you, because I thought you might laugh at me, and not believe me."

"And you were wrong, because my father already told me that you are of pure Spanish descent."

"But I often heard your mother say things by which I could plainly see she did not believe I was white. And when the dye began to wear off, and my skin got all spotted, she sent me away, because she thought I had some cutaneous disease, and she said that Mr. Hackwell said that perhaps I belonged to the 'Pintos,' and my skin was naturally spotted."

"You must forget all that. I always believed what my father said about you."

The conversation would probably have continued much longer—for Julian had forgotten the visitors announced by his mother—but that the doctor now came to look for them, and was guided by the sound of their voices to where they were.

"Lola, does not your school commence very soon?" said he, sitting on the bench.

"Yes, sir, in about four days, on the first Monday in September. I am all ready to go. Mrs. Norval says I had better go the day after you leave."

"And why so? If you are ready, let us start together. We'll take you to the convent, so that I may present Julian to the Mother Superior, and tell her that during my absence he is to take care of you. Then they will let him see you whenever he can find time to make you a visit."

It is needless to say how glad the two young people were to hear this. Lola could not repress the impulse to throw her arms around the doctor's neck again, saying he was "the kindest and dearest guardian that ever was or could be"—a performance and speech which Julian witnessed and heard well-pleased, but at the same time thinking he would like to be in his father's place.

Mrs. Norval's frowns and sneers and protestations availed naught. Lola rode off next morning between the doctor and Julian to the depot, carrying Jule in triumph.

"The deceitful, treacherous vixen! To think that she packed her trunk and got herself ready without my knowing it," said Mrs. Norval to the silent Emma, who had not failed to see Julian's radiant smile and the glow of his eyes when he handed Lola to the carriage.

Mrs. Norval's chagrin was so great that she had not one kind word to say to her husband, whom she might never see again, and to her son she coldly expressed a wish that he "might not be shot." She was indignant with both. They had plotted against her, and that she could not forgive.

Meantime, Lola and her escort arrived at the convent, where she was received most kindly. The doctor presented Julian to the Superior, and begged that Lola should be permitted to see him whenever he called. As Lola was the doctor's ward, during his absence his son could, of course, take his place with propriety.

The parting was painful, but Lola felt that she would see Julian and hear from him occasionally. The doctor promised to write also.

Next day the doctor was on the steamer on his way to Europe, and Julian was sadly riding towards the place where his company was picketed.

On the window ledge of Lola's room sang Jule the widower. But Lola did not listen, for she was thinking of his namesake.

CHAPTER XXIV

Lavinia's Experiences in Washington

Miss Lavinia and the Cackles were now experienced nurses. They had acquitted themselves with great credit for more than a year in the care of the sick and wounded. Misses Lucretia and Artemisia Cackle, assisted by their mamma, had charge of the largest ward in the largest hospital; Miss Lavinia had the next, and all did their duty—as only ladies brought up as Puritans know how—to the full measure; the gloomier the duty the better accomplished.

The winter of 1862 had come, and no tidings yet of Isaac. Lavinia wrote to her sister for instructions. Mrs. Norval answered that she thought the best thing that could be done would be for Lavvy to go in person to see the delegation from their State, and try to interest some of their political friends. She herself would have gone to Washington to help Lavvy but for the fact that, as the doctor had behaved so imprudently and absurdly, she did not think she would be well received by "the powers that be." Moreover, dear Mrs. Hackwell had just lost a child, was very ill, and she and Emma were taking care of her, as Mr. Hackwell had accepted the appointment of commissary in General Julius Cackle's staff, and was now on the Potomac.

This was news indeed. And the heart of Lavvy, if it did not gallop, trotted a little, I am sure, as if its impulse was to run towards the Potomac. Then it stopped its trot. It stood still, as Lavvy thought how cruel it was in Hack—*the divine*!—to pass through Washington and not see her! But Lavvy—as I said—was a girl who had been brought up to look rigidly at her duty, and rigidly to execute it, no matter if it went on like the Juggernaut car,[25] crushing all her feelings.

[25]The "Juggernaut car" is invoked here to refer to an overpowering and destructive force which requires blind devotion and cruel sacrifice, crushing all

Moreover, Lavvy wanted nothing better than plenty of employment for her exuberant moral energies and redundant force of will. The prospect of a tussle with a cabinet member or two, and plenty of skirmishes with delegations, did not terrify the strong soul of Lavvy.

She, moreover, felt *au fait* in all matters pertaining to high society. She had been to all sorts of receptions and parties, Presidential, diplomatic, senatorial, etc. She dressed well. Mrs. Norval stinted no one now, for she thought that if the money they were spending was Lola's, there was no need for her to economize. On the contrary, the more money they put to use, the more would be left in their hands when Lola was twenty-one.

Therefore, even poor Lavvy had *carte-blanche* now with New York milliners, and jewelers, and shoemakers, and no end of pin-money.

When Lavvy received her sister's letter of instructions, with true feminine instinct she prepared herself, as every lady should do, by making the most of her looks.

Before she sallied forth in all the glory of a careful and expensive toilet, Lavvy dutifully paid her morning visits to her sick and wounded.

She cheered the desponding, encouraged the faint-hearted, scolded the refractory, punished the disobedient, and provided for the comfort of all.

It was Lavvy's pride to hear the doctor in charge of her ward say that her sick and wounded were the best attended of all his patients. And so they were, for, as Lavinia had been properly brought up, she loved her patients. They were the impersonation of *duty*; she was, therefore, bound to love them. The more groans and sighs and lamentations she heard, the more cheerful she became in the sublime sense of *duty*. And when the amputating knife had to be used unsparingly, then Lavvy was a perfect Mark Tapley,[26] and was "*jolly*" in the midst of surrounding misery. I do not mean that the good-hearted Lavvy could rejoice in the sufferings of others, but she rejoiced in the thought that she could alleviate them.

Now, when her duties as hospital matron were over for the morning, she ordered her carriage to the door, and, stepping into it, said to the driver, "To the War Department."

in its path. The reference is to the Indian festival for the deity Jagannatha ("Lord of the World") whose massive car often trod over the pilgrims accompanying the procession. Lavinia Sprig feels her heart thus crushed.

[26]Mark Tapley, probably a well-known actor of the time, a master of dissemblance.

On arriving there, Lavinia went up to ask for the Secretary of War.[27] She was shown by an usher into a room, where a very young man (an officer of the army, to judge by his brass buttons) was writing before a desk.

As army officers used to be proverbially gallant and polite to ladies, Lavvy thought the very young man would rise and offer her a chair. But the officer was a captain, and a brevet colonel, though so *very young*, and, moreover, was "all right with the Secretary," and, therefore, what need had he of being polite to anybody? It is so refreshing to snub someone for the cringing we may have to do, and thus feel we are quits with mankind!

When Lavvy had been standing for some time, seeing that the very young man did not offer her a chair, she noiselessly took one, and sat there to wait for the young man to see her. After a long while, he suddenly looked up and startled Lavvy by saying, "Your name?"

"Miss Lavinia Sprig," said she, and her name had never sounded to her ears so insignificant, so unaristocratic as at that moment when uttered in the now historical palace, before so haughty a personage, so resplendent in brass buttons.

Evidently to the very young officer, her name did not sound any more impressive than it did to Lavvy herself, for he said, with a slight curl of the lip, "Unless you have important business with the Secretary, I cannot send in your name. Do you know him personally? Or have you any introductory letters?"

Lavinia replied that she did not have that honor, but that she wished to see the Secretary about exchanging her brother, Isaac Sprig, who had been captured at Bull Run over a year ago, and that she was the sister-in-law of Dr. Norval.

On hearing this name, the officer, who had continued to write while Lavvy was speaking, looked up and asked, "Which Dr. Norval is that? the Democrat, who has been writing letters against the government?"

"No, sir. He never could have written against the government, for he always has loved his country with all his honest heart," said Lavvy, in great agitation. "I am sure no man has done more to defend the Union. He gave the money to raise three companies, and left more for his son to raise a whole regiment. And his son, Julian Norval, is now

[27]The Secretary of War under Lincoln was Edwin M. Stanton, appointed in January 1862, to succeed Simon Cameron after the latter resigned under fire. Stanton, whose wielding of power during the Civil War and afterward provoked criticism, is the object of much censure in the novel.

lieutenant colonel of the regiment he raised with the money his father gave. If the doctor was against the government, he would not be helping to raise troops."

"That may all be," interrupted the young man with hauteur, "but, nevertheless, he has spoken and written disloyal sentiments. However, you wait here. I'll ascertain if the Secretary will see you."

When the very young man had been gone about a quarter of an hour, he returned and said, "The Secretary will see you presently," and recommenced his writing.

Lavinia was becoming very tired, and was reflecting that no matter how much a woman, in her unostentatious sphere, may do, and help to do, and no matter how her heart may feel for her beloved, *worshipped* country, after all she is but an insignificant creature, whom a very young man may snub, simply because he wears very shiny brass buttons and his uncle is in Congress. "What a miserable, powerless thing woman is, even in this our country of glorious equality! Here I have been sitting up at night, toiling, and tending disgusting sickness, and dressing loathsome wounds, all for the love of our dear country, and now, the first time I come to ask a favor—*a favor*, do I say? No. I come to demand a right—see how I am received!"

Poor Lavvy! She had no experience about asking favors of great men. She had believed all she had read in printed political speeches delivered just before election times.

Her gloomy reflections were interrupted by the laughter of several gentlemen who came out of the Secretary's room. They nodded familiarly to the blond young man (who answered their salutations with smiles and profound bows) and went out.

Lavinia wondered who these gentlemen were. The young man, anxious that Lavvy, though insignificant, might know that he was on excellent terms with the great, seemed to guess her thoughts, for he said, "These gentlemen are the greatest men of the age. All historical, every one of them."

"Ah?" said Lavvy.

"The Secretary says the lady may come in," said an usher. And Lavvy, more dead than alive, followed him into the presence of the dreaded power.

What passed between the Secretary and Lavvy no one shall ever know, for neither of them ever told it. All that is known of that episode is what the driver was able to tell. And that was not much, for he only saw Lavvy come out crying convulsively, and that is a common occurrence with the sex, and he heard her talking to herself, and that is a common occurrence with old maids, and Lavvy was past thirty-two!

The driver said he waited for some time before Miss Lavvy was able to say, between her sobs, "Drive to the Cap-cap-pi-pi-to-l!"

And to the Capitol he drove.

CHAPTER XXV

At the Capitol—Mr. Cackle at Home

With a very heavy heart Lavvy ascended the broad marble steps leading to the rotunda. She felt more sick at heart than any of the patients at her hospital, and the wounds in her spirit were deeper and bled more profusely than any of those she had bandaged so tenderly. But there was no hand to assuage her suffering. She felt very faint and lonely.

But if the flesh was weak, the spirit was yet undaunted, for Lavvy was doing this for love's sake, for her dear brother Isaac, and, until the last resource had been tried in vain, she would not relinquish her efforts. She never in her life had spoken to a senator or a member of Congress, except the Cackles and these two were so different from what they used to be at home that she did not know what the others might be like, if all had changed the same. But she was determined to see the New England senators and members of the lower House, changed or not.

As she was so intimidated by her experience at the War Office, she did not dare to face a senator. She would commence at the House. Yes, her sister had suggested her seeing Mr. Ned White, who had been a workman at the Sprig farm many years ago, and had been kindly treated by old Mr. Sprig. Of course Ned White would remember that, and be kind to Isaac, now that he was in power; of course he would, and help Isaac out of prison. Dear Isaac! Lavvy forgot how Isaac had shocked them with his fondness for foreigners and the theatre. She only thought of his being now in prison—in want, perhaps, sick, starving, without money or friends. "Why was he not exchanged? Can it be possible that he has been forgotten? I can't believe it," said Lavvy, talking to herself. "It can't be! Our government wouldn't forget him. It seems so, but it can't be so." And her temples throbbed with these thoughts as they careered through her little head.

In this frame of mind she entered the rotunda. She cast a searching glance all around to see if any acquaintance was there. Yes, she saw a friend—none other than old Mr. Cackle, now the happy father of four distinguished men.

Old Mr. Cackle was a very great man at the rotunda. He felt at home there, as if it had been erected for him especially, dome and all; its proportions suited his own magnificence and importance. Nay, there were moments when, thinking of the greatness of his four sons, Mr. Cackle felt equal to clapping that dome on his head and wearing it for a smoking cap. The addition of the goddess of liberty as a topknot, or hanging by the heels as a tassel would have been accepted kindly by the grandissimo Cackle, feeling that as a patriotic American he ought to do so. He was now, moreover, a good judge of paintings. Lavinia found him before the painting representing "the embarking of the Pilgrims," discoursing upon the merits of it to a large number of admirers, who listened to his words in silent respect.

After a while Lavinia made her way up to him, and was able to speak to him and ask if he wouldn't go with her to the House to see Mr. White.

"Bless my soul and body, my child!" said Mr. Cackle, giving his arm to Lavvy, for he now had learned manners, and could be as polite as you please. "*Of course* you shall see Mr. White! I'll fetch him to you, *of course*!" and Mr. Cackle strutted on as if he was "the boss" there, *of course*. Was he not the father of his sons? Was not Beau a leader, and had not Julius just been made major general for his Balaklava charge?[28]

As they were walking towards the House of Representatives, Mr. Cackle inquired, "But why do you wish to see Mr. White? If you want anything, why don't you ask my sons? I am sure White can't have the influence which they command."

"I have seen your sons (though not lately, for I noticed they wished to avoid me), but to no purpose. They only gave me evasive answers and very ambiguous promises. In the meantime my poor brother remains in prison, forgotten by his friends."

"Humph! ahem! It is about—about poor Isaac, is it? Ah, really! Well, we'll see Mr. White, to be sure. About Isaac! I had forgotten." And Mr. Cackle looked around him as if searching to escape.

[28]See note 20 on the British charge at Balaklava.

"Of course it is about Isaac. And though *I* can't expect to influence your sons, *you* may, and then they could perhaps help their old friend out of a horrid prison. I do wish you would speak to Beau again about dear Isaac. Will you do it, my dear Mr. Cackle?"

"Yes, yes, *of course*!" answered Mr. Cackle, again looking around searchingly.

"For whom are you looking?" asked Lavvy.

"Mr. White, to be sure. Yes, I will speak to my sons about Isaac. But mind. Be careful. I tell you this as a friend. Isaac behaved outrageously towards a very influential gentleman, and that can't bring him any good. The doctor, too, has been most imprudent in his expressions. What if his party has lost the game? They had to expect it, and they shouldn't grumble."

"You used to be of the same party," said Lavvy. Mr. Cackle gave a start, and looked around more uneasily than ever. "And as for the dear doctor, what has he done or said? I can take my solemn oath on his loyalty, whatever they may think at the War Office."

"What—what—what did you say? Did you hear any report of his disloyalty at the War Office?" asked Mr. Cackle, with increasing terrors.

"Yes, but it isn't the truth. Someone has been slandering him."

Mr. Cackle now was so overpowered by fear that, entirely forgetting his lately-acquired gallantry, he dropped his arm, and then shook off that of Lavvy resting on it and retreated a few steps, as if in involuntary dread of contagion. He thought of his son Beau's maxim of flying from unlucky people as if they were lepers, and the Norvals were not exactly in luck then. Somewhat ashamed of his cowardice however, he said to the astonished Lavvy, who regarded him with wondering eyes, "Here we are at the House. I shall take you to the Speaker's room, where *I* have the free *antray* (entrée). I will go and fetch Mr. White to you. I suppose he will do what he can for you, considering that he is under great obligations to your family. The doctor, I believe, advanced the money to pay for his tuition for three years. White must not forget that. I'll remind him of it."

"Do nothing of the kind, I beg of you. If I thought you would do such a thing, I would not let you send for him. Stay; I will send my card myself."

"Well, well, don't make such a rumpus. I'll say nothing to him, but only send your card." And, muttering to himself, "Women are so foolish! They never know how to make a good use of their capital, either in money or influence. Bah! and they want to vote! Ridiculous!" the old man went off to *order* White to come out.

CHAPTER XXVI

"Must Isaac Be Left to Starve?"

Mr. White came immediately on receiving Lavvy's card. When she saw him coming, she pulled her veil well over her face, for she knew only too well that her prominent nose—always of a roseate hue, like a high mountain reflecting the glow of a summer sunset—became almost purple when she cried. Poor Lavvy's nose had given her a deal of trouble.

Mr. White saluted her very kindly, saying he was glad to see one of her family again. "Your family, Miss Sprig, was kinder to me than my own," said he.

Lavvy said she was glad he had not forgotten his old friends, as other members of Congress of her acquaintance had done.

Mr. White laughed, understanding Lavvy's allusion, and said, most frankly, "Yes, I know they have, and I told Beau so yesterday very plainly. But I am not that sort of man, Miss Lavvy. All Congress isn't composed of *Cackles*. I shall never forget how kind your father and brothers were to me, a poor boy, so friendless. I shall never forget, either, that to the doctor I owe my education, and that he generously insisted on my going to school at his expense. He saw me studying my lessons after working hours, and he said to me, 'Do you like to study, Ned?' I told him I did, and he took my book to look at it, and said, 'Who teaches you?' I told him I taught myself. 'I'll tell you what I'll do,' said he. 'I'll let you have the funds to go to college, and when you come out, you'll pay me.' My heart gave a leap with pleasure, for I had always longed to go to college. But I told him I might die or get sick, and not be able to pay him back his money. 'Pooh, pooh, man!' said he. 'If you lose your health or your life, you lose more than I! You are an honest lad, and though I'm not a church-going man, I think it is *the duty* of honest men to help honest men. Rogues always help each other;

honest people should not let rogues be their superiors in anything but roguery, certainly not in loyalty to one's own order.' And he talked to me so kindly, and urged me so warmly to accept his offer, that I did. And I know I studied with greater assiduity because I was sure it would please him if I graduated high. So, Miss Lavinia, to your family I always shall feel that I owe everything. But I am talking about myself, and I have not asked what I can do to serve you. I'll do anything I can for you, with the greatest pleasure."

Lavinia's courage gradually returned. She began to think with Ned White that all congressmen were not Cackles, and, in her religiously-inclined mind, she thanked God that they were not.

She related to Mr. White the story of Isaac's captivity, and the seeming impossibility of exchanging him. Mr. White listened very attentively. When Lavvy had ended her narrative, he said, "I did not know that Isaac was still in prison. How strange that none of the Cackles ever mentioned it to me! I must study what to do. In the meantime, suppose we go over to the Senate and ask Senator F. to give you a letter for the Secretary of ———"

"No, no," said Lavinia, interrupting him. "I don't want to go to any department. I am afraid of Secretaries."

"But why should you be? They are no better than anyone else."

"I know that, but still I would rather not go."

"Not with a letter from the Senator?"

Lavinia reflected, and then slowly replied, "Well, perhaps a letter from a Senator might be a sort of protection. Who is that gentleman looking in?" Mr. White looked up, and a gentleman at the door made a sign that he wished to speak to him. He went, and they conversed at the door for a while. They both came in, and Mr. White said, "Mr. Blower, Miss Sprig," and Lavvy and the newly-arrived gentleman bowed.

Mr. White added, "Mr. Blower says that he knows Mr. Le Grand Gunn, who is now Second Assistant Secretary of ——— and who had something to do with the exchange of prisoners. Mr. Gunn is now here at the Capitol, and if you wish, we can go and see him, or Mr. Blower will go to see what information Mr. Gunn can give us, whilst you and I go to the Senate to see Senator F."

Lavinia said she liked this last proposition very well, as Mr. Blower could obtain from Mr. Gunn the information required better than she could. They agreed then that Mr. Blower, after his interview with Mr. Gunn, should go to the Senate reception room to report what he had learned. Lavinia and Mr. White went to the other wing of the Capitol.

Senator F. was in the chair, presiding, when Lavvy's card was handed to him by a page, and he immediately asked another senator to take his place, whilst he went to see Miss Sprig.

This was salve to Lavvy's wounded spirit. Indeed it was more—it was a delicious draught of nectar to her fainting, famished soul, so unused to kindness, yet so sensible to it.

The senator was very kind to her, and sat down at once to write the letter to the Secretary of ———, requesting him to use his influence with the Secretary of War and the President on behalf of Isaac. When he had finished the letter, the Senator said to Lavvy, "I shall see the President myself, but not for three days, for I shall be away from Washington from this evening until the evening of day after tomorrow. If it was not for this, I would go with you to see the President. However, I think the Secretary will do as well as I would. Go early tomorrow morning. Go to his private residence, before he goes to his office and is surrounded by a crowd."

Lavinia thanked the senator warmly and sincerely, promising to obey his instructions. The venerable gentleman then kindly bade her good morning, asking her to report to him what success she had, and returned to his chair.

In a few minutes Mr. Blower returned.

"White, they are looking for you at the House. Beau Cackle is foaming at the mouth because he says you promised to vote for his bill, and you ain't there," Mr. Blower said.

"Beau Cackle doesn't foam so easily," replied Mr. White. "But I'll go, Miss Sprig, if you will excuse me for a quarter of an hour. Then I'll come back, to be at your service for the rest of the afternoon."

"For the rest of your life—I thought you were going to say," observed Mr. Blower, laughing, and making the other two blush. "I'll take care of Miss Sprig, and will tell her what Gunn said to me about the exchanging of prisoners."

When Mr. White had left them, Mr. Blower drew his chair nearer to Lavvy's, and began his report thus:

"After my talk with Gunn, my opinion is that you had better make no effort to have your brother exchanged, but leave the matter entirely in the hands of the government. The government knows better when to exchange, and when not to. And there are times when it is best not to. I cannot tell you more at present, for, as yet, this policy I have just hinted at is not fully put into practice. But it will be, for *the master mind* which originated it is *the power* of the day. Do you understand?"

Lavinia looked at him in silent amazement. Mr. Blower continued, condescendingly, "I see you don't grasp the idea. Of course, ladies can't well grasp great ideas, or understand the reasons that impel men in power to act at times in a manner apparently contrary to humanity, to mercy, to justice. But in reality it isn't so. Now, let me put it clearly before you. If by not exchanging *all* our prisoners we manage to distress the rebels, who soon will be at the point of starvation, don't you think, now, don't *you think* we do right in not exchanging? For, you see, the more mouths they have to feed, the sooner they will consume what they have to eat, and then we will conquer them by famine as well as by the sword. You, the ladies, will say this policy is inhuman. But I say it is not, if it has the effect of ending the war sooner. Moreover, why should killing people with cannons be considered more expedient and less cruel than killing them with starvation and sickness? In this last-named manner we have a double advantage, for, whist leaving our people to eat up the provisions of the enemy, we keep away from their ranks those who, as prisoners in the North, have become able-bodied men, ten times better able to fight than the day we captured them half-starved. So you see how, like a patriotic girl as you are, you should resign yourself to the misfortune that made your brother one of the noble victims selected by Providence to be the means of subjugating the wicked traitors, and thus putting down a rebellion *never equaled for its magnitude and want of cause*. Reflect on this, and you will better appreciate the wisdom which originates this economic policy."

"I can understand that perhaps a general, when about to fight a great battle, might stop, *temporarily*, the exchange of prisoners, so as to keep them from the enemy's ranks. But the policy of making it a rule, as you suggest, to leave our brave soldiers there because they help to consume the resources of the South—that I can't understand."

"You, of course, reason as a lady. Don't you see that if it is well to stop the exchange once, it may be done as often or as long as it is expedient?"

Lavvy shook her head incredulously.

CHAPTER XXVII

No, Isaac Shall Not Be Left to Starve

What a debasing thing is war, when it suggests to man such horrible, ghastly ideas, and his fellow man applauds him for them, and instead of calling him an inhuman monster calls him a "*great man*"! So reasoned Lavvy, like a true woman, losing sight entirely of the main point of Mr. Blower's argument.

Her heart sank again, lower than when she had left the War Department. She could not, to save her life, see the magnanimity of the policy thus beautifully developed before her eyes. She had seen too many wounded and sick men not to be of the opinion that a quick death on the battlefield was by far less cruel. So, forgetting that her nose became purple when she cried, she gave way to a flood of tears.

"And must my poor brother, then, starve?" said she, with no other clear thought in her distracted mind. The Hon. Mr. Blower thought he must try to soothe her feelings in a gallant manner, so he respectfully kissed her hand, saying, in bland tones, "You are a good girl, and an honor to your country. If you understood this policy, I am sure you would approve it. But it is not to be expected that *ladies* would exactly appreciate those ideas, they being beyond their sphere of thought."

Lavvy humbly admitted that they were. She was very sorry for it, but she really could not see the humanity and wisdom of the course Mr. Blower pointed out. She never could see how it was that after men had been trying for so many years to govern the world, they had not yet been wise enough to settle their difficulties without killing and mutilating each other. Still, as this was the fact, and she could not help it, she tried all she could to make the evil less inhuman by taking care of the wounds which men, in their foolishness, inflicted on each other; and like a good American girl, she ended by saying, innocently, "And do THE PEOPLE of the United States—I mean *the loyal people*—do they approve of their brothers being left to starve in the South?" And her large, mild blue eyes looked at Mr. Blower straight in the face, and her red nose, shining with a pink light, pointed direct at him, as if daring him to prevaricate.

"Ahem! Ours is a popular—ahem!—government, my dear lady, but our leading men do not lay before the people *all* new great measures, some of which the unthinking multitude could not grasp at once; not until time and trial have shown their wisdom. If such practice had not been adopted from the time of Washington, who would be our leaders? This measure, however, will not be altogether unknown, and we hope it will be sanctioned by the nation."

"Then all I have to say is, that I did not know the American people, and that they don't care for their brothers," said Lavvy, relapsing into another paroxysm of sobs.

"They do indeed, but they are ready to make sacrifices to vindicate the principles upon which is founded *the best government on earth*."

"Let them go there themselves, then. They would not be so heroic if they were starving in a horrid prison on the other side," sobbed Lavvy.

"Possibly not, for the human heart is weak."

"I had the strength to kill my—my—my—dar—dar—darling can—can—canary birds, but I can't let my own brother starve," sobbed Lavvy convulsively.

Mr. Blower began to wish that Mr. White would return. And, fortunately, at that moment Mr. White was seen coming towards them.

He was surprised to find Lavvy in tears, whom he had left so cheerful. He frowned, and looked darkly at Mr. Blower for information. Mr. Blower felt uneasy, and rose to make his departure.

"I can go with Miss Sprig, if she desires it, to see the President about trying to exchange her brother, or I can get Gunn to see the Secretary of War to—"

"No, no, no!" interrupted Lavvy hurriedly. "I thank you. If they intend to do what you say, I suppose I must lose all ho—ho—hope," sobbed Lavvy, covering her face.

"What under the stars have you been telling her?" asked Mr. White, giving Mr. Blower another black look.

Lavvy, always anxious to avoid being the cause of unpleasant feeling, hastened to say, "Mr. Blower has been most kind, indeed he has, and I am very grateful to him. I thank you, Mr. Blower, believe me. Though what you said is naturally very terrible to me, I do thank you. And now, Mr. White, I'll go home. I don't see that anything can be done for my brother."

"Are we not to deliver to Mr. ——— the senator's letter?" asked Mr. White.

"No. The senator says to take it in the morning. In a day or two, when I feel less nervous, I'll try to take the letter myself. Now all I can do is to go home and lie down, after I take a look at my poor sick people."

When Lavinia arose, Mr. Blower, offering her his services "in any way, shape, or manner," took his leave, glad to get away from White's look.

"What did he say to you? It must have been very painful, to distress you so much. I am sorry I brought him to you," said Mr. White.

"Don't feel so. It is well to know the worst." And Lavvy, taking Mr. White's arm to go downstairs, related to him what Mr. Blower had said to her.

"Don't you believe a word of it," said Mr. White. "There are not two men in Congress who would vote for any such barbarous policy. The Americans are not Hindoos. We can make up our minds to fearful sacrifices, but when it comes to killing our brave boys with slow torture, then the American heart and mind revolt. If anyone says that such a thing would meet the approval of Congress, all I have to say is, that he slanders Congress. Good God! Do people reflect on what they say when they speak of such a soul-sickening holocaust? No, Miss Lavvy, don't believe in such horrors. I should lose faith in our cause if I did."

Mr. White succeeded in giving some consolation to the docile heart of Lavvy, and when he had helped her to her carriage, she—although her eyes and nose were still objectionably red—smiled on him, as she warmly thanked him for his kindness. Then she directed the driver to stop at the post office to inquire for letters, and afterwards drive home, as it was too late to go again to the hospital.

There were two letters for Lavvy, but, as they were in Emma Hackwell's handwriting, she put them in her pocket to read them when she felt better. Now her head ached and her heart felt bruised and sore. She longed for rest. From the carriage she went straight upstairs to her bedroom to go to bed.

Lavinia's prayers were always extemporaneous and multifarious, shaped by passing incidents—for Lavvy had the faith in prayer of a strict Roman Catholic. From this night, however, Lavvy's orisons became less varied. Her nightly prayer, with but slight differences, ran in these words:

"O Lord, be merciful unto *the American people*. Pour down thy blessings upon the House of Representatives and the Senate." (In Lavvy's prayers the order was reversed, and the House took precedence over the Senate.) "Bless them because they were kind *to me*, and because they will not let our people starve in awful prisons. Bless them, and keep them always in thy path and in thy light, that they may govern this thy people righteously. Bless the President, and enlighten him, that he may make a proper selection of men for *his Cabinet*, so that he may not be exposed to wicked influences.

"Forgive *the Cabinet*, O Lord, and show them the ways of thy mercy, that their hearts may not be so pitiless to the sorrowful and afflicted. Have mercy on all *the American people*, and most particularly do I beseech Thee for ———." Here Lavvy mentioned the names of the members of her family, and ended her prayer.

CHAPTER XXVIII

Mr. Hackwell and the Madam Console Each Other

The great novelist Thackeray[29] accuses his countrymen of "*a most groveling worship of success*." The free-born American resembles his proud progenitors in this so well that he is ready to do homage on his bended knees. The Eastern worshiper saying to his idol, "Crush me if thou wilt, to worship thee is my delight, my pride,"[30] is not more subservient than the "equal of kings," the *free-born* American, before *the successful man*, before the millionaire, before the railroad king—the great monopolists. During the war, the prominent politicians and fortunate generals took precedence for a short time over the moneyed men.

Thus it came to pass that the Cackles awoke one morning to find themselves famous. All New England was at their feet, proud to be there. All those who had slighted and ridiculed them the most were the loudest in their praises.

But if their old favorite Isaac had now appeared in those regions, he, the lame chicken of the henyard, would have been pecked to death by all the vicious fowls.

As for Dr. Norval, it was well he had taken the wise precaution of exiling himself, for his very name was little less than execrated. They even believed that he had no more money; that he had spent all except what was settled on Mrs. Norval. And as no one but Mr. William Sin-

[29]British novelist William Makepeace Thackeray's (1811-1863) words on his own countrymen are invoked here to draw out the assertion that "free-born Americans," too, are all like their British counterparts in their slavish cult to success at whatever cost. The Cackles here are exemplars of unbridled and unprincipled ambition, financial as well as political. Thackeray's satirical critique of the English middle and upper classes no doubt struck a chord in Ruiz de Burton's approach to her portrayal of New England society.

[30]See note 25 for "Juggernaut car" reference.

clair knew anything about the doctor's money matters, all had the right to form whatever theories they pleased on the subject.

The doctor's friends, however, bestowed upon Mrs. Norval enough respect and consideration to make up for their severity to her husband.

"She was a noble paragon."

So the popular voice said, and "the people"—Mr. Beecher[31] says—"can't make a mistake."

Tidings of a fearful nature received about this time—the winter of 1862—caused Mrs. Norval to become more and more the object of respectful sympathy and increased popularity.

Mr. Sinclair had just written (enclosing newspaper accounts) the sad report of the doctor's death. He had been killed—the newspapers said—by the Blacks in Abyssinia, with all his party, in December, 1861, several months[32] before the sad intelligence was received.

"It was a dispensation of Providence that the doctor should be destroyed by that race for whose oppressors he had manifested such culpable sympathy," said Mrs. Norval's friends.

The ex-reverend Mr. Hackwell—now reverend no longer, as he had exchanged that title for that of "captain"—was in L—— when Mrs. Norval received this terrible news.

It seemed also like a providential disposition that Mr. Hackwell should be there at that time, and should be there as a mourner, too. He had come "to pay the last tribute to a beloved wife"—to bury her. Mrs. Hackwell had died only about a week before the death of the doctor was reported.

[31]Henry Ward Beecher (1813-1887) was a New England preacher, writer and preeminent U.S. orator whose sermons drew thousands of people each week; an advocate of woman's suffrage and free trade, he was also in the forefront of the anti-slavery crusade in the North. Henry Ward Beecher was the son of Lyman Beecher, (1775-1863) a Presbyterian preacher and theologian, noted for his anti-catholicism, his advocacy of strict Calvinism, drastic domestic discipline and stand against the consumption of liquor. Harriet Beecher Stowe (1811-1896), daughter of Lyman Beecher, was the author of the crucial anti-slavery novel *Uncle Tom's Cabin*. Ruiz de Burton's portrayal of the influence of Reverend Hackwell is clearly meant to comment upon the celebrity status accorded to Protestant ministers in the U.S. during this period, as well as to the celebrated scandals in which some were involved, viz., the Beecher-Tilton affair.

[32]The original text reads: "nearly a year before the sad intelligence was received" but the novel's chronology indicates that the news reached the Norval family in early 1862.

Mrs. Norval sat at her favorite window, very thoughtful—I cannot say that she was sad: sadness implies a measure of human weakness, and Mrs. Norval's life-study had been to keep up a successful warfare on weakness and wickedness, both of which she abhorred.

So now she sat thinking very serious thoughts about her husband and his persistent inclination to take the wrong path, until it had taken him to a sandy grave in Abyssinia.

She had been thus silently moralizing for some time, when she saw her friend Mr. Hackwell coming.

He wore his uniform, and it certainly made him look ten times handsomer than did the sleek black clothes of a Presbyterian parson. But still Mrs. Norval had loved to hear him preach! Since he had left, she "did not enjoy going to church at all," she had often said.

"I was wondering if you would come back to be our pastor. I hope you may" said Mrs. Norval, when the ex-parson had taken his seat near her in the twilight.

"You are very kind," he answered, in his blandest, softest tone. "But I hardly think I will, with my home all broken up."

"You could make your home with us when Emma and Julian get married. As for little Johnny, you know Mrs. Hackwell left him under my care,'' said Mrs. Norval, probably not weighing well her words.

Long was their conversation; from one thing they glided on to another in smooth converse.

"Emma tells me you expect your daughters back next summer," said he.

"Yes, and do you know what has got into their heads? That we must go to New York to live. Did you ever hear anything so absurd?''

"Well, now, I think it is very natural for two young girls with plenty of money to go where they can enjoy it. Moreover, in New York they can make a more suitable marriage. Here there is no one whom either you or I would recommend."

"That is true, but as for their being rich, that is not so certain. You know that James never could or did economize; we always spent all our income from the farm. I don't know what his means were exactly: I only know that he left some money with Mr. Sinclair."

"Did not he make a will before leaving?"

"Oh, yes, he did that."

"Well, then, by reading his will you can ascertain what he left you."

"When Julian comes, I'll see if he wishes to open the will."

"But why do you wish to wait for Julian?"

"Because on the envelope of the will it says, 'My wife will open this in the presence of Lola and Julian and Mr. Sinclair,' and of course I can't open it now. I asked Julian what I should do, and I suppose I shall get his answer very soon."

Julian's answer did come very soon, and Mrs. Norval and Captain Hackwell sat again at the bay window in the twilight, discussing domestic affairs.

They were rather perplexed, those two good people at the window, for Julian refused to believe in the report of his father's death, and said that the will must *not* be opened until Lola was twenty-one, or her relations claimed her, or she was to be married. Otherwise the will should yet remain closed.

"It strikes me that Lola must be the principal and absorbing subject of that will. Suppose one of your daughters was to be married, and you wanted to give her a dowry—her portion at her marriage? You couldn't do it, no, because Lola is not twenty-one. It is absurd," said Captain Hackwell.

Mrs. Norval listened with eager attention. Then, with as much dislike as her regular and impassible features could express, she said, "I know that Lola was everything to him."

"The more reason, then, for you to know the contents of that will. But do not let me influence you, if you feel conscientious scruples about opening it."

They said no more that evening about the will, but next day they did, and the day after, until it was more than human nature could do to keep from opening it. Captain Hackwell's leave of absence would soon terminate. He would go in two or three days. They again sat at the bay window, and agreed to open the will that night.

They did. Late, very late in the night, they sat by the library center-table, poring over the forbidden document with more zest and excitement, perhaps, because it *was forbidden*, because they were breaking a precept. At least sinners would—that is what I mean, but not such a paragon of virtue as Mrs. Norval, or so edifying a gentleman as his ex-reverence.

His face was pale as he read; hers was flushed; the hands of both trembled, and they spoke in whispers.

The sensation was new to Mrs. Norval, and she did not dislike it.

"Did you think she had so much money?" asked he, in a whisper, though they were alone.

"No, I did not," she answered, also in a whisper. "I am surprised."

"She must have six or seven million now. It is an enormous sum."

Mrs. Norval was silent. He continued:

"But you can draw yearly over a hundred-thousand dollars, if you wish. And if I were you I would. 'A bird in the hand,' you know, and if it be left with Mr. Sinclair, he can do what he likes with it. Take my advice and draw it."

"But what will Mr. Sinclair say? And Julian? What shall I do with the money?"

"Your daughters want to go to New York, you say? Well, take them to New York. Write tomorrow to Mr. Sinclair that, as your daughters are coming and wish to reside in New York, you want him to buy you a house there, with the money you did not draw last year."

"You are a dear, good friend, indeed," said Mrs. Norval, with as much enthusiasm as it was possible for her to demonstrate, and certainly with more warmth than the *ci-devant*[33] parson had ever before seen in her.

He took her hand in his and kissed it, saying—fixing his really beautiful eyes on hers, "And has it taken you all this time to find out my devotion?"

Mrs. Norval certainly could most conscientiously have taken her oath that never in her life had she experienced a thrill like that which now went from Hackwell's hand to hers and pervaded her whole frame. She trembled like a young maiden. She blushed; she stammered.

When Hackwell saw that for the first step he had done enough, with a sigh he pressed her hand and mournfully turned his eyes upon the manuscript again. He was perfectly sure be could make the stately madam tremble like a girl anytime he pleased. Enough for the present.

Two days later, the captain came to bid Mrs. Norval good-by. She was again at the window behind the curtains, and at twilight.

"I will soon let you know what is Mr. Sinclair's answer, and when Emma and I will leave for New York. I am sorry you are to go so soon," said she.

"Are you?" said he, approaching her. She began to tremble; she did not know why. Without saying a word, he put his arms around her, and gave her a long, very long, kiss. She was so surprised at first that she could not speak, and then she felt so weak in his arms, so powerless to resist, that she did not resist. The stately lady, paragon of propriety, was as morally weak as—as—*what*?

[33]French for "former." Here in regard to Hackwell leaving behind his being "a man of the cloth" to become a Captain in the Union army and to pursue the more lucrative future of being Mrs. Norval's confidant and counselor.

It is not easy to find a fit simile for a matron who, from a chaste Lucretia[34], suddenly turns into a Clytemnestra.[35]

The captain took the night train. As he sat by the car window, looking at the gloom, he at times smiled as if amused. The flying bushes, in their grotesque antics, suggested to him the thought of seeing Mrs. Norval dance a hornpipe.

[34]The Roman figure Lucretia is often held up as a model of womanly virtue. Her suicide (509 B.C.) after being raped by the son of Tarquin, ultimately led to the expulsion of the Etruscans and set the groundwork for the founding of the city of Rome.

[35]Clytemnestra, the wife of Agamemnon, murdered her husband upon his return from the Trojan War with the aid of her paramour, Aegisthus.

CHAPTER XXIX

Lavvy's Experience as Hospital Nurse

The Misses Norval had arrived. The event was duly chronicled by the press. Their magnificent house on Fifth Avenue was all ready for them, and Mrs. Norval herself, accompanied by Emma Hackwell and little Johnny, went to the steamer to meet them.

Nothing could be more sumptuous than the Norval house. Its splendor surpassed even Ruth's ambitious desire. It delighted Mattie and frightened Mrs. Norval. She could not get used to seeing herself reflected from magnificent mirrors everywhere; it made her feel uncomfortable. She wasn't at all sure that she had done right. She certainly had not intended to ask for this magnificent abode when she wrote to Mr. Sinclair to buy her a house, but when Mr. Sinclair sent the description of several, she had chosen the one which Mr. Hackwell advised. As she had written to him, asking him to choose for her, she felt obliged, of course, to select that one. Then Mr. Hackwell had so kindly just run up to New York from Washington, for a day, and had given the orders to the upholsterers for the furnishing of it. She could not countermand his orders when they were partially executed.

But the girls were so pleased with the house, Ruth particularly, that Mrs. Norval began to think that perhaps she had done well. Perhaps all the houses in New York—of the fashionable people—were like this. She did not know, as she never had been inside of one of them, except that of Mrs. Sinclair. But her daughters had been in palaces. The Empress of France had spoken to them, and complimented them on the sweet way in which they spoke French. They knew all about genteel society.

Julian had not yet seen their new house, and Mrs. Norval was rather afraid he would not exactly approve. She was sure he would think it would cost a mint of money to keep up such an establishment.

But Mr. Hackwell had figured the expenses for her, and they did not reach forty-thousand dollars—keeping four carriages and eight horses—and said that she could draw every year, if she liked, one-hundred and sixty-thousand dollars and not exceed the doctor's allowance.

But how could she explain this to Julian without saying she had read the will?

She would write to Mr. Hackwell asking his advice, and he would certainly suggest something.

There was no danger, however, that Julian would be asking any disagreeable questions for some time to come. About the time when Mrs. Norval was moving into her new house, he was getting ready for the battle of Antietam.[36] Then he was wounded there and went to Washington, to his Aunt Lavvy's hospital. His wound had not been dangerous, but painful enough to keep him an invalid for a month. Then he was in a great hurry to rush back to his command, which was now a brigade, and he did not have the time to go to New York. He went only as far as *the convent*, because Lola had written that she was sick with anxiety, and she felt double alarm because Jule, too, seemed very sad, and hadn't sung at all for nearly two weeks. After his visit Jule sang again, and the roses came back to his mistress's cheeks.

"The girls" had lovely wardrobes, which would be a heavy loss if they went in mourning, as all their costly dresses would be out of fashion before they went out of mourning. Mrs. Norval said that Julian did not believe in the report of his father's death, and had written to her and to Lola not to put on mourning. "*The girls*," of course, did not believe it either. But Mattie, for all that, could not help crying, and would shut herself in her room at times, with papa's photograph only, and have a good cry to herself. Ruth knew better than to do such foolish things. Crying spoils the eyes; it makes the lids heavy and clouds the brightness, "and what is the use of crying? If papa has been killed (which *I don't* believe), crying won't bring him to life. And if he hasn't been killed, why should we cry?" said Miss Ruth. Mattie said, "It is so," but still would cry. And so would Lola, although she had a sort of blind faith that she would again see her beloved benefactor. "I suppose my heart means that I shall see him in heaven," Lola would say, and forth-

[36]Site of the September 17th, 1862, Civil War battle on the shores of the Potomac River, in western Maryland, it marked an important "victory" for Union forces. Days later Lincoln issued his preliminary Emancipation Proclamation. Union troops led by General George McClellan suffered heavy casualties, about 12,000, and the South's General Robert E. Lee lost about 9,000 men at Antietam.

with she would put on her black veil and rush to the chapel to pray to the Virgin Mary for "that good, *good* man."

And Lavvy, the tender-hearted maiden, how this terrible news affected her! If she had not been so frightened by Mr. Blower, she would have read Emma's letters as soon as she got them. But not imagining their contents were so fearful, she laid them on the bureau and threw herself on the bed. Presently, however, a servant brought her a cup of tea and she drank it and ate some very nice toast and a bit of cold chicken. Lavvy's courage revived and she began to think that Mr. Blower, not being a member of Congress, could not be as good authority as Mr. White, who was. And though Mr. White had admitted—as Lavvy herself did—that the exchange might for a short time be suspended, still, it could not be—as Mr. Blower said—with a view to increase the famine in the South. Yes, Mr. White ought to know better than Mr. Blower, who was only, said Mr. White, a "*lobby* man"—whatever that might be—and who, after all, repeated what he had heard Mr. Gunn say, and he might have made a mistake. With these consolatory reflections to help the tea and toast and cold chicken, Lavvy's nerves became more composed. She then began to think that she ought to have gone to her hospital to see her sick before going to bed. She looked at her watch, and it was seven o'clock. She rang and ordered a carriage immediately, and told the servant to say to Mrs. Cackle, or any of the Misses Cackle, wouldn't one of them go with her to the hospital, just to take a look at some of her sick. She would not detain them five minutes. Then Lavvy flew to her bureau and began to dress herself. When she was dressed—bonnet and all—seeing Emma's letter there yet unopened, she said, "I'll see what Emma says while the carriage comes. I hope there is no more sad news. That telegram of Mrs. Hackwell's death shocked me awfully." She then sat down to read the letter.

Mrs. Cackle was coming, all ready to accompany her, and as she was going to knock, she heard Lavvy give a loud scream. The old lady opened the door and found Lavvy fainting.

The news of the doctor's death coming when she had been all day in terror of Isaac's starvation, was more than poor Lavvy could bear, for she loved her kind brother-in-law dearly.

Of course Lavvy was too sick to go to the hospital that night, but next morning she made a great effort to rise and dress herself. She felt very anxious about her sick. Mrs. Cackle had not been in her ward, but had heard that one or two of the wounded were dying. Lavvy ate no breakfast, only drank a cup of coffee while waiting for the carriage.

As soon as she went upstairs on that wing of the hospital which was her ward, she knew that something was wrong. The nurses looked frightened as soon as they saw her.

"What is the matter?" she said, but none answered. She opened the door of the front room, and the first thing that met her eyes was one of her favorite patients lying in his bed dead.

She sat by the bedside and felt the boy's heart. It had ceased beating, but he was yet warm. She closed his eyes, still partly opened, and then, thinking of her poor brother Isaac and the doctor, burst into a flood of tears. The nurses stood by her in silent terror. Lavvy looked up; she saw that they looked guilty and a great deal more frightened than grieved.

"What is the meaning of this? What killed this boy? He was almost well."

"I don't know, ma'am," answered assistant nurse No. 1. "He was well last evening, and he commenced with convulsions about eleven o'clock, and had them all night, and died about an hour ago. The others are not dead yet, but two are very bad. The doctor has not come yet."

"When did the others commence with the convulsions?"

"About one o'clock, two of them, and the other about three," answered nurse No. 2.

Lavvy was again collected, judicious, practical, as soon as she saw that a *head* was wanted there. Straightway she began to investigate the cause of these convulsions.

"Come here all of you," said she to her staff of nurses, who, pale with fright, and not feeling altogether blameless, approached her.

"Answer truly, or I'll report every one of you, for that boy in another fortnight would have been with his musket on his shoulder"—and she pointed to the dead soldier. "He died because he ate something that was poison to him, I am sure. Who has been here since I went away yesterday?"

"Only Mrs. Cackle and the young ladies came to ask if you had returned," said nurse No. 1.

"And two ladies who brought some pickles and jellies, and some oranges," added nurse No. 2.

"And did the boy eat oranges or jelly?"

"No, ma'am, he did not."

"Who else came?"

"Nobody else, ma'am, but the two ladies' maids who carried the oranges and jelly, and—and some bottles of—of—wine."

"Good!" said Lavvy. "First there were only the Cackles; then the two ladies with jelly and oranges; then two ladies' maids; and then some bottles which make you stammer. I think I'll find more."

So saying, Lavinia began a thorough search, lifting pillows, looking behind beds and under the mattresses. The result was that she found an empty pickle jar under the pillow of the man who commenced with convulsions about one o'clock; some cheese and gingerbread under that of the man with the cramps; a box of sardines and peanut candy under that of the other with convulsions; and as she turned to examine the bed of the dead boy, she noticed that nurse No. 2 was trying to hide something under her apron.

"What is that?" Lavvy demanded quickly.

"Nothing, ma'am, but a little bit of boolon sausage."

Hard was this trial to Lavvy, whose tender conscience accused her of neglecting her duty. She should have come the evening before, no matter what the state of her feelings might have been, her conscience said, and Lavvy humbly promised never to leave her post again for so many hours. She became from that day more firmly convinced than ever that *ladies* with hearts and brains were absolutely necessary to her country's cause. Not merely *paid menials* should attend the sick and wounded, but thoughtful women, who could judiciously order as well as obey in an emergency like this, which ended so tragically.

Lavvy was no advocate of "woman's rights." She did not understand the subject even, but she smiled sadly, thinking how little woman was appreciated, how unjustly underrated. *She* could obtain *nothing* from the government—the Cackles, *all*! "To kill is better than to save," she said sadly, but not bitterly, for Lavvy had a gentle heart.

CHAPTER XXX

Captain Hackwell Becomes a Hero and Is Breveted

Again the roar of the cannon made the mountains tremble. The battle of Chancellorsville[37] was being fought.

Julian, pale yet with the loss of the blood he had left on the field of Antietam, sat on his horse at the head of his brigade, waiting for the order to advance. His forehead was pale, and his cheeks sunken, but his eyes shone with the light of suppressed enthusiasm, for he was thoroughly devoted to the cause he so gallantly defended. He hated to have to shoot down his fellow citizens, he admitted that. But if they insisted on breaking the Union, and would not come to their senses except through the baptism of blood, then Julian deemed his cause right, and was ready to defend it with his life.

He was thus thinking, when he saw a horse, apparently riderless, approaching. On coming nearer him, Julian recognized the hat and shoulders and the back of Commissary Hackwell, of General Cackle's staff. The *ci-devant* preacher, too long preaching peace to like the practices of war, was bending so close to his saddle—to afford as small a mark to sharpshooters as possible—that not until close to Julian could anyone see his face. On arriving, he gave to Julian a slip of paper, evidently a leaf torn from a memorandum-book, saying, "This is from General—."

Julian read the paper, and the word to advance went through the columns of his brigade.

But, as it is not the purpose of these unpretending pages to describe battles, we will leave Julian advancing to deal death and suffering on

[37]The Confederate victory at Chancellorsville in northeast Virginia in May of 1863 was one of the more bloody conflicts of the war.

his fellow men, and will follow Captain Hackwell, who was even less disposed to witness so closely any such inhuman havoc.

The peaceably-disposed commissary, again taking the precaution to present as small a mark to sharpshooters as he could, took his way back to headquarters. The commissary and ex-preacher and *ci-devant* lawyer was in no amiable mood now. He felt as if his back was breaking, but did not dare to sit up straight. He belabored himself mentally as roughly as he, to the delight of Mrs. Norval, used to handle his admiring congregation. And he deserved belaboring quite as much, for to his vanity alone he was indebted for being caught in the trap of delivering that order to Julian. Because he wished to be seen riding a handsome horse (which a friend of his in the Quartermaster's Department had bought cheap for him), and because he wished to go near enough to the battlefield to say that he had been there in the battle, he had approached headquarters just at the time when an aid, carrying the order to Julian, had his horse wounded, and, seeing Captain Hackwell so finely mounted, requested him to carry the order. Captain Hack would have refused if he had dared, but this was out of the question. Evidently both the aid and the horse were scarcely able to walk.

"Brutal, beastly way of settling difficulties!" soliloquized Hack on his return, and with his back almost broken." I cannot but think that the devil rears soldiers as boys raise fighting cocks, just for his sport. Curse the war and all the damned fools who got it up! But, no, those who got it up take mighty good care to keep out of it, I notice. I should say, curse the damned fools who come to get shot for other people's benefit. If I ever get away with a whole skin and unbroken back, I promise to Satan I shan't afford him further sport."

Thus soliloquizing, the captain rode on as fast as his uncomfortable position permitted. He selected a road which he thought would take him more quickly away from the flying missiles. But soon his path became so rugged as to be at times almost impassable. He was obliged to dismount, lead his horse by the bridle for a few yards, and remount. The third time he had been obliged to resort to this expedient, and within a short distance of headquarters, as he was going to mount again, his foot slipped and he fell on his knees. As he did so, one of the two revolvers he carried at his belt went off, wounding him in the right leg.

The captain yelled with pain, losing his hold of he bridle, and the horse, seeing him down on the ground, trotted off pitilessly.

The wounded captain tried to get nearer the road to call for assistance, and partially succeeded by crawling and limping painfully. Then he concealed himself in the bushes by the roadside and tried to staunch the blood. This he could not well do. He tied his wound with his pocket handkerchief and cravat, but still it bled profusely, and he felt he was getting very faint. At last, with the loss of blood and the terror of being captured, the commissary swooned away.

He must have remained in this state for several hours, as it was not until night that a party of men going by, in the humane work of collecting the wounded, saw him and carried him to the camp hospital.

This exploit, however, made the non-combatant captain a major, and a hero in the eyes of Mrs. Norval and a grateful country, who had any amount of brevets in store for him.

The captain was, at his earnest request, carried to Washington. On arriving there, he telegraphed to Mrs. Norval that he was sick and wounded, and couldn't she and Emma come to see him? He would like to see his sister and his dearest friend.

Two days before the arrival of this telegram, another one had come to the Norval mansion from the doctor in charge of Julian, saying that, "As Colonel Norval was very dangerously wounded and might die, if his family wished to see him before dying they had better come soon," adding, however, that his case was "by no means hopeless."

Mrs. Norval, of course, had started for Fortress Monroe, taking the night train so as to arrive in Baltimore in the morning and take a morning boat, if there was any.

Mattie wanted to go with her mother, but Mrs. Norval would not permit it, as she did not know that she could get any accommodation for her. She promised, however, to telegraph daily, and if Julian was worse, then to let his two sisters see him before dying.

When Captain Hackwell's dispatch came, Ruth opened it and, as soon as she read it, called loudly for Mattie and Emma to come downstairs to hold consultation over it.

"It is clear that I must go to John," said Emma.

"But he doesn't want you to go alone," said Ruth.

"Aunt Lavvy is there. Emma won't be alone," added Mattie.

"Yes, but Emma will have to travel alone. Moreover, Aunt Lavvy is so busy with her hospital that she won't have much time to spare for Em," observed Ruth. "If it was not that Julian might get worse, and ma telegraph for us, either Mattie or I could go with you."

"Then let us send for Lola," suggested Mattie. "She can go with Em."

Emma shook her head, saying, "No. I had rather go alone."

"Why, I thought you liked Lola!" Mattie said, surprised.

Emma colored as she replied, "I like her well enough, but I don't want her with me."

A ring at the front door prevented Mattie from making any other embarrassing observation about Lola to Emma, and soon after a servant came in with another telegram, which he presented to Ruth in a silver tray, saying, "Another, miss."

It was a dispatch from Lola to Mrs. Norval, begging to permit her to accompany Mrs. Norval to Fortress Monroe.

"That is cool," said Emma, livid with jealousy.

"I think it is very kind," said Mattie.

"But who told Lola that ma was to go to Fortress Monroe?" wondered Ruth.

"I did," said Mattie. "I told her that mamma was going, and we, too, might go if darling Jule got worse. And, of course, Lola wants to go, too, for she is very fond of Julian—"

"I should think she was," interrupted Emma—"which is most natural," finished Miss Mattie.

"I really don't know what I am to do, except to enclose these two telegrams to ma, and let her say what shall be done," Ruth said.

After some further consultation, the wise council of three decided that, as the mails were irregular at times, Emma should go to Washington, and they would notify Mrs. Norval of it by telegraph; they would also telegraph to her Lola's dispatch.

Ruth sat down at a table to pen a dispatch to her mother. After many corrections and alterations, and suggestions from Mattie and Emma, Ruth's dispatch as sent to the telegraph office ran thus:

> "To MRS. DR. NORVAL, FORTRESS MONROE:
>
> "Emma goes to Washington. Captain Hackwell telegraphs is wounded. Lola wishes to go with you. Can she? Let her know.
>
> RUTH NORVAL."

Whilst Ruth was writing this dispatch, Mattie was inditing another to Lola, which was as follows:

> "Telegraph to mamma at Fortress Monroe. She is there now. No further news from Julian.
>
> MATTIE NORVAL."

Mrs. Norval received Ruth's telegram very little sooner than she would have received her letter. Telegraphing, being a monopoly, commands its own price and takes its own time.

Lola, by some chance, was more fortunate, and got Mattie's dispatch soon enough to take her advice and telegraph to Mrs. Norval. Her dispatch, though it went later, was received first. Mrs. Norval read it, and, with a bitter smile curling her lips, muttered as she threw the dispatch in the fire, "The impudence!"

Towards evening, Ruth's dispatch arrived, and Mrs. Norval felt faint when she read it.

The next morning, the letter enclosing Mr. Hackwell's own telegram also arrived.

What was to be done? Julian was no worse, it is true, but the doctor did not yet wish to give her any hope. The young man lay there unconscious, between life and death.

Mrs. Norval was in despair. Suddenly a thought struck her. She would telegraph to Lavvy to come, so that if Julian got well enough for her to leave him for two or three days, she would run up to Washington to see whether Emma wanted her or not. She must want her, the poor dear girl, without mother or father. Yes, it was *her duty* to go to the dear orphan girl in her trouble.

In great anxiety she waited by the bedside of her son the arrival of Lavvy's reply.

At last it came; it ran thus:

> "I cannot go; I am taking care of Mr. Hackwell.
> Emma wants me here to help her.
> LAVINIA SPRIG."

"Oh! the vixen! Oh! the hypocrite! the miserable old maid!" exclaimed Mrs. Norval, for the first time in her life carried away beyond all decorous control. "She is after him, the bag of bones, and says Em wants her. Contemptible, to tell such lies!"

And the stately matron, always quoted by all her own and the surrounding villages as a pattern of womanly virtues, and as *a pink of propriety*, indulged in abusive language! She was alone, though, or at least nearly so, for she considered her half-dead son as incapable of hearing her, and in fact she had forgotten him for those few moments.

But Julian opened his eyes, and, seeing his mother so distracted, tried to speak.

She saw his lips move, and came immediately to the bedside.

CHAPTER XXXI

The Major Is the Object of Great Solicitude

"Dear mother," said Julian, in a scarcely audible whisper, "don't distress yourself so. I shall live. Father will come back."

Mrs. Norval shuddered. Her son's voice seemed to come from the grave to call her back to her senses. A sharp pang shot through her heretofore impassible heart. She bent over until she rested her flushed cheek close to that of her son, and for some moments she was unable to speak. Her remorse deprived her of the power to articulate.

I have read somewhere the fable of a priest holding in a bottle, and tied by a string, a lot of little devils, which he had exorcised out of different individuals of both sexes.

These imps, though powerless when thus ignominiously imprisoned and ganged together like galley convicts, would nevertheless do good service to the master who should be able to hold each one by itself. But so anxious were they to be at liberty, and so impatient of restraint, that it was next to impossible to try to let any one free without the whole gang rushing out. Thus, when the priest tried to give one his liberty, out would rush the crowd pell-mell, and his reverence was obliged to pull the string and send back his imps into the bottle, or be mobbed by them.

Mrs. Norval was now in a similar dilemma. No sooner had one of her imps escaped her control, than all rushed out unruly and riotous, and it is very doubtful whether the string by which she held them was as strong as that of the old priest. Perhaps she would never be able to bottle them up again.

When that one passion—her love for Hackwell—was beyond her mastery, all her other imps ran riot in bacchanalian freedom, and she was jealous of her sister and hated her, and she forgot her dying son, and she did not mourn for her lost husband, who had been so good and generous to her. All she now thought of and longed for was to see Hackwell, to be near him. That was the all-absorbing, uncontrollable impulse.

How insidiously that love had crept into her heart! Slowly, stealthily, through the only avenue by which it was accessible—her dark bigotry and her blind prejudices. Because Hackwell was in her opinion a very strict Presbyterian minister of the "old school," a good hater of all other sects—particularly of popery (he said)—she began to like him. He was worthy of the old Covenanters, she thought, and of course was a model of Christian virtues. He hated the theatre and all other worldly dissipations, which he said ought to have been exterminated with fire and brimstone, together with the abominations of Sodom, and be now submerged under the bitter waters of the Dead Sea. Moreover, he said he hated foreigners and all things foreign, "as every good American should," and this was the first point of sympathetic contact between him and herself. If Mr. Hackwell had been worldly, Mrs. Norval would scarcely have been courteous to him. If he had been of any other denomination or less strict a Presbyterian, she would not have tolerated him.

Now, however, he was safe to be anything he pleased. If he would turn comic actor, it is not improbable that she would have gone to see him perform. The acceptance of a position in the army, she would have regarded in any other preacher as most unbecoming. But in Hackwell it was a proof of the purest patriotism. Ah me! such is poor humanity! Cast not a stone—no, not a little pebble—at the madam, for after all, she was very womanly when she was so absurdly silly. And who is not silly when truly in love?

So let us be charitable with her—although she was never known to be so towards any one—and learn not to pitch our voices so high as she did at the beginning of her song, for we also may find how difficult it is to maintain such *diapason*.

She took her boy's bloodless hand and kissed it humbly. She felt she was not what she should be, and was meek under the lash of conscience.

Julian's lips moved; she listened.

"Kiss me," he said, and put up his lips to receive his mother's kiss. She almost recoiled, but she could not deny it. She gave him the kiss, and the pure touch of his lips was the heavenly charm which unsealed the fountain of her best feelings, her purest affections, and the tears which had not flowed for her lost husband rushed to her eyes now, and she fell on her knees, weeping by her boy's bed.

"Do not cry, dear mother. I am very weak, but God will yet spare my life." And, as if the effort to say this much had exhausted him, he weariedly closed his eyes and soon relapsed into slumber.

Whilst Mrs. Norval watched by the bedside of her son, her imps kept well "bottled up." But at about ten o'clock, Bingham, Julian's servant, came to take his nightly watch, which would last until two, and then one of the hospital nurses relieved him until seven in the morning. When Bingham came, Mrs. Norval, after giving him instructions on what to do, and charging him particularly to call her if there was any change in Julian, or if he called her, retired to her room.

No sooner was she there alone than the whole gang rushed out again to play pranks about her, the wicked imps.

It was useless to lie down. She could not sleep; that she knew. What would she do? To leave Julian now, of course, was out of the question, and yet, would it be safe to leave Lavinia there taking care of Hackwell? No. They had been in love with each other, and, for the very reason that Hackwell had been so cruelly faithless, he might wish to make amends now by marrying her.

This thought nearly drove her crazy.

Suddenly a thought came to her distracted brain. One of her imps brought the thought perhaps for the amusement of his companions. She thought she would telegraph to Lola to go to help Emma, and to Lavinia to come as soon as Lola reached Washington. She sat by a table and wrote both telegrams so that they would be ready to leave early next morning.

She ordered Lola to go immediately to Washington to help Emma, and Lavinia to be ready to leave there as soon as Lola arrived, and on the same day, if possible, to start for Fortress Monroe.

Then the madam slept, whilst her imps played all sorts of tricks with her sleeping thoughts, and she dreamed of Hackwell.

Terrible was the blow which that cruel telegram dealt at the breast of the tender Lavvy.

She had watched by the bed of her long-loved John for ten days now, and those ten days had been the happiest of her life—the captain had been so grateful, and expressed his gratitude so prettily to her.

"Lavvy," he had said, fixing his lovely, irresistible eyes on her with a tender, mournful gaze that went straight to her heart, "Lavvy, you are a good girl. I don't deserve this from you. I deserve to be poisoned by you. Yes, by George, to be shot, for I did not behave to you as I should. But, believe me, my dear, I have suffered enough for it. Yes, enough to content you. I am well punished, I assure you."

"I don't want you to suffer, or—or—anything of the kind," stammered Lavvy in confusion, as this was the first allusion ever made by him to that brief episode so indelibly stamped on her memory.

"Of course you do not, for you are the best, the gentlest of angels. Can you forgive me?"

The entrance of the doctor here interrupted the dialogue. But that night, as she bade him good night, he kissed her hand and called her "good angel."

Next day Mrs. Cackle was about all day. Came to help Lavvy—as if *she* wanted any help! But the day after, again they were alone, and then he had gone so far as to say, "Tell me, dearest, can't I ever do anything to make amends for the past?" But Lavvy had been so confused that she had not answered, and then Mrs. Cackle came. Why will a Mrs. Cackle always come at the wrong time? Oh, those Cackles! Always a Cackle!

The day after, Emma came. Still, Hackwell was very sweet to Lavvy, and Emma was very glad that she was so happy in taking care of him, as she felt no vocation for being a nurse. Two days after Emma's arrival, Mrs. Norval's telegram came, and on the third, early in the morning, Lola, pale and fatigued, made her appearance. Poor child! Little she relished to come to play nurse at the bedside of Hackwell, when her heart was by that of Julian.

Lavvy and Emma received her very coldly. So much so that though Lola had the most amiable of dispositions, she said resentfully, "I am sorry if I am *de trop*;[38] but I assure you I am as unwilling to come as you are to receive me. And as we all have to obey a superior will, suppose we make the best of the infliction and treat each other as kindly as we can."

Emma sneered, without answering, but Lavvy felt that what Lola said was true, and that it would be very unjust to make Lola suffer for that which Mrs. Norval was alone to blame.

"You are right, Lola. Jenny is a tyrant, and we are all her slaves," she said.

"Mrs. Norval is a noble woman—the best Christian, best mother, best everything I ever did see, and what she does, she does actuated by the best and purest motives. She is perfectly unselfish, and she wishes us to do what is best for us all," said Emma with great vehemence.

[38]French for "in the way", "unwelcome." Lola's use of the French is meant to mark her tact and schooling in opposition to the lack of refinement and at times rudeness of Ruth Norval, for example.

"Why, you make her almost the equal of the Virgin Mary!" exclaimed Lola, astounded.

"I should think she was! Why shouldn't she be regarded as the equal of the Virgin Mary?"

"Oh, what blasphemy!" ejaculated Lola, horrified, stopping her ears for fear of hearing any more of such sentiments.

"Come, Lola, come to my room," said Lavvy, cutting the discussion short. "Your room has not a fire; I did not expect you until this evening." And so saying, Lavvy took Lola to her own room. "Take off your things here, and lie down if you feel sleepy," she said.

"I do, for I have not been able to sleep. I never can sleep in the cars."

"Then why did you take the night train?"

"Because Mrs. Norval said, 'Go *immediately* to Washington.' I left my trunk behind, to be sent to me by today's train. The sisters will pack it and send it. I only had time to throw on my bed the things I wished to take, and I suppose I forgot half."

"I don't know what makes Jenny in such a hurry. She telegraphed to me, 'Be ready to leave on the same day that Lola arrives,' but I am not going to break my neck to obey her. I'll go tomorrow afternoon in the train that goes to Baltimore at two o'clock, and not a minute sooner. And if it were not that dear Julian is so sick, I wouldn't go until Monday. I haven't anything ready."

"Oh, how I wish I could go in your place! Why couldn't Mrs. Norval let me go to help her? I am sure there can be no impropriety in my helping to take care of Julian, when she is there herself. I should think it would be better to leave you with Emma than to send for me to come to chaperon her."

"Yes, when she is quite old enough to be your mother," added Lavvy. "But it is of no use remonstrating. Jenny has all her life been obeyed, and she would drop dead with surprise if any of her slaves had the hardihood to remonstrate. Her imperiousness drove that best of men, dear James, away. He was too high-minded to bear her mean tyranny, and, as she would insist on ruling, right or wrong, he went away. His wife had more to do with his going away than his politics. I speak thus frankly because you know it as well as I. Now try to take a nap. I'll send you your breakfast up."

The happiest man in the world was the gallant commissary that day.

As Lola was in no hurry to assume her duties of nurse, she did not make her appearance in the captain's sickroom, which was the back parlor of the house occupied by Lavvy and Mrs. Cackle, her husband and two daughters.

Captain Hackwell thus had time to pay somewhat more attention to his personal appearance, and indite the sweetest little epistle to Mrs. Norval expressive of his deep gratitude for her infinite kindness.

Although it will be anticipating a trifling circumstance, I shall here mention that this note was answered promptly by Mrs. Norval, and that when the captain, all perfumed, brushed, and shaved, sat in his bed waiting for Lola and Emma to come to breakfast with him, and read her answer, he ejaculated a long "Whew-ew!" and then fell back on his pillows convulsed with laughter. "Upon my word, this is rich!" he said between peals of laughter. "So my eloquence began the sad havoc, eh? And I am an *Ithuriel*![39] Poor old lady; then she makes herself a devil. A woman in love will make anything of herself, but I never thought the madam was a woman. *Ithuriel*, to be sure, and without any spear, but with a single kiss I caused the mask to fall. Very good, Mrs. Norval. You had better let similes alone. Miltonic quotations are not your forte, no, not more so than the biblical. But as for these, I'll warrant that you will let them severely alone, now that I have kicked against the pulpit."

The entrance of Emma and Lola interrupted the captain's mirthful monologue, but he was wittier than ever during breakfast, and all day laughed occasionally to himself.

[39]Ithuriel, in Milton's *Paradise Lost*, is one of the angels commissioned by Gabriel to search for Satan, who has penetrated Paradise. Ithuriel is armed with a spear capable of detecting deception at the slightest touch. Reverend Hackwell remarks on the fact that his "spear" has pierced the deceptive veneer of Mrs. Norval's "propriety."

CHAPTER XXXII

Mrs. Norval's Conscience Speaks Loudly

If human sorrow had a material, specific gravity, a weight proportionate to its magnitude, the Baltimore train in which Lavinia sat could not have moved unless with the addition of an extra locomotive, such was the misery of the gentle maiden on leaving the handsome, fascinating Hackwell.

But trains can pull any amount of wretchedness, and Lavinia did not in the least impede its lightning flight. And in due time she sat on the deck of one of the "Old Dominion Line" of steamers, without her sorrow causing the steamer to draw a half-inch more of water.

Next morning, at the unchristian hour of five, Lavvy was landed at Fortress Monroe, sore at heart and weary of life, wondering what she had ever done to Fate that the capricious dame should take such a spite against her.

Mrs. Norval had not thought, until too late, to send anyone to meet her sister, so there was Lavvy left on the wharf, shivering in the raw air of a misty dreary morning, without knowing where to go. Presently she discovered an officer who was talking to some men. Her first impulse was to go and ask the officer if he knew where she could find Colonel Norval. But, remembering the very young man of the red whiskers at the War Office, she forbore, and preferred to trust to the civility of a colored gentleman who was there warming his hands in his pockets.

"Can you tell me, sir, where are Colonel Norval's quarters?"

The colored citizen looked at her, scratched his head, and, turning to another darkey, said, "I say, Sam, can you tell the lady where is the quarter of Col'nel Newgo?" Sam only shook his head, too lazy to speak. The officer, however, heard the question, and, seeing Lavvy alone, came to ask if she was inquiring for someone. Lavvy told him yes, she wished to find Colonel Norval. The officer then told her that she would have to go to the government hospitals, erected near Hampton, for the colonel was in one of those hospitals, and the officer pointed the way thither, and that was all he could do.

Lavvy was ready to cry; she felt so forlorn. But we have seen what a Mark Tapley she could be in the midst of misery. So she made the best of her cruel situation, and by eight o'clock she had succeeded in getting a conveyance. As she was about to get into it, up drove Bingham, who had been sent by Mrs. Norval to escort her.

The reception which Lavvy met was not at all calculated to cheer her sinking spirit. Animosity, almost hatred, glared in the hazel eyes of Mrs. Norval. But Lavvy had no time to more than notice her singular manner, for, as she went in, her eyes rested on the pale face of Julian, who looked as if already dead.

Lavinia forgot everything at the sight of her beloved nephew. She forgot Hackwell even, for she loved Julian better than any member of her family, with all the devotion of her unselfish, loyal heart. She hastened to Julian's bed, saying, "My darling boy, is it possible that you are so very ill?"

"I should think he was. Did you ever know me to exaggerate?" replied Mrs. Norval.

Julian slowly opened his eyes, and in his weak, scarcely audible voice said, "Dear Lavvy, I am so glad you came."

"Are you, darling? I promise I shall not leave you now. I regret, in my heart, I did not realize before you were so ill."

From that moment Lavvy, now quite an experienced nurse, assumed the principal care of Julian, to whom she devoted all her time.

There was very little conversation between the sisters. One hated; the other feared.

Meantime, the task of Capt. Hackwell's nurses was quite easy; their patient was the most cheerful of invalids. He was more than cheerful; he was witty, amusing, brilliant, in his sickbed. He liked to have his two nurses constantly by him, and they spent an hour or more after each meal with him, and every evening besides. The surgeon said that though the captain's wound was doing very well, still he would not be able to walk for two months perhaps, or more. But the brave Hack received this announcement with a placid smile and a sweet glance towards Lola. She, however, received it with a feeling of dread. She feared she would be compelled to remain in Washington, when her whole soul was by the site of that other sickbed in the wooden hospital of Uncle Sam, by the ragged little town of Hampton.

By that bed now was sitting Mrs. Norval, with contracted lowering brow. Lavinia sat with her, and it is not at all improbable that the thoughts of both sisters took telegraphic trips to Washington.

Poor Lavvy! She considered that her last chance to catch Hackwell had forever gone by, and she thought that her sister *might* have thought of *that*.

So she did, but with a different result from what innocent Lavvy imagined. One thing is certain, and that is that if Julian had not been the invalid in question, Lavvy, driven to her last hope, would have rebelled and returned to Washington when she met such a cold, almost insulting reception from her sister.

But the invalid was dear Julian, now lying there so helpless, so weak, his superb eyes so sunken, his white hand resting motionless by his side. No, she could not leave him thus, for she knew that she understood better how to take care of him than his mother.

So ran Lavinia's thoughts for the thousandth time that rainy evening when she and her sister sat by Julian's bedside. He slept quietly. The fever had abated, and the doctor was very sanguine of his recovery.

"If Julian continues to improve," said Mrs. Norval, looking down uneasily, though her sister could not see her face well in the darkened room, "and if the doctor says he is out of danger, I think I had better run up to Washington to see those two girls. It doesn't look exactly *proper* to leave them alone for so long."

Lavvy thought much, but answered nothing.

"I think you can take care of Julian quite as well as I do, and with the help of Bingham and the hospital nurse you will get along for a few days. It might be criticized that I leave two girls there without a matron for a long time."

"Mrs. Cackle is in the same house, and goes to see the girls every day. Lola writes to me that either Mrs. Cackle, or Lucretia, or Artemisia, is there every day, and all are old enough to give respectability to a regiment of girls. Lola says, too, that Mr. Hackwell is very cheerful, and that, although he is not allowed to leave his bed, he doesn't even look sick."

Both sisters were silent for the rest of the evening, and at eight o'clock they made the usual arrangements for the night, which they divided into four watches. Mrs. Norval took the first, being the easiest; then Lavvy the second, from eleven to one; then Bingham the third, from one to four; and the hospital nurse from four until seven, when Lavvy again relieved him.

A few days after the above conversation, the sisters again sat near Julian's bed. He was visibly improving now. He had asked for Lola and his sisters, and if they were not coming to see him. He had been sleeping very quietly, evidently free from fever.

"I was thinking that as Julian is out of danger, I cannot conscientiously leave those two girls alone in Washington. It does not look proper, and I cannot permit it."

"I think you ought to send for Lola; *that*, I most emphatically recommend. But as for Emma, there can be no impropriety in her being with her brother. Lola is very anxious to go away, and she must have some good reason for it. She indicates as much in all her letters."

"She has the good reason that she wishes to come to see Julian, but she had better give that up, for I shall not permit it."

"I know Lola wants to see Julian, and she cries bitterly because you don't let her do so. But I know, too, that she does have some *other* reasons for wishing to go away."

"A desire to contradict me and oppose my wishes, as she has always done."

"I think you are mistaken, and, putting things together, let me tell you that though Mr. Hackwell is old enough to be Lola's father, it was evident that he was more than pleased to see Lola. He was so embarrassed, too, when she went to his bed to shake hands with him the day she arrived. He blushed and stammered like a schoolboy, and he was so excited that he trembled all over and could hardly speak."

Oh! the horrible dagger that Lavinia was thrusting into her sister's heart! Could she be saying this because she, the lean old maid, was jealous? When Mrs. Norval was able to speak, she said, "And why haven't you told me this before?"

"Because, in the first place, I was not sure that I was right, until Lola's letters have confirmed my observations. Secondly, because, when I came, you accused me of wishing to remain to catch Hackwell, and you might have said that I was slandering him out of jealousy."

"I shall go tomorrow night, and if what you say is true, I shall pack Miss Lola for her convent, posthaste."

"Send Lola to me, mother, if you care for my life," said the weak voice of Julian, who, unobserved, had listened most attentively to their conversation.

What might have been Mrs. Norval's reply to her son's appeal, we can never know, for at that moment an orderly, bringing the Washington mail, came in to interrupt their conversation, to Mrs. Norval's great relief.

Among the letters brought that day was one addressed to Mrs. Norval, in the fine well-formed characters of Lola's pen, which looked as if lithographed. With a trembling hand the lady opened the letter, and her agitation increased as she perused it.

Lola demanded to be permitted to leave Washington. She said she did not wish to put in writing her reasons for this request, but that they were of so grave a character as to justify her in going away without permission. She did not wish to do that, and hoped that Mrs. Norval would let her join her, or go back to her convent.

What was to be done? Mrs. Norval had intended to make a visit only, to Washington, and return in a few days. Lavinia could take care of Julian, but she had not been very well lately. She had had a chill and then a fever twice, and, if left alone, she might find the task of nursing Julian too much for her strength. Mrs. Norval felt as if her heart had collapsed and her brain was bursting. She felt she must ascertain the full meaning of Lola's letter or die of suffocation.

In this terrible state of mind, the dignified matron went to bed.

Lavinia had another chill that night, and fever next day. The chills now came regularly every other day. Mrs. Norval, of course, did not leave that evening—how could she?—nor the day after.

On the third day, very early in the morning, when Mrs. Norval was eating a very light breakfast—for she had lost her appetite—a boy brought in a telegram which, by mistake, was addressed to Julian. He motioned to Lavvy to read it; Lavvy did so, and read aloud:

> "To MRS. NORVAL, care of COLONEL NORVAL:
> "I leave this afternoon—will be with you tomorrow morning.
>
> LOLA MEDINA"

It was evident that the telegram had been sent the day before, but the employees of the telegraph offices had, as usual, taken their time to deliver it.

"Why, Lola will be here this morning! This telegram was sent yesterday," said Lavvy.

Julian sat up in bed and demanded to be shaved immediately. He had not been able to do more than lift his head to take his medicine and a little nourishment. But there he sat now, anxious to make his toilette.

CHAPTER XXXIII

Mrs. Norval's Conscience Waxes Dictatorial. —She Obeys.

Julian had no time to be shaved, for there was Lola at the door, inquiring if Mrs. Norval lived there. On hearing which inquiry, the stately lady arose, with more precipitation than usually accompanied her movements, and went to meet Lola. But stupid Bingham opened the door, saying, "Here, Miss Lola, here are all."

"What is the meaning of this? Why do you come away in this manner?" was Mrs. Norval's salutation.

"Because there was no other, and I couldn't stay there," Lola replied.

"What do you mean?"

"By-and-by I will tell you all."

"Mother, oh, mother, bring her to me!" said the feeble voice of Julian in the next room.

Lola did not wait to be brought to him. As soon as she heard his voice she rushed by Mrs. Norval, and at one bound was in the next room.

"Lola, darling!" exclaimed Julian, extending his weak arms towards her.

Now, if those arms had been strong, she would certainly have kept away from them, no matter how lovingly they had been extended to her. But the poor arms were so thin and weak, they seemed so to implore sympathy, that she forgot all her resolves and Mrs. Norval's frowns, and she obeyed the appeal and went straight to them, and for the first time Julian's lips touched her fresh, rosy cheek, all flushed with the morning air and her happiness.

In justice to Lola, it must be stated that she had passed the greater part of the night tracing for herself a 'prospectus' of her future conduct towards Julian, which was so strict and circumspect that Mrs. Norval herself could not have found a single fault with it. But she had not thought that Julian would look like this. He was so pale, so very weak, that she forgot the rigid prospectus, and felt nothing but the tenderest pity and sympathy.

He sank back exhausted after that grand effort, but, as Lola still held his hand, he soon revived again.

When Mrs. Norval that evening heard from Lola that Hackwell had actually *proposed* to her; that he had begged her to marry him, and had said that he had loved her always, even when others thought her an Indian; that he would die for her, do anything she ordered him to do, then Mrs. Norval's little gang broke the string and got out of their bottle indeed, and it is doubtful whether they ever went back again. Still, she spoke very calmly to Lola, for she knew that her face, which was livid, could not be seen in the darkened room. She said, "I am inclined to think that you misunderstood Mr. Hackwell. He jests sometimes, though so very dignified generally. Girls sometimes think that gentlemen mean more than they do."

"Mr. Hackwell was very explicit, I assure you, and would become impatient when I tried to turn off his words as if said in jest. I noticed, too, that Emma always left me alone with him, so I had no choice but to go away. I told him I would tell you all, so do not imagine I am acting a double part. I am not afraid of him."

"I do not suppose you are. No one can accuse you of wanting in boldness."

"You are always severe with me, madam. But what I meant was that I am so sure of my not having mistaken him, that I am not at all afraid he will think I have exaggerated or misstated his words."

"I don't know that the matter will be mentioned at all; I don't suppose he cares. But, as Emma, of course, cannot be left all alone, I shall go and see if I can get some married lady to stay with her until Mr. Hackwell can be removed to New York."

"Mrs. Cackle is there all the time, and her two daughters."

"I'll see for myself." So saying, Mrs. Norval arose with great dignity, and the interview was ended.

Lola saw that she had mortally offended the lady, but she did not know how. She had not told half of what Hackwell had had the impudence to say. And Hackwell had certainly made a fool of himself, and had gone so far as to say to Lola that *he* hated Mrs. Norval for that matron's undisguised aversion to Lola. This, Lola was too honorable to repeat, and it is well she did not, for Mrs. N. would never have believed that of Hackwell.

Julian improved as if by miracle, and the second evening after Lola's arrival, Mrs. Norval announced her intention to take that night's steamer for Baltimore, feeling that she could do so "conscientiously"—nay, more, that it was "her *duty*" to do so.

"Emma is alone, and *my conscience* reproves me. As long as Julian was in danger, *my duty* was to be here. But now *my duty* is to go there," said Mrs. Norval to Lavvy. And her gang of unbottled imps no doubt laughed and skipped about in joy, and clapped their hands, knowing that the madam would take them all to Washington, which is a city very congenial to all unbottled little imps, and where the jolly crew would have abundant fun.

They were not mistaken. They all accompanied the madam, and, having had a prosperous journey, on the second day they were with her by the bedside of the fascinating Hack, who pretended to be quite prostrate, and exhausted with pain, in order to gain time and sympathy.

But the madam either saw through it, or was too irate to be tender. So, with a tinge of irony in her tone, she said, when Emma had prudently left them alone, "What has caused this relapse? When Lola left you, you were very cheerful and quite strong."

Hackwell groaned, and said, "I have been very imprudent. I tried to walk, and it has brought on inflammation. I hope I shall not have to resort to amputation." And he watched with half-closed eyelids the effect that this fearful prospect of his hopping on one leg would have on the madam. Her face was just as hard. There was neither fear nor pity in it.

"She is angry beyond propitiation," thought Hackwell. "Very well; tyrants are cowards, as a general thing, and if that little scamp Lola has carried out her threat and told her all, then I might as well have it over now, and see who is to be the master." So he groaned again, and closed his eyes, remaining silent.

"Perhaps you wish to be alone, Mr. Hackwell. If so, I shall retire," said she, in a voice trembling with anger.

Languidly he opened his eyes and replied, "I fear it is very dull for you here, my dear friend. I thank you for your kindness. If you wish to go, please send Emma to me."

Mrs. Norval rose and left the room, too indignant to speak. Emma came in, and found her brother convulsed with laughter.

"What is the matter? Mrs. Norval was so pale when she told me you wanted me, that I thought something had happened to you."

"Nothing has happened. Shut the door and come here by me. I'll tell you what it is."

Emma closed the door and sat by her brother.

"Look here, Em, you and I are alone in the world, of all our family, except little John. Well, we will have to work for each other. I fear Lola has told Mrs. Norval all, and—"

"Of course she did; she said she would—the—the—spotted mongrel, the—"

"Hush! no abusive epithets. You know she is no more a spotted Indian than yourself. And I tell you this frankly, that in trying to win Lola away from Julian to leave you the coast clear, I got to like the girl more than is good for my comfort. But I know she is too deeply in love with the other to like me or anyone else. Now, as we cannot win Lola away from Julian, and we want money, we must try to get both Julian and money in some other way, and that way is the old woman—I beg her pardon—the madam."

"But how are we to do that?"

"Very easily, my child. Don't laugh loud, and I'll tell you a tale that doesn't require the moonlight, and can as well be told by a kerosene lamp. In short, the old lady is fearfully smitten."

"What!"

"Do you promise secrecy?"

"Of course I do."

"Well, she is in the last stages of love with your humble servant."

"Oh, John! you tell it in such a ridiculous way that you make me laugh."

"Could the thing be told in any way that would not be ridiculous? But that is not the point. The point is, that it is in our interest to humor her. She loved me—she says—for my virtues, eloquence, and edifying example as a minister of the gospel, and my patriotism in leaving my sacred calling to offer my services and my life to my bleeding country. She says all this to justify herself in her own eyes—the hypocrite—for being so ready to fall in love within two weeks after she heard of the death of her husband. But I am not the one to find fault with that, though I think it contemptible to be finding *reasons* to love, when it is well known that the truest love is generally the one that has no foundation at all. However, I don't want to preach on the subject, only you take your cue."

After some further talk, brother and sister laid down their plans and retired for the night.

CHAPTER XXXIV

Mrs. Norval's Virtuous Impulse Rewarded

Of all the jolly gangs of unbottled imps which in Washington hold nightly bacchanalian carousal, none were merrier than Mrs. Norval's. They danced and frolicked around her as she wandered in restless walk about her room, or lay down to think *and cry*, and never to sleep.

Next morning she looked at herself in the glass. She was horrified. She was so old, so very old. That would never do. What a fool she was to fret so and ruin her looks, she thought, and began a careful toilette. How was it possible to win Hackwell from Lola, so young, so beautiful, so fresh? Still, she redoubled her efforts, and the excitement gave her an animated look, which was better than the haggard one with which she began her toilette.

The charming invalid was better this morning, and, though he was rather pale, his handsome dark eyes shone clear and bright; he was very, very handsome. So thought the madam, too.

But, withal, for once his eloquence had failed to make her think just what he liked. He saw this, and, as she constantly referred to Lola, he said, "Why do you keep alluding to Lola? It is not possible that you are jealous of that child?"

"Oh, no! That, of course, was impossible." She blushed because she knew she was telling a falsehood. Why should she be jealous? she had no right to be.

"You have a right, if you wish to have it, but you have no cause."

Again the matron blushed like a girl. But she was not convinced. He continued:

"If Lola told you that I flirted with her, she told you the truth. I paid her all sorts of compliments, and told her that if I was a millionaire I would marry her and take her to Europe to outshine all the princesses there. But, you see, as there is no danger of my being a millionaire, I think I am safe in saying all that. It was all very well as long as she laughed, but the fact was that she was dying to go to Julian, and all of a sudden it struck her that my lovemaking would be an excellent excuse to go to him. Then she told me I wasn't behaving like a gentleman, and she would not stay under the same roof with me another day, and telegraphed she was going, and in two hours she was off. She was candid, though, and told me she would tell you everything. This threat, however, did not alarm me, for I thought you would see how it all was. But I fear that you do not have the confidence in me which—"

"Yes, I have. Forgive me, John—I mean Captain Hackwell—I have confidence, but—"

"But you haven't. Well, then, let my short dream be over. We will be the same good friends of old, and no more. When people are of our age, it is time they should discard foolish jealousies, as most unprofitable, and annoying, and ridiculous. If two persons who love each other cannot have full confidence in one another, they are better separated than united."

Mrs. Norval was very sorry, very repentant and submissive, and—and—very loving.

Before the week was over, they were engaged to be married. Their engagement was to be a profound secret.

"If there was any hope of Lola! But that is next to impossible! Heigh-ho! meantime, my rights of betrothed might help me. Who can tell? Fortune favors the bold—*allons*!" exclaimed the invalid.

Captain Hackwell was not the man to lose any time in enforcing what he termed his "rights of betrothed."

"Jenny, darling, we must not forget Em in our happiness. The poor child is fretting herself into a skeleton because Lola is with Julian," said his ex-reverence, a day or two after the solemn pledging of their vows.

"I'll write this very day to Lavvy that Lola must return at once to her convent."

And she did write, and Lavvy, of course, told Lola what Mrs. Norval's orders were. But Julian said Lola should not go, that Lavvy was not strong enough to take any care upon herself, and he knew he would have a relapse the very day Lola left. So Lavvy, after a day or two, sent that answer to her sister.

Immediately came flashing through the telegraphic wires an order for Lola to leave forthwith.

Julian's pale face flushed with anger.

"This is the work of that renegade parson, I know," he said. "Please, Lola, sit by that table and write what I dictate. It is but a short dispatch to mother." Lola obeyed, and wrote as he dictated:

"Lola will leave by next steamer; too warm to go by the cars.

JULIAN NORVAL."

"Next steamer will leave in a week, and then there will be another," added Julian to Lola and Lavvy, "and we will go together."

This plan was charming, and the three were very happy to wait or go together.

In the meantime, several days passed without any telegraphic orders, and that was very pleasant. One came the day they were to start, which Julian put in the fire, saying he would answer it from New York.

The first news Mrs. Norval had of the three runaways came in a letter from Ruth, in which she said that, two days previously, Julian, with Lola and Lavinia, had arrived, and that—it being now nearly the end of June—Lola had written to her convent, saying that she would not return until September, as the summer vacation commenced the 1st of July.

Mrs. Norval was too angry to speak.

Captain Hackwell would have been more so, if there had been any use in it. But the captain was a great utilitarian, and had a contempt for anything useless. He could not help cursing Julian, in his heart, for having thus checkmated them, but he would not ever waste breath in a useless oath.

Blandly, therefore, he told his dear Jemima to be calm and that, though it was a surprise to both, she must go to New York for the sake of their poor Em. Hearing which, Emma burst out crying, and her tears being very rare were of course the more effective.

Mrs. Norval lingered yet a few days; then, accompanied by Emma, took her departure.

Captain Hackwell would follow in ten days or a fortnight, as he would then be able to walk to and from a carriage. And his duties as commissary did not require any more.

Like a bombshell, Mrs. Norval fell on her family one day. But, as Julian was used to bombshells, he was not in the least disconcerted. He had, moreover, a good masked battery in the oath he had made to his father not to marry without his consent, and this battery the madam did not even suspect.

Before Mrs. Norval went to bed that night, she had obtained from Ruth a full report of Julian's and Lola's conduct towards each other. And, as her mother looked exceedingly vexed, Ruth said, "Why, ma, I thought you knew it all. Where have your eyes been, not to have seen that those two are stupidly in love with each other? And, let me tell you, Lavvy and Mattie quite favor their attachment; that much is clear, too, though, to be sure, I haven't much time to watch anybody, as I am too busy, with my summer things not half-done and July 'most here."

"Why are not your things done?"

"Because, whilst Julian was so ill, of course I did not know but what we might go in mourning, and what was the use of having such a lot of light silks made? That is why I asked you to tell me every day how Julian was. But I don't know why you almost forgot us. I would have had my things 'most ready now, if you had told me in time that Jule was out of danger."

In a few days, however, several Saratoga trunks, as big as houses, stood there, all packed full of the dry goods which composed the elegant and costly outfit of the Misses Norval for their summer campaign.

Julian, though weak yet and very pale, had left the day before, just in time to arrive at Gettysburg before the firing commenced.

"What a bother!" exclaimed Ruth, looking at her Saratoga trunks. "Now we will have to wait until we hear whether Jule is killed or not before I can wear my new things. He will surely be wounded; he always is."

CHAPTER XXXV

Messrs. Wagg and Head Travel Together

In less than a fortnight after Mrs. Norval's departure, Commissary Hackwell was ready to start for the city of New York. Through the powerful intercession of the Cackles, he had been assigned to duty as a purchasing officer in that city.

Those almighty Cackles had also demanded from a just government—ever ready to reward merit—that the gallant Captain Hackwell (who was captain by brevet only) should have still another brevet, and be henceforth called "*major*," which was done.

At the request of the Hon. Beau Cackle, the major engaged for his head clerk one Mr. Albino Skroo, a Hungarian, who married an American lady and with her thrived under the warm shelter of a high dignitary's wing. Mr. Skroo described himself as having been the bosom friend of Kossuth,[40] with whom he suffered for the love of liberty. That same love pulled him so hard to this country that he was obliged to leave the Turkish army, where he was serving with great glory. The Sultan wept with grief at "General Skroo's" departure, and General Skroo's eyes filled with tears at the recollection, making his story more plausible. Nevertheless, there was a look about Mr. Skroo which suggested the probability of his having tried the *bastinado*,[41] and afterwards, using a poetical license, spoke of the Sultan's weeping instead of his own. Mr. Skroo liked freedom.

General Julius Caesar Cackle also had his own *protégés*. He, on his part, recommended very strongly to the major for his two assistants, two favorites of his—two very nice young men—friends of the general.

[40]Lagos Kossuth (1802-1894) was a statesman, patriot and writer, who sought Hungarian independence from Austria. Skroo "drops" Kossuth's name to ingratiate himself to citizens of his newly-adopted country.

[41]Punishment consisting of a beating or caning.

These two young men had started to run with the general at the battle of Bull Run, but the general, being swifter, had distanced them. Still the general remembered that one of the young men had said, "Take that path, captain. It is shorter." And the other had said, "There is a horse and buggy, captain."

And thus Julius had found a shorter path and a horse which took him to safety, to the Hon. Gunn, and to glory.

These two young men were then privates in a zouave regiment; now they were lieutenants, and, in short, not to keep the reader in suspense—which, by-the-by, I notice is a very popular sort of *artifice* freely employed by "*sensational*" novelists—as my aspirations are humble—which these pages sufficiently demonstrate—I will at once say that these two *nice* young men recommended by General Cackle were no other than the witty Lieutenant Æschylus Wagg and the poetical and musical Lieutenant Sophocles Head, mentioned before as marching to Bull Run.

In addition to that of General Cackle, the ex-member of Congress, the Hon. Le Grand Gunn had put in his recommendation most especially in behalf of Lieutenant Æschylus Wagg, the witty.

In the opinion of Lieutenant Head, next to going to paradise was to be on duty in New York City. And if anything could add to this supreme happiness, it was that of having for companion Wagg, the witty.

So, as both youths oscillated and bobbed up and down, sitting in the same seat in the cars, on a hot July day, Lieutenant Head expressed his gratification in this manner: "I say, Wagg, it never rains but it pours. Don't it, old fellow?"

"It seems to me the sun is shining like a potful of hellfire. But you are a poet, and probably see snow," growled Wagg.

Head knew that when Wagg was in ill humor, or wished to tease him, he always used profane language, which the tender soul of Head disapproved. So he timidly explained, "I mean the good luck of being ordered to New York, and on the same duty, so that we can be together."

"I don't see either that I can call that a remarkable piece of good luck, and I don't thank that cursed Le Grand Gunn for it, d—n him. I know why he wanted me out of the way. He was afraid that if I remained, Lucinda would send him afloat. And she shall yet, curse him. He knows she is only too partial to me."

"You needn't be cursing that good gentleman, who, I am sure, is very moral and a good Christian, and doesn't care whether Lucinda is partial to you or not, for it was *I* who asked Major Hackwell to bring you. Mr. Gunn only smiled, and said you were a most gallant soldier and a worthy young man, and he hoped the major *would* bring you, because you deserved it."

"I wish he'd get what he deserves. He'd be the devil's spittoon."

"You talk awfully! How can you? Mr. Gunn spoke most kindly of you."

"You are the same old '*Soft Head*' of the red breeches, and your twaddle makes me furious. How can you be such an unmitigated fool as to imagine that because you—*Soffy*—asked the major, he brought me? Only in your *soft* head could such a blunt idea penetrate—always a softy!"

"You needn't be making fun of my name, for yours ain't any prettier, as I know of."

"Yes, and I may thank you for that, d—n you."

"I ain't your father or your godfather, as I know of. Curse someone else."

"If we were not in the cars, I would mash your *soft* skull for you," said Wagg, livid with rage, glaring at his companion.

That this interesting and polished little dialogue may be understood, it shall be explained.

When these two officers were privates in the zouave regiment, both were in the same company, and great friends, until one day, when getting ready for a review, there were many men together, and the mail was brought and letters were handed to several of them. With these letters came one addressed to "Private Æschylus Wagg." Head, being near the man handing out the letters, took, to give to Wagg, the one addressed to him. In so doing, he glanced at the address and read aloud, "Æschylus Wagg," and added, "Why, Wagg, that is my brother's name, and it makes him furious to be called Scaly—for short—but so we call him."

The men laughed, for it was known in the company that such was Wagg's sobriquet.

From that day, Wagg had occasional fits of aversion towards the mild and patient Head. One day, when Wagg had been more than usually irritable towards Head, the latter said to him, "Now, Wagg, your name ain't so bad. Just think of my brother! He will be Scaly Head all his life. And me, because my name is Sophocles, I am called Sophy and *Soft Head*; that is worse."

"And who in thunder gave you and your brother such names?" bawled Wagg.

"My father was a literary man, and he said that as he was a poor man and could not leave us money, he would leave us distinguished names."

This literary gentleman was a sexton and village schoolteacher, who led a half-starved life, but never would sell his Greek tragedies.

"A cursed old maid gave me mine, for sole inheritance, too," said Wagg.

The excessive heat and dust did not appease Wagg's ill humor, but, as Head prudently devoted himself to a new novel he was reading (there being not a vacant seat he could take), there was no occasion to renew the choice amenities of their past dialogue.

They were now approaching Wilmington. Lieutenant Wagg was feeling very hungry, and as he had exhausted almost all of his month's pay in a farewell gift to Lucinda, he felt the necessity of being economic till next payday, which was yet far off. He was sorry he had quarreled with Sophy.

On his part, Lieutenant Head, in the softness of his heart, had been thinking that it was rather hard to be called Scaly, and was, therefore, quite anxious to apologize to Wagg. He gave his irascible companion the very contrite look of a good dog who accepts opprobrium for the sake of love, at the very time that a colored gentleman opened the door and shouted, "Twenty min't's for refreshments!" And the passengers rushed out as if the car was on fire.

Useless hurry. An American traveler only requires four minutes to eat his dinner—half a minute for soup, one minute and a half for fish, two minutes for meats and vegetables, and half a minute for apple pie. Then he has laid the foundation for a life's dyspepsia, to be helped with buckwheat cakes every winter.

Lieutenant Wagg smiled. Hunger allays anger.

"Ain't you going to get out and eat something? I am awful hungry. Come, don't be mad. Let me treat, and then I shall think you have forgiven me," said Softy, the soft-hearted. And both friends went out to munch in four minutes what they should have taken an hour to eat.

That night they were in New York.

The major's room was all ready for him, and, as all the girls, including Lavinia and Lola, had gone to Saratoga, there was nothing to interfere with the madam in her hospitable efforts to make the major happy and at home.

He, on his part, lost no time in putting a little plan of his into execution. By setting the madam to make inquiries in regard to money matters from Sinclair, he soon found out a good deal more than he already knew. Then he immediately wrote to his old friend Hammerhard to give up his New England pulpit and come to New York, that he had a plan by which both could make money enough to be independent.

Hammerhard, by return mail, answered that within two or three weeks he would be with him.

"So far, so good," said the major to himself; then aloud to Mrs. Norval, "How long will the girls be at Saratoga?"

"I don't know; a month, perhaps. As they are with the Sinclairs, they will do what Mrs. Sinclair says. Lavinia will return to Washington in September, and Lola to her convent, I suppose, though Mattie told me that Lola said she is to graduate this fall. Emma and my daughters are to go to Newport with the Sinclairs, and as Julian is to have a two-months' leave, I suppose he will go with them."

The major nodded his head in approval, and Mrs. Norval was very happy.

About two weeks after this conversation, Mr. and Mrs. Hammerhard arrived in New York, and announced to their friends their intention of making the great metropolis their home.

The Rev. Hammerhard and his friend the ex-Rev. Hackwell came out of Mrs. Norval's sitting room the morning of the third day after his reverence's arrival. They had a mysterious look about them, but seemed pleased.

"She is booked now. I congratulate you on your second nuptials," said Mr. Hammerhard.

"Thanks. But, remember, we mustn't crow very loud," the major replied. "I am not so sure as Sinclair is about the news from Africa being true."

"But as long as she believes it, what more need we ask?"

"A great deal more, Ham. But 'sufficient unto the day'," etc. And the two friends again shook hands, laughing a laugh they alone understood.

CHAPTER XXXVI

The Returned Prisoners, and What They Said

Mrs. Cackle had never listened when her literary consort read those historical books from which their children derived their illustrious names. She had not heard a word, either, about the siege of Troy and the especial protection accorded to the Argives[42] by the blue-eyed goddess Minerva. Neither could she ever be guilty of approaching popery near enough to believe in guardian angels or patron saints. No sir; not she. But, as she was a good American woman, she believed firmly in "MANIFEST DESTINY," and that the Lord was *bound* to protect the Union, even if to do so the affairs of the rest of the universe were to be laid aside for the time being. Consequently, Mrs. Cackle was positive that if the North only went "ahead," and didn't stop to think or to take a breath, it would "all come out right." The war was the best thing that could have happened, for, besides setting the negroes free and chastising their owners, had it not made two of her sons distinguished congressmen and the other two renowned generals? Mrs. Cackle was perfectly satisfied, and told her daughters that Lavvy Sprig was a silly thing to be crying because so many poor fellows died in the hospitals, and so many returned prisoners came back mutilated and looking like skeletons.

"She is the silliest, most restless thing, this Lavvy Sprig, more than ever since she returned from New York so very sad," said Mrs. Cackle one day to her daughters, as she partook of a hurried breakfast. "She sent for me before I was awake this morning to go to visit a new batch

[42]Ruiz de Burton further carries out the mock epic of the Cackles, here comparing their success on the battlefield to that of the Argives, the people of Argos, (ruled by Agamemnon) that according to Homer, were favored by the Greek goddess of war and wisdom, Athena (Minerva), in their war against the Trojans.

of returned prisoners just come from the South. Ned White can't go with her, so she wants me, for which I don't thank her, for I don't relish a trip to Baltimore and back on the same day. I wish she'd give up hunting for Isaac."

"Is Lavvy yet in pursuit of Isaac?" carelessly inquired General Cackle, as he stepped into the breakfast room and overheard his mother's last words.

"Of course she is. She and Ned White go to visit every newly-arrived prisoner, always to inquire for the lost Isaac—all to no purpose. No one knows whether he is dead or alive. His name is not on any list of prisoners."

The general commenced his breakfast and said no more, but he knew very well that his friend Gunn had taken good care that Isaac's name should *not* be in any list.

The newly-arrived sick whom Lavvy and Mrs. Cackle were to see that morning were "*Union prisoners*," who had been at the Libby or Belle-Isle[43] since the beginning of the war. From the depot the two ladies drove directly to the hospital. The heart of Lavinia beat with hope and fear of what she might hear about her poor brother, now gone more than two years, and never once heard of.

Ascertaining that the sick were doing as well as could be expected, and that they were all pretty comfortable, accompanied by one of the hospital matrons and Mrs. Cackle, Lavvy went up to the "sick-rooms" to commence her investigation.

After the usual inquiries about the state of their health and comfort of several of the patients in the room—a long one, containing forty beds, all of which were occupied—Lavvy asked one of the men, who seemed brighter and stronger than the others, whether he had ever met Captain Isaac Sprig, who was captured at *the first* Bull Run.

"No, ma'am. I was most of *my* time at Belle-Isle, and maybe he was at the Libby."

"*I* was at the Libby. Who is that you want to know about? I know all about him," said a man sitting up in great precipitation, and he was so attenuated that he looked like a skeleton rising from the grave.

"Shut up, Scrogs. You know you are crazy," said a shrill voice at the opposite side of the narrow room. And a boy holding his arm in a sling sat up too, as if to be ready to hold Scrogs silent.

"No, I ain't crazy, neither. I only want some ice cream," said Scrogs pleadingly.

[43]Libby and Belle-Isle were Confederate prison camps at Richmond, Virginia.

"Shut up your ice cream; the lady wants to know something," insisted the boy. "Jim Suky can tell you more, ma'am; he ain't crazy, and he was at the Libby, too. Get up, Jim, and tell the lady if you ever heard of Captain Sprig."

A fair, light-haired boy made two or three attempts to rise, but he was too weak to do so, and he fell back on his pillow.

Lavvy and Mrs. Cackle ran to him, saying not to trouble himself to rise, that he could speak lying down.

"It is no trouble," said Tom of the arm in the sling. "Let him try again, and he'll get up. I never get up myself until I have tumbled down two or three times. You see, ma'am, we are so starved that we ain't got no more strength than so many sick kittens." And the boy laughed, amused at their weak condition, and his laugh seemed contagious, for almost all the poor sick wretches near his bed joined in it, particularly Scrogs, who shook with hilarity until Tom again, in imperious tone, cried to him, "Shut up, Scrogs. Don't laugh so much; it will hurt you." Hearing which, Scrogs became serious on the instant.

"You have Mr. Scrogs under good discipline," said Mrs. Cackle to Tom of the arm in the sling.

"His name ain't Scrogs, ma'am, but we call him so because he was so hungry that he forgot his name. And when he saw some of our boys eating frogs, and he wanted to ask them for some, and for scraps of anything to eat, he cried, 'Scrogs, scrogs!' meaning scraps of frogs, ma'am, that's all. But his name ain't Scrogs."

"What is his name, then?" Lavvy asked.

"We don't know, ma'am, nor he either. What is your name, Scrogs?" asked Tom.

"Scrogs Ice Cream," answered Scrogs, with a military salute.

"You see, ma'am, he is crazy. Hunger made him so, and he don't know his name."

A sob arose to Lavvy's lips. She pulled down her veil and hurried with her inquiries. No one there, however, knew anything of Captain Sprig. They were very sorry they could not give the lady some information, but they had never heard of him.

Seeing that she was going away so sad, to cheer her, the boy with the arm in the sling and authority over Scrogs, said, "You ought to be glad, ma'am, that we never saw him, for if he had been with us, he might now be crazy with hunger, like Scrogs, or his feet and hands eaten up with frost, like me and Sammy."

"Are your feet eaten up with frost?" asked Lavvy, sitting by him again.

"Yes, ma'am, both of them, and this one hand in the sling, too. But Sammy Doggy has his worse than mine. All his toes are gone."

"But why did you let the frost eat up your feet so badly? Why didn't you cover them?" Mrs. Cackle asked.

"Because we only had a piece of a blanket, and my companion was dying of hunger and cold, and I gave him my share of the blanket, ma'am. Poor George! he was so good and patient."

"And what became of him?" asked Lavvy.

"He died, ma'am. He was too weak to be so badly disappointed, like. He was quite cheerful when we were going to Aquia Creek, but when we got there and we found no rebs to change with, and no steamer to take us, and they brought us back to Belle-Isle, then George seemed to have lost all the little strength he had. That night he said to me, 'Tom, it is no use. I'll never see the dear faces of the Union folks no more. I can't stand it. This has gone to my heart. But if I only could see my dear mother and my little baby sister, and kiss them good-by, I wouldn't mind it so much. Good night, old fellow. My love to the Union folks, if you ever get to see them.' And he turned over the other side, and it was bitter cold, so I put our little blanket over him, for I was stronger than he, and by-and-by I didn't feel the cold, and I fell asleep. Next morning, very early, I spoke to George, but he didn't answer me. And, as he was always so civil, I thought something was wrong, that he didn't speak. I moved him, and he was stiff. He had died in the night, ma'am, of hunger and cold, and because his strength gave out, like, ma'am, when he had hoped to go home and they didn't exchange us. He had no more courage anymore; it seemed to him as if the Union folks had forgotten us, and he felt it awfully, and his strength gave out entirely."

The ladies were so affected by this simple recital of Tom that for some time they wept in silence and were unable to speak. Presently, however, Mrs. Cackle asked Tom, "And because you gave your share of your little blanket to your friend George your feet got frozen?"

Yes, ma'am, because it could not cover both of us. If I had known that poor George was dead, I would have taken the blanket myself, for it was no use to him no more, ma'am, you see. But I thought he was asleep, he was so quiet, and I felt sorry for him, and I covered him all I could, and my feet got froze up. But my hands will be all right. I ain't as bad off as Sammy Doggy. He has his fingers all chopped off, and his toes all eaten up, gone, with the frost."

"But was there no wood for you to make a fire?" asked Mrs. Cackle of the man designated as Sammy Doggy.

"Very little, ma'am, and the fellows who were strong would take it. Sometimes we had a little more, when the James River floated down sticks and left them on the shore around the island. Then we gathered them up and put them to dry to make a fire. But, as I was so weak, the other fellows pushed me off and took the sticks from me, and so I had no fire."

"The wicked rebels, to take a few sticks from a poor sick man!" exclaimed Mrs. Cackle, indignant.

"No, ma'am, it wasn't the rebs; it was our own companions, ma'am. But we were so cold and so hungry that we didn't care for nobody, and we quarreled for a bit of anything to eat, or a bit of wood to make a fire."

"His hands wouldn't have got frozen, ma'am, if he hadn't held on to his dog after his hole in the ground caved in," said Tom.

"What does he mean?" asked the ladies, growing more shocked and more curious every moment.

"He means that I dug a hole in the ground to sleep, for I had no wood nor blanket. And one night it rained very hard, and the hole caved in, and the earth held me there until next morning, and my hands got froze up."

"Yes, but why don't you tell the ladies that your hands was froze up because you wouldn't let go your dead dog?"

"But why did you wish to keep your dead dog so much? Did you love him so very dearly?" asked Lavinia, thinking of her own dear poodle, abandoned for her country's sake.

Here Scrogs began to laugh immoderately, and his laugh again seemed contagious, and for some moments nothing but laughing—as loud as could come out of such carcasses—was heard in the whole room. The ladies could not see the joke, and waited until the laugh should subside, which it did as soon as Tom said to the leader of it, "Shut up, Scrogs. I tell you, laughing will hurt you."

Then Sammy answered, "No, ma'am, I didn't love the dog, but we wanted to eat him."

"Oh! oh!" exclaimed the ladies. "Whose dog was it? Where did you catch it?"

"The dog belonged to a rebel officer who came to see how many of us had come back from Aquia Creek. The dog was running about, and I caught him by the hind legs and killed him. Then I carried him to my cave and kept him until the officer went away. When he was gone, we took the dog out and skinned him, and divided him among the fellows of my company, and we ate it up."

"You ate a dog!" Mrs. Cackle ejaculated.

"Yes, ma'am, skin, tail, ears, legs, entrails, all, all. And we only wished it had been a bigger dog. When my house—the hole where I slept, I mean—when it caved in, I had my piece of dog with me there, and just had time to save it, and held it in my hands, though my legs were buried. That is the way my hands got frozen."

"But didn't the rebels give you any meat?" asked Mrs. Cackle.

"Yes, ma'am, once in a while. But we were so hungry that we rushed to the meat cart when we saw it coming, and we took all we could, without waiting till they gave it to us, and so the weak ones didn't get anything, and sometimes they starved to death."

"But didn't the rebels give you any other kind of food at all?" again asked Mrs. Cackle.

"Yes, ma'am, a little. They gave us corn or flour sometimes, and a bit of bacon, or molasses, but not much of anything."

"The wicked, horrid creatures!" exclaimed Mrs. C.

"The truth is, ma'am, that they didn't have much to give, and nothing to spare. They complained that we were eating them up, because we helped to consume the little they had, and so we were starving them. When I was first taken prisoner, they gave me some kind of bread made of oats and corn meal. It was very hard, and I threw mine away, and the reb sentinel taking care of us picked it up and began to eat it. I asked him how could he eat such dry husks, and he said to me, 'When you have been longer in the Confederacy, you will be mighty glad to get such dry husks as these.' And so I would, afterwards. They are all starving down there."

"But they fight as if they ate four regular meals of Old Nick's flesh every day," said Tom.

"That is truly so," said Mrs. Cackle. "They seem inspired by the Evil One to destroy the best government on earth, the last hope of mankind."

And here Mrs. Cackle took occasion to deliver a lecture on patriotism to the sick and maimed men, who listened to her attentively, resting their mangled and frostbitten extremities upon pillows. What a parody, Mrs. Cackle! You should kneel down before those pitiful, bleeding stumps wrapped up in rags, for they are sacred symbols of that love of country you are bleating about. They speak words which easy patriotism cannot say, neither from the pulpit nor the tribune.

So thought Lavvy, and, interrupting Mrs. Cackle's effusions of comfortable patriotism, they took their departure, with cheering and kind words from Lavvy, with exhortations to vengeance from the Roman matron Cackle.

A long war was good for the Cackle family.

Lavinia did not wish for vengeance. She had seen suffering enough. Her heart only yearned for her lost brother. Where was he? Was he dead? Lavvy asked herself these questions a thousand times. She now began to think of going South to hunt up Isaac herself. If he was sick, she would stay to take care of him. If he was dead, she would bring his remains to bury them decently at home. Like sweet, devoted Antigone, she would go "beyond the gates of Thebes" to bury the dear remains of her Polynices—in the face of the wrath of Creon, who had said, "Let all the traitors and rebels be devoured by vultures around the walls of Thebes."[44]

[44]In Sophocles' tragedy, Creon, king of Thebes, decrees that the body of Polynices, son of Oedipus, is to remain unburied. When his sister Antigone dares to go against the king to fulfill the rites due the dead, she is condemned to be buried alive. Upon learning of the decree, Antigone and her fiancé, Creon's son, commit suicide. Though somewhat forced, the parallel between Antigone and Lavinia is meant to underscore the heartlessness of the "high officials" of the Union government who allow her brother Isaac to languish in prison.

CHAPTER XXXVII

Mrs. Norval's Mental Debut

Julius Caesar Cackle had often slid downhill, carrying on his sledge close to his heart the fair young form of Ruth Norval, and his heart had not throbbed any faster than it was natural it should, going up a steep hill, dragging a heavy sledge, and then downhill at lightning speed.

Now, however, General Cackle's heart behaved more like a heart. After a ride in Central Park, in a most elegant turnout, by the side of Ruth—though not nearly so close as in the sledge—it throbbed. And when, after the ride in the Park and down Fifth Avenue, there followed an exquisite dinner at the Norval palace, and then the opera, with its charming, bewitching aristocratic bustle, its dazzling lights, and more dazzling toilettes, then the general's sluggish heart commenced to give responsive beats, and grew civilized all so quickly that it began to knock at his stupid head and talk to it. He thought all at once that it was "very queer" that when he had Ruth Norval on his sledge he never once had had the notion of squeezing her—very queer, indeed! "She is mighty fine-looking! I suppose because it was so infernally cold!" muttered the son of Mars to himself—thereby showing a poetical turn of mind very creditable to himself and illustrative of the theory that "great minds will always in kindred thoughts meet," for he had never read the *Divina Commedia*, and yet he had Dante's idea of the infernal regions.

No, there was no doubting that if the general's susceptibilities had lain torpid in the cold North, now they awakened with a leap by the side of Miss Norval, in Mrs. Norval's proscenium box.

Ruth saw the evident admiration of the general, and was pleased thereat because they were in full view of the Misses McCods, the Misses Pinchinghams, the Misses Squeezphat, and more so of the pretty Mrs. Van Kraut, who had the proscenium box opposite and could see the general's "yellow buttons" so well.

Ruth and Emma spread their costly silks (all bought with Lola's money) in magnificent array, flanked by the general and Major Hackwell, who certainly looked very handsome in his uniform, and prepared themselves to stare and be stared at.

With elegant nonchalance Ruth raised her opera glass and surveyed the house—the boxes first, of course. Yes, there they were, all the fashionable wives and daughters of the railroad kings and princes of the gold room. Some of the princes themselves were there, and their hopeful sons, "the youth of New York." But Ruth had seen too many real princes of the blood and danced with too many *bona fide* dukes and counts of aristocratic foundation to care for these whom a tumble in the stocks might dethrone tomorrow. Still, though she affected—as a lady who has traveled abroad should—a contempt for "*Shoddy*,"[45] she was gratified to see that their glasses were directed constantly to her box. She was sure the Norvals were making an impression.

"This is a mighty pretty sight, this opera house, Miss Ruth. I am sorry Miss Mattie and brother Beau didn't come," said the general.

"Yes, I like the opera better than those crowded receptions, but Mattie likes dancing and prefers the balls. I believe she means to go to three tonight."

And Ruth now began to point out to the general the notabilities of fashionable society, the major and Emma occasionally adding their observations, whilst back of them silently sat Julian and Mrs. Norval, who certainly had no wish to be there. Julian was too annoyed and Mrs. Norval too much out of her sphere to enjoy that elegant din. But that force of circumstances which whirls us poor mortals like chips round a whirlpool, had brought them there—the madam for the *first time*.

Let it not be supposed for one moment that she had lost her old horror of the theatre which had made her deplore Isaac's *penchant* for it. No, as yet she would not have gone, unless the major positively desired it, to see a play *spoken*. But she could effect a compromise with her relenting conscience by going to hear it *sung*, particularly as it would be in a language she did not understand, and she would not know what they said. That seemed to her not so wicked, only very silly. And this idea grew in her mind as she sat there listening to what to her seemed a Chinese din, and seeing those people singing to each other that they were happy, or sad, or angry, or sick, or well, until she was

[45]Here Ruth Norval attempts to mimic high-class disdain for showy, ostentatious over-dressing.

ready to burst out laughing. But no one had ever seen her laugh aloud. She did not like to laugh. Still, those people were too much for her gravity, and when Adalgisa and Norma[46] sang their grand duo and separated in despair, Mrs. Norval said, laughing quite loud, "What is the matter? I thought they were going to fight. But I suppose someone is sick and they have run for the doctor."

"Oh, mother, hush! for gracious' sake!" said Ruth, afraid that she would be heard.

But Mrs. Norval did not stop there. After a while she asked, "Why did she beat that gong?—for dinner ?"

"Oh, ma! it is the sacred shield. She is calling her warriors to drive off the Romans," said Ruth in despair.

But Hackwell was amused at her remarks, and this made her so happy that she almost felt tempted to leap upon the stage and begin to sing her own love as being exactly similar to that of Norma, only greater, truer, than any ever sung or wept for by any matron before or after Norma.

It was very fortunate that the "leg opera" had not yet blossomed on the New York stage, as it lately has, else his ex-reverence might have been tempted to take the madam there, just to test the strength of his power and to measure the length of his tether—for he was fond of experimenting. The madam then, though she would never utter the word "*leg*" would have seen five-hundred bare ones, in entangling evolutions, like so many polypi let loose to crawl on the stage, cuttlefish dangling merrily their tentacula, with a sure instinct of fastening on poor, gaping oysters, which would be sucked dry. But the advent of the yellow-haired nymphs of the "eighty-leg opera" was yet retarded and Mrs. Norval with the rest of the community was spared from that *improvement* on the drama.[47] Therefore I cannot tell what would have been her sentiments on seeing those half-nude females tossing their limbs so promiscuously, if she had observed that they pleased her adored John. I fear she would have been willing to pirouette, too.

Julian could certainly appreciate music much better than his mother, but his mind was too anxiously preoccupied to enjoy anything.

He had arrived from the Army of the Potomac that morning very unexpectedly, and had requested his mother to see him in her room alone. But the major overheard him, and as he arose from the breakfast

[46]Adalgisa and Norma are characters that appear in the opera *Norma*, by Vincent Bellini (1831).

[47]The September 1866 debut of the Broadway musical *The Black Crook*, featuring 100 dancing girls in pink tights, caused a sensation in New York.

table to go to his office downtown, he whispered to her, "Don't promise anything to Julian until you consult with me."

To be on the safe side, Mrs. Norval had made several excuses to Julian to put off the interview until the next day. They were going to have a dinner party that day, and she had ever so many things to attend to. Wouldn't it be the same tomorrow? Julian sighed and said, "Very well." He could afford to wait a day, considering that he had made up his mind what to do. So he said no more, and joined the dinner party, rode in the park, and went to the opera, perfectly indifferent as to how he spent the intervening hours.

After the opera they took an ice at Delmonico's,[48] and then rode home, Mrs. Norval and her *husband* in her cozy little coupé, and the young people in the large carriage. At the door the general bade them good night, and as he drove to his hotel in the soft cushioned carriage of the Norvals, his thoughts reverted again to the hard old sledge, and he sighed, thinking he would "like *mighty* well" to have Ruth now as close as then to his heart.

That young lady, meantime, ran up to her room and told her maid to undress her. Miss Ruth could not undress herself now.

"Did Miss Mattie's dress fit her well?" asked Miss Ruth when she undressed, all but her "rats and mice"[49] to come off.

"Beautifully," answered Mina, the maid, commencing to take dozens and scores of hairpins from chignon and rats. "Mademoiselle looked superbe, comme une véritable princesse. And Monsieur Cack was charmant, so pleased, so passionné, il est profondement épris de Mademoiselle Matti."[50]

"Never mind that; describe her dress, for I did not see even the stuff before it was made up."

"It is a white satin, with silver fringe, and above it a narrow silver galloon for a heading; the skirt full and with a long trail; over it a tunic of pale-green gauze, trimmed also with silver galloon and fringe; under the fringe is a deep d'Alençon flounce."

"That is too much. Mattie must have looked loaded; I am sure she did."

[48]Ruiz de Burton here refers to the famed Delmonico's Restaurant in New York.

[49]The term "rats and mice" refers to the hairpieces worn by fashionable ladies to complete their elaborate toilette.

[50]Mina, Ruth Norval's personal servant, here remarks, in French, that General Cackle is taken with Ruth's sister, Mattie.

"No, miss, she looked royal—magnificent. The sleeves and corsage are also trimmed with point d'Alençon to match, the ends of the Alençon fichu falling over a large Alençon sash, in the back, over the green tunic. It is lovely!"

"Too much stuff; too loaded," said Ruth, jumping into bed. Since she became a fashionable lady she had no time to say her prayers; she was too tired—too busy.

As soon as she put her head on her pillow, she began to plan several dresses which would eclipse those of Mattie. From that her thoughts naturally went to the opera and to General Cackle, and ran in this manner:

"Who would have thought that Ciss Cackle could ever look so well? Wonderful *metamorphosers* are those yellow buttons. But more yet, MONEY! Yes, money is *everything*. I wonder if the Cackles have made as much money as it is said? They ought to, with so many fat government contracts at their disposal. He wouldn't be a bad catch, if they have money besides the stars in the straps." And Ruth laughed to find herself thinking of Julius Cackle as a catch—he who used to plow with her Uncle Abraham and drive their wagons to market full of pigs, or poultry, or apples, or hay, or vegetables. But this thought Ruth never uttered even to the pillow; she drove it off quickly, and tried to think of the opera, and the sensation they had made, to judge by the number of glasses directed at their box. These thoughts would again take her to the general, and in spite of herself to those old times of which he too had thought, when they used to slide downhill together and walk up arm-in-arm.

"Who can fall in love freezing?" exclaimed she aloud. "And with such clothes as we wore? I remember I used to look like a fright in my Solferino hood which Aunt Lavvy knitted for me, and my nose about the same shade. Poor aunty! She, too, had a Solferino hood, and her nose was purple. Ugh! I hate poverty!"

And she began to think that they must be very rich, because their mother never objected to their buying anything, and she used to be so very economical. "Yes, papa must have left heaps of money." And, lulled by this delicious thought, she fell asleep.

CHAPTER XXXVIII

In Which the Major, like Yorick, Was a Fellow of Infinite Humor[51]

"Ring for me as soon as you are ready," Major Hackwell said to Mrs. Norval as they alighted from their coupé on their return from the opera.

Mrs. Norval had, as usual, obeyed, and rang a little silver bell which was on the center-table of her bedroom. A minute after, from the closet next to Mrs. Norval's bed, emerged the handsome major in his costly dressing gown and slippers, smoking a most expensive meerschaum, and sat in an arm chair opposite to a similar one occupied by Mrs. Norval. This lady had changed more within the last five years than any of her metamorphosed family. She had grown younger and improved in appearance rapidly since her arrival in New York. She dressed now at the height of the fashion, as John admired finely dressed women, but she always dressed in dark, rich silks, and in a sort of dignified style which suited her very well. Every day her hair was crimped, perfumed, and curled by a hairdresser. Her *robes-de-chambre*, even, were most costly. No more ugly wrappers now, made of old merinos and faded delaines, against which the doctor had protested in vain. John liked to see her well-dressed in her bedroom; so she wore rich *peignoirs* of costly silks and velvets for the winter, and of batistes for the summer. Mrs. Norval, with all this magnificence, and though sure that no one suspected her clandestine marriage, still had a sad look about her face. But even this sad look capricious fate turned for her to good account, causing it to enhance the respectful sympathy which everybody felt it to be her due, because society said in its wisdom, "How is it possible for her to recon-

[51]From Shakespeare's play *Hamlet. Prince of Denmark.* Hamlet addresses the skull of the deceased jester Yorick. Sterne's *Tristam Shandy* also has a character named Yorick, a humorous parson, who claims direct descent from Shakespeare's Yorick.

cile herself to the horrible fate of her husband, who perhaps was not only murdered but eaten by the barbarians of Africa? It was so noble in her not to wear mourning, to prove that the brave soul will cling to hope to the last." There was always a respectful murmur of approval when Mrs. Norval entered her spacious drawing rooms, her long trail sweeping slowly after her majestic form. Even Hack *almost* admired her.

Now Mrs. Norval sat waiting to hear what John had to say. He refilled his pipe and said, "I think it is very silly to postpone the marriage between Em and Julian."

"I have done my best, John dear, but he says he promised his father not to marry, and that he is sure that his father is not—not dead."

"And he is a damned fool for thinking so."

"That may be, but you know, my darling, that I cannot force the boy. He says that Emma did not accept him when he offered himself; that she rejected him, and he has never renewed his offer, and Emma can't hold him to it after rejecting him; that he will leave it up to Emma herself to say whether or not this is the true state of the case."

"Yes, the puppy, because he knows that Em is too proud to hold him to a promise he wants to break. But I, as her brother and protector, will see that the rascal doesn't trifle with her. He was hardly civil to her this evening, and scarcely spoke to her at the opera. But I tell you what, madam, my patience might give out, and you might regret it if it does."

"But what can I do? Only tell me what I must do, and you know I shall obey you. You told me to send Lola back after they came from Fortress Monroe, and I did. But the doctor said she needed change of air, and I was obliged to let her go with the girls to those watering places."

"Yes, and Julian was with her."

"Only a little while. After the battle of Gettysburg, you know, Julian had a relapse, and did not come for five weeks. Then, when he came, I sent Lola off."

"They were together nearly a month."

"That, of course, was unavoidable. They were with Mrs. Sinclair, and I couldn't help it."

"No, you can't help anything. But I will and shall. If Julian doesn't settle this matter now, I will take Em to Europe, and you and I, madam, must part, for a long time, or perhaps forever, as I shall not return while Em has a particle of this foolish love for your false-hearted son. And I fear she is like her brother; she knows how to love constantly and deeply, but not how to forget!" said he, combining in his tone and manner the eloquence of the pulpit and the forum.

Mrs. Norval—would the reader believe it?—clapped her hands to her face in the most feminine manner, as Lavinia, or Mrs. Cackle, or any other weak creature of the subservient order of females would have done—clapped her hands, as if ashamed of having become so womanly, and began to cry.

The major smiled, pleased, and, drawing his chair closer to hers, said, caressingly, "There, there! don't cry, Jenny! I didn't mean to say anything harsh." And he put his arm around the stately form of his wife.

She felt a thrill through her entire frame, just as might have felt one of those creatures—whom she so abhorred—who go to parties in low necks and short sleeves, and go to theatres, and, in their wild chase after worldly pleasures, do court such thrills. She, a strict hater of popery, a pious, proper churchwoman, felt just the same. And who was the man who had the power thus to thrill her whole being and set her heart throbbing in such unmatronly, unpresbyterian tumult? No other than her spiritual adviser, the man trusted by their congregation and held in reverence. She was not shocked at this, at him, or herself; he had educated her mind in such artistic graduations, that she liked, she enjoyed, this antithetical position with her former self. She put her arm around his neck.

"Oh, John! you have such power over me!" sighed the mature inamorata.

"Why shouldn't I? Who has a better right than your husband?" answered the ex-divine, kissing her with a mock passion that almost made him burst out laughing at himself.

Was it Hackwell alone who had caused this change in the rigid pink of blue propriety, or had external influences—MONEY—helped him? If so, it would have been better, perhaps, that those heavy boxes and that little black girl had never come, and that the magnificent palace in Fifth Avenue had never been built, and that Mrs. Norval's heart had never thawed. But she did not think so: she loved this new state of being. She had so far degenerated that she regarded her youth as misspent, her life a blank, until she loved Hackwell, until she was past forty. Poor woman! to have been a chrysalis all her days! Who would not excuse this avalanche of the snows of forty years?

And viewing the matter thus—and that is the way in which Hackwell taught her to view it—he had been her Prometheus[52]—her creator.

[52]Prometheus, one of the Titans in Greek mythology, stole fire from heaven and brought it to man, for which act he was punished. More appropriate to the context here is the legend, according to some stories, that Prometheus

"Such is woman!" moralized Hack, with his head resting on her shoulder. "There is more latent passion in one of those women who live with frozen-up souls half of their lives, than in those impetuous, susceptible children of feeling who have burnt their hearts to a cinder before they are thirty-five."

And Mrs. Norval, instead of being shocked as she would have been last year, loved to hear her John comment upon the strength, depth, and ardor of her passion for him, just as much as she had loved to see him work himself up into a holy frenzy inveighing against parallel cases. She rejoiced that she had kept this volcano in her heart, closely covered over with layer upon layer of snow, which the devotion, the generosity, and the kindness of the doctor had failed to melt, but which her "Ithuriel" had charmed away in one instant!

"I must go," said Hackwell, starting up, kissing the hand he was holding in his. "I must send my letters."

"Don't, don't go," said she, holding his arm. "Please don't! It is so sweet to sit by you and let you lean your head on my shoulder while you talk to me. Sit down by me! Please!"

But, my darling, those letters are urgent, and some are about your affairs. Remember, I am your lawyer downtown, as well as your husband in this room."

"Yes, you are mine, my own in every respect—my lawyer, my lawgiver, my lord, my all. If I were like some of those irreverent women with foreign, loose notions, I would say, my God on this earth. Come to me; your caresses take away my strength. I cannot hold you by force."

Hackwell knelt on one knee on the footstool before her chair, and she clasped her arms around his neck. "Now is my chance," thought he, and, again leaning his head on her shoulder, he said, "How cruel it would be to separate from you!"

"Don't you ever say the word separation to me. I would rather die than live without you."

"And yet, my own dearest, what is the alternative? I certainly cannot let my sister remain here, jilted by Julian, and you say he won't marry her."

"But he will. He must, he shall! I can sympathize with Em, for I know it would kill me if you were to slight me or be indifferent to me. I shall see him tomorrow, and will give him a piece of my mind. He shall

was the creator of man, fashioning him from mud. Here Mrs. Norval's transformation into a "Yankee Popocatepetl" is laid at the feet of Rev. Hackwell.

decide tomorrow. I refused to have any talk with him because you told me not to. But we will settle matters tomorrow, be sure of that."

"Good!" thought Hack. "That point is settled. Now for the next." He changed his position from resting on the left knee to rest on the right, so as to be more comfortable, and at the most suitable times press his wife to his heart. She, meanwhile, played with his curly hair, glossy, brown, without a single white line in it.

CHAPTER XXXIX

Julian Carries the War into Africa

"You are so good and so generous," said the major, with his elbows on the arms of the madam's chair. "Your heart is bigger than this house. You are so good to my little orphaned sister. I don't know how I can ever pay you for your kindness."

"I only ask your love," softly whispered the metamorphosed matron, kissing him.

"And that you have fully and truly as ever man gave to woman. Good night, dearest; I shall see you tomorrow. It is late. You go to sleep, and I to my unpleasant task."

"What task is it? Why can't you put off your letters until tomorrow?" said she, retaining him closer.

"I cannot tell you. Don't ask me."

"Why not ? I will ask. I shall know. Tell me."

"Well, if you must and shall. But—really I don't like to. Well, it is this: that I have lost money in a foolish speculation, and had to borrow, thinking I would soon recover my losses. But I didn't, and now I have to write to Chicago to sell at a great sacrifice some town lots I bought there some time ago, to meet my notes, which will be due in two or three days. There! you have it now, you inquisitive darling. Go to sleep. Good night!" And he gave her a most emphatic unparsonlike kiss, rising as if to leave her.

"But why sacrifice your town lots? Haven't I money enough in the bank to meet your notes?"

"I deposited to your credit sixty-thousand dollars yesterday," replied he, smiling.

"Well, will not that be sufficient?"

"You are right royal, but, I assure you, I don't like to use so much of your money."

"Is not everything I have, myself included, yours and only yours?"

Hack was a good comedian, so he was properly overcome. And after all this natural emotion had subsided, the madam signed an order to her bankers to deliver to him twenty-five thousand dollars.

He would have put double the amount if he had dared, considering that she never looked at the figures (and she used to count the eggs the doctor and children ate!) but he was afraid of arousing Mr. Sinclair's suspicions.

"Now you will not have to sell your Chicago lots or to sit up working all night," said she, lovingly.

"No, my precious! Thanks to you, my angel!"

Next morning, when the major entered his office, Mr. Hammerhard—who also had given up pulpit-preaching and only gave lectures on miscellaneous topics—was there waiting for him, and saluted him by saying, "What news have you? You look happy."

"By George, Ham, what a woman she is! Whew! Don't you know that that woman almost frightens me?—and I ain't easily frightened," added he, with a wink,—"she loves me so!"

"Who would have supposed such a Vesuvius covered over with New England snows, eh? A Yankee Popocatepetl!"[53] said the Rev. Hammerhard, rubbing his hands gleefully. "Tell us all about it; it must be rich sport!"

"*Tell* you! Bah! As if her intensity could be described! Why, she is a Clytemnestra, a Medea, a Sappho! She is so earnest, and her love for me so fervid, that she almost makes me forget that she is thirteen years my senior and *compels* me to love her. Yes, just kind of sucks me into her furious love maelstrom. Whew!"

"Take care, Hack. Love is contagious."

"By Jove, I should think it was! If those superb eyes of Lola were not here maddening me," said Hack, striking his forehead—"if I did not think of that girl night and day, I believe the old woman would succeed in kindling me with her conflagration, for I don't deny I *am* combustible."

"Look out! Remember the fate of Pliny for going too near Vesuvius. Don't go to sleep within reach of an eruption. The doctor might pop out some bright morning before you are out of bed. I tell you, whilst she is in that Clytemnestra mood you describe, make haste to feather our nests; you have no time to lose."

[53]Ironic reference is made here to the snow-capped volcano *Popocatepetl*, found outside Mexico City. The volcano, dormant since 1802, reaches a height of 17,887 feet and on occasion sends up its plumes of smoke and ash.

"I know that. Did you burn all those letters? If the doctor should pop in, he must believe his letters never reached New York. I am glad that the old lady really believes him dead, and so does Sinclair—he hasn't the slightest doubt. He is shocked because the Norval girls go to balls and theatres and don't wear mourning. I am glad he is so firmly convinced. He will be good collateral evidence. Still, you had better bring me those letters. I, being the most interested, will burn them myself."

"I would have burnt them had you not told me you wanted to keep them as trump cards in our game with the madam."

"Yes, but I see now that her own volcanic love is sufficient for all our purposes, and those letters might be used against us. I am always afraid of black-and-white evidence. I'll give you five-thousand dollars it you bring them to me."

"Ah, I see you have been sweet to the old woman, and she put you in fresh funds! How much did she give you this time?"

"Twenty-five thousand—*as a loan*."

"Which you will pay *with interest*, of course. And you only give me five out of twenty-five!"

"Look here, Ham, don't be unreasonable. I fear we shan't get hold of Julian's money, for he doesn't want to marry Em. I'll try to make him pay something if I can, but that is uncertain. And if the doctor should be alive, you know, this most charming major might have to bolt. So he had better send a little money across the Atlantic."

Whilst the two worthy reverends carried on this edifying conversation, Mrs. Norval had descended to the breakfast room to have the anticipated *talk* with Julian, who was quietly employed in reading the *Herald*, like a good American citizen. Mrs. Norval could not repress a shudder of indefinable terror whenever she saw Julian reading the newspapers. She believed her husband dead, and yet she had an instinctive dread that, at some unexpected moment, there might be something in the papers about Lola's friends looking for her, or about her husband not being dead. And this highly proper, rigid stickler for decorum and the Presbyterian Church, derived a new incentive and zest in spending Lola's money, and her love for Hackwell grew in intensity as she contemplated these two possibilities.

"Put down your paper. You said you wanted to have a talk with me, and *I*, too, want to have a very plain one with you," said she. And Julian obeyed, and looked at his mother, waiting for her to speak. Was it her conscience, or was it Julian's resemblance to his father, that troubled her? Her embarrassment lasted only until her idol's image arose before her. Hack's last terrible words were yet in her ears: he "would go!"

"I hope what you want to tell me is that you have resolved to obey the dictates of honor, and stop this trifling with Emma."

"I never have trifled with Emma, and never disobeyed the dictates of honor, mother. I wish you would cease accusing me of acting dishonorably towards Emma. I am sure she does not say or think so herself, and she cannot."

"Emma is not a girl that says much, and she never complains, but she suffers the more for being so silent."

"All I can say is, that I regret from my soul that my boyish foolishness should have caused her any pain."

"That is a very poor excuse, and very mean reparation. I do not see how you can find it in your heart to ruin a girl's happiness for life, and not offer her the only reparation you can."

"What! to marry her?"

"Certainly."

"That is absurd."

"And why so, sir?"

"Because I don't love her. I think I have told you that plainly enough."

"Yes, I am sorry that my son is dishonorable enough to say so in my presence."

"Look here, mother," said Julian, standing up, "I did not come all the way from camp to talk about Emma, or be abused on her account, and it is best that we omit her in our conversation. I came to speak about Lola, not Emma."

"I thought so. Your insolence is unbearable," said Mrs. Norval, trembling with rage. "I suppose you came to ask my consent to your marriage with the mongrel."

"Oh, no," said Julian, smiling, "considering that I am not able to obtain hers, and *that* is the one to be obtained first."

Mrs. Norval was so angry that she could not speak. Julian continued, "What I wish to say, and what brought me here, is, that as you almost drove Lola away to the convent when the dear child was not fit yet to recommence her studies, I think that now that she has graduated, you ought to write a kind letter asking her, of course, to come home."

"Never, unless you pledge yourself to marry Emma."

Julian laughed aloud, and continued, as if he had not heard his mother's interruption.

"Write to her to come immediately, for there is no excuse for her remaining in the convent, she being no longer a scholar, and to remain there she would have to disclose to the nuns that you don't want her here."

"Let her disclose it, then. I don't care."

"Yes, you do, for the only excuse you have for spending Lola's money so freely is the supposition that this is her home."

"You are positively offensive. I do not wish to hear any more."

"But you must, mother. You must *hear* and *think*; you must *know* that Lola, though the Norvals flourish with her money, has no home to go to. And listen to me. If you do not call her here *immediately*, and most kindly and most courteously, I will go there and *marry* her *immediately*; *marry her*!"

"This is too insolent, and I will not listen to it," said Mrs. Norval, rising, though scarcely able to stand up, trembling with rage.

"Very well, mother. Do not listen. But you will be sorry if you do not. If Lola had wished it, I would have married her before coming here, but she would not. She believes, of course, that my father will return, and wishes his consent. But if the poor child finds herself homeless, she then cannot have any reasonable objection to marry and have her own home. I tell you frankly that your opposition to her coming is just what *I* want. But I pledged to her my word of honor—and I do have honor, mother, though you say I have not—I pledged her my word that I would first see you and ask whether you had any objection to her coming here—to *her* house. If you *refuse* to have her here, then she promised she would consider whether she will marry me or not. That is what I came to tell you. Now you can do what you deem proper."

"If that is not a clear case of 'your purse or your life,' there never was one. She is a good Mexican, surely, and knows how to put the dagger to the throat," said Mrs. Norval with a hoarse laugh, sitting down again.

"Pshaw!" ejaculated Julian, taking his cap and walking towards the door. "In this instance the simile is bad, for we have appropriated the purse, not she."

"Anything else you would like to call me, besides a thief?"

"Oh, mother, this is too painful! I do not wish to be disrespectful to you, but I will most certainly protect Lola. She is not only the woman I love, but she was put under my care by my father. I have said all I have to say. About one o'clock I shall return for your answer. If kind, I shall telegraph to her to get ready to come. But if you insist on denying her the shelter of her own roof, then I shall go and beg and beg until she consents to be my wife." And Julian walked out without waiting for a reply.

No sooner was he out of the house than Mrs. Norval rang and ordered her coupé. About an hour later, she was driving down Broadway to Major Hackwell's office. On arriving there, she sent for that charming personage, who was still discussing her and a meerschaum with Hammerhard.

The major came to the coupé rather hurriedly and not a little surprised, but as soon as he saw her face he felt reassured. She was angry, but not frightened. It was all right. No tidings from the doctor. All right. He got into the coupé and sat by her, and she commenced to repeat her conversation with Julian, watching his face closely. He felt she was watching him, and was provoked with himself, because he knew he had betrayed more emotion than he could well explain away.

"You turn red and then pale," said she. "Does Lola's coming affect you so much?"

"Lola's coming? She is not coming, is she? Poor Emma!" And here he closed his fists and set his teeth, as if in a terrible rage. "This is too monstrous! I really am at a loss what to advise you. It is evident that Julian wants to act like a villain, and will only be too glad of the pretext to outrage Em to the degree of going off to marry the other."

"He said that, very clearly."

"But, dearest, that must not be. It will almost kill Em. He must at least give her the privilege of refusing him."

Mrs. Norval shook her head.

"Then I must take Em away."

"I thought you promised me you would never say *that* again?"

"But what can I do? I leave it to you."

"I suppose we cannot help letting Lola come. (How I do hate her!) Better that than to allow Julian to marry her."

"Yes, I suppose so. And yet—"

"And yet what?"

"I think you once felt a kind of jealous feeling for her, and your peace of mind is dearer to me than anything. Could we not manage it somehow to keep her away without the danger of Julian running his head against a stone wall? Think! can we send her somewhere?"

"No, nowhere, without having to give some reason. As for my being jealous of such a little mongrel, you need not fear that. I hope I have too much self-respect to place myself so low as that." The major stooped to kiss her hand and hide his broad smile. He was too amused and too pleased to keep his gravity.

After some further conversation, they agreed that it would be wiser to capitulate to Julian and write immediately for Lola; the major adding, "And we must try to make it appear that we are glad to see her. She must never have a pretext to run up to Julian with complaints."

The madam looked sober, but assented, and the worthy pair separated—she to write to Lola; he to say to Hammerhard, "Ham, you could knock me down with a feather! By Jove! she is coming!" and let himself down on a chair.

Yes, she came. Julian saw her *politely* received in her house before he returned to camp.

Mattie was an ally of theirs; Ruth a neutral power, acting occasionally as spy, and the madam, flanked by Hack and Em, was at present *in statu quo*. So Julian bade them good-by.

CHAPTER XL

The Major's Staff

Sophocles Head was certainly a very nice young man, and Mr. Skroo had found him useful; his friend Wagg had proved him to be patient and forbearing. Mr. Skroo did not care for the drama, but he cared very much for a game of poker. Mrs. Skroo was inclined to be fashionable, and, as the doors of the upper ten were locked and bolted for her, she took nightly consolation by going to the theatre. Mr. Skroo had always free tickets to the theatres, and considering gentle Sophy as good an escort for his wife as her grandmother would have been, he gave him almost daily invitations to accompany Mrs. Skroo and her sister to the theatre, much to the chagrin of Wagg, who, not being good, was not so favored, which goes to prove that virtue *is* once in a while rewarded in this world. Sophy, therefore, was having quite as good a time as he had anticipated in that new paradise called New York: going deadhead to all the theatres whilst Mr. Skroo played poker.

But the favorite amusement of Sophy was his ride from their office, down by the Bowling Green, up to Central Park. You should have seen how gracefully he sat his gray horse, "Beau Cackle" (so called in honor of the distinguished statesman to whom Sophy owed his advancement in the military career). And Beau pranced and went sideways like a crab, or stood on his hind legs like a circus bear waltzing, pawing the air for nearly a minute, taking nearly a half-hour to go the length of three blocks, dancing as he went, with Sophy sitting in the saddle with an arm akimbo, to show the girls what a good rider he was, not to lose his graceful poise whilst Beau danced his hornpipes on the pavement. Thus they went up Broadway—starting from the Bowling Green about three, to reach the Park by five—every afternoon. On reaching Fourteenth Street, Sophy turned to the left, following Fourteenth Street until he arrived at Fifth Avenue. Here, right opposite Delmonico's, Beau performed a few extra *pirouettes*, then turned the corner and went up Fifth Avenue. On reaching Twenty-third Street, opposite the Fifth Avenue Hotel, again Beau acted as if madly bitten by the tarantula, and must dance or perish, Sophy quietly sitting—"still sitting"—in the saddle, never moving. From Twenty-third Street they went along Madison Square up Fifth Avenue, quietly enough, until they arrived in front of Mrs. Norval's palatial mansion. Here again Beau seemed seized with a frenzy for dancing, and hopped about as if the ground was hot, hotter than anywhere else, and fifty tarantulas had stung him! When his hoofs resounded on the pavement, a window sash was thrown up in the second floor, front, and a fine-looking girl, with an exquisite headdress, always appeared at the window and smiled sweetly on gentle Sophy, making his heart beat a regular tattoo and dance more furiously than Beau. Sophy was sure he had captivated one of the rich Misses Norval, and his enthusiasm for his Dulcinea[54] had reached such a pitch that he had on various occasions determined to ask the major to present him to the family. But he knew that Mr. Skroo had several times more than hinted the same request in behalf of his wife, yet the major would never take the hint. An introduction, then, in the modern conventionalism, was out of the question, and Sophy was strongly tempted to take his guitar and go to her window—a large bay window—and, like a "good knight of old," sing his lone dirge to her. "But the neighbors might laugh," said gentle Sophy, sighing, and then he would tune his guitar and sit in front of his stove—upstairs in his room above the office, in which he lived for reasons of economy—to sing to the stove his love ditty, and appease the wild throbbings of his docile heart. He imagined *she* listened to him, and he endeavored to give all possible emphasis to his broken French and fragmentary Italian. In four different languages Sophy sang his love to the stove, and as the stove listened attentively, not laughing or tittering, he felt much encouraged, and sure he was progressing in the languages.

Thus mild Sophy consoled himself for the hopelessness of his love and the bullying of Wagg.

It was established by the major as one of the rules of the office that the two lieutenants should take turns, and not leave the office at night at the same time. One of the two had to stay alternately, keeping two clerks and two orderlies with them, as there was a great deal of government property in the building which might be stolen, and for which he was responsible.

[54]Dulcinea del Toboso is the ladylove of Don Quixote in Cervantes' *El Ingenioso don Quixote de la Mancha.*

When Sophy's turn to remain at the office came, he stayed at home, and sang in broken French, bruised Italian, and maltreated Spanish to the stove (the sole confidant and impersonation of his love) and he never saw Wagg's face. But when the turn of this latter gentleman arrived, then many an evening Sophy stayed to keep him company, and Wagg rewarded his amiability by teaching him to grunt like a pig, or bray like a donkey, or neigh like a horse, or imitate any other animal, for Mr. Wagg excelled in the gift of mimicking animals as well as people.

Sophy had, on one or two occasions, remained with his friend Wagg for the double purpose of guarding the government property and the person of Wagg himself, who had been "rather wild lately"—as mild Sophy mildly expressed it. In consequence of this wildness, Wagg had a touch of wild fancies—called by some people "delirium tremens."

Wagg did not see rats or mice (though any sober man might, as Sophy, only drunk with love, could hear them running about when he sang in Italian); Wagg was not so bad a case as that. He only fancied himself excessively tall, which was natural to the ambitious Wagg, and then microscopically small, which was not natural.

"Sophy! I say. I couldn't go through that door if I was to double in two," said Wagg one night when he had his wild fancies, sitting up in bed, by the side of which Sophy sat watching him,. "I'll be damned if I could now! And what the devil am I to do tomorrow? How shall I get out of this hole?"

"We'll manage it for you. Go to sleep now. That is a good boy," said Head soothingly.

Wagg was not convinced, but he lay down, to start up again with some other idea, ridiculous and painful to hear. He thus talked and laughed all night. Towards morning, after a short doze, he exclaimed, looking at Sophy, frightened, "What is the matter now? What the devil have you done with me? I am so little I can't find myself. My! haven't I dwindled, though? I am going, and no mistake; passing away, like my month's pay. Sit there and write, quick. Are you ready? First, I must say good-by to Lucinda. Commence, 'Darling Lucinda.' Have you written that?"

"Yes. What next?" said Head, humoring him.

"Say, 'I am dying, Egypt, dying.'"[55]

[55]This line is a quote from a death scene in William Haynes Lytle's play *Anthony and Cleopatra*. "I am dying, Eygpt, dying, Ebbs the crimson life-tide fast, And the dark Plutonian shadows, Gather on the evening blast." Head cautions Wagg after his overwrought lament that Lucinda, the quadroon object of Wagg's affection might take exception to the mention of her African blood.

"She'll think you are alluding to her African origin, and she won't like that."

"Yes, she will like it. And tell her I leave her my horse, and my dog, and 'the sword of Bunker Hill.' Do you hear me?" roared Wagg. "I don't hear myself, I am so little." And so he continued for hours, Sophy never losing his patience.

In a few days Wagg was again about, and Sophy resumed his incomprehensible ditties to the silent stove, and his rides up Broadway and the Fifth Avenue, sitting gracefully on the saddle, with arm akimbo, whilst Beau danced his *fandangos* and *tarantulas* in front of Delmonico's, opposite the principal hotels, and in view of Mrs. Norval's palace.

One afternoon, whilst Beau was performing a complicated crab—*pas seul*—if I may so describe it—opposite that window, Sophy's constancy was rewarded by seeing the sash of the window go up, a white hand salute him, and then make a sign to stop.

Sophy was bewildered. He was thinking what he would do with all this good luck thrown at his head, when he saw the very pretty girl who had saluted him come out and direct her steps downtown. Sophy wheeled the astonished Beau, who, unused to this performance, thought he must rear up and dance vigorously, and did not know what to do. But Sophy did not want any hornpipes now, and so he intimated to Beau, who soon understood he was to trot like a sensible horse for a block, then stop and let his master alight. Then Sophy walked up and met the lovely girl, who was smiling and showing him very white teeth.

"You are very kind to take the trouble to dismount," said she with a lovely foreign accent, which Sophy thought she must have acquired in speaking foreign languages. He, too, would show her that he understood several languages, though he did not speak them fluently, for want of practice.

"Jay suisong galan Tom; of course I delight to speak to a lady," said Sophy.

"Est-ce que monsicur parle Français?" said she, in lovely French.

"Ong poo. But parlongs anglay, sill voo play. Jay ney pa de la practick."

Here she complimented him, and told him be spoke French beautifully. And from that they went to other topics, and conversed for a long while. But as to be conversing on the sidewalk, holding a horse by the bridle, rather attracted the attention of the passersby, they agreed that next day Beau's hornpipes should be omitted, and Sophy would ride up in the omnibus and she would be in Madison Square walking and they would sit down and have a *tête-a-tête*. Then they separated, delighted with each other.

"The major may keep his introduction now," said Sophy as he remounted Beau and rode back to the stable.

Next day, at the appointed hour, all brushed, shaved, and perfumed, Sophy sallied from his room over the office and took the omnibus, like any other ordinary mortal, and rode up to the corner of Twenty-third Street and Madison Avenue. Here he descended the high, breakneck steps of the 'bus and directed his course towards Madison Square. The charming young lady arrived in the other 'bus bound downwards, and entered the shared walks of the square. They passed a very delightful hour in conversation, which pleasure was repeated almost daily. In a few days Sophy learned a good deal about the Norval family: all about the magnificent entertainments already given, and those in prospect; who were the young ladies' beaux, and who were not; how they treated Miss Emma Hackwell and Miss Lola Medina—everything, in short, except who the young lady herself giving all this charming information was. That Sophy could not penetrate, she so cleverly eluded inquiry on that one point. But Sophy was determined to find it out—which he did.

CHAPTER XLI

Isaac in the Southern Confederacy

If Isaac's friends had apparently forgotten him, that is no reason we should forget him, and, since he can't come to us, we must go to him.

All the efforts of Lavinia to rescue or even hear of him having failed, it seemed clear that he had to be left to his fate, hard though that were. At first, Mrs. Norval had often thought of her favorite brother, but, from the time that she went from Fortress Monroe to Washington, escorted by her merry crew of unbottled imps, the memory of poor Isaac grew faint in the matron's heart. In fact, it got trampled out, pushed off, when her new lord took full possession of that heart and enthroned himself there absolute and supreme.

Left to himself, Isaac began to think what to do. Catch a Yankee boy in a tight place without immediately setting himself *to work* to get out of it!

Poor Isaac! he had been very ill with a bilious fever, contracted soon after he was captured, and, neglected and friendless and penniless, he had suffered much. Isaac the stylish dandy had disappeared under the rags of Isaac the forgotten prisoner. But his spirits, if depressed, were not broken. With returning health he regained something of his old cheerfulness and much of his genial good nature, and of course became a favorite with his fellow prisoners, and even with his guards. His amiability and patient good humor also gained the friendship of an "American citizen of African descent," who was *a power* in the prison-yard and a body servant of the officer in charge of the prison. This distinguished citizen was called Caesar, hearing which, Sprig had remarked to him that he had a friend by that name.

"Y'u don't say! And what's y'u calls him? Massa' calls m' *Sar*."

"We call him *Ciss*," Sprig answered. And Sar was convulsed with laughter.

"That's a gal, that is! How funny them Yanks! 'tis so, he! he! *Ciss*!" laughed Sar. But from that day he took Isaac under his protection, which he testified by an occasional hoecake, or piece of bacon, which were to Isaac most welcome love offerings and coveted luxuries.

"Lots more of dem Yank pris'ners," said Sar in a confidential whisper to Sprig one day, soon after a great battle had been fought. "I say, masa, p'r'aps y'u 'ab friends 'mong dem."

Many of the prisoners were brought there, but Isaac found no one he knew—no friend, not one among them. But he found something more useful—a friend in a rebel.

With the new batch of prisoners came a rebel officer. After delivering them, he was going to mount on horseback when the wistful look of Isaac's s large blue eyes made him think he knew someone with just such eyes. Then, casting a glance over Isaac's tattered garments and emaciated limbs, he thought how that poor fellow must have suffered, and remembered his own dreary life in Northern prisons. He mounted his horse, but, as he did so, he again caught Isaac's eyes fixed on him. He was sure he had seen those eyes before. He came towards Isaac and said, "How long have you been a prisoner?"

"Since the first battle of Bull Run."

"You are among the poor fellows we haven't been able to exchange. What is your name? Tell me, please, have you any relatives in the army?"

"I had a nephew, Julian Norval. Some persons have told me he was killed at Chancellorsville, but again I hear that he is a brevet-colonel and lieutenant colonel of the —— Regiment in the Sixth Corps."

"That is so. He was not killed, though I thought *I* had killed him at Antietam,'' said the officer, dismounting and coming closer to Isaac. "I know Colonel Norval; I owe him my life, though I tried to kill him. I'll tell you how it was. We had made a furious charge on the Yankees, and I was left lying badly wounded right in front of the Yankee line. The canister of two full batteries was flying over me, and I could not move. Every instant I expected and hoped would be my last. I raised my hand several times that the Yankees might see where I was and shoot that way. But, instead of that, I noticed that the order to stop firing was given. I was faint, and had closed my eyes, when I felt someone stooping over me. I opened my eyes, and I recognized the Yankee officer in command of the battalion. I had my pistol cocked in my hand. I raised it and fired at him, right at his breast. The wound must have been severe, for he fell back. But he arose again and said to me, 'I had come to lift you up and try to serve you, and you shoot me. Surely, war makes us worse than savages.' His men came and raised him, and he directed them to take me, too. They carried us to the rear, and then they recommenced the firing. The officer was Colonel Julian Norval, who had stopped the firing to pick up a few wounded rebels who were near him. But I owe more yet to him. When they came to take him to the hospital, he requested I should be put in the same ambulance and carried to the same hospital. There, his aunt came to see him, and, finding that I was a rebel prisoner, she came to ask me if I knew you. I told her I did not, and she seemed sadly disappointed. But she was very kind to me, and personally tended me, as if I had been her brother. When I was convalescent, and was ordered to prison, I thanked her for her great kindness to me and told her I would like so much to be able to repay even a small part of her favors. 'You may,' she said. 'If you ever meet my poor brother in the South, be kind to him, and you will pay tenfold all I have wished to do for you, which is much more than I have done.' I promised her I would be kind to you if it should be my good luck to meet you, and, with God's permission, I'll keep my promise. I owe more than life to Colonel Norval. I owe him the chance to endeavor to atone for my ingratitude towards him at first. I shall not rest now until I see you free. Here are twenty dollars, good money; please take them and get something to eat. I'll send you something more, and if you tell Sar to come to me, I'll send you some clothes right away." And, without giving Sprig time to thank him, the officer rode off.

Sprig did not find it necessary to tell Sar to go for the clothes. Sar had been an attentive listener to the officer's recital, and started off after him at a trot.

"Here, massa, put 'em on, for de Lo's sake, an' look like a gin'leman ag'in," said Sar, delivering into Isaac's hands a large bundle containing a full suit of clothes, with extra underclothes besides, and a very nice pair of shoes—things not easily found in the Southern Confederacy in those days. Sprig dressed himself in no time, giving himself "a good scrubbing," and he slept soundly that night.

But days and days passed, and with the exception of some money he received from the officer, Isaac had no more tidings of him.

One day Isaac was sitting on a stone in the prison yard, watching Sar in the process of cleaning his master's pistols, whistling merrily in his work. Providence seemed to have made Sar's lips especially for that purpose, and *Abe*, Sar's poodle dog, was apparently convinced of that fact, and respected his master more when he whistled, as he then was fulfilling his mission. Abe would occasionally lift his tail and let it down with a flap, as if to say "*bravo*," and continue to give him his respectful attention. Isaac was amused watching Sar and his dog, and did not perceive anyone's arrival until his friend, the rebel officer, was close by him, saluting him. Isaac arose and shook hands with him, truly most glad to see him again.

"I have been working for you, though it seemed as if I had forgotten you. My efforts to effect your exchange have been fruitless. Have you for an enemy some influential man in Washington?" asked the rebel officer.

"Not that I know of," answered Sprig. "But wait. Yes, I think I have one. Why do you ask me?"

"Because you could have been exchanged long ago if someone there had not opposed it. Your name is not in any record of prisoners, and someone has had a hand in taking off your name from the lists. I find your name in our lists here, but not there. Who is your enemy, if I may ask?"

"Well, I may be wrong, but I think it must be Le Grand Gunn, to whom I gave a whipping once. He had me dismissed from the department in which I was a clerk, and maybe he has done this."

"Depend upon it; he is at the bottom of this mischief. However, I am going to set you free now, if you give me your parole that you will not bear arms against us again, unless exchanged. I had to promise that in your name, and I think it was but right I should. Don't you?" Isaac replied that it was, and most willingly and solemnly pledged himself not to bear arms against the Confederacy. Then quietly and unobserved he was taken by his rebel friend to a house nearby, where a saddled horse was waiting for him.

Here the rebel officer gave him a pass to cross the rebel lines, and some money. Then, shaking hands with him and wishing him a safe journey, he said, "My best and most grateful regards to your sister. The resemblance of your eyes to hers called my attention to you and enabled me to redeem part of my promise. Tell Colonel Norval that 'When this cruel war is over, I pray we may meet again.' Meantime, the ungrateful rebel that shot him at Antietam, sends his blessing to him. Good-by, and God bless you!"

"Won't you tell me your name?" asked Isaac, holding his hand.

"What's in a name?" said he, laughing, and, bowing to Isaac, went away.

Isaac met with no accident. His journey was as short as could have been expected. He reached Alexandria, and there he left the horse to be sent back to the rebel officer, when that could be accomplished, and took the cars for Washington, where he also arrived in safety.

CHAPTER XLII

"Shake Not Thy Gory Locks at Me. Thou Canst Not Say I Did It."[56]

The Hon. Le Grand Gunn was sitting by his beloved Lucinda one afternoon, when, without the ceremony of ringing the front doorbell, or knocking at the parlor door, Isaac Sprig walked into the room—the same room where three years before he had given to the Hon. Gunn such a terrible beating in the presence of pretty Lucinda. There he was now, the very man Isaac wished to find.

Lucinda screamed. She thought Isaac was his own ghost. The Honorable stood up, pale and trembling.

Isaac had made up his mind, on leaving the South, to stop in Washington only a day or two. He thought he would go to his boarding house (which was kept by Lucinda's mother), take his trunk and a few other things, and go to New York to embark for Mexico. He would try to find Lavinia or Julian that day and the next, and then go off. He was sick of his country and countrymen, for what he thought their heartless ingratitude in leaving him forgotten in a prison. He longed to get away. Thinking where he could go, he bethought himself of once having had a notion to go to Mexico to carry the manuscript found by Cackle at the dead-letter office. As soon as this recollection came to his mind, he resolved to go to Mexico at once and seek his fortune there, and get away from ingrates.

Nothing, therefore, could have been more pacific than Isaac's intentions when he entered that room. But no sooner did he see his old foe, Gunn, sitting by Lucinda, than the memory of all that he had suffered in the Confederacy rushed upon him.

"You cursed hypocrite and coward—damned old knave!" said Sprig, striding up to the trembling Gunn, who shook with fear because

[56]The reference is from Shakespeare's tragedy *Macbeth*, Act III, scene 4.

Isaac was not his ghost as much as Lucinda had shaken thinking that he was. "I am glad you are the first dog I meet on arriving, you infernal scoundrel! I'll pay you for leaving me to starve, you vindictive snake! I'll draw your fangs out, viper! I'll make you feel! I have plenty of strength yet, though half-starved by you."

"I didn't! I didn't! I know nothing about it!" cried Mr. Gunn in mortal terror. But Isaac had collared him and was shaking him.

"Ca-all a—a—a po-o-liceman, Lucy da-a-r-ling!" exclaimed Mr. Gunn as Isaac shook him, holding him by the cravat.

But Lucinda, in her fright, instead of running to the front door to call for help, ran upstairs to her room, leaving her devoted ex-congressman in the hands of the infuriated Sprig, who, the more he pounded his old foe, the more bloodthirsty he felt, and did not leave off beating him until Gunn offered resistance no longer. When Sprig was satisfied that he had given his persecutor a worse beating than the previous one, he walked upstairs to his old room, which Lucinda had occupied in his absence.

He told Lucinda to give him the key to his trunk and go and lock the front door to prevent anyone coming without ringing and discovering Mr. Gunn, who was lying insensible on the parlor carpet. Lucinda obeyed Isaac's orders, and in a few minutes he had changed his dress, taken the gold that he had left in his trunk two years and a half before (which Lucinda had faithfully guarded), and the manuscript. Then he went towards the door, and deliberately downstairs.

"Have you nothing to say to me, Isaac? Not a word, even?" said Lucinda to her beloved and never-forgotten Isaac, with tears in her pretty eyes.

"Yes, that about half an hour after I go, you sprinkle some cold water over the lovely face of your young lover to bring him to. This mauling was worse than the other. I suppose your love will grow in proportion. Good-by! I wish you joy!" So saying, Sprig went downstairs and to the nearest hotel, where he took a hack and drove to the depot. There he arrived just in time to catch the New York train.

It had been the intention of Isaac not only to try to find Lavinia or Julian in Washington, but, on arriving in New York, to go to Mr. Sinclair's and make inquiries about the rest of the family. The day he arrived in New York, Mr. Sinclair was out of the city, and, as the Havana steamer would leave the next day, Isaac thought he had better go then (for he did not know to what extent he might have injured Mr. Gunn), and not wait till Mr. Sinclair returned.

He went back to his hotel to write to both his sisters, his father, and to Julian, telling them he was alive and well, and on his way to Mexico;

that on his arrival there he would tell them how and where to address him. He carried the letters to mail them himself. Then he bought his ticket on the Havana steamer, and next day by twelve o'clock he was going out of New York harbor.

At Havana, Isaac took passage on an English steamer, and, without meeting any accident or unusual delay, he arrived safely at Vera Cruz. Here he began to make inquiries about Don Felipe de Almenara and Don Luis Medina, who were the persons mentioned in the manuscript, and from the readiness with which his questions were answered he inferred that these two gentlemen were well-known men and he would have no difficulty in finding them.

As soon as he reached the city of Mexico, Isaac, after installing himself at the Iturbide Hotel, went to inquire where to find the two gentlemen he was in search of, and was delighted to hear that they lived a short distance from the capital and often spent some time at a house Don Felipe kept always open in the city, ready to receive them when they should come. Now they were at their country seat, some three or four miles from town. Isaac inquired for the hacienda mentioned in the manuscript as being situated in the northern part of Sonora, and was told that it had not been visited by its owners since 1846, when a fearful calamity had befallen the family there, and the hacienda, though a most beautiful place, was now left in the care of a major-domo, who lived and grew rich there, but who had to keep the hacienda as a besieged fortress, with a garrison always on the alert because the government of Mexico, being a free and independent government, lets its Indians live as they please, and its more civilized citizens take care of themselves as best they may.

The morning following his arrival, Isaac, after partaking of a good breakfast, called for a hack and directed the driver to take him to Don Felipe de Almenara's house.

"Don Felipe is not at his house in town, sir. Shall I drive to his country residence?" said the polite driver, hat in hand, a thing which our drivers would rather perish than do. And we have to be very thankful if, after cheating and robbing us, and being insolent, they don't apply their whips to our backs, which, I think, the public well deserves for submitting so tamely to all their gross impositions.

Whilst Isaac, leaning back on a well-cushioned carriage, enjoys the magnificent scenery on his route, and builds innumerable castles on the classic ground of Montezuma the timid and Cortez the daring, we will see what the two gentlemen he is in search of are doing, and hear what they are saying. They are sitting in the library by a table loaded with papers, books, reviews, pamphlets, etc. They are reading letters of great interest, to judge from the eagerness and attention with which they read them, and these letters have arrived by the last mail from Europe. When they opened a letter in English or German, the younger of the two, who was Don Luis Medina, translated to his father-in-law, the older man, Don Felipe de Almenara. In French or Spanish, Don Felipe read them himself.

CHAPTER XLIII

Isaac in the Land of the Aztecs

When the allied troops of France, England, and Spain landed at Vera Cruz in 1862, Don Felipe de Almenara at once resolved to offer assistance to the government, in money, to drive off the invaders, he being too old to recommence the life of a soldier and take the field against them. But his son-in-law, Don Luis Medina, immediately joined the army and took an active part in checking Laurencez's progress, and in the obstinate and gallant defense of Puebla.[57]

Don Felipe and Don Luis, therefore, had been among the firmest and most prompt supporters of the republican government up to the winter of 1863. In December of this year, however, and just about the time of Isaac's arrival in Mexico, these letters which the two gentlemen perused so eagerly as Isaac was riding towards them had come. These letters said that there was a very strong probability—almost a certainty—that the Archduke Maximilian would accept the proposed throne of Mexico; that he still hesitated, but that, as a great field for a noble and lofty ambition was thus opened to him, and he was known to be of generous impulses, the friends of monarchism anticipated that he would accept in the hope of effecting a great good by giving the Mexican people a stable government, which would bring to them peace and prosperity and raise them to a high rank among the civilized nations of the world.

No argument could have been more specious to Maximilian's heart and mind.

"This is rather too much of a dilemma for me, I must say," Don Luis Medina observed. "Whilst the question is of repelling the French,

[57]Puebla, site of a battle (May 5th, 1862) by Mexican republican forces, headed by General Ignacio Zaragoza, that were victorious against the French invading forces led by General Latrille Laurencez.

or any other nation that comes to Mexico as a hostile invader, I shall not hesitate in giving my all in the defense of our country. But, though I am Mexican at heart as well as by adoption, I shall find it too difficult to make up my mind to fight against an Austrian prince, and above all Prince Maximilian. My Austrian blood rebels against fighting him."

"I am not an Austrian. I was born on Mexican soil," said Don Felipe. "But if it is positive and certain that the Archduke will accept the crown of Mexico, I shall be only too happy to be the most loyal of his subjects. And, what is more, not only will I consider such an act perfectly honorable and patriotic, but I would consider it wrong to oppose the re-establishing of a monarchy in Mexico under a Hapsburg, for the Hapsburgs were, and are, the legitimate and lawful heirs of the glorious Isabella and the great Charles V."

"Such an opinion however, would only be derided in Mexico. The right of succession is laughed at nowadays," Don Luis replied.

"I know it; I know that loyalty is well-nigh extinct all over the world. But I am old-fashioned, and, what is more, I am a true Almenara. No one can make me believe that the Bourbons have, or ever had, a right to the throne of Spain. Neither can any one dissuade me from the belief that the House of Hapsburgs has—if not an absolute and admitted right—at least a foundation for a claim, a valid justification, to entitle them to re-establish a sovereignty in Mexico. How do we know that Mexico would have declared her independence from Spain if she had been under a Hapsburg instead of a Bourbon dynasty? The Mexicans did not want a republic; they wanted a good and just prince. Witness all the efforts of Iturbide and his party to induce some of those timid Bourbons to come here. Under a different dynasty, we might now have been an independent kingdom. Ferdinand would have done a much more manly and wise act by coming here to establish a glorious and mighty empire than by putting himself, like a poor woman, under Napoleon's protection. I have no patience with those Bourbons. To their pusillanimity Mexico owes all her miseries—to their neglect and indifference. And what makes all this more aggravating *to me* is, that they were never entitled to govern, or misgovern, Mexico. The Hapsburgs were cheated out of Mexico by Louis XIV's intrigues, as much as they were cheated out of all the other lands belonging then to Spain. Therefore, to my mind, a Hapsburg is not in the least wrong if he endeavors to repossess himself of some of these lands unfairly wrested from his family. I honor him for it."

"That is not, however, the ground upon which the Mexican Commission has based its invitation to the Archduke. Nor has Prince Maximilian himself made any allusion to a possible claim of his as a descendant of Charles V, or to the fact that the will of Philip IV made Margaret next heir to Charles II, and Charles had no right to change the succession."

"Of course not. I did not expect it, and, in truth, I am glad he has not. To base his throne upon the will of the people is more suitable to the ideas of the present time. This pleases me the more because (as you know) I am convinced that a republican form of government is not suited to the Mexicans, and it is well that the change be made with *their free approval*. On the other hand, this change is even more acceptable, because a Hapsburg is the prince selected, his house being the only one that, by the established and accepted principles of Europe, can be said to have any *hereditary* claim to a land conquered by Isabella's soldiers. Such a monarchy can have nothing—ought to have nothing—objectionable to the Mexicans. Of course the ideas of this continent are different from those of Europe, but we all know that such would not be the case if the influence of the United States did not prevail with such despotic sway over the minds of the leading men of the Hispano-American republics. If it were not for this terrible, this *fatal* influence—*which will eventually destroy us*—the Mexicans, instead of seeing anything objectionable in the proposed change, would be proud to hail a prince who, after all, has some sort of a claim to this land, and who will cut us loose from the leading strings of the United States."

"Half of our leading men love and kiss these leading strings," said Don Luis, smiling.

Here a servant interrupted their conversation, bringing in a card, which he presented to Don Felipe, and retired to wait his orders. Don Felipe saw the card, but, it being in English, he did not understand it, and handed it over to Don Luis, who translated as he read: "Isaac Sprig, an American gentleman, would like to see Don Felipe Almenara, if he is the father of Doña Maria Theresa de Medina, who was carried off by the Indians in 1846."

"Great God!" Don Luis exclaimed, starting up. "Where is this man?"

The servant came forward and said that the stranger who had given him the card was outside, waiting. Don Felipe told him to bring him in, and in a few minutes our friend Isaac walked in, preceded by the servant.

"Tell me, sir, is my daughter living?"

"Where is she now?"

"I am her father."

"I am her husband."

These were the words with which Sprig was saluted. The two Mexican gentlemen—forgetting, for the first time in their lives, I venture to say, all their civility—never thought of saluting Isaac or offering him a seat. He, however, understood their feelings, and kindly answered, "Please, gentlemen, speak English, for my knowledge of the Spanish language is very limited."

Don Felipe shook his head in token of his inability to speak English, but Don Luis was more fortunate in that respect, and said, in good English, "It is a long time since I spoke your language, sir, but I shall endeavor to speak it now. At least I hope I'll understand all you have to say about my wife, whom we have mourned for more than sixteen long years. Tell me, sir, without delay what is it that you know about Doña Theresa de Medina?"

"All I know is what I learned from a manuscript I casually found in Washington at the dead-letter office."

"Was the manuscript addressed to me? Who wrote the manuscript?"

"It was written by a man named Adrian Lebrun, and dictated by Doña Theresa herself. But *to whom* it was addressed I cannot tell." And here Isaac related the manner in which the manuscript was found and kept by him. Also, that he had been made a prisoner, and on being released, feeling discontented, and having before had the notion of visiting Mexico, he bethought himself of the manuscript, and resolved to find the gentlemen therein mentioned, and show it to them, believing that if he could be of assistance in the matter, the gentlemen, in return, would help him to find some honorable employment in Mexico.

Don Luis translated to Don Felipe all that Isaac said, and both assured him that he was not mistaken in relying upon their gratitude. Then Don Luis asked where the manuscript was now, and when Sprig answered that he had left it at his hotel, both gentlemen expressed a wish to accompany him to the city to get it at once, and immediately prepared to start.

Don Felipe rang for a servant and told him to serve some refreshments to the gentleman, and to order the carriage in which they always went to town, whilst Don Luis collected and, with trembling hands, tried to arrange the papers scattered on the table.

When the carriage drove to the door, the two anxious men were already in the hall putting on their gloves and hats. Seeing that, Sprig reluctantly gave up the delicious lunch he was enjoying, taking a parting glass of the best wine he had ever tasted in all his life. They told him not to hurry, that they could wait until he finished his lunch, but Sprig was too polite to make them wait. Then the three got into the carriage whilst the hack which had brought Isaac followed empty behind. Two servants rode outside with the coachman.

The winter days being short, it was already dark when the travelers stopped in front of the Iturbide Hotel, where Sprig alighted to get the manuscript, which Don Luis received with hands trembling with eagerness.

They asked Isaac to come to stay at their house and make his home with them whilst he was in Mexico. Isaac blushed a little—more with pleasure, perhaps, for his purse was not overly full—and, after a slight hesitation, accepted the kind offer. He went back to the hotel, paid his bill and gave directions where to send his trunk, got into the carriage again, and they went on to Don Felipe's house, which was a very handsome and commodious one.

On arriving home, Don Felipe ordered his servants—all of whom were males, with the exception of an old housekeeper—to take the best care of the *Señor Americano*. Then with signs and bows, and Spanish very distinctly pronounced, Don Felipe begged Isaac to make himself at home; that supper would be served to him as soon as he pleased, but that he and Don Luis felt no desire to eat, and hoped Isaac would excuse them; that they were very anxious to read the manuscript.

Isaac bowed also, and made signs that he would take care of himself, and the gentlemen need not stand on any ceremony, etc.

Don Felipe then saluted him, and followed Don Luis to the library, locking the door after him to exclude inquisitive servants.

When Don Felipe went into the library, Don Luis had read the first two pages, and was now, with his head upon the table, weeping like a child, like a weak woman. But he was not ashamed of his tears. It seemed to him that he had not realized all the horror of his wife's fate until now—all the life-agony of his pure and beautiful and accomplished Theresa. And he had not, for he had mourned her as dead, and only occasionally the fear that her fate might have been worse would come to his mind with a frightful distinctness. And it *had* been worse, a million times worse! She, the pure, the high-minded, refined, and delicate Theresa, to meet such a fate! It was horrible as well as terrible! The two proud gentlemen bowed their heads low in shame and horror and pity!

Long they remained thus bowed, but the task must be done. They must read on and know all—all. They must drink drop by drop the bitter chalice, all, all—to the dregs.

And who has not drunk more or less deeply in some, if not many, bitter chalices? Who has had *only honey* in his or her cup. I would like to see that person, and ask how many summers he or she has counted. Certainly not thirty.

Misery is, undoubtedly, "the lot of mortals," *but* there is no doubt, either, that in some countries certain kinds of evils are impossible. If Mexico were well governed, if her frontiers were well protected, the fate of Doña Theresa would have been next to an impossibility. When it is a well-known fact that savages will devastate towns that are not well guarded, is there any excuse for a government that will neglect to provide sufficient protection? Does a plea of economy counterbalance an appeal for life? How fearful is the responsibility of lawgivers and law executors.

Thinking of this, the mind is led to the thought that—with some exceptions, of course—a nation can, with a good government, avoid the majority of those misfortunes which we now call "*unavoidable* human sorrows." If we were to trace our troubles to their veritable source, we would often reach, more or less directly, their origin in *our lawgivers*. Not only the dwellers of the frontiers, not only the victims of lawsuits, not only— But I am no political philosopher. I am wandering away from my humble path. We must go back to the readers of the manuscript, and accompany them in their sad task.

CHAPTER XLIV

Bound for the United States

All night the two unfortunate gentlemen sat by that table, one reading and translating, when he could command his voice sufficiently to speak, and the other listening horrified; both weeping for pity, tender, holy pity, for her, their best beloved. Yes, there she seemed looking at them from that portrait. The beautiful radiant face smiled on them as if saying, "Do not weep for me. Do not mourn. I am an angel now. I was always pure, for my soul did not sin, although I was insulted by a savage. I was a martyr; now an angel."

They came to a passage where Doña Theresa said that although suicide is a wicked sin, she would have committed it if she had not been restrained by the thought that thus she would kill her own child before it was born, and afterwards by the hope that if she lived, she might rescue her little daughter from a fate like her own; whilst if she died, her child could perhaps never leave her horrible captivity. "At this hour of my death," Doña Theresa said, "and when about to appear before my Maker, I forgive the horrible savages who inflicted upon me the most terrible torture that the human soul can know—the agony of living in degradation forever on earth. But I trust that with the hourly suffering of these ten long years, I have purchased for my child, my husband, and my father, the happiness that was denied to me. Good-by, my beloved three. It is well I go now to a better world, for how could I follow my child, or bear the sight of my Luis? Never! No! Shame would strike me dead at his feet, never to rise again!"

When in broken accents Don Luis translated this passage, so full of the sorrow and shame of the high-toned lady, the two gentlemen arose and paced the room in vain endeavor to suppress the grief that convulsed their strong frames. Don Felipe sank down into a chair and no longer restrained the tears that flowed on his venerable face. Don Luis fell on the sofa, utterly crushed, and he too gave vent to the grief he could no longer contain. How long they wept and mourned thus the two men did not know.

The gray dawn pushed timidly through the lattice a pale ray of light, but the two sorrow-stricken mourners took no notice of the coming day. The morning twilight went by and the sun came in, and they did not know it.

About eight o'clock in the morning, Nacho, Don Felipe's valet, ventured to knock at the door. He, too, had watched all night, for he had a suspicion that something was wrong, else his master would have been in bed by ten o'clock. Now he came to see if his master would have a cup of chocolate; this Don Felipe, and also Don Luis, refused. Charging Nacho again to take good care of the American gentleman, and to say for them that they would see him at dinner, they dismissed him and returned to their heart-rendering reading.

"The darkest hour is when near daylight." Thus, in that horrible night of mental agony there came a sweet consolation. The image of a child, Theresa's child, was the saving angel: it came to save those two unfortunate men from the madness of despair. Yes, a beloved fruit of that pure and transient love, of that happiness so tragically terminated, was living. Don Luis could scarcely restrain his impatience when at the end of the manuscript, Doña Theresa again begged that "*the Doctor*" would make every effort to find Lolita's father.

"It is plain that Theresa commended our child to *a doctor*. Where can he be?" Don Luis exclaimed. And he hastened to ring the bell to send for Isaac. Nacho answered the bell.

"Has the American gentleman gone out?" asked Don Luis.

"No, sir; he is breakfasting," Nacho replied.

"Tell him I beg he will come here as soon as he finishes breakfast," said Don Luis, and Nacho left, to return soon after with Isaac, who had just finished a delicious breakfast after a night of calm repose.

He bowed to the two pale, sorrow-stricken gentlemen, on whose faces the traces of the fearful suffering of that night were but too distinct. Don Luis said, motioning him to take a seat, "This manuscript, sir, says that—that there is—a child—a—"

"Yes, I know. A girl named Lolita," interrupted kind Isaac, seeing that Don Luis was so agitated that he could hardly speak. "I read the manuscript myself, as I told you, but I made no inquiries about the little girl for two reasons: the first, because I did not have the necessary time, and the second, because I thought I would first ascertain whether you lived and I could find you, who were the most interested. Then the next step would be to find the child."

"And can we do that, when you say that the address of the manuscript was lost?"

"I think we might get a clue by advertising, and, if you wish, I can write today to the United States to friends to insert for me the advertisement at once. We can also advertise in San Francisco, in California, inquiring for the doctor who took the child, and in France we can advertise for Lebrun, who wrote the manuscript as Doña Theresa dictated."

Don Luis said he liked Isaac's idea very much, and translated to Don Felipe the suggestion. This gentleman also approved it, and now the three sat by the table to form a plan together for future operations.

It was decided that Don Luis would immediately retire from the army, and, as soon as his resignation was accepted, he would go, accompanied by Sprig, to the United States in search of his daughter. In the meantime, Sprig would send advertisements to be published all over the United States, but principally in New York and San Francisco, also in Paris, for Adrian Lebrun. Don Luis sat at a desk to write his resignation, whilst Isaac wrote his letters to the United States containing the advertisements for New York as well as those to be published in Paris and San Francisco.

As the French were already in possession of the city of Mexico, and Don Luis and Don Felipe both belonged to the Liberal party, they had to keep their visit to the capital a profound secret, and deemed it prudent to return to the hacienda that same night. They did so, after seeing that the resignation of Don Luis was forwarded to the republican government, then at San Luis Potosi.

This government, however, refused to accept the resignation at first, and much as Don Luis wished to leave immediately for the United States, he was compelled to wait over two months before he succeeded in being allowed to leave Mexico. There were rumors that he wished to join the French—rumors which, considering that he was an Austrian, could not be said to be altogether unfounded. About the 1st of March, 1864—after great difficulties and delays, and only when he pledged his word that he wished only to resign to go in search of his lost child—a leave of absence was granted to him. With this he was obliged to content himself, and, accompanied by Isaac, to whom they were now very much attached, they started for Vera Cruz *en route* for New York.

Isaac did not regret their delay. He had sent his advertisements two months in advance, and was thus, moreover, enabled to write a very kind letter to Lucinda, begging her pardon for his parting words and laughingly inquiring for the health of Le Grand Gunn.

Lucinda promptly answered that though the Hon. G. had been obliged to stay in bed for three weeks, he was now well and anxious to hush up the little episode.

That was all Isaac desired.

CHAPTER XLV

How Julian's Patriotic Song Was Cut Short

Julian led the chorus, and about a dozen clear, ringing voices took it up and followed. Song after song was poured out by the careless singers, as if tomorrow's night might not spread her dark mantle over their stiffened corpses. Julian, being the host, was kept busy "mixing drinks" for his thirsty guests. He had just mixed a new batch of "cocktails," and again led the boys of the Sixth Corps in a clear baritone—

"Hurrah for the Union, hurrah, boys, hurrah!
Down with the traitor and *up* with the *stars*!
And we'll rally round the flag, boys,
And we'll rally once again,
Shouting the battle cry of '*Freedom*!' "[58]

An orderly came in and delivered to him a long envelope, sealed, which Julian took, and, without stopping his song, waved the paper over his head as he emphasized—

"Shouting the battle cry of '*Freedom*!' "

Then, leaving the singers to continue the song, he approached a camp table, where a lamp was burning, to read the document just received.

He read twice, then again, before he could comprehend the meaning of it. He turned very pale as he began to understand, and felt very giddy and sick, and he staggered as he silently and slowly walked out

[58]Ruiz de Burton here incorporates one of the most popular Civil War songs of the North. Composed by George Fredrick Root, *The Battle Cry of Freedom* was written in 1863.

of the tent to tell his orderly to saddle one of his horses and bring it to the tent of General ——. Meantime, he went there himself on foot.

"I wonder what made Norval stagger and look so pale as he went out?" said one of the thirsty convivials.

"The fire makes the tent so hot," replied another, "for he never drinks liquor."

"No, he never touches liquor, but I guess he got news from his father. You know, report says he was killed last year," added a third.

"Two years ago, the report goes. But Norval doesn't believe it."

Another song was started, and all joined in, soon forgetting Julian's paleness and the probable cause of it, whilst he walked to the general's tent.

"Good evening, general," said Julian, walking in. "Can I speak to you for a few minutes?"

The general was alone, writing; he looked up, and seeing Julian looking so pale, he said, kindly, pointing to a seat, "Sit down, colonel. What can I do for you?"

"You can tell me what all this means. It can't be to *me* that this communication is addressed! Is there not some mistake about it?"

The general cast a glance over the paper which Julian held in his trembling hand, and said, with evident reluctance, "No, it is not a mistake, but the adjutant need not have sent it to you this evening. I told him I wished to notify you first that I had received that order, as to give you a few days to communicate with your friends. They might have it rescinded."

"But what have I done? Why am I dismissed without at least knowing what charges are brought against me, or by whom, and without giving me a chance to defend myself?"

"That I cannot tell you, for I don't know it myself. I wish I did."

"General, I am not guilty of any crime, or deed, or thought whatsoever, to bring this disgrace upon me. I beg you, as a man of honor, to allow me just sufficient time to go to Washington, and if this order is not rescinded by telegraph, then you may publish it. I shall not be in this world to know it. Will you do that?"

"Yes. But go now, this instant. You can catch the train which leaves Brandy Station at eleven o'clock and be in Washington tomorrow morning."

"I thank you, general," said Julian, in a husky voice. He wished to say more, but the words died on his colorless lips. The general arose and took his icy hand, which he kindly pressed with both of his, saying, "Courage, my boy. These things will happen in all countries in unhappy times like the present. We Americans are not angels, to be exempt from wrong, and injustice will visit the innocent among us, as it has among other peoples in all ages. Be of good heart, for this, after all, might be something that you can explain away at once. Go and see the President in person, for as the dismissal, you see, is '*by the order of the President*,' he can, if he likes, rescind his order without delay."

"Thank you, general, with all my heart. I shall do as you say, and, come what may, I shall be your devoted friend as long as I live," said Julian, pressing the general's hand.

But a few minutes sufficed Julian to ride back to his camp and take from a traveling trunk in his back tent some money. The he told his orderly to go with him to the station to bring back the horses. Putting on a heavy overcoat, and a revolver in the pocket of it, he started to take the eleven o'clock train, which was just moving off as he jumped upon the platform.

On arriving at Washington next morning, Julian endeavored to eat some breakfast, but his throat seemed to have contracted and refused to swallow more than a cup of coffee. This done, he called a hack and told the driver to take him to General Cackle's quarters.

He found that renowned soldier surrounded by his obsequious staff, with whom he was about to ride out to visit the troops around the capital.

"Can I speak with you alone, general?" said Julian, after shaking hands with the hero of the brilliant charge.

"Certainly," said he condescendingly, stepping aside.

"Have you heard any unpleasant rumors about me?" commenced Julian, looking the hero straight in the face.

"Well! What do you mean? What kind of rumors?"

"General, you *do* know something about me, and you must tell me what it is."

"Well, do you mean the talk about your disloyalty, and about being dismissed for it?"

"Yes. What is it?"

"All I know about it is that you have been talking against the President, saying that he is usurping powers; that he had no right to issue the emancipation proclamation, and—Hush! here comes Beau. Not a word to him that I mentioned a thing to you," said Ciss, lowering his voice. Then very loud: "Yes, I heard that you are getting ready to break camp. I envy you. I love the bustle of camp life. I am sick of 'fancy duty.' I shall apply to be sent to the field again."

"Good morning, Colonel Norval," said the Hon. Mirabeau Cackle, who certainly would not have approached so near if he had sooner recognized Julian. But the latter being with his back to the door, his face was not seen by the eminent orator until too late to retreat.

"Good morning, Mr. Cackle," said Julian, shaking the proffered hand of the great leader. "You came just in time, for I was going to your house to try to catch you before you went to the Capitol."

"Were you? I'll see you this evening, if it's all the same to you. Now I am on my way to see the President on appointment," he replied.

"It is precisely to get you to go to the President's with me that I was going to look for you."

The Honorable winced and looked around as if in search of someone who would do him the favor to take Julian to the devil. He hesitated, then said, "You can go with me, if you like, and take your chance of seeing the President. But he is very busy and sees very few people except on pressing and important business."

"My business, I assure you, is of a most important nature," said Julian, very firmly.

"Come along, then; we'll try," said the patriot and statesman, hurrying out of the room for fear that Julian might tell him what this business of his was, which the orator knew better than he, but didn't want to hear.

When they arrived at the White House, Beau told Julian to walk about in the East Room, or in the vestibule or lobby, or look on the avenue from the East Room windows, but not to go upstairs to the reception room, for he would get tired of looking at the anxious faces of people who had come there day after day in the vain hope of seeing the President.

"And why don't they see him?" asked Julian naïvely, laboring under the delusion of old times, when the President held it to be his highest honor to be called *the servant of the American people.*

Beau smiled at Julian's verdancy, and replied, "The President is too busy with weighty affairs to be bothered with all the old women who have their sons prisoners, or can't be found, or a thousand other trifles."

"They are trifles to you, but not to them, and *ought not* to be to the President," said Julian. "They are ready, perhaps, to give their heart's blood for these trifles. In a country of equals, every man's concerns are as important as any other's."

Beau shrugged his shoulders and ran upstairs, leaving Julian to his antiquated political philosophy.

CHAPTER XLVI

"Oh, Romeo, Where Art Thou?" "Je Pleure, et le Roi S'amuse!"[59]

This was the first time that Julian had cooled his heels in any great man's antechamber, and he did not do it patiently. A whole hour elapsed before Beau came out and told him that, as it was Tuesday, there would be a cabinet meeting, and the President would not be able to see him until tomorrow. Julian did not like this. He had seen several men go in smiling and come out laughing—doubtless at the President's jokes—and their business could not be so pressing as his, else they could not smile, much less laugh. Why, then, see them in preference? He said as much to Beau, with the grand simplicity of a true American who has accepted—*au pied de la lettre*—in all sincerity the lofty theories of republicanism, and honors his country and his government with a manly reverence truly noble.

Beau smiled, again repeating, "Tomorrow you will see him. Come early."

But tomorrow passed, and the next, and the next, and now it was Saturday, and Julian was sure that on the morrow—being Sunday, and the order dismissing him not having been rescinded—he would be disgraced before the world. The order of his dismissal would surely be read out by the adjutant before his regiment, ay, before his brigade, before the whole corps, before the Army of the Potomac! And Lola! She would know it; she would know that he was disgraced like a coward before the world. And she would pity him, but be ashamed of him. No, he did not want her pity.

"You will not see me alive, Lola. Your lovely eyes shall never behold me a disgraced man."

[59]"Oh, Romeo, where art thou?" from Shakespeare's tragedy *Romeo and Juliet*. "Je pleure et le roi s'amuse": "I weep and the king is amused" (source unknown).

And Julian examined carefully a little pocket five-shooter he carried in an inside pocket of his coat. Then he buttoned up his coat, thereby setting off the symmetry of his tall, graceful form. But he thought very little of the admiring glances which followed him as he went through the parlors of the hotel, looking for General Cackle, who had promised to meet him there with his brother Beau to go to the White House with him. He walked up and down the long corridor, vainly waiting for the Cackles, and his handsome pale face grew paler, and his dark-blue eyes darker, whilst the emotions which agitated him gave a glowing intensity to his gaze. But he was utterly unconscious of his great manly beauty. He looked with a sort of stern disdain on everybody, for he was in despair. His finely cut lips, always so full of *bonhommie*, had uttered but few words, and not once smiled, since he left camp.

The ladies at the hotel, who after breakfast had assembled in the parlors to hear and to retail gossip, were hushed when they saw him enter and look all around anxiously for someone. His gaze, so sad, so full of thought and feeling, went mournfully over the heads of the admiring groups, resting on no one, unconscious of the tremor it sent through so many hearts.

Seeing that the Cackles did not come, and it was getting very late, Julian left the hotel to go to the White House alone.

Several of the ladies ran to the window to see him go out; to see if he would walk, or drive, or ride on horseback. "Who could he be? Never had they seen such a handsome man! Oh, he is superhumanly beautiful!" said a young miss just out of school and who wrote poetry. He, meantime, had gone out. He crossed the street. There was a lady. He was going towards her. She stopped. She comes to meet him. And she extends both her hands, which he takes. And-and-she kisses him. Oh, who can that happy, happy woman be?

"Aunt Lavvy, dear, I am so glad to see you!" said he (but his admirers did not hear it), taking her arm and placing it most affectionately in his. "I am on my way to the White House; walk that way with me. It is not very gallant to make such a request instead of offering to walk with you, but I haven't a minute to spare, having lost all the morning waiting for the Cackles, who promised to come to go with me."

"The Cackles! Which of them? They are the same, however. Don't talk to me about any Cackle whatsoever. Their heads are completely turned by prosperity—all, all, commencing with the old man and the old woman. And to think Julian, how much they owe to your father! But don't talk to me about Cackles. Tell me what brought you to Washington. How long have you been here? Why haven't you been to see me?"

Answering all these questions, Julian walked up Fourteenth Street with Lavvy to the corner of "F" Street. There the admiring eyes at the hotel windows lost sight of him, as he and Lavvy walked towards the Treasury building, then around the corner on Pennsylvania Avenue to the gates of the White House. Here Julian bade Lavvy good morning, promising to go to see her in the evening and report the result of that day's efforts.

Fortune did not seem in a more propitious mood this day than the previous. Julian saw the morning pass by, and the afternoon came whilst he yet waited. Presently he heard music quite near, and wondered where it could be. But he did not know. From the windows of the East Room he saw people come and go around the house to the other side. Where could they be going, laughing so merrily, so gayly dressed? He looked at his watch: it was nearly four o'clock.

He could wait no longer. He rushed upstairs, determined to see the President. He talked to himself as he ran up and walked through several rooms.

"What!" muttered he, "have we free-born Americans turned into slavish courtiers, and are we to dance attendance at the antechamber of a despot? I will see the President, or know why not. He shall tell me why he dismisses me and sends me branded before my fellow men. By the heavens above, I shall know *why*?" And Julian entered first one room, then another, but not even a clerk was to be found.

Turning to go downstairs again, he met the page who had daily opened the door for a whole week to him.

"Look here, my good man, I am sick of waiting. I must see the President. Where is he?" said the despairing Julian.

"He is at dinner now, and he doesn't like to transact any business after dinner. You'd better return on Monday," the man answered. Julian laughed a loud laugh and pushed the man aside. "He is crazy," thought the page, not knowing whether he ought to stop Julian by force. But as two gentlemen, who were liberal patrons of his, now appeared at the door, he turned his back on the pale-faced, distracted Julian, who evidently had no influence, to run smiling towards those who had. Julian, thus left to his own resources, went hurriedly about the house in search of a servant whom he could bribe; yes, he would give him five-hundred dollars to take him to the President. But good luck did not bring him against any servant.

"To wait until Monday! Oh, God! did you hear that? Until Monday! And tomorrow my ignominious dismissal will be announced, and I shall be forever disgraced! I will not leave this house alive until this man rescinds his inhuman order, or at least gives me a fair trial! Why should I not have a trial? by heavens! why not? Has *might* usurped the place of *right* in this free, beloved land of ours? Am I a free man, or an abject slave? I want to know *that*." Thus soliloquizing, in a not very low tone, Julian came into a room hung with red damask. He crossed it, and entered an octagonal room hung in blue. Crossing this, he found himself on a piazza fronting upon the greenswarded lawn, where the Marine Band was playing, and a gay assemblage was listening to the music, walking or standing in groups, or alone, or sitting on benches under the tree.

Nothing could be more joyous than this scene, but a single rapid glance only did Julian bestow upon the gay crowd. Here, close by him, sat the object of his anxious thoughts and wild search. The President sat there listening to the music and looking at the people—*his* people.

CHAPTER XLVII

Julian States His Case to the President

The President held in his hand a gold-headed cane, which had just been sent to him by a lady in token of gratitude, and he tapped his teeth with the gold head of it, keeping time to the music. His leg hung over the arm of his chair and dangled regularly, like a ballistic pendulum, also keeping time. When the base drum gave, at measured intervals, a sound as if a young cannon were exercising its lungs for sport, the leg of the First Magistrate oscillated up and down, and dropped with the emphasis of a pile driver—for the foot of the lamented President was not small.

The music stopped as Julian came out upon the piazza, and the President, hearing his step, looked around. Julian hastened to apologize, saying, frankly, that he had not expected to find him there, but was glad he had, for he must see him before night that day.

"And why so? My working hours are over now, and I want to have some rest along with everybody else," said the President, pointing to the crowd on the grassy lawn. "We might not have another fine day like this for outdoor music until the last of May, and we might, I think, put off work this afternoon a little earlier."

"Mr. President, if it were not a matter of *more* than life, believe me, I would wait until Monday. But tomorrow morning, before ten o'clock, I shall be disgraced before the Army of the Potomac if you do not hear me *now*. So, as an American who will not cast a fellow citizen down into a mire of disgrace, and as a man who will not let a fellow man perish in despair, you must hear me *now*, at once."

"What is it?" said the President, letting his dangling leg stop its swinging and glide gradually on the floor, and turning to face Julian squarely.

"Mr. President, you have dismissed me from the army without a trial or sentence from a court. I want you to give me a chance to defend myself and vindicate my good name. Why have you dismissed me?"

"I haven't dismissed you. Or, at least, I don't remember. What is your name?"

Julian smiled sadly. What bitter philosophy he was learning from the leading men of his country; from the Cackles; from the First Magistrate! American citizens as *individuals*, then, had lost the importance, the sacredness, of old. Now they only counted as masses on which leaders might tread to stand high—as masses to be hurled at the cannon's mouth. It seemed to Julian that a case like his should be indelibly stamped on the mind of the American nation; forever stereotyped there, commencing with the President then down to the humblest peanut-vender, because a case of dismissal without a trial should be so exceptional, of such odious singleness in the United States, that no one should or could forget it. He thought, too, that it was of ominous augury for the liberties of the Americans if a man who was on the field defending that Union loved by all so dearly, exposing his breast to the bullets of its enemies, should be dismissed and the case be considered so unimportant, or of so common occurrence, that it was immediately forgotten! Rapidly these sad thoughts crossed his mind. Then he answered, "My name is Julian Norval, Mr. President. I am a lieutenant-colonel of the —th Regiment, and I belong to the Sixth Corps."

"I remember now something about your being a sympathizer with the Secesh."

"Strange sympathy, sir, which is shown by mowing them down—the poor, half-clad, half- starved fanatics!"

"Yes—something, too, about your saying that I had no right to issue the Emancipation Proclamation, and that I am usurping powers, and that some members of my cabinet tyrannize over the people, and I let them do it, and I don't know what else."

"If I had said all that, sir, I think I would still have the right to a trial and defense (supposing that such utterances are to be considered treason). But I never said such things. All that I ever said was that if you, being the executive, and not the legislative, did not have the right to issue that proclamation, as a commander-in-chief of the army now occupying the South, you had the right to make the law in the conquered soil. But, I assure you, I paid so little attention to this conversation (it passed a year ago) that I had forgotten it. I know I only said that much to get rid of some of the officers who were discussing those things, and pressed me to give my opinion. I was about to start on picket duty; my saddled horse and my orderly were waiting whilst I ate a hurried breakfast. This is all that ever occurred."

"Then it has been greatly exaggerated, and on Monday I'll speak to the Secretary of War about it."

"Sir, the order dismissing me has been at the headquarters of my corps for over a week, and it will be published on parade tomorrow morning unless the general is notified that you rescind it. If you do not, I shall be disgraced." And Julian felt sick, and staggered a step or two, and leaned against a pillar of the portico.

"But now it is late, you see, and the Secretary of War and the Adjutant General have gone home. I don't see what is to be done."

"Then you yourself telegraph to my corps commander that the order is revoked. Or give me authority to telegraph myself that such is the fact."

"Very well: say that I rescind the order, and that the revocation will be issued on Monday."

"Thank you, sir! you have saved my life!" said Julian in a husky voice.

The President, always glad when he had finished a disagreeable job, would, no doubt, have told Julian some funny anecdote, but Julian, saluting the President, and repeating his thanks, hurried off to send the telegram immediately to his corps commander.

In less than twenty minutes the words announcing that the dismissal was revoked were flying on the wires, and Julian then thought of dinner. He went to the dining room and sat at a table, and for the first time since he came from camp knew what he put in his mouth, or thought of drinking a glass of wine.

After dinner he met the Honorable Marcus Tullius Cicero Cackle—called, for short, Tool—and this gentleman informed him that both of his distinguished brothers, Beau and Ciss, had gone to New York, which was the reason they had not fulfilled their promise to go with Julian to the President's.

As Julian walked with Tool Cackle on the hotel promenade, he was again the object of unanimous admiration. But he was unconscious of it, and, without deigning to return one sweet glance, coolly left all to go and spend the evening with his dear Aunt Lavvy!

Whilst Julian talks to Lavvy, we will see what they had been doing at home this week so painful to him.

CHAPTER XLVIII

"Hooker and Skinner, Solicitors and Attorneys-at-Law"

The motto heading this chapter is transcribed from an inscription over the door next to Major Hackwell's office.

Hooker and Skinner, solicitors, had a different entrance to their office from that of the major's, but there was a secret communication between the two offices which made private transactions very easy and convenient for the major, who was a silent partner of the firm.

About a week before Julian went to Washington, soon after the major reached his office, Mr. Hooker came in through the private passage to the inner room of the three which formed the office of the purchasing commissary. Mr. Hooker sat close by the major, and in a low tone said, "I have received a very curious letter this morning. Who do you think it is from? You'd never guess. It is from Isaac Sprig, who writes from Mexico, inclosing advertisements which he wants us to publish for him. He advertises for a girl found among the Colorado Indians. Is there not a young lady at Mrs. Norval's with some such history as that? Read what Isaac says."

With very shaky fingers the major grasped Isaac's letter and eagerly read it.

"Don't publish these advertisements until I tell you. I'll find out more about our young lady's history, and perhaps we might get the money which Isaac says her father will give. I'll let you know in a day or two what I find out."

When Mr. Hooker went back to his own office, he said to Mr. Skinner, "Depend upon it, the major is more interested in those advertisements than he would own up. He shook as if he had the ague when he read Isaac's letter, and his nerves are not weak generally."

The major's nerves were weak all day. That night, however, they got in better tone after a talk with the madam, sitting close by her in his gorgeous dressing gown.

After those gallant preliminaries which he so well knew how to employ, and when Mrs. Norval was so happy sitting by him thinking of their love, the major told her that advertisements for Lola would soon be out if they did not stop them.

The matron was, of course, perfectly terrified. Oh, that Lola! She was always the reptile in the innocent paradise of Mrs. Norval! What was to be done? Oh, Isaac! Of course no good could come of his unnatural liking for foreigners, and of all foreigners, the least of all, the Mexicans?

Such were Mrs. Norval's lamentations, which Hackwell wisely permitted to be poured out freely, for it suited him that the madam should be made perfectly docile by terror. When he saw that she already imagined Lola's father in New York asking for Lola's money and that she was ready to do anything to avert such a catastrophe, he told her that if she would advise Lola to be guided by him he thought he could yet fix matters so as to avoid giving up Lola's money,—at all events, not until she was twenty-one—even if her father claimed her.

"But how can you do that?"

"Have you confidence in me?"

"Why, certainly."

"Then leave the matter in my hands and be guided by me. All you have to do now is to *advise Lola to do everything I suggest to her.* After breakfast tomorrow, I'll feel my ground and tell her all I deem proper. Then when I go downtown, you speak to her, and if she refuses to trust me after you have spoken to her, you can either send me word or wait until I come home in the evening."

Soon after, the worthy couple was sleeping in the tranquillity of a clear conscience.

Next morning after breakfast, the major approached the piano where Lola was practicing. As it was the first time he had done this, Lola looked up from her music, surprised.

The major smiled and blandly apologized for interrupting her, only he had something of importance to tell her. Lola stopped playing, and waited to hear what he had to say.

"Miss Lola, if I could persuade you to dislike me less, and have a little more confidence in me, I think I could put you in the way of obtaining information about your father."

"My father!" exclaimed Lola.

"Yes, your father. But you hate and distrust me so much that really—" Here he hesitated.

"Oh, I shall not hate you! I don't hate you! But do tell me how I can hear about him."

"Will you trust me and be guided by me?"

"Indeed I will!" said she, earnestly.

"Very well. You may have to go with me *in person* to the office of the men who can give us the information. This is unpleasant for a young lady to do, as *only married* ladies go to such places. But you can put on a thick veil, and cover your sweet face, and no one need know but what you are old and ugly. Would you be willing to pass for that?"

"Certainly. You don't suppose I would hesitate to go where I can obtain information about my father for fear of being taken for old and ugly?"

"And married?"

"And married. What do I care for that?"

"All right then. But first I shall endeavor to obtain the information myself. And only in case I fail will you have to play the role of ugly and old and married. I shall let you know this evening what success I have. If it is necessary that you go in person, I will let you know that also. But I trust it will not be."

It is needless to say that Mr. Hackwell did find it necessary that Lola should go *in person.* That night, after a day spent by Lola in the most excruciating agony of suspense, she was told by the major that the people who had the information refused to impart it to anyone but the interested party, and to that one only on being well identified; that they were about to publish advertisements, but he had begged them to wait until tomorrow, as it would be so disagreeable for her: "The notoriety of being described in the newspapers as found among the Indians, and your mother being—"

"Hush! hush! Of course it would be horrible! No, no! They must not publish any advertisements! I'll go! Will you go with me?"

"Certainly. And I'll ask Hammerhard to be there to identify you."

"Thank you. You are very good."

"And you don't hate me so much?"

"No, I don't!" said Lola, laughing. "And I am going to try to think you are my friend, and love you accordingly."

The color mounted to Hackwell's forehead. To be told, even in jest, that she was going to try to love him was too sweet to hear composedly.

"Very well: I accept the promise, and tomorrow you will go with me and pass for old and ugly and married—will you? It is hard for one so young and beautiful, but—"

"Oh, I know it will be an awful sacrifice for one so vain as I, but I'll do it!"

There was no need of Mrs. Norval's exhortations to induce Lola to trust and be guided by the major. Her own anxiety to obtain information about her father, and her dread that those horrible advertisements describing her mother's capture and life among the Indians might come out if she did not go in person to stop them, did all that the major wished. She was ready to do as he directed. She would go with the major next morning, immediately after breakfast, and learn all.

She scarcely slept that night, and the night seemed so long to her. It seemed very long to the major also; he, too, wished the day to come. He feared something might derange his well-concerted plans.

CHAPTER XLIX

Lieutenants Wagg and Head Enter the Grand Monde

The night, although so long to Lola, was at last succeeded by day—the day in which she would hear news from her father. She was too nervous to wait. She thought she would write to Julian. A whole week had passed without hearing from him. What could be the matter? She jumped out of bed and ran about her room in her bare little feet, so pink and dimpled. She went to the window to peep out and see if the Fifth Avenue world was awake. It was not. She opened the register to let the warm air into her room, and sat near it to write to Julian. Yes, she would tell him the good news; though, after all, she didn't know much yet. She would leave the letter open to finish it when she returned from her trip downtown. Meantime, she would tell him about their last balls and receptions, and that Mrs. Norval was to give her last evening reception, which would terminate with a German, that day.

That was the Saturday on which Julian had his interview with the President on the portico.

After writing a long letter, and when she had finished her toilette and descended the stairs in street dress, Lola heard the breakfast bell, and a few minutes afterwards the steps of the other ladies of the family, who were coming downstairs.

"What is the matter with us all?" said the major, taking his usual seat opposite to Mrs. Norval. "Are we going to turn over a new leaf and be early risers? I believe this is the second time in six months I have had the pleasure of breakfasting with the Misses Norval or Miss Hackwell."

"You may thank my dressmaker for the pleasure of breakfasting with *me*," said Ruth. "Her ladyship sent me word that if she did not try my dress on before eleven, she could not finish it by four."

"My case is very similar. Sincerity compels me to say that not alone the pleasure of your company got me out of my bed," added Mattie.

"I am nevertheless grateful to the circumstance which brought you," the major replied politely. "And you, Em, what made you so *smart*—as we say in Yankee-land?"

"Nothing particular," Emma answered.

"I wonder if our reception will be as brilliant as the last?" said Ruth. "I hope it will, for I want it to be better than that of Mrs. Van Kraut. By the bye, major, you must come early, and in uniform."

"I see that General and the Hon. Mirabeau Cackle arrived yesterday," said Mrs. Norval, reading the newspaper.

"That is fortunate, for I shall immediately send cards and write them to come," said Ruth. "Receptions always look brilliant when there are many officers in their uniforms."

"That's so. Why don't you bring your two lieutenants to help the shine with their brass?" Mattie added, addressing the major.

"Are they good-looking?" Ruth inquired.

"So so," the major replied."

"That is to say, their beauty is as big as a piece of chalk." Mattie observed.

"Just about," answered the major.

"Are they agreeable? What are their names? Are they accomplished?" inquired Ruth.

"Their names and their accomplishments are about the same," replied the major, with a laugh.

"What do you mean?" Emma asked.

"Yes, what do they do?" asked Ruth.

"And what are their names?" Mattie added.

"The name of one is Wagg, Head the other, and—"

"Wagg-Head, you say?" interrupted Mattie.

"No, one is Wagg, and the other Head—"

Exclamations and laughter interrupted the major, then he continued: "The combination is funny, but their nicknames are more so. And if I am to bring them, I had better not tell you what these are."

"Oh yes, yes. Do!" said the young ladies.

"You will laugh at them, and the poor fellows are very sensitive about their names."

The young ladies promised not to laugh, and the major told them the nicknames, which of course brought out a burst of laughter from everyone, even the madam.

"Are their names appropriate to their looks and dispositions?" asked Lola.

"Yes, I think they are. One is sentimental, and the other is a wit."

"Sophy is the sentimental and Scaly Wagg[60] the wit, I suppose," said Mattie.

"Exactly," the major answered.

"I think they must be interesting. Describe them a little, major," said Ruth.

"Well, Sophy has a round Dutch face and rounder head, both perfectly meaningless. Wagg has greenish, protruding eyes, yellow hair, yellow mustache, and a chest as flat as a plank. Both are great equestrians and lady-killers, only they ride their horses and kill the ladies in different ways. One rides *á l'Anglaise*, and trots, pounding his horse; the other rides *á la Méxicaine*, and prances. One plays the guitar and sings in foreign languages (which the ladies don't understand), and the other crows like a rooster to perfection and imitates several other sounds, all of which constitute his stock in trade with the fair sex."

"I suppose it is Sophy who prances," said Lola.

"And Wagg who crows," added Mattie.

"Do they know anybody in town? I have never met them anywhere," said Ruth.

"No, they don't have many acquaintances. As far as I know of their amusements, it seems that when Sophy is on duty he stays at home and sings French and Italian or Spanish love songs to the stove and the rats about the office. And when off duty he is 'on guard' near Mrs. Skroo's person, and that of her red-headed sister. Wagg, when he is off duty, goes with Skroo to play poker, to which both he and Skroo are very partial. And when he is on duty, he teaches Sophy to crow, or quack, or bray, or some other of his accomplishments, to fool Sophy into keeping him company."

The young ladies thought the two ex-zouaves "lovely," and made the major promise to bring them without fail to their reception.

Breakfast being over, the ladies hurried to their different affairs, and when no one but Mrs. Norval was downstairs, Hackwell called Lola and told her it was time for them to go downtown.

How the poor child trembled as she got into the coupé! The major, too, was visibly agitated. This was the first time that he had been alone

[60]Ruiz de Burton here is obvious in her pun on "scalawags," the deprecatory term applied principally to refer to white Southern office seekers, supporters of northern Republican Reconstruction policies.

with Lola since she had run away from him in Washington. And never, since she was a child, had he been so near her.

"I hope you are a good actress," said he as soon as they started, "and that, if it is necessary to pass for married, you will act your part well."

"I shall try. But why must I be married, if I only have to be my father's daughter?"

"Just to avoid delays, perhaps, as they may wish to know who is your guardian, and all that sort of thing, before they give you any information. They would perhaps require Julian's presence before they said anything, and what we wish particularly is to avoid delay and prevent them from advertising. When we have obtained the information, I'll manage them; leave them to me. But they are very sharp. If we have to pass you for married, suppose you pass for Hammerhard's wife, or the wife of one of my lieutenants? But wait. They know Mrs. Hammerhard, and that Wagg and Head are not married."

"I'll have to pass for *your* wife then," said Lola, laughing and blushing.

"That is a happiness I did not hope to obtain even in jest," said the major with more truth than he generally used in his sayings and doings.

"Try to see if we can get the information without this marriage farce. I don't like the idea of it, and I think these men ought to give me the information as Lola Medina."

"And so they will; only as my wife you will require no further witnesses, which you might as a young lady, if they chose to insist on it. Do you understand me?"

"I can't say I do, but I'll do as you tell me. Mrs. Norval told me to obey you implicitly."

The major did not wish to give any more reasons, and as soon as he saw that Lola would do what he told her, he changed the conversation and tried to divert her mind from the object of their drive. This he succeeded in doing, and, conversing on different topics, they arrived in front of the door over which were the names of Messrs. Hooker and Skinner.

The major helped Lola out of the coupé, and was about to escort her up to Messrs. Hooker and Skinner's office when he suddenly changed his mind, and said to Lola, taking her to the next door, "Let us go here first. I'll leave you here whilst I go to ascertain if the gentlemen have come."

So saying, they walked up to Major Hackwell's office. Lola, perfectly ignorant as to where she was going, followed—a little nervous, but happy that at last she was to hear of her father and would prevent the terrible advertisements from going to tell the world, through the columns of a newspaper, the shame and grief of her adored mother.

CHAPTER L

Lola Hears Important News

Three gentlemen were in the room into which the major ushered Lola; two of them were writing, and one was reading a newspaper. Lola was so thickly veiled that her face could not be seen, but all seemed to expect her. She could not distinguish their features through her double veil. She asked the major, in a whisper, if she could remove it.

"Certainly," said he, presenting a chair to her, then added, "Do you recognize your old acquaintance, Mr. Hammerhard?"

"Of course I do, although I have scarcely seen him since I went away to school," she replied.

Mr. Hammerhard advanced to shake hands with her, and the major said, coolly addressing the two other gentlemen, who were writing, but who now stood up, "My wife, gentlemen. Lola, Mr. Wagg, Mr. Head, my two assistants." The gentlemen bowed, and Lola looked at them and burst out laughing.

Mr. Hammerhard, in all seriousness, again took her hand, calling her "Mrs. Hackwell," and congratulated her on the "happy event."

"And when did it happen? I have been west for the last month, and I had not heard of this," he said. And he spoke the truth thus far—that, as he lived west of Fifth Avenue, he had been west—at home. The major smiled, saying, "We have kept it secret, and mean to keep it so for some time. So, gentlemen, though it is of no material importance, still I wish you to do me the favor not to mention having seen my wife."

The gentlemen bowed in assent.

Lola looked a little alarmed, and blushed very red. She looked at Hammerhard; that worthy divine gave her a very unclerical, but very encouraging, wink, and she felt a little more reassured. Then she looked at Sophy and Scaly, and thought of their nicknames and idiosyncrasies, and again felt a great desire to laugh, and did not dare to speak.

The major told Mr. Hammmerhard to sit by *the madam* and talk to her; that he would be back in a few minutes.

He thereupon left the room. In less than ten minutes he returned, accompanied by two other gentlemen, to whom he said as soon as he entered, "This is the lady, gentlemen," and then to Lola, "My dear, these are the gentlemen," and he invited them to walk into the adjoining room, closing the door carefully after all had entered.

One of the gentlemen, Lola noticed, had a large book like an account book under his arm and a roll of papers in his hand. Very imposing to Lola were that book and those papers, and so was the man carrying them—he was so villanously ugly. This was Mr. Skinner. He stammered painfully, so he always let his partner, Mr. Hooker, do all the talking. Mr. Hooker had the "gift of gab" in a high degree—more than would compensate the firm for Mr. Skinner's stammering. He commenced business.

"Madam," said he to Lola as soon as they were seated in the major's inner office, "we have very important information to impart. But first we wish to be sure that we impart it to the right person; so you will excuse us for making a few inquiries, if you please."

"Certainly," said Lola, frightened as she saw Mr. Skinner's dim eyes and coarse big nose aimed at her fixedly whilst he held a pen in his hand over the imposing book, as if ready to put down there her heart's pulsations.

"What is your name, if you please?" continued Mr. Hooker.

"Lola Medina," she answered. The major coughed and little moved uneasily in his chair, but he did not add anything.

"Are you married or single?" Lola blushed, but hesitated to answer. Mr. Hooker added, "I do not ask you out of impertinent curiosity, but only for this—that if you are single we may have to see your guardian, should you be under age, and if you are married, then we may have to see your husband. We must not only be sure that we have found the right person, but we must be sure, too, that this transaction is done fairly. Someone has to be responsible to us for our remuneration."

"I shall be responsible to you for that," said the major, giving Lola a very expressive look.

"Yes, the major will answer for that," said she.

"Is he related to you in any way? Is he your guardian or your husband?"

"Yes, sir, he is my husband," the poor child replied hurriedly, afraid that if she did not say that, she would not hear from her father, and thinking of the advertisements.

"In that case, of course, we feel no hesitation in telling you all we know," said Mr. Hooker, who then proceeded to tell Lola a long story, the substance of which was that a manuscript had been dictated by her mother and directed to an unknown person, had been found (he did not say by whom) and carried to Mexico to her father, and that her father was now making inquiries for her, and that they—Messrs. Hooker and Skinner—guaranteed Lola to put her father in the way of coming straight to Fifth Avenue to find her.

"And now, Mrs. Hackwell," added Mr. Hooker in conclusion, "please do not accuse me of wanting in courtesy if I again ask if you are what you tell me."

"Of course I am," said Lola, firmly. "My name is Lola Medina, and Don Luis Medina is my father. I remember perfectly well that my mother told me that such was his name, and my grandfather's name is Don Felipe de Almenara."

"And you are married?"

"Ye—es," answered Lola, blushing.

"Oh, do not be afraid that we wish to speak of your marriage," said he.

"My dear," said the major, "the gentlemen might doubt you if you hesitate to tell them your are married."

"Why should they doubt? Did I not say I was your wife?"

This last answer seemed to satisfy all the gentlemen, for they bowed and rose to leave.

Mr. Hammerhard also bade them good morning. The major and Lola were left alone.

"You dislike me so much, that even to obtain this information, you hated to pass for my wife," said the major in a mournful tone, standing in front of Lola with arms folded over his breast in Napoleonic style.

"No, I don't hate you, but I hate to tell a story," said Lola, blushing again.

"Lola, how I do worship you! I know it is madness, but I can't help it. You are my destiny; you are the only woman I ever did or ever shall love."

Lola looked at the door, alarmed.

"Do not be afraid. Let us go. I shall not be so mean as to take advantage of your coming here under my protection to torture you with expressions of a love so disagreeable to you." And the major walked towards the door to open it.

Lola laid her hand on his arm. She felt very sorry she could not be more grateful to him than she was, and thought she would at least show that she did not wish to hurt his feelings after his rendering her a great service.

"You are not angry with me?" said she. "Please don't be. Indeed, I appreciate your kindness."

He looked at the little hand lying on his arm; he took it, and, as it was gloved, he kissed the little wrist with avidity many times.

"Oh, Lola! my darling angel! Can I ever hope? It seems to me I am capable of doing anything to obtain your love. It is burning my very soul. You must be mine, somehow or other."

"Let us go, major. I cannot stay to hear you talk so," Lola said, opening the door herself.

When they came out in the street, he was pale and agitated, and Lola was afraid to ride with him. She told him that she would take an omnibus, as she wished to do some shopping before going home.

"No, you get in the coupé. I don't mean to force my company on you. I shall remain. Good morning."

"We will see you early this evening, and your two specimens of humanity, I suppose?"

"Yes, I shall take them if they'll amuse you," he replied, bowing to Lola as he closed the door.

CHAPTER LI

Mademoiselle Mina's Accident

"By Jove, Ham, I feel shaky!" said the major, returning to the office of Hooker and Skinner, where his three confederates waited for him, and had watched from the window the ceremony of his escorting Lola with great deference to her coupé and closing the door of it with a most profound bow.

"Allow me to congratulate you on this last *coup-d'état*," said Hammerhard. "You beat Prince Pöllnitz;[61] for he made marriages for others, whilst you make them for yourself."

"Hush, Ham. No frivolity just now; it is too serious. She repeated *twice* that she was my wife: didn't she, Mr. Skinner?"

"Ye—ye—yes, to—to—twice. I—I—I not—tis—ticed it par—par—part—ti—tic—cu—cu—cu—cu—cu—"

"Particularly," interposed Mr. Hooker; "and, as we have done our part and given your wife information so valuable, I hope you are satisfied, major, and will now close our agreement."

"Certainly, certainly," answered the major. "Sprig says in his letter that Don Luis Medina will give ten-thousand dollars. Well, as a member of our firm I have my share of that. I'll give my share to you three, and two thousand besides, so that you will have twelve thousand to divide among you. But, mind, if I have to make fight, I shall require you to appear as my witnesses. Julian is a stubborn boy, and terribly smitten."

"Of course we shall be your witnesses. But if you can manage the business without going to law, I shall like it better," said Mr. Hammerhard.

"So will I," added Mr. Hooker.

[61]Prince Pöllnitz (unknown reference)

Mr. Skinner opened and shut his mouth and gasped, which might have meant that he was of the same opinion.

After a half-hour more of innocent converse, the four partners separated, apparently highly pleased with their transaction.

The reception at the Norval mansion that evening, Mrs. Grundy[62] said, was the most brilliant that had been given in New York City that season. Mrs. Norval surpassed herself and everybody else in the magnificence of her entertainment. Everything was in the richest style—the rooms, the table, the dresses, etc.

Mrs. Norval came downstairs to receive her guests robed in a rich lilac velvet trimmed with point d'Alençon. No one could have recognized in this superbly dressed lady the gawky girl the doctor saw for the first time counting the eggs to send to market, nor the rigid Puritan who had scorned the frivolity of lace or a bit of ribbon around her neck. Mrs. Norval looked young for her years. If in earlier life she could have felt the passions to which now she was a constant prey—her ambition, her remorse, her bitter hatred for Lola, her blind love for Hackwell—she might now have been an old, old woman. But the cold selfishness and unloving impassibility of her previous nature had preserved her young, as the ice she used to put around her turkeys to pack them for the Boston market kept those fowls fresh, though she made it a rule to "do her killing" a week before Thanksgiving Day and a week before Christmas. She had had only one passion—her religious bigotry—which had inspired her with a strong hatred towards everything and everybody that was not Presbyterian. She had felt but one ambition—that of saving, saving, saving—putting away more pennies and five- and ten-cent pieces than any of her neighbors. Aside from these two feelings, which alone could be said to have had in her strength enough to be called passions, there had been no other to shake her soul. Her life had flowed smoothly on in peaceful current, without any other disturbance than an occasional ripple caused by some unsuccessful revolt of the doctor or some escapade of the truant Isaac. So it was that her soul only warmed into life under the Promethean breath of Hackwell, and it leaped from its lethargy like those lizards imbedded for ages in granite which geologists say resuscitate when brought to the sun and air. And there was she now, majestically bowing to her obsequious guests.

[62]A fictional figure, Mrs. Grundy, is invoked as the arbiter of taste and morals in a given community.

The young ladies of the family were also richly dressed on this last grand reception, all except Lola. Her simple costume consisted of a white tarletan dress, with bunches of forget-me-nots in her hair. Mrs. Norval as yet had given her none of her jewelry.

As she and Emma descended from their rooms in the third floor, they met Ruth coming out from hers in the second, followed by three other young ladies richly attired who had come "to receive with the Misses Norval." They saluted Emma with warm kisses, and bowed to Lola very coolly. Then all stopped in the hall to comment on each other's dresses and admire themselves before a large mirror placed in front of the stairs. All eyed Lola, but said nothing to her.

"Why, Lola, you look perfectly lovely!" exclaimed Mattie, coming out of her room. "But why haven't you any jewelry—at least earrings? Ah, I know!" And she ran into her mother's room and returned bringing a pearl necklace and earrings, which, in spite of Lola's resistance, she clasped on her neck and fastened in her ears, saying, "This is the prettiest girl in these United States. No wonder my poor brother wishes the rebs may shoot him if he can't have her."

"And you might shoot us all, for, as the major says, you are a perfect blunderbuss," said Ruth, irritated.

"Dearest Rooty, if you had any good looks '*to speak of*,' you wouldn't mind my blunderbussing about them. But the trouble is that you haven't, sister of mine; I am sorry to blunderbuss that to you. And as for the major, I know where the shoe pinches his reverence, and if he wishes it I'll blunderbuss him the spot. Talk of Spanish women being dark! Can anything be whiter than Lola's neck and shoulders?" added Mattie, addressing all.

"Lola is not Spanish; she is Mexican," said Ruth.

"I think Lola might teach us the secret of that Indian paint that kept her white skin under cover, making it whiter by bleaching it. I would bargain to wear spots for a while," said Emma.

"And well you might, for a freckled neck is no beauty, and easy to please must be he who will kiss a freckled hand," Mattie replied.

The voice of Mrs. Norval calling them downstairs happily interrupted their dialogue, and in silence they descended.

When they entered the drawing rooms, several friends had already arrived. Among them were Mr. and Mrs. Hammerhard, who had driven up in a handsome carriage, very different indeed from the squeaky vehicle of yore owned conjointly by the two *poor* parsons.

The two Generals Cackle were also there, resplendent in brass buttons and smiles. And now the stream of elegance poured in, bringing princely speculators, military celebrities, fashionable belles, and all half smothered by shoddy. Major Hackwell came too, as he promised, followed by his two lieutenants, whom he duly presented to the ladies of the family. They were politely received, but soon found very uninteresting. They could not shine advantageously there, as Wagg could not crow or neigh in the midst of this elegant assembly, nor Head sing in impossible Italian. They were soon forgotten behind a door.

"I say, Head, wouldn't I throw a bombshell in the midst of this gay bivouac if I were to peach about the major's farce of this morning, eh? Wouldn't I like it, though? I'd like to see the rascal's face, and the young lady's, too," said Wagg.

"There you are again, suspecting that good man," said Head reproachfully. "But hush! here comes his wife," he added, seeing Lola come towards them. She was the only person who had taken any notice of them; she came to invite them to the dining room to partake of refreshments. There she left them under the care of the headwaiter, and ran upstairs to her room.

She wished to be alone. The unkind words of Ruth and Emma were still ringing in her ears, and had taken away all desire for gayety. If she had had more of her sex's vanity, she would have consoled herself, seeing that those cruel words had also added brilliancy to her beauty by heightening her color and making her black eyes dazzling in their glorious lustre. But Lola did not think of looking in the glass. Straightway she went up to Julian's picture to talk to it. Then she prayed to the Virgin Mary for the doctor's return, and fell to weeping, as she often did when harshness recalled to her mind more vividly her loneliness, making her feel more keenly the loss of her kind protector. She had been for some time lost in sad thoughts, forgetful of the gayety downstairs, when angry voices calling her name close to her door roused her from her reverie.

"Who wants me?" said she, opening the door. And as she did, so she beheld Major Hackwell and Lieutenant Head wrestling by the door of Emma's room, which was next to hers. Livid with rage, the major was endeavoring to wrest Lieutenant Head from the doorknob, to which that chivalric zouave, flushed with champagne and native heroism, clung resolutely with one hand in desperate effort to keep the door closed, whilst with the other arm he warded off the major's blows and prevented his approach to the door. At the sound of Lola's voice the major turned quickly around, and his hands relinquished their furious hold on his lieutenant, and his arms fell powerless at his side.

"I will defend the lady with my life!" shouted Head.

"There is a door between Em's room and yours, isn't there? Speak quickly, and tell the truth," said the major to Lola, imperatively.

She, however, first surveyed him from head to foot with a derisive smile that made her dimples very saucy, then slowly answered, "No, sir, there is not."

The major thundered louder, "How, then, did you get through? Or who is the lady?"

"Which lady?" said Mrs. Norval, appearing at that moment at the head of the stairs, followed by Ruth and Lieutenant Wagg. "I heard your voice in the dining room, major, calling Lola very loud," said she.

Quick as a flash the major saw his position. He answered, "I thought there was a communication between these two rooms, and I was calling Lola to go into Emma's room to see who is the woman my worthy lieutenant is hiding there. I think it is that little grisette, Ruth's servant."

"I am no 'grisette,' sir, nor a 'servant,'" said Mina, opening the door and confronting the major. "You are angry with me because you mistook me for Mademoiselle Lola, and you wish to insult me."

"Hush this instant, and go to your room," said Mrs. Norval. "If you are not a proper girl, I shall not permit you to remain as my daughter's servant. For a *servant* you are."

"A servant!" exclaimed Head, aghast, "a servant!"

"A *servant*!" repeated Mina. And stepping nearer Mrs. Norval and shaking her fist close to that matron's nose, she said, "A *real* lady never calls a waiting maid a '*servant*'; only women whom we call *parvenu* [63] in Europe do so."

"You may call servants countesses in Europe, and free grisettes ladies, but we don't do so in America, and we expect servants to know their places," said Ruth.

"The ladies don't know theirs any better," retorted Mina.

"That'll do," said the major, pushing Mina towards the stairs leading to the garret. "Go where you belong."

"You wish to send me off because you are afraid I shall repeat to madame what you said, thinking I was Mademoiselle Lola. You said, 'I'd rather die than see this,' and then you said—"

"That it was likely Miss Lola would behave like a grisette," interrupted the major, "and allow my second lieutenant to put his arm around her waist, for such was the situation when I came."

"Mina does look like Lola, decked in that cast-off old finery," said Ruth, pointing at Mina's dress which was one given to her by Lola.

Mina's eyes flashed at Ruth, but she answered the major's imputation, that being the more offensive. She said, addressing Mrs. Norval,

[63]French for newly-rich, coarse and unrefined in manners and taste.

"No, madame, that is not true. I was standing by the bathroom door when Monsieur 'Ead came out from the dining room, saw me reflected in the mirror in the upper hall, and came to salute me."

"A French way of saluting," interrupted the major.

Mina continued, "Very soon after, monsieur, the major came running upstairs, abusing Monsieur 'Ead. I was frightened, and ran to 'ide myself in the nearest room. As I entered the door, I 'eard the major say, 'I saw you in the mirror, Lola! this is infamous!' Then I—"

"Then you have lied enough, and should be discharged from a service you can only disgrace by your lies," said the major.

"You—a—monster—a—a—horrible man—" said Mina, and, overcome by the impetuosity of her anger, she fell forward, fainting.

"She is drunk," said the major, and a new expedient suggested itself to his mind to extricate himself from his awkward position. "Wagg, call two waiters to carry this woman to her room."

Lola, who had caught Mina's form as it fell, said, "No, sir, don't call servants. Lieutenant Head, you and your friend will please help me carry the poor child to my room. I'll take care of her until she regains consciousness."

"Bah!" ejaculated Ruth, running downstairs.

"Birds of a feather flock together," said Mrs. Norval, following her daughter.

CHAPTER LII

Julian at the White House

Julian was not so fortunate as he had anticipated, and whilst his mother and sisters gave brilliant entertainments, he passed miserable nights.

Five days had elapsed since his interview with the President, and he had not been able to learn whether the dismissal was or was not officially rescinded. He passed in and out, and saw anxious faces—those of sad-looking ladies, more particularly—patiently waiting day by day. "Can they be the same people?" Julian thought. "They all have the same weary expression. Yes, they must be the same, or else there are more miserable people in this land than I had any idea of. Why should they not be the same? Have I not waited days and days with a halter around my neck?"

Friday came, and, that being cabinet day, it offered but small hope of his seeing the President. Still, Julian went, and sent in his card.

"The President is too busy," said the usher, and Julian knew it was useless to spend the day waiting.

That night he again examined his little five-shooter—a present from Major Hackwell—and sat down to write two telegrams: one to his corps commander, asking him to wait a little longer; another to his own adjutant, to send him any letters which might have come to camp for him since he left—to send them by that night's mail, so that he might get them next day.

"Oh, I hope there may be a letter from Lola!" said the miserable Julian as he threw himself on his bed.

Saturday dawned. Julian felt that on this day his fate had reached a turning point. It was a bright morning in the early part of April. If the President did not see him (thought Julian), he would go to his own senator and *demand* justice. He would not rely for co-operation or support on any Cackle. On that he had resolved. And if he failed! He shuddered as he thought of the little five-shooter he carried so close to his heart, and despair darkened his soul. "You should know who is your calumniator, and if you plunge into eternity he should go before you," whispered one of those "unbottled imps" which unseen walk alongside of people at times like a persistent little beggar that will have his penny. Julian tried to reason with the little imp, as will a harassed pedestrian protesting that he has no change, and he argued that in this free country calumniators have no trade; they have no power to disgrace and ruin an honest man; the fountains of justice are not dry or poisoned in this free land; underhanded persecution is abhorrent to the American mind, argued he. "Why, then, are you dismissed without a trial? And why is it that you, an American citizen and a patriot defending your country, can't even see the guardian of the people?" said the persistent little invisible one. Julian clinched his fists and set his teeth close together, as he perceived that the imp was getting the best of the argument, and, pale with suppressed emotion, he walked up the steps of the Executive mansion.

So absorbed was his attention with his unseen interlocutor that he did not notice three gentlemen who approached the steps from the other side of the semicircle of the front entrance, until one of them, putting his hand on his shoulder, said, "Why, Julian, my boy! what makes you so pale? Have you been sick?"

Julian turned, and saw that Mr. Sinclair, his father's best friend, was speaking to him, and that with him were Senator ——— and General Cackle. They all shook hands very cordially with Julian, and the Senator also asked him if he was sick.

"I am sick—yes, sick of waiting," Julian answered. "No courtier of Louis XIV of France, or serf of the Russian Emperor, could have waited more assiduously than I, a free-born American, have waited (with somebody's foot upon my free-born neck) in vain hope of seeing his absolute excellency the President, who we are told is 'the servant of the people,' and treats gentlemen as if he had bought them, branded them, and was sure they will not stray from his pasture grounds. Surely we Americans have got to be great liars, or else some fearful lies are being told to us."

The three gentlemen looked at one another, and then looked around them to see if anyone was near enough to have heard the reckless boy express himself so imprudently.

"Do not fear for me, gentlemen," said Julian, with a laugh, and as if amused at their terror, "there are depths of misery in which a wretch can feel perfectly secure. I have reached that depth. I am down in a deep well where I need not be afraid that sunshine can reach me, any more than sticks thrown at me. I feel perfectly secure. Only a dim instinct of what is due to others, and a faint memory of what I *was*, impel me to make one last effort today. But I assure you I feel perfectly independent; I will say what I please. No one can do me any more harm *now*."

The Senator took Julian's arm and placed it under his own, then drew the boy towards the door. As they went in, he turned to Mr. Sinclair and the general, saying, "You go up to the President; I shall follow in a short time. First I must speak with Julian; there is something wrong with him." And, holding Julian's arm tightly, as if afraid that the crazy boy might take a notion to run away, he went into the East Room, taking his prisoner to the recess of the farthest window in the spacious room. Here, seating himself, he made Julian sit by him and tell him his sad story, to which he listened with the closest attention, his dark bright eyes shooting out a flash now and then.

"Why didn't you come to me as soon as you arrived in Washington?" asked the senator.

"Because I trusted from day to day that I would see the President, and that the thing would be arranged. And—to tell you the truth—because I hated to speak about it, or to think that any one of my friends should know of my disgrace."

"Disgrace! Pooh! pooh! What are you talking about? *Disgrace* can be brought upon us only by our own acts. And, what is more, a man who has fought for his country as you have, and only brought honor to his nation as you have, can't be disgraced because he is accused. And he shan't be, either, whilst I can prevent it, and prevent it I will. Come, you shall see the President at once." So saying, the senator again took possession of Julian's arm and walked upstairs to the President's room with him.

Besides Mr. Sinclair and General Cackle, the senator and Julian found two other gentlemen with the President. These gentlemen Julian knew by name, and by a description which Lavvy had made of them. He recognized them with feelings of anything but pleasure.

In their presence Julian felt great repugnance to speak of his case. But the President, who always regarded squeamishness as entirely unnecessary, when he had answered the salutation of the senator, turned to Julian, saying, "Your case is pretty bad, colonel. So, at least, these two high officials say."

A flash shot from Julian's eyes as he looked towards the gentlemen pointed to by the President and designated by him as "*high officials*." He replied, with firm voice, and averting his gaze from them, "At least,

I can be tried by court-martial, I suppose. When I entered the army, I did not imagine I had surrendered the right which our institutions give to thieves and murderers even—the right of defending themselves, the right of trial. That right I, as an American citizen—for I *am* an American citizen, Mr. President, by the grace of God—that right I demand, and you can't deny it to me, for I only ask for common justice!"

"Of course you can have a trial. At least, I suppose so—can't he?" said the amiable President (wishing to please everybody), looking towards the high officials, both of whom were now very busy looking at some papers in the recess of a window where they had stepped when Julian began to speak. With evident displeasure at having the President ask their opinion, one of the two, the dark one—the other was blond—answered, whilst the other continued to read,—

"You can judge as well as we, Mr. President, since you are acquainted with the case."

The President turned to Julian, and said, "It seems that, besides your criticising my right to issue the Emancipation Proclamation, colonel, you have been abusing me for suspending the habeas corpus.[64] I don't care, so far as I am concerned, how I am criticised or abused. But such a way of talking is very injurious to the discipline of an army, and very mischievous anywhere in times like the present."

"Abusing you for suspending the habeas corpus?" said Julian, musingly, trying to remember when or where he had ever expressed any opinion on the subject. "I pledge you my word, I never did such a thing."

"Such is the report," said the President.

"And who is my accuser? As we can't possibly have established the old Spanish Inquisition in the United States, I suppose I can know who accuses me?"

The senator was afraid that Julian, in his reckless despair, would utterly ruin his case: so he said, "I think there is a mistake in the man, Mr. President. It was the colonel's father, Dr. Norval, who was a very uncompromising Democrat, and it was reported he spoke against suspending the habeas corpus, and other things. I think they have mixed up the two men."

It was fortunate that the Senator thought of this probability, for it gave the good-natured executive an excellent chance to settle more gracefully a case which might become disagreeable, as Julian was evidently disposed to make a fight. But it was a very painful ordeal for Julian. He loved his father with almost the tenderness of a girl, and

[64]see note #24.

since the fearful report of his death, though he did not credit it, he could not hear him mentioned without the most profound emotion of tender love and acute pain, for a crowd of doubts and fears rushed to his heart. When the senator mentioned the doctor, the expression of intense pain was so marked in the pale, handsome face of Julian, and his vain effort to master his feelings was so evident, that everyone noticed it. He looked down; he clinched his fingers; his breast heaved with swelling emotion. But he stood like a good soldier, erect and immovable, as he had stood facing the fire of the desperate Southerners.

"Very likely it is as you say, senator," said the President, looking towards the *high officials*, as if anxious to ascertain their opinion. But they "gave no sign," and the President continued, "And the colonel has been mistaken for his father. I shall make inquiries, colonel, and if it is as the senator says, of course then your case is quite different from what has been reported."

Julian's pale face flushed, and the deep blue of his eyes looked black as he stepped nearer to the President, and, in a voice in which there was a slight tremor, but great firmness, said, "Mr. President, I told you a week ago today that if the order of my dismissal was not rescinded, it would be published on the following morning. The publication has been suspended for a whole week, because, by your authority, I telegraphed to my corps commander that you annulled the order, and that it would be so announced to him by letter. Nothing has been done since, and if my statement is not confirmed by your authority, or that of the Secretary of War, I fear the general will not feel authorized in delaying any longer. Therefore, if on this very day you do not cause my dismissal to be formally rescinded, tomorrow it may be too late. I do not ask you to do this with any intention of urging my services upon the government. On the contrary, as soon as you revoke my dismissal, I shall be glad to resign. But I am an honest man, Mr. President, and I should feel very great shame at being sent from the army in disgrace."

There was an awkward pause. The President broke it, saying, "I don't think the order will be published tomorrow, and we will see about your case leisurely on Monday."

"No, Mr. President! Now or never! The order, once published, I do not care to have it withdrawn," said Julian, hurriedly, interrupting the senator, who was about to speak.

"Why, young man, do you wish to dictate to the President?" said one of the two *officials*—the blond one.

"No, sir, I would be sorry if my words even seem to want in respect. But I feel I have a right to defend myself, and since a proper trial is denied or withheld from me, and there is no chance to vindicate my good name, I must endeavor to show to the President that there is no time to be lost if he would do me justice. I repeat"—said he, now addressing the President again—"I have no wish to force my services upon a government that casts them and me off. But I must not be sent away branded, disgraced. Give me a trial, or rescind the order. It is but simple *justice*, and I pledge you my word that in either case I shall not continue services so little wanted. I shall resign immediately, but *acquitted*."

"But we don't want you to resign. Our state is proud of you, for no one has fought more nobly for the Union, colonel," said the senator.

"And see how a grateful country rewards me!" said Julian, with curling lip.

"The President will see you righted, for I repeat that your state speaks with pride of you."

"If my state is proud of me, that is one more reason why I should leave the service, for, I assure you, I shall never again feel the enthusiasm for my flag I have felt heretofore. I have fought, thinking myself a free man fighting for freedom, and I awake from my dream to find that I do not have even the privilege granted to thieves and cutthroats. And these straps," said he, trying to pull one off his shoulder. "These, I thought the insignia of honor; I find that they are the mark of slavery, of proscription. For if I had committed murder or vile theft without them, I would still be a citizen and have the right to defend myself. But, as I have them, I am a Pariah. No, I must resign. I wish to have my freedom. If the negroes have it, why shouldn't I? I did not bargain to surrender my freedom to give it to Sambo. But this affair must be settled first. Disgraced I will not be. If I have served my country with sufficient credit to entitle me to any favor from my state, all I ask is justice, and the protection which our free institutions give to everyone under our flag."

Nothing could have been more injudicious than Julian's speech, and he knew it. But he was in despair, and very angry. He was surprised that he was not ordered out of the room, though he returned defiantly the indignant looks of the *high officials*. He was surprised, too, that the President seemed thoughtful, but not angry.

The senator, though evidently pained by the unfortunate turn Julian had given to the affair, said, in a firm voice, "Your state will certainly give you all the protection and support she is always happy to accord to her meritorious sons. But this matter the President, I am sure, can arrange at once by telegraph. I suppose, Mr. President, you can telegraph *now* that the dismissal is entirely revoked, can't you? I am sure there is nothing against Colonel Norval. At all events, you can suspend the order and call a court of inquiry or court-martial to investigate his case, or try him."

"Good morning, Mr. President," said the *high officials*, going. The blond added, "We will return this evening when you will be disengaged."

The President followed them to the door.

CHAPTER LIII

Julian's Fortune Takes a New Turn

The door remained ajar as the President went out, and Julian saw that the Hon. Beau Cackle had joined the group talking near it. But he could not hear what they were saying. The senator, being nearer, heard the President say, "I think it is best to let it go; it don't amount to anything even if he said it, which is doubtful, and the ——— delegation might take it up. The senator was in earnest." The high officials were apparently of a different opinion, but when the President asked Beau if he did not think the ——— delegation would take the case into their own hands if the senator insisted on it, and Beau said, "They will certainly do it," then the high officials concluded it was best to let Julian off that time, and the President returned to the room, followed by Beau, who shook hands with Julian cordially. Julian regarded his *empressement* with supreme contempt.

The President resumed his seat, and putting over the arm of the chair his long leg, which immediately began its oscillatory movement, he said to Julian, "I suppose if I telegraph now to your corps commander, colonel, that I revoke the order, the affair will be arranged to your satisfaction at once?"

"Yes, sir," Julian answered.

The President drew his chair nearer to the table, took his glasses out of their case, put them on his prominent nose, and, again hanging his leg over the arm of his chair, wrote a telegram himself.

"Here it is," said he when he had finished writing, handing the dispatch to Julian, who took it and bowed, saying, "Shall I carry it to the War Office?"

"Yes, give it to the Adjutant General and tell him to forward it immediately. And do wait there for the answer. Let us finish the business now."

Julian again bowed, and left the room. He went downstairs to the vestibule, to the front portico, and took his way across the grounds to a little gate and through it into the grounds of the War Department.

As he went downstairs, he again noticed in the East Room quite a number of distressed-looking people, among whom were some of his old acquaintances of ten days past who had kept him company in his sad anxious hours. These poor people—all—all—looked weary with waiting. And to think that many must, after that long suspense, go away disappointed made the sympathetic heart of Julian feel for them. There were some ladies, too, in deep mourning, and in widows' caps, and with dim red eyes, the luster of which had all been wept away! They were waiting, perhaps, for a little pittance, called a *pension*, to help them; a little pittance which Congress, in its fits of economy, grudges them so cruelly to give in the next hour hundreds of millions to rich monopolists. Or perhaps the poor things had sons dismissed and disgraced, calumniated and persecuted; or a father killed or prisoner; or a brother turned out of office to starve with a large family because it had been reported at the War Office that he sympathized with rebels—because he had been heard to express opinions which he, as an American, had been proud of all his life!

Julian grew heartsick at the thought of these poor people and their sad faces, and the prospect of being freed from the horrible obloquy, so terrible to him to think of, did not cheer him. He was disenchanted. He acknowledged that to himself, and felt that it would take a long time before he should again believe that in America there is not as much despotism as in Europe—"despotism of a worse kind, because we pretend so loudly the contrary. If we didn't say so much about freedom, the thing wouldn't be so bad. We are hypocrites and impostors besides," said the embittered Julian, walking towards the War Office. "We are living on the credit of our fathers and squandering the inheritance of liberty left to us, but we want to humbug posterity by loudly insisting that we have greater riches, more freedom." He laughed. "Here I am at the Juggernaut temple," he said in a louder tone than that of the previous soliloquy, and he entered the War Office.

The dispatch was sent the minute the Adjutant General received it, and Julian sat down to wait for the answer, which he was told would return in ten minutes if the general was in his tent, or, if not, as soon as he should be found about camp.

Julian took a newspaper to read whilst waiting, but scarcely had he cast his eyes over the columns of it and read the few headings when the general's answer arrived.

"It is all right, colonel," said the adjutant. "The order is rescinded. Allow me to congratulate you."

"But had it been published?" Julian inquired.

"No, I don't think it had. I'll ask."

But whilst they were walking towards the telegraph desk, another dispatch came ticking through the wires. They stopped to wait until it was finished. The operator wrote it and handed it to Julian. It was from his corps commander, and said, "I congratulate you. It is all right. Nothing has been published. I reviewed your brigade this morning. It is in splendid order. No hurry for your return. We will not march for ten days, until the Lieutenant General comes."

Julian heaved a sigh of relief. He felt as if he had for years been bent down under a heavy load, almost crushed under its weight, and now it was off.

He thanked the adjutant, and slipped a twenty dollar note on the sly to the operator, thanking him, too. Then he left, taking the answer to the President.

As he stepped out in the hall, a clerk came up to him with two letters, saying, "These have been here for some time, colonel."

Julian took the letters, and, without noticing the handwriting on the envelopes, put them in the breast pocket of his coat. This, however, made him think that the letters he had telegraphed to be sent from camp must now have arrived and be waiting for him at his hotel. He hurried to the White House, with thoughts quite different from those he had had when coming. He was now thinking of Lola, and that thought made everything lovely.

Julian had been away a little more than half an hour, and in that short space of time what a revolution had taken place in his fortunes! He had left, trembling lest he should be too late, for his dismissal might have been published, and, though it were revoked, would nevertheless be publicly known. Now, when he returned, he was met with congratulations from Mr. Sinclair, Beau Cackle, and the senator, which he did not well understand, as he had not yet given to the President the answer to his telegram. But the senator soon explained why they congratulated him, by putting a paper in his hand and saying, "Here, my young friend. The government whose service you wished to leave because you thought it would not do you justice, has done more—has rewarded your merit, as it always will. This is a commission of colonel, which the President has just given you."

Julian's surprise was such that for a few moments he could not find words to express his thanks to the President. But when he did so, his sincerity was so genuine that it could not be doubted. The President certainly believed it, and it pleased his kind heart to see that he had in a measure made amends for the young man's great mental suffering of the last few days.

"It is a darned sight more agreeable to give commissions than dismissals,'' said the renowned Executive in his own peculiar style—again putting his leg over the arm of the chair, of course. "I can tell you what, colonel, you have made me feel very bad with your pale face and those mournful big eyes. I reckon you are very successful with the ladies, ain't you?" Julian blushed crimson, and the majestic foot over the chair began, as usual, to oscillate quite waggishly. "Take my advice. When you want to bring to terms an obdurate charmer, you just manage to get pale, and you look at 'er as you looked at me last Saturday on the back portico. She'll come to terms, and be as manageable as you'd like to have 'er. This reminds me of a story I once heard a bargeman tell when I was going down the Missouri River in a flatboat." And here the redeemer of his country told one of his characteristic stories, which the distinguished men of the day had duly applauded scores of times, but which might not be so well appreciated now, though at the time it made even the grave senator and the anxious Julian laugh.

When Julian left the White House, Mr. Sinclair and the two Cackles went with him. As they walked towards the gate, Julian asked, "Will you tell me how I came to be promoted, when I was so near being dismissed?"

"You are promoted because you deserve it, and because your state is entitled to give some appointments, and the senator asked the President to promote you, there being a vacancy to be filled. Brother Beau and Mr. Sinclair joined the senator and urged the President to promote you now, and he had to give in," answered General Cackle.

"The President was well disposed, and the request of the senator would have been sufficient without our co-operation—at least, without *mine*," said Mr. Sinclair.

"Don't you ever underrate yourself," said the great Beau. "Nothing is ever gained by doing oneself injustice. For my part, I think we *did* help the senator some, though he would eventually have got the commission. Still, we precipitated matters, and the thing was done at once. And, by the bye, Norval, let me tell you: I would have helped in this matter of yours before, but I did not think you would have any trouble or delay in arranging it satisfactorily. Caesar and I were obliged to go to New York on Thursday, and we only returned last night. We saw your mother and sisters, and had a grand time with them. How very pretty that little girl Lola has got to be!—and so very white! She is superb. I—''

"I came with this gentleman," said Mr. Sinclair, intentionally interrupting Beau, "and I am charged with a secret commission of great importance, of which you must be made acquainted as soon as possible, Julian."

"Then come into my room at once. Here we are at my hotel. Where are you staying?"

"Here also."

"We are all here," added Beau.

"We will see you both at dinner," said the general.

"Yes, pretty soon, as I have had no breakfast,'' said Julian, and, followed by Mr. Sinclair, he went up to his room.

On the center table there were several letters, and on two of them Julian recognized Lola's writing.

"Before you read your letters, tell me how long it is since you heard from Lola.''

"About ten days."

"I see. That accounts for it. The girl is almost crazy because you have not answered her last two letters. She told me to say to you that if *you* don't go at once to save her, something *worse than death* will happen; that she *begs* and *implores* you not to delay a single day. She is almost wild. Something has gone wrong, I am sure, and her father's arrival seems to have precipitated a disaster."

"Her father? Has Lola's father been found?"

"Why, yes. Didn't you know it? Lola wrote you all about it the same day. He came nearly a week ago, and guess who found him and brought him to the house. No other than your Uncle Isaac. But read your letters. All I wished to say is, that you must go to Lola immediately, for she certainly is in some distress, of which she did not wish to speak to me or to her father—only to you. The little thing made me promise to go to camp to bring you to New York, and if I had not found you here I should have taken this evening's train for Brandy Station to fetch you to her."

"Then go I must. I'll run back to the War Office to get a leave of absence if I can, and if I cannot, I'll go without it."

"No, that won't do. You read your letters and eat your dinner while I go back to the White House to see if the senator is still there. If he is, he will go with me to the War Office to get you a leave, or I'll try it myself."

Mr. Sinclair met the senator as he was coming out of the White House. He told him why Julian must have a leave, and both went to the War Office to get it. While they waited for that important document in the secretary's reception room, Julian, at the hotel, read his letters.

The two from Lola troubled him. What could that great calamity be which she said poisoned the pleasure of meeting her father? Julian could not imagine. In trying to find what it could be, he thought of the letters given him at the War Department. Perhaps these letters might give a clue. He took them from his breast pocket and broke the seal of one.

What! Did his eyes deceive him? There, there it was! Was it so? Could it be so? He looked at the heading and signature again, and a great sob arose from his heart, and he fell on his knees by the sofa and bowed his head and wept. Then, with the simplicity of a child, he raised his hands to heaven and offered humble thanks to God.

The letter was signed,

"Your affectionate father,

JAMES B. NORVAL"

But now a terrible shadow darkened Julian's happiness. "Perhaps I did not read the date right," he thought, and arose, trembling, to approach the window to see the writing more clearly. He looked again.

No: he was not mistaken. The letter was dated London, 6th of March, 1864. He opened the other; that also was from his father, and dated March 10th, 1864, four days later. No; there was no doubt his father was alive! How glad his dear mother would be! thought Julian, and sat down to read his father's letters leisurely, forgetting that he had not yet had his breakfast and that it was now after three o'clock.

But how could he think of eating when he *almost* forgot Lola? His father would leave London for New York in a few days! Perhaps he was on his way now. He had heard of the report of his death in Egypt, and had written immediately contradicting the report—the doctor said—and hoped that his wife had long since received his letters. And so she would, if Mr. Hammerhard had not been keeping them for his friend the major—if she had not married so hastily.

Julian had just finished reading his father's letters when Mr. Sinclair, accompanied by the senator, came in, saying, "Here is your leave. Off with you. But don't desert, for I pledged my word you would not, though I have my misgivings that you would do it if Lola wished it. But what is the matter now?" he added, seeing traces of tears in Julian's eyes.

For sole answer Julian extended one of his father's letters to him, and the other to the senator.

"Who would have thought it?" exclaimed both on looking at the signature.

CHAPTER LIV

"So, Instead of a Pistol, He Cocked His Tail. 'Aha!' Quoth He, 'What Have We Here?'"

Byron: *The Devil's Ride*

We must now go back a few days in the course of this truthful story in order to explain what had happened whilst Julian yet waited—what had filled Lola with such wild terrors and surrounded her with difficulties from which Julian alone could extricate her.

From the day on which the major had taken Lola to his office to obtain the information concerning her father, his active brain had known no rest. He did not hope or expect to win Lola by fair means. He did not pretend to, but he was perfectly ready to use unfair ones. He cared not, provided he succeeded, and she was his.

The more he studied how to accomplish this object, he became convinced that he would have to shut her up in some house or carry her off by force and stratagem, by contriving some such story as the one which induced her to go to his office. This was difficult, but Hack liked to conquer difficulties. Yes, he would contrive to induce Lola to go on board a steamer, and take her to Cuba and there force her to marry him. And, wild and absurd as this idea was, to the heated brain of the major it seemed quite practicable.

"If Lola is distrustful, the madam can accompany her and make our departure quite proper and most decorous." And the *ci-devant* expounder of the gospel laughed to think that Mrs. Norval would help *him* carry off Lola.

"I'll threaten the old woman to let the doctor know of our sweet private relations if she proves obdurate. Still, I hate useless cruelty, and if I can make her believe that, for both our sakes, we must get rid of Lola and send her off before her father comes to the United States, then so much the better. That is far preferable. Now, then, first to get out of Uncle Sam's clutches." And, saying this, he sat down to write his resignation, which he sent off to Washington by that evening's mail.

That done, the major stepped into Hooker and Skinner's office to ascertain how much money he had in the bank in New York and how much in London. The figures were not as large as he had anticipated, but still they were by no means small, and, as he could not afford to quarrel with his honest partners, he made up his mind to be satisfied.

The major then went to Mr. Skroo's desk and told him to get his accounts all in order, for he found he had a good deal of private business to attend to, and at any moment might be obliged to leave the service. Mr. Skroo gave the major a very peculiar look out of his round yellow eyes, and muttered to himself, "I, too, will leave the service, and that before you do it." That night Mr. Skroo had a long consultation with his wife, and with her approval decided that if the major was to leave the army, Mr. Skroo had better write a certain document which—to avoid delays—Mrs. Skroo would in person carry to Washington.

Which she did, for she had a powerful friend there who wrote lovely letters to her and would do anything she asked.

After finishing that day's business, the major got into his crimson-cushioned coupé—a present from Mrs. Norval—and drove home.

With light step he ran up the grand *perron* of the Norval mansion, and, taking a passkey from his pocket, he opened the door and went in. He divested himself of his spring overcoat and hat in the hall, and, passing his fingers through his glossy chestnut-colored locks, stepped into the reception room, hoping to find Lola there.

And she was there! But how was she? What sight was that before his eyes? Lola was sitting on the knees of a man whose back was turned to the door, so that the major could not see his face. But he saw plainly enough that Lola was kissing his eyes and his forehead, and that he had both his arms around her waist.

The major was struck dumb with horror and amazement. He staggered and held to the door to keep from falling. He thought the man could be no other than Julian, and, as the thought flashed on his brain, he instinctively carried his hand to his breast pocket, where a little pistol—the mate to the one he had given Julian—lay always ready. Lola looked up, and exclaimed, "Come, major; here he is. To think that when we went to inquire for him, he was so near New York! Papa, this is Major Hackwell, the gentleman who interested himself so kindly in helping me to obtain information about you."

Like one in a horrible dream, Hackwell shook hands with the gentleman whom Lola called father, but who did not seem to be such, for his hair was very light and his eyes were blue, whilst Lola's were jet black. Moreover, he seemed too young to have a daughter eighteen-years old.

Hackwell made this observation to himself, but his usual fluency seemed all of a sudden exhausted. He muttered something about being very glad at Lola's happiness, left father and daughter, and walked upstairs to Mrs. Norval's boudoir. He knocked at the door, and the madam's voice said, "Come in." His ex-reverence went in, and casting a glance around the room to see if the madam was alone, and another to the door to see that no one had followed him, he locked the door. The expression of his face told so many terrible things that Mrs. Norval stood up frightened.

The dark demons and hideous monsters, the untamed, ferocious beasts of passions, the poisonous reptiles, and repulsive, crawling things of wicked propensities and sinful desires, which formed a perfect "*happy family*" in the breast of the exquisite Hackwell when all were well fed and allowed to gambol at pleasure and live in unchecked freedom, now arose infuriated, and howled and hissed as if they would devour the heart of their indulgent protector and tear his breast to pieces. But their roar and hissing were heard by no one but himself. Mrs. Norval did not suspect that her darling carried with him this horrible menagerie (no wife ever does); she only saw in the expression of his face the shadows of the monsters. She was terrified, and with colorless lips she asked what had happened.

"It is all up with us; that's all."

"Has the doctor come?"

"You are a fool!" thundered the bland gentleman. "Who puts such notions in your head?"

"Forgive me, John darling. You know that Julian and Mattie are always saying they don't believe their father is dead. And, though Mr. Sinclair and yourself are sure of it, I can't help feeling uneasy at times. And now, when you came in so pale and agitated, and the expression of your face was so terrible, I—I—I thought that some dreadful calamity had—"

"Ha! ha!" laughed darling John pitilessly. "So you would regard it as a *calamity* if your good husband were to turn up, eh? Pretty good, madam! *very* good! Who would have thought it? Not those dear, good souls of *our* congregation, surely; not those good Puritans who regarded you as a model of matronly virtues and a stickler for *propriety*. But no; let your *pure* heart be easy, *as yet*, on that score. I only wish to tell you that as your interesting brother did not go to hell, as he ought to, but only to Mexico—which is next door—to bring Lola's father, the man will claim his daughter and her money along with her."

"I know it, John darling. That is why, when I heard you come in, I left Isaac with the girls in the library, and ran up to see you here. I was in hopes you had arranged matters."

"*Arranged matters*? And how can I, when it is not a week since I got the first intimation that Lola's father was advertising for her? And here your cursed brother brings him. I tell you plainly, we are beggars if you flinch. Do you hear me?—if you flinch! For I must have at least a whole week."

"What must I do? Tell me darling!" said she, more and more terrified.

"You must, or course, look for your husband's will, high and low, everywhere, and—"

"But, John, how can I find it, when you took it, my dear?"

"Fool! damned fool!" hissed the smooth Hackwell between his set teeth, then aloud, "And who tells you that you are to find it? I say you must *look* for it. But of course you cannot find it; or tell where it is; or who stole it; on all of which assertions you can take your oath, for you certainly don't know where the will is now, and no one stole it since you gave it to me, and you could not find it if you searched until doomsday, for I alone know where it is."

"I'll do just as you order me, only don't be angry with me: *that* almost kills me."

"Zounds, madam! because I damn your accursed brother from the bottom of my heart, must you apply all my words to yourself?"

"I will not anymore, dearest. Forgive me; you know it is because I love you so devotedly, you, my angel. You are superbly beautiful in your anger, and, though you terrify me, I adore you only the more, my divinity."

And here the matron arose to throw her arms around her husband's neck.

The major received a few caresses quite patiently, and even courteously, but when he saw that she was about to pour forth a torrent of them, hypocrite though he was, he could not tolerate the infliction with a semblance of pleasure. He averted his face, pushed her and arose to walk up and down the room.

His heart was swelling with suppressed emotion. His brain throbbed at the thought that Lola would be taken from him—Lola, that radiant, magnificent creature, to keep whom from marrying Julian, he had plotted, lied, and stolen. He had cherished the thrilling, intoxicating hope, though with savage spells of rage and wild longings of despair, that she would be his in spite of Julian. For if Julian would not marry Emma, he, to save his mother's good name, and his father from a shame that might kill him, would certainly surrender his aspirations to Lola. Then the only opposition would come from Lola herself. And she was so generous that to save Julian and the doctor from the shame of exposure, she would sacrifice herself, and he, Hackwell would soon succeed in consoling her for the loss of Julian. Of this he was sure. He had been too successful with the fair sex not to be convinced of *that*. Moreover, Hammerhard, who was a shrewd man of the world, had often told him that he had the whole game in his hands, particularly since Lola's visit to his office.

Hackwell had passed all these things in review many times, never once shrinking from the disgusting array. It was "all fair in love and war."

But now "the accursed blue-eyed Mexican" came to overthrow all these beautiful combinations. Who ever heard of a blue-eyed Mexican? "I wish I could choke the rare specimen," muttered Hack, pacing his wife's chamber.

Suddenly an idea came to his fertile brain, and gradually he grew more composed. He had hit upon a plan to carry off Lola, and on the instant he resolved to carry it out. The plan was better, less risky, than the other. He smiled, and Mrs. Norval, who was watching him, felt happy. She, too, smiled.

CHAPTER LV

His Ex-Reverence Shows the Cloven Foot

The major did not inquire for particulars of the manner in which Isaac found Lola's father, and so successfully brought him to Mrs. Norval's house. But Lola was too happy to resent this seeming want of sympathy, and very good-naturedly volunteered a full account of the whole affair up to the time that "Mr. Sprig came in, and she walked into the parlor, and Mattie presented her, saying, 'Lola, this is our Uncle Isaac, whom we thought dead, and who now comes from *your* country. Uncle, this is Miss Lola Medina, a Mexican young lady.' Whereupon Mr. Sprig was so surprised that he was for the moment speechless, but as soon as he was able to speak, had said, 'Lola Medina, did you say? And was she found among the Indians? And did her mother leave her in the care of a doctor?' 'Yes, yes! papa was the doctor,' Mattie said. Whereupon Mr. Sprig, without saying a word, seized his hat and rushed to the door, and when he got there turned and said 'Miss Lola, I am going to bring your father,' and ran out into the street, to come back in half an hour with papa."

The major listened very attentively, thinking how fresh and red her lips were, and how sweet her breath, never giving one thought to what she said, except inwardly to curse Isaac and wish that he and "papa" were at the bottom of the Gulf of Mexico. But he seemed so interested in Lola's narrative that she became more animated and sat close to him to tell him all, for had he not interested himself so much in her obtaining information of her father? Of course he had, and he must be pleased, of course. But he alone knew that his private menagerie was howling and tossing and scratching, and that the closer Lola sat by him, the wild beasts got more ferocious and unmanageable, as if that sweet breath was poison to them. The major heroically dug his nails into his flesh, to keep his beasts quiet, and promised them a nice carnival by-

and-by to silence them, whilst he smiled placidly on Lola's lovely face, radiant in her happy laughter which dimpled her rosy cheeks and displayed her pearly teeth.

The whole family seemed to sympathize with Lola in her happiness. And perhaps they did, for diverse reasons. The major and the madam had resolved to retain the money as long as possible by the pretended loss of the will, and had now made up their minds to invest as much money in the major's name as they could obtain from Mr. Sinclair. It was politic to be very amiable to Lola and her father, and detain them as long as possible. So the major smiled, listening to Lola, and the rest showed their satisfaction in other ways.

Mattie laughed and talked the loudest, for she really loved Lola and was happy because Lola was. She walked about the rooms with her uncle, telling him how lovely Lola's character was, how talented she was, etc.

Ruth was quite smiling and gracious, for she saw that Don Luis had a *distingué* look which would bring *éclat* to the Norval mansion.

Emma was delighted, for she hoped that now Lola would immediately go away.

Whilst Isaac and Don Luis were the happiest of all in having succeeded beyond their most sanguine expectations.

After her interview with the major, Mrs. Norval dressed for dinner and came downstairs to join the rest of the family.

For a wonder, her entrance did not cast gloom or seriousness over everybody. On the contrary, she seemed to take part in the general contentment. Mattie went on walking about the rooms, hanging on her uncle's arm, whilst Lola kept giving her account to the delighted major, and Ruth and Emma conversed—charmed—with Don Luis.

No family dinner ever passed off more delightfully than this one, the *first* that the lamented Isaac partook of in his sister's house.

"If only darling papa and dear Julian and good Lavvy were here," exclaimed Mattie, "wouldn't we be the happiest mortals in Yankeeland?"

Lola and Isaac warmly assented, and Ruth and Emma said, "Of course." The madam looked at the major. He said, raising his glass to drink with Isaac, "As we are eating the fatted calf in your honor, Isaac, here is to you, and may you never leave us." All drank to Isaac.

After dinner many visitors came—as usual—and the young ladies had music, dancing, and singing. The married ladies and older men had card-playing; a few played billiards or conversed. About eleven o'clock, refreshments of the choicest variety—from capon with truffles to biscuits glacés—were served, with rare wines and choice fruits.

When Isaac retired to his elegant sleeping chamber, he looked around, and involuntarily exclaimed, "Why, Jenny lives in paradise!" But Isaac did not think that there could be a serpent in it.

Next day the major had a long and most animated conference with his confederates, Messrs. Hammerhard, Hooker, and Skinner. They came to the conclusion that to carry off Lola forcibly would be, if not impracticable, certainly very difficult and dangerous. It would be better to intimidate her into compliance by proving to her that she was entirely in the major's power; that he could have a writ served on her father if he attempted to take her away; that to resist the major's wishes would only force him to an action which would bring upon her a much worse notoriety than what she had dreaded before; that her mother's history would be all brought to light, and as she and the major lived in the same house, and she had admitted that he was her husband, of course the case was very clear.

This certainly was a better plan than to take her by force. Still, the major hired a yacht for six months—to sail about the bay during the summer, he said—and gave orders to get it ready to go to sea at once.

That evening, after a sumptuous dinner given in honor of Isaac's return, to which only intimate friends were invited, all were assembled in the spacious drawing rooms, which early began to fill with visitors. The major made himself very agreeable to the company whilst he watched his chance to speak to Lola alone, unobserved by Mrs. Norval's eyes, which followed him always.

Two of the most fashionable ladies were announced. Taking this opportunity, when Mrs. Norval advanced to receive them, to speak to Lola, the major said, in a whisper, "I am going into the library; follow me presently. I have something of great importance to tell you."

With a slight inclination of her head, Lola signified assent, and ten minutes after, in great trepidation and amazement, she went into the library which was on the other side of the hall.

The major had stepped out upon a little balcony around the bay window of the library and called Lola thither. With great reluctance Lola went as far as the window and stood waiting to hear what he had to say.

"Come out here. The light shines on your dress, and you will attract attention standing there. The night air is very mild. Come out, please. Do not fear me."

Lola hesitated, but she went out. The major was very calm and his manner was very respectful.

"Lola, when does your father say he is to take you away?" he asked.

"He says we had better take the first steamer, as we will have to wait too long for the next."

"The first steamer leaves in four days."

"I know, but it will not take me long to get ready."

"But why such haste?"

"Papa is anxious to get back on account of the coming of the Archduke Maximilian, he says. I heard Mr. Sinclair say to him this evening after dinner that he was ready to see papa tomorrow. And papa said that Mr. Sinclair could take his own time, as he (papa) was in a hurry to return, but in no hurry to receive a fortune of the existence of which he had had no idea. And with the exception of one-hundred thousand dollars he would give to Mr. Isaac, that he was willing to leave in Mr. Sinclair's hands everything as the doctor had arranged until I am of age."

The major was silent, though evidently agitated. What Lola said was good and bad news to him. After a while he said, "Listen to me, Lola. I know you love Julian, but you can't marry him because he has given his word of honor to marry Emma. And if he is a man of honor, he must fulfill his promise."

Lola was silent.

"Don't you believe what I say?" asked the major.

"I don't know. But suppose it is so?"

"Then why will you not try to give me a little love in return for all I have given you ever since you were a mere child? See how patiently I have borne your indifference, and even dislike, hoping that sooner or later you would appreciate my devotion."

"Indeed, major, if it was to tell me this you called me here, I must go. You know how I feel about this—this—matter; it is very disagreeable."

"You spurn me, then? Take care!"

"Do you threaten me?"

"No, but I caution you."

"I can't imagine why you should caution me because I can't love you," said Lola, moving towards the window to return to the library.

The major caught her hand to detain her, and immediately lost his calmness and self-control. His wild beasts began to toss, and leap, and howl, and in an instant the whole menagerie was in a tumult—all, all—the slimy crawling things as well as the unruly ferocious beasts. The touch of that pure hand did it all—the little, soft palm, which sent through his whole being an electric thrill and made him feel that he could commit murder, theft, perjury, or anything else to which his menagerie prompted him. And yet the major laughed at Mrs. Norval's infatuation! There is a law of compensation, surely, though it is to be hoped for the sake of the major, that we don't pay for everything. The agitated ex-divine said, "Lola, have pity. Don't drive me to despair, for a desperate man will do anything. Listen. Do not go away yet. We can find plenty of excuses to induce your father to leave you a little while with us."

Lola looked pensively down, thinking it was very bitter to go and leave Julian without seeing him again. If she stayed, she might see him! But no! Was he not to marry Emma? Better never to see him again! She looked up, and answered, "No, major, it is best that I go now."

"You know that the doctor left a will to be opened in case your father claimed you. I am sure you ought to stay until the will is found, and Mrs. Norval has not yet been able to find it."

"Papa doesn't care for that, nor I either. Everything will be left in Mr. Sinclair's hands."

"And is that your sole answer to my prayer?"

"What else can I say, major?"

"That you will try to love me a little."

"No! I cannot say that, nor stay either."

"But you must do both, and you shall. I have *the power* to compel you to stay and to hear reason. But if you stay a little while, I will not use my power; I swear it."

"Pshaw! you speak in riddles which I don't understand, but which do not intimidate me in the least," said she contemptuously.

"Spare me your contempt, and, since you are so defiant, let me tell you that you are legally married to me. By the laws of this state you are my wife, for you so declared before five witnesses."

"This is infamous! When did I declare such a thing? When were we married?"

"We were married by the fact of our having said before witnesses that we were man and wife. Surely you cannot have forgotten that you repeated at my office several times that you were mine!" And the major, trembling with emotion, tried to clasp Lola to his heart. She, however, quickly springing back, eluded his grasp, saying, "Miserable viper! Is it possible that you can be so treacherous as to avail yourself of so flimsy a subterfuge? You become repulsive to me."

"To win you and make you mine, I'll do anything; I'll commit murder or anything else. 'All is fair in love,' you know. All I care for is to secure you, no matter if you say you hate me. You will love me afterwards. I'll make you. See if I don't."

"Never! I loathe you, and I don't believe what you say. If you will commit murder, you will then certainly *lie* to obtain your wicked purpose. I don't believe you."

"Very well. The day you attempt to leave, I shall detain you by force, if necessary. My witnesses are ready to give me their sworn affidavits, or to appear in person, to prove that you admitted freely that you were my wife. If your father attempts to take you away, I shall have him arrested for kidnapping my wife."

"This is horrible!" exclaimed Lola, sitting on one of the rustic chairs in the balcony and covering her face—feminine fashion—with both hands.

"Lola, again I say, pity me!" said the major, kneeling by her. "I promise I will not take any steps to force you to stay, or tell any one I have this hold upon you, if you will remain for a short time and let me try to win your love. Give me a chance. If in six months—say if by that time I can't persuade you to be my wife and convince you that you cannot marry Julian, then I promise I shall not oppose your departure."

"I could never trust you. Now you promise this; in six months you would break your promise as easily as you betrayed me into a wicked snare."

"Then there is no hope of my winning you?"

Lola shook her head in the negative and rose to leave.

"Very well, I shall have the consolation of knowing that you are tied to me, and no one can snatch you away. We will drag our chain together, and, by Jove! that is something," said he, rising from his knees more agitated than before.

Without waiting to hear more or saying another word, Lola passed him and ran upstairs to lock herself up in her room to pray and weep. Then she rose to write to Julian and entreat him to come.

The major returned to the gay company, smiling, just in time to meet Mrs. Norval, who, having missed him and Lola, was looking for him anxiously.

"You are a dear darling," said he, putting her arm in his.

CHAPTER LVI

"He Awoke One Morning and Found Himself Famous"

Sophy Head jumped out of bed one morning and crowed! His surprise and delight at this sudden burst of a new faculty were extreme. He flapped his elbows against his ribs in imitation of a rooster's wings and crowed again and again in proud exultation. Feeling much encouraged, he tried neighing and braying and grunting, in all of which, to his delighted amazement, he found himself efficient. No discoverer—and I don't expect Columbus, Vasco da Gama, Newton, or any other of the glorious and immortal host—was ever so proud or elated with his newly-found world as Sophy. He would now eclipse Wagg! And what more glory need a man achieve in this perishable world?

Sophy was so happy that he ordered his servant to saddle Beau and at three o'clock bring him around to the office door. For the first time after his mishap with Mademoiselle Mina, Sophy felt a desire to sally forth in his glory.

On her part, Mina had carefully noted the days of his absence and wisely concluded that her soft-hearted and soft-headed admirer was about to slip through her fingers. To do Miss Mina justice, I must say that she did not wish to entrap Sophy into matrimony. Nor had she any idea of being a poor man's wife. Not she. She had a great deal nicer time as a rich lady's maid, and meant to stay so until she could marry some rich grocer or retired shoemaker who would adore her and give her all the ribbons and laces she wanted. She, therefore, did not mourn for the loss of Sophy, only she did not like the way it was brought about, and swore she would revenge herself on the major for calling her a "grisette" and a "servant" before her devoted admirer, and she would punish Sophy for deserting her so meanly afterwards. But how could she do this? She had no other means than Sophy himself. Yes, she would find out about the major's mode of spending his days, and she would make Sophy tell her all, and then she would, perhaps, find a way of paying them off together. The first step was to get hold of Sophy, and Sophy came no more. As the mountain would not come, Miss Mina wisely foresaw that she would have to go to the mountain.

And she went.

Sophy Head came on the curveting, pirouetting Beau around the Bowling Green, thinking he would go up to the park by way of Madison Avenue instead of Fifth Avenue, when, as he turned to go up Broadway, he saw a lovely figure standing there holding by the iron railing and looking at the fountain. The figure was beautifully dressed and closely veiled, and had one little foot resting on the curbstone a little higher than the other, so that Sophy could see a lovely ankle and the high instep of the tiny little foot.

The figure bowed; Sophy checked Beau, and, respectfully lifting his cap, approached her.

"Bonjour, monsieur," said the melodious voice of Mademoiselle Mina, and though Sophy ejaculated a terrified "ah!," still, as he always was a "galang Tom," he could not run from a lady.

He alighted and tried to make apologies, which she received with a sweet, lovely grace which enchanted him. She had no difficulty whatever in making him feel truly repentant, and more in love than before. As they both had much to say to each other, they thought they had better adjourn to the Astor House and have a long talk in one of the parlors. Sophy went back to the office to send away Beau with an orderly, and then rejoined the lovely Mina. After spending two hours in sweet converse at the Astor House, they walked up Broadway together, stopping to take an ice on the way.

From that day Sophy lived for Mina only. They went to the theatre together, took lunches and drives, and spent every afternoon from three to five, and every evening from seven to ten or eleven, or later, always with each other. She was necessary to Sophy's existence. The half of her object was thus accomplished. Now for the major, thought Miss Mina, and she felt she was on his track.

As Mina got in the habit of going out so often, and staying so late, Ruth began to remonstrate. This Miss Mina rather liked. She never had loved her cold-hearted mistress much, but since the night of the ridiculous misadventure and fainting, Mina positively hated Ruth because she had so cruelly ridiculed her. The little French maid wanted only a good excuse to leave Ruth.

"Mademoiselle," said Mina, courtesying to Lola, "I wish to know if you would be willing to take me to Mexico as your maid?"

"If you were not in Ruth's service, yes, Mina. But never would I take you if you left her to come to me."

"I am going to leave Miss Ruth, and, as I would like to go with you, I wish to know if you will take me, so that I may not look for a place elsewhere."

"I fear, Mina, it would seem as if I had enticed you away, particularly as I have often told Ruth that I wished I had a maid like you, and that I envied her having you. No, Mina, I am sorry, but it wouldn't look right. It is such a mean sort of treachery to entice anyone away. I shrink from the appearance of it even."

"I am sorry. I shall leave Miss Ruth anyway. I suppose if I were out of employment, you would take me?"

"You are a little sophist," Lola said, laughing. "But I dislike to make any such promise."

Mina, however, saw that if Lola could be satisfied that Ruth would not attach any blame to her, she would consent to take her. She therefore *gave notice* to Ruth that she would leave her service and went out to meet Sophy.

Mrs. Skroo had returned from Washington in a very happy mood. She had accomplished her mission successfully. Herself and sister, with Miss Mina (whom Sophy presented as a young lady *staying* at the Norvals'), made a party that night to go to the theatre. Mrs. Skroo was charmed with Mina, and as Mina dropped several hints about the usages of the grand monde, and about dressing, Mrs. Skroo pricked up her ears, and in about two seconds she made up her mind to cultivate Mina. When they separated, she kissed Mina, and would not let go her hand until she had promised to call on her next day.

Mina, on her part, had also picked up hints dropped by Mrs. Skroo. For instance, Mrs. Skroo had sneered when Major Hackwell's name was mentioned, and afterwards had said that perhaps the major would "come down from his high horse some of these days; that Uncle Sam sometimes inquired where his money went," etc., etc., etc.—desultory remarks, which would have meant nothing to a mind less analytic than that of Mina, but which in hers formed a concrete mass of varied threads to lead her into a labyrinth of facts—valuable facts.

Of course she accepted Mrs. Skroo's invitation.

CHAPTER LVII

Who Would Have Thought It?

Who is that traveler standing there in stoical indifference to the drenching rain and the mud with which the passing hacks bespatter him? No other than Julian Norval, just arrived on the Washington night train at dismal Courtland-Street depot. As there is no place where a passenger can wait under shelter for a carriage to drive up to him and he get into it without going in the pelting rain, Julian had to submit to the infliction, as everybody else does, will do, and has done. He was drenched and bespattered with the rest of the traveling community, and, like everybody else, submitted silently meekly, for in this free country we are the subjects of railroad kings and other princes of monopolies; we obey their wishes and pay our money.

Julian was waiting for a hack which a policemen had politely volunteered to procure him, for during the war *even policemen* were civil to gentlemen wearing the uniform of army officers—a phenomenon which disappeared with the war. But Julian was too restless and anxious to get home to wait much longer. He crossed the slippery street and took the first vehicle he met, which was a groaning, wheezing, hack pulled by two asthmatic Rocinantes,[65] which fell down as they started, but were galvanized into a sickly trot by the electrifying oaths of the driver. The ground being slippery, and the horses in the last stages of consumption, it took Julian nearly an hour to arrive home.

But at last the Rocinantes stopped in front of the palatial mansion of the Norvals, where Julian dismissed the dilapidated turn out and, carrying a portmanteau in his hand, which contained all his baggage, he ran up the broad steps and rang the bell. It being only about seven

[65]Reference is made here to Don Quixote's bony, worn-out horse, on whose back the chivalrous knight rides out to do battle.

o'clock and Sunday morning, he had to wait for some time before a servant in his *undress uniform*—for the Norval mansion made its servants dress in livery—came to open the door.

As the hack had driven up, however, a white little hand had opened the lattice of a third-floor front window, and two lovely eyes had seen him alight and come up the steps. Thus, by the time he came in, Lola was nearly dressed and ready to see him. She had given her wavy hair a twist and pinned it with a comb, fastened a morning wrapper around her small waist, and with but little more than this, her toilette was finished, for she had just come out of her bath and had no ablutions to make.

"Why Mr. Ju—"

"Hush! don't wake anyone," said Julian, interrupting the servant's ejaculations, as he foresaw they would be emphatic and loud. "Are they all well?"

"Yes, sir, all well, and Miss Lola's father is here. And he took all our breaths away, he and Mr. Isaac. They fell on us like—"

"I know! I know! Take my portmanteau upstairs, and I'll go to my mother's room."

Julian was so agitated that he had to lean against the door of his mother's bedroom before he felt calm enough to go in and give her the startling news of his father's arrival in London.

Presently he summoned courage to knock gently, fearing lest he might startle her unpleasantly, and thus render her less composed to hear the glad news.

He then knocked a little louder, and ventured to say, "Mother dear, will you let me in?"

Since the arrival of Lola's father, Mrs. Norval had slept very little because she had noticed that her dear John was very restless and had hardly slept any at all. On Saturday night she and her husband (as she supposed) had had a long talk and had not gone to sleep until near daybreak. They had been discussing whether or not they should announce their marriage. The major, after apparently yielding to Mrs. Norval's wish to do so, had decided they had better wait until Julian came home and let him be the first one to know it.

"Very well, John. I frankly confess to you that it is very sweet to have you here all to myself and no one know it. But at the same time, I am in constant dread that something might happen just on account of our having kept our marriage secret," Mrs. Norval had said.

"And what do you imagine might happen?" the major asked, smiling.

"Well, I don't know, but you and Julian might get into a quarrel, and—"

"And you think that this would be avoided if Julian knew I am his papa? How little you know your boy! He would only hate me worse."

"But he would respect you for my sake."

"Peut-être!" said he, rising to go to bed. "But I don't believe it."

"Moreover, it doesn't look *respectable* to be married clandestinely—doesn't look *proper*."

"Bah! I thought you had forgotten your cant of old times. Good night. I have to be in my clothes early in the morning; I must retire now." And he was soon sound asleep.

That was, however, only about four hours before Julian knocked at the door.

Mrs. Norval awoke with a start. Julian's voice resembled that of his father so much, that even after he repeated, "Mother dear, will you let me in?" she could not believe it was Julian and not his father. Like one seized with ague, the madam shook with fright, and in terror rushed to the major's room, exclaiming, in a hoarse whisper, "John, did you hear that voice?"

"Of course I did; it is that of the boor, your son. If I had been dressed, I would have gone around to tell him to behave like a gentleman. But I couldn't well go through your room." And the major laughed, as Mephistopheles would have done. "Bah!" added he, pitilessly, "you see '*gory locks*' everywhere. I thought you hated popery too well to be superstitious. Did you not want to announce our marriage? Why not take this opportunity?" And he felt more than half a wish to announce it himself, and dictate a compromise with Julian by which he would stipulate silence on condition of Lola's hand. But he would not have had time to put his wicked wish into execution, as Mrs. Norval now had recovered her presence of mind and bolted the door between their rooms, hastening to let Julian in.

"How soundly you sleep, darling mother!" said Julian, kissing her.

"What brings you home so unexpectedly? I hope you have not got into trouble."

"No, mother, trouble doesn't bring me, though I have had plenty of it for the last two weeks. It is over now, I hope. What brings me, dear mother, is a great joy." And Julian broke down, and leaned his head on his mother's shoulder, unable to say any more.

"What is it, then?"

"Prepare yourself to hear something very, *very* startling, but which is going to make us very happy."

"Well, tell me, then. What is it?"

"What your heart would ask of the Lord to grant to us; that is what it is. Don't you guess now?"

"No, I can't. For Heaven's sake, tell me," said she, turning very pale and beginning to tremble so vehemently that Julian became alarmed and hastened to say, to appease her, "Well, dearest mother, our prayers have been heard, and a noble-hearted man was spared. My beloved father is in London. I have just received two letters from him. He might be here in a few days—perhaps this week."

With a piercing cry, Mrs. Norval threw her hands up and fell back in Julian's arms.

"Who would have thought it?" shrieked the wretched woman, as she swooned away.

On hearing her shriek, the major, shrugging his shoulders, began to dress, saying, in loud soliloquy, "Murder will out. I reckon she won't tell Julian he has a second papa! I wonder if Julian has received any letters directly from his father. I suppose so, and I'll have to finesse like the devil. Heigh-ho! Here it goes!" said he, thrusting into his pantaloons that leg which had been the subject of Mrs. Norval's anxious solicitude when it got wounded. Then he continued soliloquizing:

"If I finesse right, I might yet get Lola without violent measures—which I detest; too brutal for my taste. They might all help me, for Julian must hate exposing his mother, and she must be terrified. And Lola is generous and self-sacrificing, and all that sort of thing." And the major laughed, feeling that in the midst of difficulties he was in his element.

CHAPTER LVIII

The Major before Mrs. Norval's Chair

Slowly Mrs. Norval returned to consciousness, to life, to know that she was wretched. A short twilight of reason revealed to her in all its horror the debasement of her situation. She saw around her the pale faces of her distressed children; she saw Lola, Isaac, and Emma, and at the foot of the bed she saw the major. A shudder, a feeling of horror came over her; she tried to speak, but could not; she raised herself, and with another shriek again fell back. Nature succumbed; she was delirious; fever took possession of her brain, and she did not know any longer that she was a miserable woman.

The palatial mansion of the Norvals, lately so gay and brilliantly illuminated, was now a vast mass, darkly, ominously silent. The joyful news brought by Julian had turned music and laughter into maniacal ravings and timid whispering. The gay dancers now walked about in noiseless tread.

At noon the doctor called to attend Mrs. Norval said she had a violent brain fever, which might deprived her of reason, if not of life. Still, she might possibly recover.

Julian telegraphed to Aunt Lavvy to come immediately. When the family was happy, no one missed the kind Lavvy. But as soon as misfortune came, Lavvy was indispensable. She telegraphed back that she would take that night's train and arrive in New York next morning.

Weary and enervated with the painful excitement of that long dreary day, Ruth and Mattie felt exhausted when night came. Lola begged them to lie down and try to sleep, that she and Emma would watch in the sick room. The major gave his sister a very significant look, which made Emma join her persuasions to those of Lola.

"I thank you," said Ruth. "I guess it is the wisest thing we can do, and since you are so kind I think I'll go to bed. Aunt Lavvy will be here tomorrow to help us with mamma, so you will not have this trouble again."

Mattie, however, refused pointblank, saying that it was her duty to stay by her mother.

"But isn't Julian here, you goose?" said Ruth.

"Yes, but he can't be up all night."

"Let me tell you what ought to be done," said the major, looking at his watch. "It is now nine o'clock. Julian and Isaac will watch until one o'clock, and then Emma and I will take their place until daylight, when, if Mrs. Norval is quiet, Hannah, her woman, can relieve us and watch until eight or nine, and then Ruth and Mattie will be up."

"And when is my turn? You leave me out entirely," said Lola to her hated worshiper.

"You look as pale as Ruth and Mattie. You ought to go to bed now," the major replied.

Lola gave a toss of her graceful head, which the major thought enchanting, as she insisted, "I will not be sent to bed. I will help Julian and Mr. Isaac or Emma."

"Let Lola and me watch with Julian and uncle," Mattie said. But the gentlemen approved the major's arrangement, and that was the one adopted.

When everybody had retired to rest and Isaac and Julian were alone in the sick room, a white little hand pushed the door open and Lola walked noiselessly into the room. She approached Julian, and said, in a plaintive tone of earnest supplication, "Julian, *do* let me watch with Mr. Isaac. You traveled all last night and have had no rest today, and Miss Lavvy wrote to me that you had some trouble in Washington—which I can see by your face, for you look very haggard and weary. Please do take some rest, at least, on that lounge there," said she, pointing to a lounge at the opposite end of the room.

Julian made no answer, but, taking the little soft hand she had laid on his shoulder, kissed it and drew her towards the lounge. Passively she followed. He sat down, and motioning to her to sit by him, and drawing her still closer towards him, compelled her to sit down *very* close to him. She gave a half-scared, furtive look towards Isaac.

"Never mind him. He knows all. Mattie told him we love each other, and he is our best friend. Now, tell me what is the matter; why did you call me? There must be some trouble. What is it?"

Lola hung down her head and blushed until her temples were crimson.

"What is it, dearest?" said Julian, putting his arm around her waist and stooping to look into the downcast eyes. "Surely it must be something very serious, to trouble you so much."

"If it wasn't very serious do you think I would have been so earnest in my entreaties?" said she, and hid her face on his shoulder to prevent his seeing the rising tears. But, bitter as the confession was, it had to be made, and she told Julian all about her adventure of passing herself off for the major's wife, and he for her husband; and how Mrs. Norval had told her not to question the major, but be guided by him in entire confidence; and, finally, what the major had told her in the balcony about stopping her father from taking her away by accusing him of kidnapping Major Hackwell's lawful wife, etc., etc.

In horrified silence Julian listened. He had always suspected Hackwell of being a rogue and a hypocrite, but he had not imagined he was capable of such villainy. Julian did not know what to think.

"I will see Mr. Sinclair tomorrow," said he, after thinking in silence for a while, "and I will consult Mr. North, who has for years been my father's lawyer, and with them I will decide what we had better do. Hackwell is a very smart lawyer himself, and there must be some pretext on which he can build up a case, I suppose. Tomorrow I will have a talk with him before I see Mr. Sinclair and Mr. North."

"You will have to see him early, because Mina told me that he has been ordered by telegraph to report to the War Office."

"And how did Miss Mina learn that?"

"Oh, as for that, she knows everything that passes at the major's office. Lieutenant Head tells her everything, and what he doesn't know Mrs. Skroo does. And she, too, makes a confidante of Mina."

"How judicious their choice!"

"Very. Mina says, too, that Mrs. Skroo is sure that the major will be dismissed, because he has defrauded the government, and that (Mrs. Skroo says) she hopes to see the major flat on his back."

A piercing shriek from Mrs. Norval, which made Julian and Lola spring to their feet, put an end to their conversation. For a whole hour the poor woman raved about her darling buried in the sand, and the horrid negroes and the ugly Indians, and then became calmer again.

At one o'clock precisely, Emma, followed by her brother, came into the room. Julian's blood mounted to his temples, but, being in the dark, the major did not notice it. He frowned darkly at seeing Lola there when he had thought she was in her bed asleep.

Julian felt a great desire to take the villain by the throat and pitch him into the street, and he had an almost invincible repugnance to leave him in the room where his mother was lying so helpless, as if he were quite capable of murdering her. He did not know why, but he had for a long time felt that his influence was injurious to his mother. And now, though he could not bring a proof "as big as a mustard seed," he was sure that by some process he had undermined her fortitude and deteriorated her well-balanced brain until she was unable to stand even the shock of such gladsome news. Poor Julian! How near and how far from the truth he was!

But he had no reasonable excuse to give, and, to fly from the entreaties of Emma—Emma, who had become absolutely repulsive to him—he hurried out of the room, saying to Lola, "Come, Heaven knows what he will do to my poor mother!"

When the last sound of their retreating steps had died away, the major went to the door and peeped out. No one was in the hall. He locked the door and walked straight to Mrs. Norval's desk. Turning to Emma, he said, "Please have the kindness to sit on the other side of the madam's bed, and not follow me with your eyes. *I don't bear watching.*"

Wisely, Emma did as her brother said, and with the high footboard and drapery of Mrs. Norval's elegant bed between them, she did not see what he did. Then he took a bunch of small keys from his pocket and opened Mrs. Norval's writing desk. From a secret drawer he knew how to open, he took some letters and some bank-notes, and in their place he put a long envelope, sealed in three places. This done, he arranged the papers and everything else as they were before, and locked the desk, muttering, "There, the doctor will find his will unopened."

Then to Emma he said aloud, "Go to sleep on that lounge. I can watch her, and if she gets to raving and tries to get out of her bed, I can call one of the footmen."

Emma was too sleepy and too accustomed to obedience not to be perfectly docile this time. Without a word of remonstrance, she went to lie down upon the lounge as she was told. He then unlocked the door, and, taking a book, seated himself in front of a well shaded lamp which was on a round table near the fireplace.

The major was very pale, and looked anxious, and trembled. But let no one suppose that such a trifle as Mrs. Norval's sudden and—to all but himself—mysterious illness disturbed him. No. What troubled the major was a telegram received about noon from Washington, and the contents of which Mrs. Skroo seemed to have *clairvoyantly* read and communicated to her friend Miss Mina, who, in her turn, communicated them to Lola, and Lola to Julian.

The telegram informed the major that his resignation could not be accepted until he answered some charges made against him in a report addressed to the War Department by his head clerk, Mr. Skroo. He accused the major of having appropriated government funds to his own use, alleging that there were many false vouchers signed by the major, and a balance of nearly half a million against him. This telegram was followed immediately by another, ordering Major Hackwell to report to the War Office, in person, without delay.

These two telegrams made the major pale.

After his threat to Lola, he felt he had put Julian on his guard; the doctor might now arrive at any day, and yet he must go to Washington.

His spirit chafed like a chained mastiff. Bitterly he laughed at the wisdom of man, which punishes man when innocent and rewards him when guilty on *the sole condition* that he be SUCCESSFUL! With his gaze fixed on the open book, not a word of which went any farther than the retina of his dilated eye, the major began to mutter to himself, a bitter sneer curling his lip.

"I think the sooner we give over to women the management of public business, the better it will be. If we did not have such brute arrogance and unblushing conceit, we would long ago have seen the justice and propriety of hiding our diminished heads. But no. Because we have the physical force to beat women at the polls with our fists, we maintain that they have no right there as thinking beings. And because we make the polls indecent with our profane language and drunkenness, we remain masters of the field. Glorious! Behold the result! How well the world is governed! What sagacity and strict adherence to honor are everywhere displayed! Our own glorious government, in its grand *rôle* of 'MODEL' presents several shining examples. I wish I had made a confederate of that scoundrel Skroo, and stolen two or three million. I never yet acted honestly—that is to say, like an ass—that I did not have occasion to repent. And I hate repentance. I fully sympathize with Satan in that respect. But such at present is the humiliating fact, and I have to beat my breast like a good friar, and to say, 'mea culpa.' If I had been less true to the government, and more so to that poor woman—" Here he glanced towards the bed where the invalid moaned, and was silent for some minutes. Then he recommenced his monologue with another sentence. "And what and who is the government? At present, of course, *our* government is the Secretary of War: that we all know. But I mean, speaking in general, what is a government? Ah! it certainly is a terrible impersonality if a republic—an irresponsible tyrant that can neither blush nor be guillotined. And for this reason we call ourselves *a free people*! And with perfect sang-froid we can see a cabinet officer make a cat's paw of a President! And we say we are the '*model government*,' because, as long as the mob is cajoled, no matter how much *individuals are tyrannized over*, a cabinet officer can crush anyone opposing him and make it all right with the President by telling him and the mob that it is done for the glory and interest of *the people*." And Hackwell laughed bitterly, then continued. "Yes, so goes the miserable world, wabbling along as it rolls on impelled by man's hand. If the whole external world was guided by the same hand, it would wabble, too. Some of our wise legislators would make laws to have winter for ten years and give to a rich company the monopoly of collecting all the ice, then would decree to have summer for ten years so that the ice job should pay well, no matter how many wretches froze to death, or died of exhaustion in such prolonged heat, and the ice so dear."

Again Hackwell broke off, and was silent, then recommenced, "What a contemptible, hard-headed brute man is! How I despise my sex! for I am behind the scenes with him, and know what he really is. No woman can ever fathom the dark depths of man's heart. And it is well she cannot, the poor thing!" He stood up. He would have liked to walk about the room. To sit still when his brain was working with lightning speed was torture indeed, but he endured rather than disturb the invalid. He sat down again and leaned back in his chair opposite to the one always occupied by Mrs. Norval when they used to retire to the privacy of her bed chamber to have their cosy talks as man and wife, which she enjoyed so well. The major passed his hand across his eyes, as if to shut out the sight of that vacant chair, so eloquent in its emptiness, and a sickly feeling came over him. "Bah!" he exclaimed, looking fixedly at the chair, as if he answered the mute piece of furniture. "Nothing on earth can be more useless than repining! Curse remorse! I hate it and despise it! It is a mean '*rechauffé*'[66] of one's sins, in which even the sweetest turn sour by the miserable warming-over. It is a dish which cowards alone should eat. The brave fling it to the dogs. Only the bigoted Roman Catholics believe in the efficacy of remorse, which they call *Contrition*." Here a shriek from the sick woman ended the monologue. As if the last word had gone through her heart like a dagger, she stood up, holding her hand to her heart. Hackwell laid her softly down, but her shrieks and ravings continued until daylight.

[66]French for "reheating." Hackwell has no use for dwelling on the righteousness of his actions.

CHAPTER LIX

Julian and Hackwell Vis-a-Vis

The major was in his office early next morning. He wished to take the half-past twelve train for Washington, and had many papers to sign, some letters to write, and many to burn up before leaving.

"Good morning, major. You left early this morning," said Julian, walking in.

"Good morning," said the major, with his accustomed courteousness. "Glad to see you. Take a seat, please. I'll be through in a minute. Yes, I left very early because I have several things to attend to this morning before I go, and I wish to get to Washington tonight." Then he handed the *Herald* to Julian to read while he finished what he was obliged to do at once.

"The Lieutenant General will soon be on the Potomac, and the army put in motion," Julian read, and his blood flowed with a quickened impulse, for he was a great admirer of the hero of Vicksburg, and longed to fight under his orders. The major now turned, as if ready to enter into conversation, and Julian, with the newspaper in his hand said, "General Grant will soon be with us now. We will finish the war in double-quick time." The major shrugged his shoulders, as if to say, "What is that to me?"

Julian added, "As I am anxious to be with my brigade before the army moves on, I hope my business with you will be arranged soon."

"And what is your business?" coolly asked he.

"I wish to know what is this farce of your marrying Lola. Have the kindness to explain the matter to me before I speak with her father about it."

"By whose authority do you question me?"

"You know very well, major, that my father constituted me her guardian during his absence, and, moreover, I am engaged to her."

"You are engaged to Emma. You cannot insult my sister in my presence by avowing yourself engaged to another."

And so saying, the major carried his hand to his breast. Julian did the same, saying, derisively, "Have a care! You forget that you presented to me the mate of your little five-shooter."

The major withdrew his hand, saying, "I cannot comprehend how, if you are a gentleman, and what is called *man of honor*, you can come here to tell me to my face that you are engaged to Lola, when you have been for years pledged to my sister."

"I see very well that you have an object in wishing to turn this matter off and again make a cat's-paw of your sister. But my time is too precious to allow you such play. I will give you full satisfaction on the score of my engagement to Emma (if *she* says such exists) afterwards, but now I must insist on your acquainting me with all the particulars of your pretended marriage."

"And what if I consider your questions impertinent, and refuse to answer them?"

"Then I shall take steps to oblige your accomplices in the plot to tell me, and perhaps this will complicate matters for you in Washington. I am not a lawyer, but it seems to me there must be some way in which we can frustrate your plot."

The major reflected for a minute, and, seeing that he could not afford to provoke hostilities until he returned from Washington, said, "All I can say is what Lola has already told you—that is to say, that we are married, and Lola admitted the fact before five witnesses."

"And do you intend really to force Lola to recognize you as her husband because with your lies you caught the poor child in a vile trap?"

The major turned livid with anger; he said, "It is my turn to say have a care! As long as you speak to me with some courtesy, I'll answer you. But if you forget yourself, I may do the same."

"No, you won't. Forgetting one's self is generally the fault of honest people."

The major shrugged his shoulders, and Julian continued, "But I'll humor you. I'll put my question thus: And are you going to attempt to force Lola into this new-fashioned marriage because you made her believe that in saying she was your wife she was using a harmless subterfuge to obtain information which you assured her she could not obtain otherwise?"

"Lola said before five witnesses, several times, without compulsion, that she is my wife. If a court of justice is to admit that I used unfair means to entrap Lola, can't it also be admitted that you may be using unfair means to seduce my wife from me?"

"Major," said Julian after a short pause, "it must be clear to your mind that all you will gain in this matter will be to drag Lola into a terrible notoriety, which will be agonizing to one so sensitive and bashful as she is. But let me assure you, on my word of honor, that when we have exhausted all the means we can command to save Lola from you, if we fail in all else, then we will meet you on your own ground, and defeat you, too."

When he had said this, Julian rose to take his leave. The major rose also, and said, "You will find it more difficult than you think to defeat me. Lola and I have lived for months under the same roof. Can any one prove that we have not lived most intimately?"

Scarcely were the words out of his mouth when Julian dealt him a blow on the head that sent him reeling to the ground. But the major had his hand on his revolver when speaking, and as he fell he fired. The ball passed close by Julian's head, and before the major had time to revolve the pistol to fire again, Julian had wrested it from his hand, holding him down by placing his knee on the breast of the fallen adversary.

"Infamous scoundrel!" said Julian, shaking the ex-parson by a very gaudy cravat, "I have a great mind to scatter your vile plotting brains with your own pistol."

"Do it, if you are coward enough to shoot a man fallen on his back," said the major defiantly.

Julian arose, and spurning the prostrate major with his foot in no gentle manner, he said, "Arise, viper! I won't kill you, though I feel I am doing society a wrong by not crushing with my heel such a venomous reptile." Then, without waiting to see the discomfited hero arise, or hear what more he might have to say, Julian walked out of the office, putting the captured pistol in his overcoat pocket.

From the major's office he stepped into that of Messrs. Hooker and Skinner, where he met an old acquaintance, no other than his ex-reverence Hammerhard. "The firm" politely gave Julian all the information he wanted, adding, moreover, that Lieutenants Wagg and Head would no doubt be very happy to tell the colonel all they knew. Julian thanked them, saying that he would call on the lieutenants some other time. Then he asked Mr. Hooker how he came to have the information about Lola's father.

"Mr. Isaac Sprig was an old client of ours, and he wrote us from Mexico about the matter," Mr. Hooker answered.

"And why did you require so many precautions to acquaint Miss Medina with what you knew? You certainly could not have doubted her identity?"

"Why not? We did not know her."

"But you knew the major, and that she lived with us."

"Yes, but we were not bound to part with information which was valuable to us, without some security. The reward offered was ten-thousand dollars."

"That is not the point, and you know it as well as I. The point is, that you connived with the major to deceive Lola into the belief that she could not obtain the information unless she said she was married. It is an infamous plot, and lawyers who lend themselves to such vile purposes should be kicked out of the bar." And Julian walked leisurely out of the office.

At the corner he took the omnibus and rode up to Mr. Sinclair's house, as it was not yet ten, and he never came to his office until half-past ten or eleven. He was not sure, either, that Mr. Sinclair had returned from Washington.

The servant that came to the door informed Julian that Mr. Sinclair had returned on the previous evening, and was now at breakfast. Julian sent his name in, and told the servant he would wait in the library. He did not have to do that long, for in a few minutes Mr. Sinclair made his appearance. He had been informed by Mrs. Sinclair of Mrs. Norval's sudden illness, and expressed to Julian warmly his regrets. After thanking him, Julian went at once into the matter which brought him there. Mr. Sinclair listened with all the attention and surprise which the subject merited, and after hearing all that Julian had to say, seeing that the best adviser would be a lawyer, he told Julian that his coupé was at the door, and the best thing they could do was to go and consult Mr. North. They found this gentleman as he was taking off his overcoat, just arrived at his office. Again Julian went over the whole of the hateful story. When he had finished, Mr. North told them that he had no doubt but that they would, in the end, defeat Hackwell, but that there was no denying that he had trumped up quite a case, and Lola could not escape notoriety.

"Then we must defeat him with his own weapons, and plot to extricate Lola out of his clutches," said Julian. "He has bought a yacht, and has given orders to have it ready to sail at any moment. Suppose we too hire a yacht to have ready to chase his if he attempts to abduct Lola?"

"Yes, your idea is good," said Mr. North. "But if such is his intention, his taking affidavits must be only with a view to defend himself in case you stop his taking *his wife* with him. Have you any idea how he contemplates to take Miss Medina from the house?"

"I suppose he intends to decoy her, as before, with some trumped-up story," said Mr. Sinclair.

Julian had been silently studying out a plan which he thought would certainly circumvent Hackwell. When he had organized it in his mind, he communicated it to Messrs. Sinclair and North, both of whom approved it.

Mr. North was commissioned to hire a yacht and have it made ready to sail immediately. Also he would write to Mr. Hooker, proposing to commence negotiations with a view to entering into some agreement with their client, the major.

Julian would inform Don Luis and Lola of the whole matter that day, and what they had decided to do.

Mina had left Miss Ruth's service, and was now heart and soul engaged in Lola's.

She had sworn vengeance on the major, and had *ordered* her meek slave, Sophy, to watch "the firm," and report to her all they did, or intended doing. Sophy blindly obeyed. His infatuation for the little *grisette* had completely clouded the dim light of his nutshell intellect. His little head throbbed and his mild submissive heart ached when she did not smile on him. The slightest frown was torture to his tender soul. She was his queen, and he her abject slave. She was his oracle, which, the less he understood, the more he reverenced. She did not want matrimony; she scorned such slavery. She was the prettiest advocate of *free love*,[67] and he her most devout proselyte.

On the other hand, Mina's new friend, Mrs. Skroo, gave her all the time valuable bits of information, which were faithfully transferred to Lola.

"Mademoiselle," said she to Lola, two days after the incidents narrated above, "the major has telegraphed that he is coming from Washington, with or without leave, to stop your going away, and Sophy says that they know that Mr. Julian has a yacht to take you on board the Cuban steamer; they telegraphed that to the major."

Lola ran to Julian to report the news.

"Good!" said Julian. "I like that. Let them get ready to stop our taking you off *in the yacht*. Let Mina confide to Sophy that such is our firm intention."

[67]"Free love" was a scandalous notion, much in vogue at the time, in part due to the efforts of Victoria Woodhull, et al.

Then he went to see Mr. North. They agreed to redouble the preparations in the yacht.

"The yacht will be ready tonight, and Mr. Hooker and I are to have our first conference in a day or two," said Mr. North, laughing.

CHAPTER LX

"Il N'y a Que les Morts Qui Ne Reviennent Pas!"[68]

Jule, the widower, sang merrily in his cage, as if he wished to celebrate his impending journey. But Jule was ignorant of the fact that he was to sail next morning in the steamer bound for Cuba. So, that night, when Lola came and broke his dignified repose by opening his cage and taking him bodily out of it, Jule's memory flashed back to the dark day when Lavinia, converting herself into a she-Herod, had slain so many innocents. Jule had no reason to suspect Lola of similar murderous intentions, but had he not trusted Lavvy? With this thought, Jule shook, frightened, and Lola's affectionate kisses on his little beak, and pet names of *queridísimo*, and *Julito precioso*, only increased his distrust. With the native sagacity of the male sex, he distrusted one woman because *another* one had given him cause to do so. He saw his cage wrapped up in a shawl, whilst he was put to nestle under Lola's, close to her heart. Then he could see no more.

Next morning the Cuban steamer began to get up steam by nine o'clock, but Hackwell's satellites were well informed, and knew that she would not start until ten.

The spies of the firm of Hackwell & Co. had kept for days a close watch on the Norval mansion. That day they would redouble their vigilance and begin it earlier.

About eight they saw a carriage drive to the door and two closely-veiled females get into it. The first one came leaning on Colonel Norval's arms; the second was carrying a bird's cage, a satchel, and some shawls. A gentleman in citizen's dress, with a Spanish cloak wrapped

[68]Quote from *Rapport à la Convention*, of 26 May 1974, by Bertrand Barère de Vieuzac (1755-1841); "only the dead do not return," here referring clearly to the unexpected —and by some feared— return home of Dr. Norval who was believed killed in Africa.

around his shoulders and his hat well over his eyes, came out last and followed them into the carriage. They kept down the avenue until they reached Fourteenth Street. Then they turned to the left until they got to the Bowery, and went down towards the South Ferry. The spy was sure now. He was not disappointed. The stupid party stopped right in front of the yacht "*Dove*" and went on board.

The firm laughed triumphantly. Mr. Hooker ordered their yacht, "*The Giant*," to sail towards Jersey City, where he and Hackwell would embark. Then he went to meet the train, which was to arrive at nine, bringing the major from Washington.

At ten o'clock the Cuban steamer began to move off. The yacht "*Dove*" sailed by her at a short distance; "*The Giant*" a little in advance, keeping them both under a watchful eye.

"Are you sure that we have the law on our side?" said the major to Mr. Hooker.

"There is a limb of it, and two more are taking breakfast down in the cabin," replied Mr. Hooker, pointing at a gentleman who sat whistling and looking at the steamer abstractedly, and to whom he said, "Captain Jones, you think we will certainly catch them, don't you?"

"I have no doubt of it. But, of course, we must wait until they get on board the steamer. While they go in on one side, we pounce on them on the other."

"Hadn't we better board the yacht?" said the major, looking very pale.

"I think not," answered Captain Jones. "We can't prove that they are kidnapping the lady only because they are sailing in a yacht inside the harbor. But if they go on board, then we have the dead thing on them."

"Isn't that a blue veil and a parasol I see on deck?" asked the major, trembling visibly as he recognized Lola's parasol held over a head closely veiled.

Mr. Hooker smiled proudly as he answered, "Of course it is. We have fooled them beautifully by pretending that we gave up the case and were willing to compromise matters for a sum of money. I am to have an interview with Mr. Sinclair or Mr. North at twelve today and talk about our terms."

"Why, Hook, they mean foul play! Mr. Sinclair is in Washington now. The President had given me three days' leave, when Sinclair went and told him a lot of trash about me (all of which I'll make him eat afterwards), and then the President ordered the leave to be withdrawn, and I was obliged to take *French leave*.[69] I suppose they'll dismiss me

[69]Here "French leave" means the desperate Hackwell left Washington against explicit orders not to go on leave. He is willing to risk dismissal, that is to go "absent without leave," in order to pursue Lola.

for it, but I don't care, provided I get Lola. How can you see Sinclair when he is away, tell me?"

"The agreement was to meet either Mr. Sinclair or Mr. North," said Hooker.

They had been sailing now for more than two hours. They had passed Staten Island, left behind Fort Lafayette, Coney Island, and Sandy Hook; they were out of the harbor. On they sailed. The day was clear, the air soft, the sea smooth. All was propitious to Hackwell. Still, he was anxious. He was silent for a while, then he looked at his watch; it was one o'clock. He felt more anxious yet. The steamer began to put on more steam; her speed began to increase. But the "*Dove*" did not seem to notice it, for it sailed at the same distance. A European steamer appeared in sight. It came on, on, growing as it neared. It had its flags, which meant something, but Hackwell did not trouble himself to understand it, and he sailed on, watching the "*Dove*."

"I don't understand this dilly-dallying," said the major, again looking at his watch. "It is nearly four hours since we started; we are miles off New York. I will board the yacht and ascertain what it all means. You be ready, Captain Jones, to come when I call you."

They approached the other yacht and hailed it. Julian stood up to answer. The gentleman in citizen's dress, with the Spanish cloak, was talking to the two veiled ladies, with his back turned. He was watching the steamer.

"Can I speak with you a few minutes?" said the major.

"Certainly," Julian answered.

"May I ask where you are going?"

"Yes, you may ask."

"Well, where?"

"If you will do us the honor to continue following us, as you have done for four hours, you will see."

"Will you let me come on board your yacht?"

Julian looked at the receding steamer. It had increased its speed, and was fast getting beyond reach. He then spoke to the pilot something which the major construed into an entreaty to put on more sail. His supposition was confirmed by the fact that more sail was put on the "*Dove*," and she steered directly for the retreating steamer.

"Julian pretended not to hear my last question. I think we had better stop them."

"We can't prove they are abducting the lady," said Captain Jones.

"They can't catch the steamer now," said the man at the helm. "The wind is changing."

"Yes, they are getting left," said Hackwell, with renewed excitement. "In half an hour she will be almost out of sight. I fear there is foul play somewhere, or Julian is more stupid than I thought him to be. Let us hail them again."

"*The Giant*" again came alongside the "*Dove*," and the major again addressed Julian, who, leaning on a mast, watched the steamer with a very sad gaze.

"Colonel, I think your yacht is a very poor craft," said the major.

"Mine is better; take it if you wish to overtake the steamer, for in yours you can't do it unless the steamer is to wait for you."

"Could your yacht overtake the steamer now, think you ?" asked Julian.

"It is rather doubtful now," the major replied, "but yours certainly cannot."

"Perhaps not."

"You had better accept my offer. Your only chance to overtake the steamer is in taking my yacht, and every moment you lose counts against you."

"I think not, but I am very much obliged to you for your civility." And Julian again looked anxiously towards the receding steamer.

"In five minutes it will be too late," the major said.

"Yes, I think it is too late now. But, as we came to board the incoming steamer instead of the one leaving, there is no need of troubling you."

"What do you mean?"

"I think Julian is very tantalizing to keep you from running after Lola, now that you can't catch her," said one of the veiled ladies, rising and removing her veil, revealing to the astonished major the features of Miss Mattie Norval. "As it is useless to accept your very kind offer, I'll return your civility by inviting you to come to our yacht—though not so fine as yours—and meet papa with us. I hope that will repay you for the disappointment of not catching Lola."

The major did not know whether he heard aright, or whether Mattie was jesting.

"What is the meaning of this?" said he, with pale lips, turning to Hooker, who, with scarcely anymore color in his, answered, "I can't imagine."

The polished major swore a fearful oath, saying, "I shall soon know," then aloud, addressing Mattie, added, "Since you are so kind as to invite me, I will go on board your yacht."

"Come, major!" said Mattie, as he leaped aboard the "*Dove*." "In a few minutes you will be face to face with papa. See how near he is." And she pointed to the approaching steamer.

The major tottered and turned paler. He was incapable of superstition, and scorned remorse, but the words of Mattie of being "*face to face*" with the man whom he had so deeply injured, smote him with a force the more powerful as it was to him unknown.

One glance he cast in the direction indicated by Mattie, and now only one steamer loomed up with rapidly increasing magnitude, but it did so as the other carrying Lola away became at every second smaller and smaller. Punishment approached as hope receded. If he had been a heathen of classic times, he would have exclaimed: "Nemesis! Retribution!"

But as he was a *Christian*, a modern sinner, an unpoetical breaker of the ten commandments, he merely shrugged his shoulders. And though he felt very sick and shaky, and weak in the knees, he averted his eyes from the black smoke which seemed now a long, black finger from one steamer to call his attention to the other, and he looked anxiously at the other lady, who still kept closely veiled.

"It is my Aunt Lavvy," said Mattie, with a chuckle of half-suppressed delight. "Take off your veil, Aunt Lavvy: the major doesn't recognize you. There is no object in our fooling him any longer."

Lavvy took her veil off and bowed to the major. He removed his hat and also bowed. Then he looked at the gentleman with the Spanish cloak, who still kept his back towards them.

"Turn this way, uncle. There is no need of your acting the part of Don Luis anymore," said Mattie, laughing heartily.

Isaac turned and also bowed to him.

Hackwell was too anxiously preoccupied to care much for ridicule, or to give much thought to the absurdity of his plight. Still, for one moment, the humiliation of being thus duped almost equaled the rage at losing Lola—perhaps forever!

"I don't understand," he stammered.

"Of course you don't. You are too nonplussed," said Mattie, laughing mercilessly in his face. "But I'll explain to you. We came to meet papa, and to wave our handkerchiefs to dear Lola, who is now almost out of sight. As Julian knew you were intending to stop her going away, he thought he would fool you by pretending he was to carry her off in the yacht and put her on board the steamer outside the harbor. So he made all that fuss about getting the yacht ready, and, as you see, it was a good bait, and you swallowed it hook and all. You have the satisfaction, however, of having made Lola cry all day yesterday, for she knew that papa was coming in this steamer, and she hated to go without seeing him. But as she hated worse the idea of being entrapped into an odious marriage with you, she submitted to the cruel alternative of going without seeing papa. Julian took her and her father and Mina to the steamer last night, and stayed with them until midnight. Then he left the poor child almost brokenhearted, for she loves Julian as much as she hates you."

The major was silent, and no one else seemed disposed to break the awkward pause.

Mattie continued: "You used to preach very hard, bigoted sermons when you played your *rôle* of parson. Let me preach you a little one now, by calling your attention to that black line of smoke from the steamer carrying Lola away. Without taking the trouble to be very poetical, or dealing you poetical justice, we can very well see it looks like a black dividing-line between you and Lola, traced by Providence to separate you and tell you to cease persecuting her."

"The major laughed a horse laugh, saying, "The black line looks more like the finger of my friend Satan pointing the way for me to follow her."

Then he turned his back on them, and, without any leave-taking, stepped back into his yacht, which a few minutes after was sailing back towards New York as the "*Dove*" approached the English steamer.

It had been as Mattie said.

Lola had cried all day because that night she must go to the steamer to elude the vigilance of Hackwell's spies, and she could not see the doctor.

But Don Luis said he would not run the risk of being detained and losing that steamer, and as for waiting for the next, he would not hear of it. The death of his daughter scarcely seemed to him more a calamity than a law suit with Hackwell, in which the names of his wife and child would be dragged into a mire of publicity.

About eight o'clock Lola had left the Norval House—her house—accompanied by her father and Mina. They got into a hack and drove to a hotel. There they dismissed that hack, waited a while, and ordered another to the side entrance, in which they drove to the steamer where Julian was waiting for them.

Their rooms were ready. Lola put Jule into his cage and sat down to talk with Julian.

At midnight, Julian must go.

Up to that time Lola had been cheering the desponding Julian, who felt crushed by the blow of the approaching separation. But now, when he at last arose to part, all her fictitious fortitude gave way, and she sprang up and flung her arms around his neck and clung to him. Both of course (as all lovers do) wished to die then and there.

"No, no! I cannot! Don't leave me! Why, why can't you go with me? Why not resign? Oh, I may never see you on this earth!" sobbed Lola.

"Yes, you will, dearest. My life will be spared, and one month after the last battle is fought, I shall be in Mexico. I could not resign now, when my brigade is waiting for me, and all the army will be marching in a few days."

"But the war might last for a long, long time," pleaded she, with her soft cheek close to Julian's mustache.

"No, it won't. You will see what quick work the Lieutenant General makes of it, and in a little while I shall be with you."

"Oh, I don't believe it! I shall die! I shall die!" she sobbed, clinging to him. And Julian, with scarcely any more strength than she, pressed her to his breast and kissed the sweet pale lips as if he would draw from the petals of a rose long draughts of honey, of nectar, to give his heart the courage to leave her.

But Don Luis wisely came in to put an end to such despairing adieus, and Julian left her. And as he walked away, he felt a great desire to fling himself into the dark water below.

Lola sobbed and moaned all night. Her sad father sat by her and tried to soothe her, whilst he thought how much he would have loved to have found his child before she had so entirely given her heart away! "She can't love me much now," he thought, as he held the little hand in his. "No child ever loves the parent after *such love* has entered the heart. There is nothing left but the dregs. Be it so; it is God's will and God's law." So ran his thoughts, while she sobbed, thinking of Julian with intense love, and of Hackwell with aversion. And the gray dawn gently glided over New York Bay!

CONCLUSION

"Upon what meat doth this our Caesar feed,
That he hath grown so great?"
—SHAKESPEARE[70]

Julian joined his brigade the day before the Army of the Potomac began the campaign of 1864 under Lieutenant-General Grant. If this campaign had not been so imminent, he would have resigned his commission the day on which his dismissal was rescinded. But to leave when battles were so near at hand Julian could not do—no, not even to follow Lola. Now, however, he had followed the hero of Vicksburg and Donelson to the Appomattox tree; General Lee, with his brave army, had surrendered; now Julian considered the war ended, and himself at liberty to leave a service he no longer loved. He tendered his resignation and went home to prepare for his departure to Mexico.

Hurriedly, Julian made his arrangements to leave. There was nothing to detain him at home now, as his mother was steadily improving under the wise treatment and careful watching of his father. But there was great urgency in his being in Mexico. Don Luis had written that all remedies having failed to restore Lola to health, he feared he would have to resign himself to lose his child; that the doctors said her malady was nothing but a profound melancholy, which could only be cured by the cause of it being removed. The cause of it being the absence from Julian, it was clear that Julian's presence would be the remedy, and so it was.

A few days after he arrived, the roses and dimples which had fled when she went to Mexico returned with the Yankee lover. The coral

[70]The quote is from Shakespeare's tragedy *Julius Caesar*, Act 1, scene 2.

lips parted in merry laughter again, showing the pearly teeth. And the lustrous black eyes (which so maddened Hackwell) were once more brilliant with happiness or languid with love.

But Julian and Lola were not the only ones of our acquaintances of these truthful pages to be made happy. Mattie and young Mr. Sinclair, the son of the banker, were also to be made one. And Ruth and the renowned Major-General Cackle, in a very matter-of-fact way, agreed to do likewise.

Yes, by the smoky rush-light of his intellect, the great hero had at last plainly discerned that Ruth was "a mighty fine girl," and that if he had not seen this fact thus plainly years ago, when sliding downhill on that sledge manufactured by brother Beau, it was "because who could when so infernally cold?"

He said as much to Ruth one afternoon while driving in Central Park. And as she had been praising or criticising the elegant turnouts which they passed, or passed by them, he, with commendable *naïveté*, added, "And if you marry me, Miss Ruth, you needn't think you'll have to give up your handsome carriages, *nor* your rich dresses, *nor* your fine house, for I'll get you just as fine ones. I guess I have the stamps. Brother Beau and I have made a handsome thing this year out of our salt-pork and lard contract. In fact, this last year he and I cleared a good half-million, besides what we are making together with father and Tonny and Tool. Beau thinks in another year we can go railroading if we like. We are fast coining money, Miss Ruth. So says brother Beau."

Ruth required no further arguments. No key could open her heart but the one used by the clumsy hand of the heroic general. He stumbled right into the keyhole of that metallic heart of Miss Norval, and the organ, thus by chance opened and galvanized into action, sent the same sort of vitality to her brain, and the heavy features and bushy head of the modern Darius became beautiful, glorified, to her sight as he sat by her side talking of *lard* and *salt-pork* contracts! In an instant Ruth saw her life dream realized. She saw herself the leader of American *bon-ton*,[71] quoted and imitated by all the fashionable belles of New York and Washington, of Long Branch and Newport—all the well-dressed women who have a perfect right to be stupid, because their husbands have brains; who have a perfect right to be silly and trifling, because their husbands conduct the mighty affairs of the nation; who have a perfect right to be spendthrifts, because their husbands have, by extortion and driving hard bargains, accumulated princely fortunes—all

[71]French for "good taste" or "high class".

these beautifully dressed ladies who slander as they drive by in *their own* carriages, richly cushioned in damask, who backbite from their bay windows hung with costly satin; who snub and ignore old acquaintances if seen driving in the Park in a hired hack—all of this fortunate class Ruth wished to lead, and she felt equal to the task.

With great candor and a frank laugh, she said to the hero of the involuntary heroic charge, "I am glad to hear you are so rich, for I confess I hate poverty; I always did; I do now."

"So do I!" chimed in our Caesar. "I hate poverty and *I hate poor people*! I wouldn't for the world go back to plowing and manuring the farm, and taking care of the cows and horses and pigs, and—"

"Hush!" interrupted she, in genuine alarm. "There comes Mrs. Van Kraut. She might hear you!"

A few weeks after this memorable drive of the great general and Ruth in the Park, Mr. Cackle, the father, dressed in the finest broadcloth, resting his yet firm hand upon a gold-headed cane, sat on the velvet-cushioned chair by the library center-table of the Cackle mansion in Washington. The four sons, the pride of the Cackle family, and leaders of the nation, surrounded the proud father.

At home, these four illustrious scions are called *brother Beau, Ciss, Tonny, and Tool.* But a grateful nation respectfully designates them as—the honorable Mirabeau Demosthenes Cackle, the heroic Major General Julius Caesar Cackle, the renowned Brigadier General Mark Antony Cackle, the distinguished Marcus Tullius Cicero Cackle.

It was a sight that would have done your patriotic heart good, reader—for I suppose you *have* a patriotic heart—we all have in this country—to see this brilliant cluster, this radiant galaxy, formed by Mr. Cackle the elder and his illustrious sons. Beau, the leader, at home as well as in Congress, was speaking. He was saying, "Even if I should have to make it a *personal* matter, I shall tell the Secretary that Hackwell must not be dismissed."

"I tell you what, Beau," observed the celebrated Mark Antony, "make Le Grand help you with the Secretary. He'll do it, for if Hack was to tell tales out of school, old Gunn would *bust*. He'll get his nose clipped."

"And Gunn and the Sec. are great chums," added Marcus Tullius, with a wink as a sign of his great sagacity.

"Of course they are," rejoined Mark Antony. "Don't you remember how he kept Isaac in the Confederacy for three years, and wouldn't allow him to be exchanged, though poor Lavvy moved heaven and earth to do it?"

"And many a good laugh we had thinking of the dandy Sprig in tatters, and the epicure feasting on hoe cakes," laughed Julius Caesar.

"Le Grand, of course, has influence, but you all forget that he is a great friend of Skroo, or of his wife, which is worse yet. At the earnest request of Gunn, I recommended to Hackwell the rascally Hungarian, who, I believe, has gone to Europe with all his family, because *he is* the defaulter," replied Beau.

"What are we to do if Skoo doesn't return? He might take a notion to remain in his own country," said Ciss.

"No, he won't; he will return. I know him well. But still, his absence will cause delay, and the Secretary very properly remarked that a justly indignant nation will demand a speedy punishment of the guilty. And who are the guilty?" said Beau.

The four illustrious brothers looked at each other, and their proud father looked at them in silence.

Beau, the leader, broke that silence. He said, "Brother Ciss, I fear that your two pets, Wagg and Head, must go by the board."

"Poor fellows! I don't like that," answered Ciss.

"I know that when you took to your heels at Bull-Run-the-first, one of these two showed you the shortest way to run to Washington, and the other told you where to find a stray horse and buggy. These were eminent services at that critical moment, services which formed the foundation of your good fortune, and you deserve great credit for not forgetting them. But, for all that, when it comes to a matter of necessity to find the defaulter or defaulters, what then? Hackwell and Skroo *won't* be. Shall we?"

There was again a silence in the galaxy, which the elder Cackle broke by observing, "Beau is always logical."

But Lieutenant Wagg was not, and though the great men swore on their sacred honor that when appearances were saved and the howl of the newspapers was silenced, he and his friend Head would be restored to their rank and money put into their pockets, and though many more fair promises were made, Wagg was unmanageable. He refused point-blank to do anything except to keep silent as long as they testified their friendship to him by an occasional bank note. He knew too much; he could be insolent. He had accompanied Mr. Skroo night after night to certain places, and had made a careful memorandum of the times when Mr. Skroo had lost at draw poker stakes ranging from five-thousand dollars upwards. He had overheard conversations between Major Hackwell and his friends, Messrs. Hammerhead and Hooker and Skinner, in which it had been freely admitted that the major had pretended to be Lola's husband to terrify her into acceding to be his wife in fact. Lastly, Lieutenant Wagg knew all about certain lard and salt-pork contracts of the Cackle brothers, beside other contracts of rotten blankets and of shoes made of burnt leather which they had sold to the *best of governments*!

Altogether, it would have been inconvenient to make Wagg an enemy, for he was reckless and *drank*. So they, instead of that, gave him some money, whereupon he was very gay for some time, and had the usual visit of wild fancies, called by some people *delirium tremens*. His friend Sophy, of course, took care of him, and beguiled the hours of his watch writing sad verses to Mina. Sophy was very miserable, so when Wagg was too stupefied with laudanum to object to the monotonous sound of the guitar as he repeated hundreds of times, in Spanish and French, that he was *dying* and would *surely die* if Mina did not return, he arranged his "*farewell to Mina*" to the doleful tune of "*The Flying Trapeze*."[72]

Sophy was peacefully occupied singing before the silent stove one evening, and the rats, as usual, restlessly ran about, much excited by his music. For the thousandth time Sophy was repeating his ode to Mina. And he was proud of his verses and believed he had shown good taste in interpolating the same with Spanish and French words, inasmuch as Mina was French and she had gone to a Spanish country. For this reason, and for the great sympathy Sophy felt for "*The Flying Trapeze*"—whose fate he thought similar to his own—the tears rolled down his cheeks, as at the end of each stanza he repeated:

> "Il faut que je meure si tu ne reviens à moi!—yes, yes,
> Me muero, me muero si tú no vuelves a mí!—yes, yes."[73]

(The word "yes" he thought rhymed beautifully with "*trapeze*.") And the sympathetic rats sped around the room in mad career, as if frantically searching for means to avert the sad catastrophe and save mild Sophy.

This harmless excitement had lasted about an hour when it was interrupted by the entrance of an orderly who brought to Lieutenant Head a communication from the War Office. The communication informed Lieutenant Head that he was cashiered. The terror of mild Sophy can better be imagined than described. He looked at the writing, at the stove, at the rats, in stupefied silence. The guitar scraped his fingers and tumbled on the stove, and the strings got burned but he did not

[72]Extremely popular song of the 1860s, written by George Leybourne with music by Alfred Lee, celebrating the acrobatic exploits of Jules Leótard, "That daring young man on the flying trapeze."

[73]Sophy Head's equally poor French or Spanish poetry reads: "I'll die if you don't come back to me. Yes. Yes."

know it. When the music ceased, the frantic careering of the rats also ceased. But they came stealthily to peep and roll their little eyes at Sophy, distending their nostrils inquisitively, wondering what that smell of burnt strings could mean in conjunction with Sophy's silence.

This silence, however, was now broken by a heavy step heard coming upstairs. Sophy, as well as the rats, listened. He did not know why he listened. He expected *nobody*; he hoped *nothing*. He heard a step and a hiccough, then another step and a hiccough, and so on until he counted ten or twelve steps and the same number of hiccoughs.

Then there was a pause and then a loud laugh, and the voice of Lieutenant Wagg was heard saying, "I say, old Sophy Head! How would it do to hang by the banister like a bat, eh? and sleep here, eh? The devil a bit I *hiccup* when I don't lift my legs, but as soon as I begin to climb these nasty stairs I *hiccup* like all possessed." And, as if to illustrate his assertion, he began to ascend and hiccough.

The patient Sophocles ran to meet his beloved friend, thinking that in all probability he would have to nurse again his wild fancies. Such, however, was not the case. On the contrary, Mr. Wagg was sufficiently sober to notice that his friend was in great affliction.

"Out with it, old woman," said he. "What is it now? Not the French lark, is it?"

And when he understood what troubled Mr. Head, he said, pushing his friend towards the door, "Come along with me; this couldn't have happened in better time. Those three little angels, Beau Cackle, old Gunn, and Parson Hackwell, are just now downstairs. They sent me to bed. I'll make a bed for them if they don't stop their nasty tricks. Come along." And, still afflicted with the hiccoughs, he dragged his friend after him until he reached Major Hackwell's private office.

The renowned gentlemen, designated by Wagg as "little angels," were there. In no very choice language Wagg laid before them his friend's case, and would not leave the room until the Hon. Beau and the all-powerful Gunn sat down and wrote most urgent letters to the Secretary of War, asking him to withdraw the order cashiering Lieutenant Head. This, in due time, was done.

In the course of time Mr. Skroo returned, and Major Hackwell's accounts were settled, and his honor saved from the slightest imputation. The major then feared no one. He, moreover, was rich now, very rich. He rode and drove beautiful thoroughbreds, very different from the yellow *masetudo*[74] of old, which squinted and lolled out his tongue

[74]Term referring to Hackwell and Hammerhard's old hag of a horse seen in Chapter I.

so ridiculously as he dragged the squeaking vehicle owned conjointly with Hammerhard. He lived well—yes, he led what is called a "gay life," but he was very miserable. Whilst waiting for Skroo to come from Europe and enable him to settle his accounts, Hackwell had been forced to remain in Washington, and Julian had gone to Mexico, and was already there before he knew that his hated rival had left the Army of the Potomac. The bitterest drop in Hackwell's bitter cup was the thought that, as Wagg had spoken so publicly of his marriage having been a *sham*, when Lola should come as Julian's wife he could hardly dare to institute legal proceedings against her. The affair of the marriage was too well-known now, and he would only make himself ridiculous.

With an undefined idea that if he acquired *power* he might yet win Lola, or at least ruin Julian, and with the blackest despair filling his soul, Hackwell plunged into politics and became the warmest friend of the Cackles, like one of them in fact, a true Cackle, and so he is now. But he hardly ever mentions the Norval family. The name of Mrs. Norval has never crossed his lips. As this poor woman became very violent once that at the request of Ruth he went to see her, the major took this incident as an excellent pretext never to darken the Norval door again.

But he is a friend of Ruth—now that she is Mrs. Julius Caesar Cackle. The major and Emma were the only friends of the Norval family who supported Ruth in her efforts to send her mother to an insane asylum, and Mrs. Julius Caesar—as the major is rich and a great friend of the Cackles—has not forgotten it.

About the time when Sophy's plaintive ditty to Mina, sung up in the garret to the silent stove and noisy rats, was interrupted so cruelly by the orderly delivering him his dismissal, at the same hour, in the upper part of New York City, Misses Ruth Norval and Emma Hackwell were busily engaged assorting and arranging various articles of a magnificent wedding trousseau just arrived from Paris.

Miss Ruth was saying, "Isn't it provoking that pa won't let me have a handsome wedding. As if my having it is going to make ma worse. If she had been sent to an insane asylum, she might have been well by this time. Pa is so obstinate."

"Mattie and Julian are as much opposed to it, and so are Mr. Isaac and Miss Lavinia," said Emma.

"I know it. They didn't even want to let me send for my trousseau to Paris, but, as I told them I would not marry if I didn't, Ciss insisted on it. They are a pack of obstinate fools, and I am glad I am going to Ciss, who will pay more attention to my wishes."

❖ ❖ ❖

When gentle Sophy was reinstated to his rank in the army, and Wagg was appeased, and the major's accounts settled, and Mr. Skroo dropped easily, the conscience of the Hon. Beau was satisfied. He felt that justice to the best government, and meed to merit, had been measured rightly, and he had now a better right than ever to turn his attention to his own brilliant career and that of his illustrious brothers. In consequence, their success has been uninterrupted. Like the forest of gourds overtopping the young cedars and oaks, they hold their heads high in their transient glory. Perhaps, like the prophet's gourd, they will wither on the third day. But that day has not arrived. In the meantime, they march in the front rank, leading the American people. Shoulder to shoulder with them also march the Honorable Le Grand Gunn, and the Honorable Mr. Blower—whom the reader may remember as a very warm advocate of the humane policy of starving the Union prisoners in the South, together with the stubborn, wicked rebels, in order that the war should be ended sooner. The Honorable John Hackwell also marches with them. They form a glorious phalanx.

At this very hour, when these humble pages are drawing to a close, the mighty phalanx is marching about the country under the immediate leadership of General Julius Caesar, but under the instructions of Mirabeau the Honorable.

As General Cackle believes that from the moment of his birth it was decreed by fate that his destiny should be influenced by horses, his motto is—"A Kingdom for a Horse."[75] This shows how original *our Caesar* is. With that motto on one side of his banner, and on the other written, "On to Cincinnati," he leads the glorious phalanx to that city of celebrated pigs.

In that city the phalanx delivered several eloquent speeches. Of these, one of the most remarkable, and quoted as a specimen of powerful oratory, was delivered by *our Caesar*. The concluding words of the modern Darius were as follows:

"Fellow citizens! have we not, we the Cackles, have we not led you triumphantly for twelve years? Look among you, and you will see how many we have enriched. Why, then, will you not follow us now? Have you forgotten that brother Beau is the father of our party, and that as such he must lose his patience when his children don't obey him?"

[75]The quote by which Ruiz de Burton pokes further fun at the ignorance of the Cackles and yet at the same time marvels at their success is taken from Shakespeare's play *Richard III*, Act IV, scene 7: "A horse! a horse! My kingdom for a horse!"

"I remember that twelve years ago brother Beau said to me and Tonny and Tool, 'Let us *teach the young to shoot*, and to shoot properly, all over the country. And we did, though at first neither Tonny nor Tool nor I understood what brother Beau meant. But you forget now all that we, *the Cackles*, have done for the country, and you go on forever talking of the siege and surrender of Donelson, of the siege and surrender of Vicksburg. Ain't you tired of it? *I am, and so is brother Beau.* Suppose Grant *did* conquer Donelson and Vicksburg. What of that? *I*, on my gray charger, or brother Tonny, could have done the same thing. Have you forgotten my furious charge which won to our arms one of the most important battles, and for which the newspapers called me the modern Darius? Yes, you forget *that*, and what brother Beau has done for our party. And now that *we want to purify it*, you won't let us! But, mark my words! If you don't let brother Beau guide you, the party will go to pieces, the country will be ruined, and it will go down so low that it will never rise again. Therefore, follow us, and help us in our work of purification. We have worthy and able coadjutors in the persons of the distinguished Hackwell, Gunn, Skroo, and Mr. Blower, and others equally notable. This Mr. Blower is the celebrated patriot of 1862 to whom the country (that *is*, our party) gave a *niche* of honor for the memorable words he uttered. Speaking of the rebellious South, he said, '*We'll make it a solitude and call it peace*,' and he—"

Here someone pulled the coattails of our Caesar, whereupon he lost the thread of his discourse, and became confused, and hurriedly wound up, saying, "Therefore follow us blindly, and stop talking about how Grant treated Lee when he surrendered, and all that sort of thing we are tired of hearing. You know what I mean. Now, give me three cheers!"

The cheers were given. The band played loudly "Glory, glory, hallelujah!"[76] and Julius Caesar took his seat in the midst of the deafening applause thrown at his head by his ardent admirers.

What the hero of the compulsory charge meant by saying, "Stop talking about how Grant treated Lee when he surrendered," was this: that he wished to exhort all the American nation, but especially the Southerners, to forget the soldierly courtesy, the gentlemanly consideration, of General Grant towards the vanquished enemy. The moderation and good sense shown then by General Grant were enthusiastically praised by the grateful South and held up in striking contrast with the

[76]The band plays Julia Ward Howe's *Battle Hymn of the Republic* (1862) —perhaps the most famous of Civil War songs— based on the Union Army song *John Brown's Body*.

spirit of vengeance and unforgiveness which unhappily at the time pervaded this country. The Southern press, the democratic journals of the North, and the more liberal of the Republican journals, all spoke in high praise of the man who in the height of success, and when he could have dictated any terms he pleased, never sought to be cruel or revengeful; all lauded the soldier who, in the flush of victory, never forgot what was due to a great but less fortunate general, to a brave but exhausted army.

This is what Julius Caesar asks the Americans to forget, this and all the other memorable events which the Americans remember with pride, and which to forget, the nation will have to forget also that it has a history, a glorious past, a future full of promise, and that on the brightest page of that history the name of Grant will go down to posterity.

All this, however, is nothing to the Cackles. The phalanx continues its march, whilst Beau shakes the very walls of the Capitol in frenzied denunciations of all who are not Cackles.

"Father," said the Honorable Beau when, after one of these exhausting philippics, he went home to hold a family council with his father and brothers. "I fear we must be sweet to the Democrats. I fear, indeed! You know how I hate them and despise them, but what can we do? We must try to make up with them, or be defeated. Tonny, and you also, Tool, must not forget to be sweet to them. I wrote to Ciss about our *new departure*."

"You are always logical, my boy," replied the elder Cackle, emphasizing his approval with a vigorous thump of his gold-headed cane upon the carpet. "*We must and shall be sweet to the Democrats*!"

"For you know that by fair or foul means the Cackles must hold to their power," added Beau.

"You are always logical, my boy," said the elder.

"And be careful not to say one word of this before mother or the girls, for they will be writing to someone about it. Remember what a scrape mother got us into by writing about 'the great man who put the habeas corpuses all in irons, and had a right to ring his little bell under the Constitution,'" suggested the wise Beau.

"He won't hurt anyone now; he is a gone coon,"[77] said Tool, derisively. "He won't bully any of us as he did in those times."

"No sound can awake him to glory again, my dear boys," added the elder Cackle. "But, nevertheless, it is well not to tell mother we mean to be sweet to the Democrats."

[77]Tool Cackle here deprecatingly refers to deceased President Lincoln as a "gone coon," i.e., out of the picture, as he recalls the conflict surrounding the Habeas Corpus Act.

"And now, my dear boy," continued Mr. Cackle, addressing Beau, who looked as if his philippic had exhausted him as much as he had wished to exhaust his subject—"now you go and lie down and take some rest. You are used up."

Beau shook his head despondingly as he replied, "That is not the worst of it. The worst of it is, that it might be of no use. But I'll keep it up."

"You must not despond so. You certainly were most eloquent. I and your mother thought several times that you were going to have a fit, you got so purple in the face. But by-and-by we saw it was all pure *eloquence*, '*the Cackle eloquence*' so celebrated by the American people. And then we were proud, but not frightened. Your sisters felt particular pride in the persistent modesty with which you brought up your name—*our* name, *the Cackle name*—before the public. 'What a pity,' we all said,—'what a pity that the whole nation could not have been here with us, listening to our Beau's words of wisdom and *unselfish patriotism*!' "

"The whole nation shall read those words! The whole world shall read them!" Beau replied. "Thirty-five million copies of a pamphlet containing my speech are now printed, and shall be distributed over the land!"

"So soon! Why, you just now made that speech two hours ago!" exclaimed Mr. Cackle and Tool and Tonny, astonished.

"'Strike while the iron is hot' has been one of my rules always, so I had the thirty-five million copies of the speech printed before I delivered it. I ordered a cartload to be brought here for the use of our family. I ordered three tons to be sent to Boston, one ton to New York, two tons to the West, and so to be distributed that everybody can have a copy. Here is one I brought for you," said Beau, drawing one from his pocket.

"Read it to me! Oh, read it to me!" exclaimed the fond father. And, as Beau is always ready to read his own productions, though much exhausted, he began to read, as follows:

"CACKLISM *vs.* GRANTISM"

"Mr. President—You will observe that my natural modesty, and the bashful delicacy with which I always speak of *myself*, will preclude all desire to bring myself forward during this oration, unless it should be absolutely necessary. But I have no hesitation in declaring *myself* the father of our party—the creator of it. There isn't another senator that can be compared to *me* in point of ability and of meritorious services to the country (*I* mean of *our* party, of course). All admit that *I* beat them all in brains. It is well-known that *I* began in the beginning. *I* never cared about the color of the skin or about the character of my followers. All *I* cared for was to have power, so *I* intertwined *my* very bowels with the party! It breaks *my* tender heart to see its original character changed. It harrows *my* sensitive soul to find *I* can't manage it now as *I* used to, and that it will go to destruction, to ruin, the disobedient child! Therefore *I* pray and implore a kind Providence (for I am a religious man, Mr. President), I pray that the danger may be averted! Oh, *I* nursed the little darling in its cradle! I sung to it the first lullaby! Oh, don't let me follow its hearse!"

Here, Mr. Cackle the elder, as well as Tool and Tonny, being overcome by their feelings, Beau interrupted his reading to recommence again. But, not having much space, I cannot transcribe all the speech. I shall only quote those passages of it which seemed to affect the Cackle father and brothers most particularly, or to bring out their applause most enthusiastically. First Beau came to a place in his speech wherein he describes the applause he received twelve years ago, when he delivered, *as father of the party*, his first philippic against "*the oligarchy*" of the South. Then he contrasts *his* great ability with the want of it in the President, and *his* great love of freedom with the tyranny of the same magistrate, and corroborates these charges with authority of no less magnitude than that of E. M. Stanton,[78] a man well-known to the country for the mild and impartial use he made of his authority. Beau read from his pamphlet as follows: "I am not alone in the opinion that Grant is usurping all power, and that he has not *my* ability. Edwin M. Stanton thought so, too. He told *me*, Grant cannot manage this country as you or I can. The whole world knows that there never was a man who abhorred tyranny as E. M. Stanton did. He was always law-abiding, and never assumed or usurped any powers. It is true that the newspapers used to call him the 'barnacle of the War Office' because he resisted the order of the President to leave the office. But that President was a Copperhead,[79] who should not have been obeyed, and E. M. Stanton felt it was his duty to disobey him and take into his hands the power so misplaced.

"Besides other horrible misdemeanors, do you know what President Grant has dared to do? My blood curdles with horror! My brain reels with indignation! I can hardly articulate, but it must be told. He has dared to slight a colored gentleman! No less distinguished a citizen of African

[78]Ruiz de Burton, at the end of the novel, lashes mercilessly into what is considered to be Stanton's authoritarian abuse of power.

[79]"Copperhead" or "Peace Democrat" were terms disparagingly used to refer to Northerners who opposed the war policy and sought some sort of negotiated resolution to the North/South crisis. Here Ruiz de Burton has the Cackles

descent than Mr. Fred. Douglass.[80] Yes, this monster of tyranny, this horrible usurper (observe, Mr. President, how mild is the language I use), this Ulysses Grant, not only did not invite Mr. Fred. Douglass to a diplomatic dinner, but he did not order to be destroyed the steamer in which Mr. Douglass was refused a seat at the dinner table. Can the country tolerate this monstrosity? We impeached President Andrew Johnson for offenses far less heinous than those committed by the present incumbent. Why can't we impeach this President, too? Please let us try it! I beg! I entreat! Remember that in selecting his cabinet he did not appoint a single Cackle to it. He is utterly unmanageable; I can't do anything with him.

"The Democratic party is dissolving. Now is the time for us to catch the falling pieces and join them and shape them into *Cacklism.* If we don't do so, we will be very foolish.

> "Cuando te den la vaquilla,
> Corre con la soguilla,"[81]

says Sancho Panza, very wisely. So *I* say, now that the Democratic party is about to disappear as a political organization, let us absorb it, and let us raise the banner of 'CACKLISM *against* GRANTISM!'"

"Aha!" ejaculated Mr. Cackle, "do you see now, boys—you, Tool, and you, Tonny—do you see why *we must be sweet to the* Democrats? You are always logical, my boy," said he to the Hon. Demosthenes Mirabeau Cackle—"always logical. You know it and so does the nation."

THE END

term President Johnson, a "copperhead" not to be obeyed, as they seek to legitimate Stanton's near usurpation of power while at the same time inveighing against President Grant's "tyranny."

[80]Frederick Douglass (1817?-1895), an African-American abolitionist and journalist. A former fugitive slave, Douglass fled north and became an important speaker in the movement against slavery. Here Ruiz de Burton mentions President Grant's failure to invite Douglass to the White House, an event the Cackles see as proof of Grant's "lukewarm" stance towards Black enfranchisement.

[81]quote from Cervantes' *Don Quixote* in which Sancho Panza says: When they give you the calf, run with the rope" pointing to the Cackle's unrestrained political and economic opportunism as they now side with Greeley's Liberal Republicans, later to be endorsed by the Democratic Party.